CORDELIA'S SONG

David Stanley

Morris Publishing Australia

CORDELIA'S

SONG

ISBN: 978-0-6457598-8-4

Morris Publishing Australia
www.morrispublishingaustralia.com

Dedication

To Linda Shields, a wonderful colleague and friend.

NOTES

Cordelia's Song is completely fictional. All characters, locations and names used in the book are fictional and bear no intentional resemblance to any person known to me, living or dead, although in my mind, as I developed Cordelia's story, it was set in the Australian state of New South Wales. The fictional names for the magpie (mytre) in the book were all invented by the author, and if they bear any resemblance to First Nations words or indeed words from any other culture, it is purely coincidental.

I believe that all creatures have their own language for the important things in their world. In my story the Australian magpies refer to themselves as 'mytre', a unique name that I created as their traditional and ancient name, and this name is used throughout this book. As well, I have created words that my magpie (mytre) use to refer to humans and human things, their Gods, and their relationship with important things in their world. These are listed in the glossary.

Set before you is a story that comes completely from the author's imagination. The valley and the station locations are completely fictional, although visiting a conglomerate of similar places across rural New South Wales fed my inspiration.

The birds like leaves on Winterwood
Sing hopeful songs on dismal days
They've learned to live life as they should
They are at peace with Nature's ways.

Don Mclean – 'Winterwood' (1971)

Contents

GLOSSARY

A list of Magpie (Mytre) words used in this book.

MAGPIE (MYTRE) WORDS:

GODS:

Egnaro	The God of the moon, the night the bringer of cold and darkness
Elppa	The God of the sun, the day the bringer of light and warmth
Korzela	The God of wind
Xervinu	The God of rain

TIMES OF DAY:

Ksud	Dusk
Nwad	Dawn
Nwod	High sun or noon

OTHER MAGPIE (MYTRE) WORDS USED IN THE STORY

Elpitlum	Community/combined clan meeting or large gathering of birds.
Keere	Monster or evil thing
Mytre	Magpie
Norzela	Humans
Norzela Nest	Human House/Home
Norzela Park	Human Golf course
Picture Window-Box	TV
RFS	Rural Fire Service (in New South Wales, Australia)

THE VALLEY CLANS

Cor Clan:

Corzell (Clan Leader), Corselia, Cordelia, Coruel, Corxell, Corhelia.

Dart Clan:

Dartvada (Clan Leader), Dartspadd, Dartkull (Youngling)

Kar Clan:

Karmann (Clan Leader), Kardelia, Karbett, Karcelia.

Wayt Clan:

Waytbill (Clan Leader), Waytjulia.

Yat Clan:

Yatnolia (Clan Leader), Yatdoll.

Invaders:

Krat Clan:

Kratt (Clan Leader), Krattac, Kratatora, Kratthood (the Emissary), Kratjoa.

On the Station:

Chris (Station owner), Mary, (Chris's wife), Lilly (Chris and Mary's daughter).

Animals: Bruce (The station owner's chihuahua), Gary (A wedge-tailed eagle), Trev (A Pied Currawong), Sid (A Pied Currawong), Yrarbil = (A Snake).

The Valley (Map)

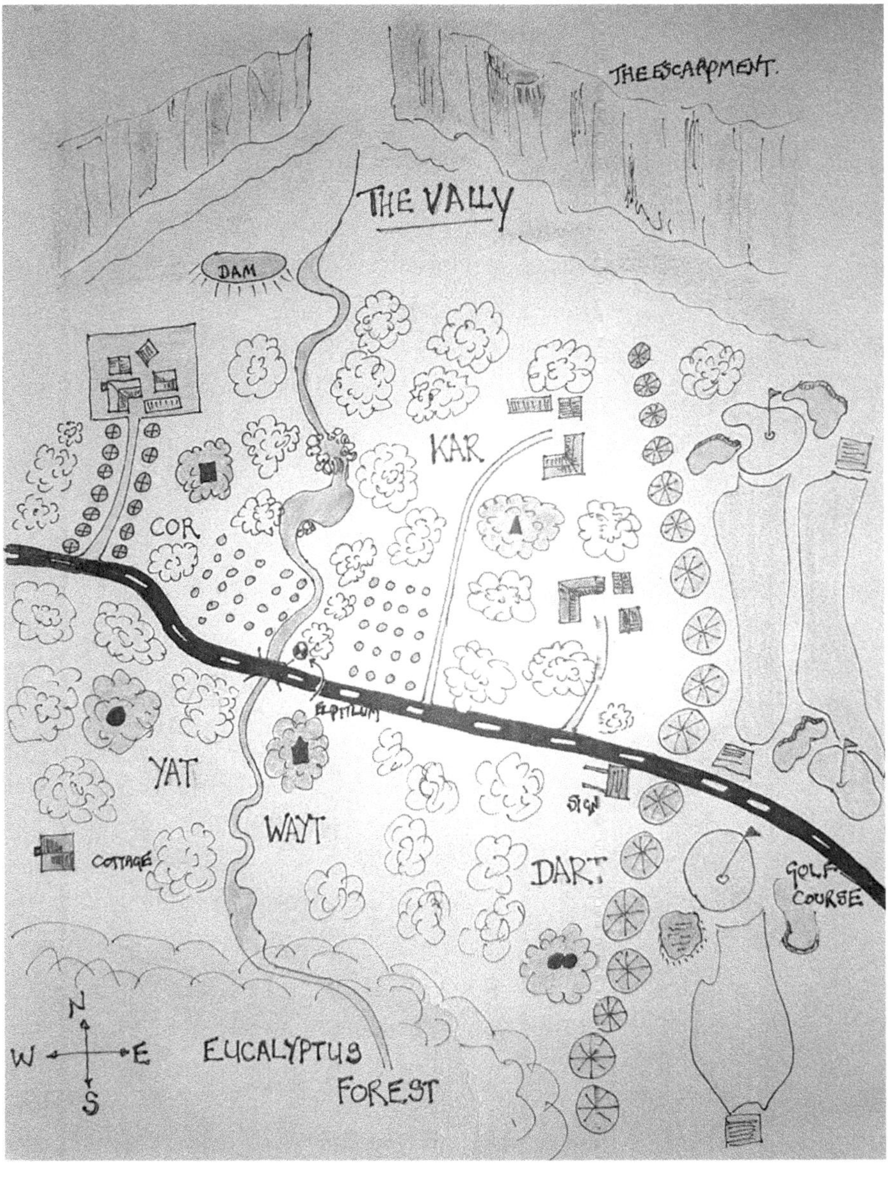

Clan Nest Trees =

PROLOGUE

Unseen

Stand upon the mountain,
Raise your wings up high,
Cast aside the chains of fear,
Trust and you will fly.
Rejoice now in the knowledge,
Returned to you this day,
You've always had the power
To simply fly away.

Robert Longley – 'Fly' (2014)

THE TWO BIRDS STRODE leisurely across the short cut grass of the putting green. About them, the crisp, still air at the end of the day helped them hear the slightest movement from the worms and grubs that burrowed and tunnelled under their claws. In places, crystal-clear water droplets clung or hung from the taller blades of grass that stood out above the generally even cut lawn.

They had timed their arrival at the green to coincide with the retraction of the automatic sprinkler system and the green was still damp where the water had recently sprayed the area. The putting green also fell under the shade of a tall Norfolk Island Pine that loomed over the western end of the norzela park (human golf course) and the shade and moisture were sure signs that worms and grubs would be easy picking for the pair.

Dartspadd, a male mytre stood still and alert, with his beak pointed like a dart at the ground. His partner, Dartvada mirrored his stance. To a passing observer they would have looked like statues posed, frozen, black, and white against the dark green of the lawn. Both stood perfectly still, listening, and watching for their prey to betray their location. The air about them cooled as Elppa (*the sun*) sank lower in the west.

Dartspadd picked up some movement, low and to his right. Stealthily he stepped lightly across the lawn and drove his powerful, pointed slate-grey beak-tip into the soil in search of a meal. As Dartspadd withdrew his beak it held the squirming upper part of an earth worm. In one movement, the mytre tossed his head back and swallowed the unlucky worm.

Dartvada looked across at him enviously. She strode quickly over to where he was standing and propped on one leg as she also listened intently for the faint sound of underground movement. She lowered her head toward the ground and within a moment, she could hear the soil being drilled as a worm burrowed below her. Like her partner, she plunged her hard, sharp, pointed beak into the soft, moist, soil and withdrew a long thick earthworm. She too threw her head back and swallowed the unfortunate creature. The two birds looked at each other for a moment, satisfied with the start of their hunt, before each broke into song.

The pair had known each other only two seasons and their songs were still forming, still immature and disjointed. Slight inconsistencies and bars of ill coordinated metre showed that these mytre were in the early stages of their relationship.

However, their song attracted the attention of their son, Dartkull, who had been born the season before. He had remained in the valley to help them secure their territory, their clan lands. The Dart clan land had been established on the small area of the valley to the west of the Wayt clan and south of the main road that separated them from the larger Kar clan lands to their north.

The Dart clan lands consisted of a small area of open bush land, the lower part of the line of Norfolk Island Pine that separated the bush from the norzela park and a small dam that sat on the western fringe of the norzela park.

Their lands were small and lacked any access to norzela nests (*human homes*), but they'd been welcomed into the valley, and they had settled into their small territory without incident.

Dartkull landed on the putting green and immediately his parents stopped singing. His father, Dartspadd turned his head and acknowledged his arrival. The three birds assumed the statuesque stance of a hunting mytre. Each bird listened and remained still and focused on their search for food under the turf of the green.

Dartkull had not found a meal before a small black and white bird swooped in, flapping vigorously as it snapped the air above the head of the younger mytre. As it did, it cried with a short, shrill, crisp, piercing call then it dropped down to the lawn and waited a moment before repeating its manoeuvre. The magpie lark again flapped and darted over and swooped at the larger black and white mytre, playing the game it did most days.

The younger mytre ignored the bothersome bird and continued to step and listen as it moved carefully over the short cut lawn of the green.

The magpie-lark teased and pestered the bigger bird, as if in a ritual dance, rather than an actual act of irritation or as a threat. In truth, the bigger magpie could easily drive the smaller bird away, but their relationship and the game they played had been one they had learnt from each of their forebears, and it amused the bigger bird to feel the game was still worth bothering with.

The smaller bird darted and dived in and out of the space in front of and above the mytre, and tried to peck and fluster the bigger bird, as Dartkull tried to concentrate on the sound of underground movement.

Becoming frustrated with the game and having their mealtime disturbed, Dratkull's father, Dartspadd, snapped his beak up at the magpie-lark and flapped briefly into the air to drive it away.

The smaller bird was fast. It rose, pivoted away from the bigger bird, and was away, avoiding its powerful beak before there was any contact. But this too was part of the game to the young bird, and the magpie-lark returned a moment later and resumed his mock attack on Dartkull. About every third dart and dive, Dartkull responded with a flash of his wings or a hop into the air, as his father had done. But nothing they did deterred the invaders' cries, calls or dives at their heads.

"Just ignore it," Dartvada said, sounding mildly irritated, before driving her beak into the soil at her feet to retrieve a moist worm. It squirmed and twisted in her beak before she flicked her head back and swallowed it in one gulp.

"I'll try," Dartkull said, sounding disheartened. Before adding, "Although, I don't mind, we play like this every day." The younger bird enjoyed the game. He was the only youngling in the Dart clan and his games with the magpie-lark were his only opportunity to play before he advanced to adulthood and took on more of the responsibilities that would come with life in a new, small clan on the valley land.

"You should go now," Dartkull shouted to his magpie-lark friend. "We can play tomorrow."

The magpie-lark chirped a shrill cry and said, "Tomorrow, mate." He flew off, toward the tall Norfolk Island pine closest to the putting green, and toward its own nest. The three Dart clan birds continued to stand, listen, and strike as the evening passed toward night and a blanket of darkness sank over the valley.

-0-

Perched high in the branches of the Norfolk Island Pine, another mytre sat still and inconspicuous as he observed the dance of the small magpie-lark and the young mytre on the putting green. He was a large mature bird with a strange white patch of small feathers emblazoned on his forehead. From high in the tree the strange mytre took note of the playful behaviour of the young bird and of his parents as they focused on their hunt for worms. *It'll be easy*, he thought. He looked about to be sure no one had seen him.

He watched the magpie-lark fly to its nest a few dozen branches below where he was hidden, and he too waited for the night to drape the valley in darkness. Then he dropped silently from his high branch, diving between the branches of the tree before leveling off and skimming the ground gracefully without needing to flap his wings. He moved quickly and in a straight line towards the open bush land and disappeared into the thick forest of eucalyptus trees to the southwest of the Dart clan lands. He was soon out of sight in the dark, close, forest.

Easy, the big mytre thought, as he stealthily glided into the cover of the trees, unseen. *Easy*.

PART ONE:
INVASION

1

Nwad

"Hope" is the thing with feathers —
That perches in the soul —
And sings the tune without the words —
And never stops — at all —

Emily Dickinson - 'Hope is a thing with Feathers' (1861)

THE BRIGHT ORANGE-GOLDEN orb appeared slowly, tipping the crest of the low hills on the eastern side of the valley. A shadow lay still, across the norzela park that covered the eastern hillside's lower slopes. The light grew slowly on the tall branches and leaves of the trees on the western side of the valley's slopes and was soon gracing the upper branches of the Cor clan's nest tree, a tall Spotted Gum whose leaves rustled and whispered to each other in the gentle breeze.

Other flora graced the slopes, sides, and floor of the valley. This included a line of rigid Port Jackson Pines, used to create a wind break along the driveway that ran up to the homestead on the Cor clan's territory, and an occasional handsome, straight Cedar Wattle that grew near the creek line.

A whispered breeze ran through the small stand of stumpy Cootamundra Wattle and green trunked Black Wattle from the same gentle wind, as they stood freely across the western fringe of the lower valley slopes. Low shrubs of Rubiaceae, Woombye, Handsome

Flat Pea, and the purple open flowers of the Kangaroo Apple grew in clumps and isolated islands at the bases of the taller trees or near the rocks along the creek line.

Tooth-leafed Heath Banksia and silver-leafed Silver Banksia spread out along the shaded areas at the sides of the sealed road that split the valley north from south. Weeping Bottlebrushes and Mudgee Wattle hugged the lower eastern slopes of the valley, before the stately, steady trunks of the Norfolk Island Pines that separated the norzela park from the private lands of the valley and acted like a line of giant sentinels looming from the brightening gloom.

Two mytres of the Cor clan, Corzell and Corselia, raised their heads from their deep nest and began a chorus from their home in the Spotted Gum, to welcome the return of Elppa, (*the sun*). "Quardle oodle ardle waddle doodle," they sang simultaneously. As a mated pair with a long history of successful breeding, they sang in almost perfect unison.

Their nest tree or home tree was always the first in the valley to be blessed by Elppa's light. Elppa was the bringer of light, and warmth. He was the God of day, of summer heat and winter warmth. The shrill call of a kookaburra had told them that Elppa was coming, and the birds of the valley were already awake, eagerly awaiting the growing glow of nwad (*the dawn*).

The kookaburra was always awake before Elppa's arrival and his crass, raucous, course, cackling, laughing call seemed to the mytre's ears, to mock Elppa. The kookaburra was loud, uncouth, and unwelcome in the valley by most of the mytres there, although Corzell tolerated his early morning calls and was even willing to share their home tree, affording the kookaburra a clear view across the valley floor.

More than once, the kookaburra had picked up and eaten a small brown snake or young goanna or monitor lizard, plotting to climb up their nest tree and steal Corzell and Corselia's eggs or young. The kookaburra had sometimes also called out a warning of an approaching wedge tailed eagle or brown goshawk.

Corselia and Corzell had only ever known this kookaburra as 'the kookaburra' because in all their years in the valley they'd only ever met this one. But they also knew his name was Bill. Corzell knew there were other kookaburras in the area, but they all seemed to keep their distance or keep to themselves, although they often heard the nwad and ksud (*Dusk/Evening*) calls from others.

The two black and white feathered birds coordinated their vocalising and as well as celebrating Elppa's return. They carolled to thank Bill for his unusual vigilance, friendship, and for his help to protect their nest tree.

As Elppa rose into the lightening, clear blue-sky, Corselia shuffled for comfort on the eggs where she had spent the night. She now sat comfortably on the three eggs that she'd laid weeks before. Corzell hopped over, through the still dew-dappled branches, to take a place next to her by their nest. He leant in and placed a grub on the lip of the nest for Corselia to snatch up for breakfast. After swallowing the fat, white grub, Corselia moved in the nest and fluffed out her chest feathers before she settled back to her nursery duties.

"Shall I take your place?" Corzell offered seeing his partner moving for comfort in the nest, although he knew she would say no.

"No," she said.

Corselia was his partner and while she would welcome an opportunity to fly off and gather her own food, even if only for a short time, she knew her place and her responsibility was to sit with her three eggs and with the young ones until they hatched, right up until they had feathers. She looked up, thankfully, at Corzell, and repeated, "No dear, I'll be fine here as long as you keep bringing those juicy fat grubs." Then she added cheerily, "I felt some movement in one of the eggs."

"Soon then, if Egnaro and Elppa bless us," Corzell said gladly, as he reached out a feathered wing to touch his partner as she wriggled again, before settling down, finally, over the eggs.

Corzell had been on guard all the previous night and after his short flight to bring the grub back for Corselia's breakfast, he found himself feeling tired and drawn.

"I hope they come soon my love, I get quite stiff and tired, perched here in the nest tree in the chilly night air. Egnaro has no pity for an old mytre in a high tree."

"Old… you're not old," Corselia said, with a chuckle, dismissing his concern.

Corzell was not old. He had seen only ten summers, and he was still in his prime. As he stretched out each wing and arched his neck up and down to loosen the stiffness, Corselia studied him. *He is still a handsome bird*, she thought.

Corzell was as big as mytres get, he had a dark black chest, and his wings were almost all black, apart from what looked like a racing stripe along each shoulder and down across to each wing tip. While most mytres had a white band of feathers on the nape of their necks, Corzell's white band extended from the back of his neck and head to join at his throat in an almost complete circle of white feathers. It looked like a bandana tied under his chin and draped back over his neck. His eyes were the strong amber of a mature adult, and he held his head proudly. His beak was powerful and white apart from the pointed tip, which was a pale black.

Corzell was considered big for a mytre, although in spite of his size, he was also lean in flight, so that he could fly swiftly and his inflight manoeuvrability was legendary, at least amongst the mytre's of the shallow valley they called home.

"I feel old now," he said, adding, "During Egnaro's passing it was cold, and I had a sense of…" he hesitated. "… a sense that something strange… something odd… something… sinister is coming." He hesitated again. "The valley seems uneasy… a change, a calamity, something new or something dangerous is coming."

Corselia regarded him with concern. Her partner had a powerful sense for activities in the valley and a gift of foresight that she or he could not explain. She'd been his partner since her adolescence.

They'd raised eight previous clutches of chicks who had all grown and flown because they were a good partnership. Four offspring from an earlier clutch still lived in the home tree and two of their first clutch of young lived in the gum tree next to their nest tree.

It meant the Cor clan were the second largest in the valley. Others of their offspring had joined with clans of the valley or flown to make their life in other parts of the district. They were one of the most successful partnerships in the valley and she knew her partner well, she trusted his judgments, his feelings and she worried now about his anxiety.

"What is it?" she asked in a whisper, as concern gripped her.

Corzell felt foolish upsetting his partner this way, before Elppa had warmed their nest, and before the other clans had joined in the nwad celebration of Elppa's return. He stretched high on his black legs with his claws holding firmly to the branch. He sang out a short chorus to the eastern hills and the growing glow of Elppa. Then he said reassuringly, "It's nothing… just a feeling… I don't know, it might be nothing, or the cold in my feathers. It's probably that… the cold." He began to swipe his long thick beak on the sides of the branch at his feet. As he did, his beak clicked and knocked on the wood. "It's just Egnaro's cold talking," he said at last, "ignore me."

She could see he was putting on a brave face. She knew him too well to be reassured by the dismissal of his feelings as, 'Just Egnaro's cold getting to his feathers'. But she also knew better than to press him on his concerns. "He'll tell me when he knows more," she told herself.

Slowly, around them the valley was coming to life as the rays from Elppa spread across the valley floor and up the far slope, over the norzela park and to the eucalypt forest beyond. The mytres from other clans, and many other birds, had started their nwad welcome celebration, singing, and carolling the arrival of Elppa's warmth and light.

Corzell could clearly hear the chirps and cries from other residents of the valley. A tribe of splendid fairy-wren had their nests in a bush next to the norzela nest *(human house)*. The fairy-wren also welcomed Elppa's arrival and although Corzell couldn't see them nervously flying out to the gravel drive and snatching up ants or small flying insects, he could hear their distinctive and sharp *tsit* cries and short reel of pips and trills as they began the days hunt.

Near them, a small family of willie-wagtails lived in a hedge near the back of the norzela nest. These fidgety, small black and white birds fed on spiders and tiny insects around the garden, and the mosquitoes that swarmed up from the dam after the rain or when the air was still.

He looked skyward and saw a flock of galah fly sleepily over the home tree and turn as one, to spiral down and land near the orchard on the far side of the creek. Their pink and grey feathers flashed brightly in Elppa's rays as they turned and twisted in a feathered mob, ready to land. Almost as one, they let out a loud strident *chee chee* that was shrill and sharp to Corzell's ears. It sounded like a wounded bird calling out to others in distress, but he knew it was the distinctive cry of the galah. He scanned the area as each bird started to waddle about between the fruit trees, pecking and scratching in the short grass and fallen leaves.

As he watched, a speedy Welcome Swallow flashed past his gaze and rolled and spun as it chased its prey on the wing. The small glossy black bird caught his eye as it was rare to see them this far from the norzela's nest and the water of the small dam on the north side of it. Corzell knew that they had their nest of mud under the eaves of the norzela nest's roof and they were most likely to stay in the vicinity of their nest site, as it was homing season.

The swallow banked swiftly and sang out to Corzell in a sharp high pitched *tswit tit-swee* as he passed. "Morning, Sir, Elppa's greetings to you," the swallow chirped as a rapid morning greeting. The swallow didn't wait for a response from Corzell. As quickly as he'd appeared, the bird dived low under the lower branches of the home tree and speared its way back to its mud nest under the eaves of the nearby norzela nest.

Corzell was fast in flight, and could manoeuvre well on the wing, but he knew he could never hope to match the dark, fork-tailed mastery of the swallow in agility and speed. Other birds were coming out from their nests or sleeping perches, and as Corzell continued to look out over the valley, he could hear the various birds fill the nwad air with chirps, twitters, warbles, and carols to welcome Elppa's light and warmth.

Far off, a flock of little corellas sang *curr-ur-up* as they drifted noisily over the treetops of the eucalypt forest to the south. In the lower branches of the nest tree a pair of magpie-lark cried out with a piecing *peewee* song, sung back and forward between a new mating pair. They had made their nest under the veranda of the norzela nest on the northern side of the property and were eagerly chasing flying insects and singing of their bliss.

All the birds also sang at the finish of the day, at ksud (*evening*) and although the birds loved the God Egnaro as much as Elppa, there was something altogether more joyful in their nwad chorus, something glorious, almost spiritual in the renewal of the day and the warmth that Elppa brought. Corzell drew strength and hope as the day opened across the valley, under the bright spring sun. Sitting high in the home tree, he felt like Lord of all the valley, although he knew he was not.

If any mytre was Lord of the valley, it was Karmann. He was the elder statesman of the valley mytre and leader of the largest clan, the Kar clan, to the east. Corzell and Karmann were old friends, but Corzell was glad not to have the responsibility of valley leadership, and as his feathers warmed, he felt calm, proud, and at peace. He soon forgot his feelings of unease and disquiet. A gentle breeze blew the feathers on his breast, and he took a deep breath and sat up to stretch his neck.

Corzell quickly looked out across the valley that had been his home since his birth. He had been born in the same tree he now sat in. It was where his family had grown and lived for as long as the tree had stood.

The valley was green and lush, with open grasslands and sporadic tussocks of Kangaroo Grass strewn between the stands of scattered Wattle, Marblewood, Cooba, and various types of Eucalyptus tree.

A shallow creek ran the length of the valley from north to south, and on either side of the creek before a sealed road spanned the valley east to west were two small orchards of fruit trees. Corzell's tree was on the western side of the valley, near a gravel road that ran up to the rural property that marked the upper limit of the Cor clan's territory.

He watched as two male norzela children came from the norzela nest on bikes. The property had a large norzela nest, and a few sheds or smaller outbuildings, including a wooden kennel for the norzela's old, lazy golden dog. A small dam had been built behind the norzela nest and Corzell knew that the two boys were from the property at the end of the gravel road. He'd watched them play before the norzela nest or ride their bikes up and down the gravel drive for years. His tree sat in an ideal location for overlooking the gravel road, the norzela nest, and the majority of the Cor clan's territory. From his perch in the home tree, he could see the sealed road running past the two orchards before it rose a little over a small bridge and then disappeared into the heat haze in the east.

The creek that ran along the valley floor formed the main boundary between the Cor clan's territory and the bigger, Kar clan to the east. The small creek ran well in winter or if spring rain blessed the valley, but in summer the creek became a long train of disconnected pools. Still, it was there to quench their thirst and it offered a clear delineation between the two clans above the road.

Three norzela nests had been built amongst the trees and fields of the upper valley. One was on the Cor clan's side of the creek. The other two norzela nests were across a wide grassed area above the creek. They both sat in the territory of the Kar clan.

The Kars had been in the valley before any of the other mytre clans and their elder, Karmann, had been a respected leader when Corzell's father had been young. The Kar's side of the upper valley occupied the largest of the mytre's territories in the small valley, and along with the two norzela nests, their territory had access to the east side of the creek, the other small orchard of fruit trees near the sealed road, and ample open grassland and groves of banksia and eucalyptus trees. It also boarded the norzela park that made up the far-eastern limit of the Kar clan's land. Corzell could also see as far as the territories of the other three clans in the green, still sleepy, shallow valley.

The other three clans were all smaller, with nests in the lower reaches of the valley. Yat clan occupied the area directly south of Cor clan across the sealed road. They also had access to the west side of the creek as it ran south, but a thick forest of eucalyptus and other trees, only a few hundred metres below the road, limited their territory, meaning Yat clan had access to no current norzela dwellings or orchards.

However, an old derelict cottage sat on the fringes of the eucalypt forest. It had long been abandoned and it offered no benefit to the Yat clan. The other clans, Dart and Wayt had territory in the south-eastern corner of the valley. Wayt clan had the smallest territory near the bridge and below the sealed road from Kar clan. While they had access to the eastern side of the valley creek, the great eucalyptus forest to the south also restricted the Wayt clan. Thick stands of Bangalay Gums, Eurabbie Gums, Dunn's White Gum, Flooded Gums, Yellow Box, Tallowwood, and occasional tall Spotted Gums covered the forest. The trees made a forest of rich nesting sites, and ample food, however, it lacked the open grassland and open areas that mytre enjoy for family gatherings, discourse, play, and foraging.

Dart clan was the newest clan to come to the valley. This clan occupied a narrow strip of territory south of the sealed road and next to Wayt clan with the same extensive eucalyptus forest limiting their expansion to the south. However, to their east, Dart, like the Kar clan, had unrestricted access to the lower reaches of the norzela park beyond the Norfolk Island Pine line, and to the green, bunker, hole, and water trap of the single hole adjacent to their territory.

The winter had brought overcast, cold, grey days, and frequent rain and as Corzell looked out over the green and golden valley he felt blessed by Korzela, the God of wind, Xervinu, the God of rain, and by Elppa, the God of the sun and day. He called out a short chorus of clicks and chortles to celebrate the Gods' work and care for them.

Corselia looked out from the nest and echoed her partner's song in perfect pitch and with exact accuracy. It was a song they had perfected together, singing out their parts of their hymn each nwad and nwod (*High sun or Noon*) to celebrate Elppa, and each ksud to celebrate Egnaro.

Then he saw the two boys riding their bikes along the gravel driveway, towards the home tree. Suddenly, he remembered his anxiety and he steeled himself for the tests of the days to come.

2

Protecting the Nest

Rose up this morning, smiled with the rising sun.
Three little birds pitch by my doorstep.
Singing sweet songs of melodies pure and true.
Saying, "'This is my message to you-ou-ou."

Singing, "Don't worry about a thing.
'Cause every little thing is gonna be alright.
Singing, "Don't worry about a thing (don't worry)
'Cause every little thing is gonna be alright.

Bob Marley and the Wailers – 'Three Little Birds'' (1977)

THE NORZELA BOY threw the rock high up into the branches of the Spotted Gum tree. He missed the magpie nest by three metres. But Corzell wasn't going to wait until the norzela child's arm grew stronger or his aim better. The big male mytre hopped across the tree branch near the nest and looked back at his partner. She gave a short squawk of encouragement, and he moved further out onto the fringes of the tree branch, drawing the attention of the troublesome child away from the nest.

"Aim at the big magpie," the second child called excitedly to his brother.

Corzell could see both boys at the base of the massive, grey-dappled eucalyptus tree's trunk. One was looking about at the ground for a second stone, while the older boy used his hand to shield his eyes from the sun's glare as he surveyed the branches above.

"Be careful," Corselia said as she watched her partner walk, clawed foot over clawed foot, along the thinning branch, exposing himself with each stride.

The nest was over twelve metres in the air and well hidden amongst the leaves and foliage of the tall Spotted Gum. The two norzela boys had tried to climb the lower reaches of the great gum's trunk, months earlier. They had failed but stayed to watch the two magpies re-build their nest in anticipation of the coming spring.

Corzell and Corselia were in their eighth season as a mated pair, and they had chosen their nest site well. Experience had told them to find a high safe place, downwind to protect the nest from the strong winds that blew up the valley. They also chose a narrow fork between two strong branches in the towering Spotted Gum that would hold their nest firmly and protect their eggs and their young from even the most determined predators, and from the wind, the rain, and the stones thrown by the small arms of troublesome norzela children. Although they had not anticipated the boy's rambunctious behaviour, Corzell determined quickly to attack the norzela boys and drive them both off before they did any real damage.

He glanced back to the nest, where Corselia was snuggled comfortably on their eggs and almost out of view behind the rim of the well-built, deep, and thick nest of twigs, small sticks, and threads of cotton pulled from an old blanket near a dog's kennel.

The eggs were almost ready to hatch and the last thing they needed was the disruption and potential damage caused by these small norzelas. The valley had been a quiet place to live and for the past few seasons they had raised their chicks to adulthood without losing a single fledgling.

Sitting high on the exposed branch, Corzell watched the bigger boy pick up a stone from the ground. One of the boys stepped back and looked at where he was going to lob the rock.

The flock of grey and pink galah that had settled on the grass at the edge of the orchard earlier in the day caught sight of the norzela boy and sensing the boy's potential for mischief, they took to the sky in a flurry of feathered flight. As they did, a car roared along the sealed road at the edge of the property where the boys lived. Corzell hated the fast, wheeled, killers and he watched the noisy vehicle speed away into the distance as the flock of galah lifted into the air and flew away, squawking, to the east.

The boys also saw the car drive past and watched as the flock of galahs filled the sky with flashes of pink, and grey, and noise.

As Corzell watched the birds rise quickly into the air a shiver ran down his spine and the same chill sense of foreboding gripped him as it had earlier that morning. *Had he foreseen the trouble these norzela boys would cause, or was it something else?* Troubled as he was, he couldn't see clearly what doom loomed for the valley.

The sound of a rock crashing through the leaves and branches of the gum tree disturbed his thoughts. The rock arced through the air and clattered through the tree only a few metres from his perch. He refocused on the boys at the base of the tree. One of the boys was now bent over, reaching for a new stone.

Corzell hesitated a moment, called in his mind for the speed of Korzela; the God of wind, then, he fell off the branch, tucked his claws into his body and flew at the boy. He spread his wings, then pulled them in to his chest as he dived directly at the child. He made no sound or screech, it was a sudden, silent dive aimed specifically at the boy's head.

The boy didn't see him coming until the last moment. Then he screamed and dropped the stone from his hand as he placed both of his hands over his head while bending low to the ground. Once the swoop was past, the child moved in a semi-stoop and started to run away, back to the gravel path that led to his home. His younger brother was quicker or had seen the impending attack early and had already taken to his heels. Both boys rushed for the pushbikes they had left, at the side of the gravel driveway. There they scooped up their bikes and began to peddle like mad for their home.

Corzell flapped violently just beyond the boy's reach, now screeching, and squawking loudly causing each boy to duck, dodge, and dive to avoid his impending strike. Corzell knew he had them on the run, and he held the final strike back until the norzela boys slowed their pace or became tired.

Both children were peddling as fast as they could. Heads down, arms wide, backsides lifted off the bike's saddle as their little legs pumped at the peddles.

"Is it gone?" the younger boy asked breathlessly, as he looked about and slowed his speed.

Just then Corzell jabbed at the younger boy's backside, causing the boy to squeal and twist as he renewed his pace.

His older brother slowed a little, not wanting to look foolish or fearful any longer. He held on to the pale blue handle grips on the handlebars tightly, as he skidded out his back wheel and came to a halt 50 metres from their front gate.

The younger boy peddled on a few metres further and came to a halt. He rubbed the strike point on his backside as he turned around cautiously. Both boys then sat still astride their bikes and looked back at the tall Spotted Gum. Neither could see the magpie.

"Stupid bird," the younger boy said angrily to mask his fear and the shock of pain caused by the strike. "Is it gone?" he asked his older brother, again.

Then Corzell struck once more. The mytre dropped from a nearby tree branch and dived at the older boy's head. As the bird neared the point of impact, he drew his wings in to increase his speed, like a streamlined spear he flew at the child. A moment before impact the magpie drew his feet up and thrust his wings wide catching air, creating an updraft that slowed his approach and pulled the bird up short of the boy's helmet.

"Duck," cried the younger brother as he watched the black and white bird drop from the tree branch and stream towards his older brother's head. It was too late. The bird's beak tapped the white plastic of the used ice-cream tub the boy was using as a helmet. It almost fell off his head as the bird's beak knocked into the plastic with a sharp hollow 'tonk'.

The bird struck again as the boy screamed and tried to peddle with renewed fury, in full retreat, back to his home. Corzell darted away from his attack and swooped in an arc back up toward the tall home tree from where he'd been watching before his swooping dive. Settling on a long branch he watched as the two boys rode their bikes away up the track, towards their home's front gate.

"Every bloody time," shouted the younger of the boys as he discarded his pushbike violently on the front lawn beyond the gate. The older boy tossed his bike to the ground too and they both ran inside.

"Mum, can you drive us to school?" the older boy shouted as they clattered into the kitchen. "That magpie won't let us past to get to the bus stop."

"I saw you!" their mother said, glaring at them, her hands on her hips. "Why do you have to tease those poor birds?"

"What?" said the older boy with an expression of innocence.

"I saw you throwing rocks at the birds, it's no wonder they fly at you like that. Leave them alone or it will be my hand across the back of your heads in future?

"What?" The older boy protested weakly.

"I told you we should 'av just gone to the bus stop," the younger brother said quietly.

Their mother shook her head in exasperation. "Come on you'll be late for school. I'd better drive you now."

The two boys gave each other a high five and each said, "Yer."

"Oh, so that was your plan all along, was it?" their mother said, putting her hands on her hips and regarding the boys with mock disdain. The boys looked chastened, before she smiled at them and drew them both into a hug. "Come on, you rascals, into the car, or you really will be late for school."

The boys took up their school bags and raced off to the car, parked in the driveway. As the car drove slowly down the gravel driveway toward the turnoff at the end of the drive and onto the sealed road, Corzell sat high on the branch and began to sing. His partner soon joined him in song and together they celebrated his victory over the schoolboys.

"You know they can't fly?" she said sarcastically, from the comfort of the nest.

He looked at her incredulously. "It's my job to protect the nest."

"I know, but they won't do any harm to the eggs from down there will they?"

"I like to let them know that they are not welcome while the young are in the nest, and one of those rocks could have found its mark."

Suddenly, Corselia felt a twitch from within the nest. She rose a little on her feet to look at the three eggs.

"It's time," she said, sounding delighted. "One is getting ready to hatch, and another looks almost ready."

Corzell flapped his wings and jumped over to investigate the nest and to see for himself.

"Praise Elppa," he said with a chorus of chortles and cries.

Before he had finished his song, the tip of a beak was protruding through the shell of one of the eggs and a small black claw kicked and pushed the shell fragments on the second egg, pushing the egg wall back. Only the third egg remained unmoving and uncracked.

3

The Kookaburra Calls

When I was young
My heart was young then, too

Anything that it would tell me
That's the thing that I would do.

But now I feel such emptiness within
For the thing that I want most in life is
The thing that I can't win.

Anne Murry - 'Snowbird' (1969)

THE THIRD EGG had taken a long time to hatch and both of Cordelia's brothers, Coruell and Corxell, were crying and straining for food before the female chick had shed the shell casement.

"She is so small," her father said, as he looked over the rim of the nest at his new daughter.

"But she has spirit," Corselia replied, "Look at her tenacity." She paused and considered her youngling. "I'm going to call her Cordelia," she announced boldly.

Her partner looked surprised, but nodded in agreement, and said, approvingly, "A wonderful choice."

Corselia started the process of removing and discarding the broken eggshells from the nest, knowing that a tidy nest gave her young a better opportunity to survive. She pulled at a loose twig that was sticking into the nest and tossed it vigorously over the side of the nest's rim. She even collected one of the chick's faecal sacs and dropped it from the nest, making sure that the nest was a clean and comfortable place for the hatchling chicks to feed and grow.

Having successfully raised eight broods of young, she had learnt early that in the first few weeks, a key part of her role, as their mother, was to keep the nest clean and to keep her chicks warm and safe. It was a task of which she never tired.

Already her brothers looked to be twice her size and Corselia knew from the moment of Cordelia's birth that she would need all her strength to survive and thrive in the confines of the nest.

The new smaller hatchling knew that while she was smaller and weaker than her brothers, she had one thing she could use to get her share of the food: her voice. Therefore, from the moment she was born, Cordelia began to squark, to cry, to push and to demand food from her parents, and while she was often trampled to the bottom of the nest or squashed between her two larger brothers in the battle for their parent's attention, she never gave up, and she never stopped crying and squawking.

"She really is small," Corzell said again as he dropped a worm into his daughter's wide-open beak. "I'll have to work twice as hard to keep this one fed."

All three chicks were blind at birth, and naked. Their pink skin meant they couldn't regulate their temperatures and all three moved to crawl under their mother's body for warmth.

Cordelia almost always found herself at the edge of her mother's chest, shivering as her bigger, stronger brothers pushed or dug with their growing feet and claws in their attempt to be in the warmest, central part of the nest.

All three chicks had inordinately large feet and long necks, but in contrast to adult beaks, their beaks, as chicks, were short and broad allowing them to open their mouths in a wide gape. The boys grew quickly, gulping at any morsel dropped in the nest or snatching at anything their parents presented to them. Cordelia looked to have no chance and her small size soon seemed to be a hinderance to her survival.

But as her mother had observed, she never stayed down, she never gave up. She pushed and fought for recognition, and for her share of the food, and for her mother or father's attention. Corselia stayed in the nest with the three small pale chicks for the first two weeks, keeping them warm, and continuing to keep the nest clean and tidy, while their father was constantly flying to and fro, with food for all his family, including his partner. Both parents knew what was required of them, and they worked well as a team to ensure that the chicks were kept warm, fed, and safe.

Cordelia's parents were a successful pair because, like all mytres, they practiced consecutive feeding, meaning that they didn't just favour the chick with the loudest voice or the most insistent cry. When returning to the nest, Corzell would determine which chick was in line to be fed and not favour any one above the others. They knew that in this way the three chicks would all grow and mature at the same relative rate, allowing for a more balanced approach to fostering and building their young family.

But because her brothers were bigger and more insistent, Cordelia found even with her parents' best intentions, more food was going to her older siblings. It was all she could do to open her beak and gape, straining her neck and vocalizing with all her might.

When mytres are born, it can take up to four weeks for their highly vocal calls to be heard with them making only weak vocal peeps in the first few weeks. But Cordelia, in spite of her small size, was determined to reach almost mature vocal cries and calls within a few days. It was this that forced her parents to respond with more food and attention, beyond their instinct to feed their clutch evenly. Soon, every fifteen minutes, when Corzell returned to the nest with food for his young, it was Cordelia that was always the first of the three chicks to sense his return to the nest, as if she knew he was coming before he arrived. She also felt even the slightest movement of the nest when Corzell landed with food for them, and she responded more urgently than her bigger brothers.

As soon as she was aware of her father's return, Cordelia would let him know where she was, and how hungry she was. She waited with her beak agape and with her sharp high pitch calls ringing out above the low peeps of her brothers.

Seeing Cordelia's small size and hearing her increasingly loud vocalisations, Corzell began to respond with growing quantities of food. Her father eagerly delivered earthworms, grasshoppers, crickets, spiders, ants, bees, weevils, cicadas, snails, caterpillars, and a host of other treats. Soon Corzell, in spite of his natural urge to feed all his chicks evenly, found that he had a special affection for Cordelia. While he presented all three chicks with food that they each eagerly devoured, he always gave the largest grub, or longest worm, the fattest grasshopper or caterpillar to his daughter. They all grew rapidly, and even Cordelia showed signs that she was going to grow and thrive alongside her bigger brothers.

Corzell and Corselia were also blessed with a 'helper' at feeding time. One of their now mature chicks from last season's brood had stayed with the family in the nest tree and was willingly flying back and forth alongside Corzell with food for the three chicks. This was not uncommon in mytre families and their habit of keeping an offspring about from the previous clutch meant they could increase the frequency of food deliveries to their young. This season, their daughter from the last season's clutch; Corhelia was helping Corzell bring food back to the nest.

Corhelia had watched her parents build and reinforce the nest, share the duties of protecting and defending their territory and prepare for the current nesting and clutching season. She'd learnt from both her mother and father where to build a nest, how to find twigs and sticks, how to care for eggs and feed hatchlings. Now she was putting into practice what her parents had taught her. While helping her father feed her brothers and sisters from this season, she watched Corselia keep the nest in pristine condition.

The weather had begun to grow warm, and they had not had rain in over two weeks. Their nest was well protected from the valley wind and the chicks had started to become covered with light plumage. Pinfeathers had shown on the wings and tail of the boys by the end of the first week, although Cordelia's feather development was a few days behind. By the third week, downy grey feathers had started to show on the small birds' rump, head, and back. Again, Cordelia was a few days behind the boys and her overall size and weight remained lower than her brothers. But Corselia and Corzell were both delighted with the health and growth of their clutch.

Only one thing stood out as different from their other clutches. Cordelia had a strange configuration of feathers above her upper beak. One feather or a small gaggle of small black feathers had grown out above her beak, so that it looked like she had a small horn on her otherwise smooth forehead. It was Corselia who noticed it first and she thought to remove the unusual shock of feathers. But her partner had discouraged her and said it made her appear more tenacious or even fierce, and so it was that Cordelia's small feathered 'horn' remained.

After two weeks, Corselia felt able to leave the chicks and help gather food for her young, with her partner and their helper, Corhelia. Corselia could see the small hatchlings had started to grow more feathers and although Cordelia's 'horn' was even more pronounced, she remained still noticeably smaller than her brothers, Coruell and Corxell. Corzell reassured their mother that they would all grow, and he and Corhelia redoubled their foraging efforts.

As the time for fledging approached Corselia's contributions to the feeding and foraging parties greatly increased the size and growth of her chicks. As well, she was feeling it was time for her to fly again after weeks of sitting on the eggs and cleaning the nest. All birds love to fly and, as before when she'd been on the nest, she missed the feel of the zephyr in her feathers and the freedom that flying brings. Contributing to her chicks' development now allowed her to fly and search with Corzell and her pride in her brood grew with her contribution.

-0-

Taking a break between trips back and forth for grubs and grasshoppers, Corzell was perched on a branch near their nest when Bill, the kookaburra, flew up and settled a few metres away from him on an opposite branch.

"Elppa's greetings," Corzell said in a formal almost gruff tone.

"Err… yer, same to you," Bill said awkwardly, before adding, "How's the better half?"

"Well," Corzell replied stiffly.

"She was a chilly night mate, wot der yer reckon?" Bill continued.

"Yes, it was," Corzell agreed, still in a formal tone and still shaking off the chill that had settled on his quills from the night before.

"How are yer clutch com'n on mate?" Bill asked cheerily.

Corzell wasn't surprised by the question. They had talked of little else each morning now for a few weeks.

"Fine," he replied, adding, "All three are growing and showing their feathers, thanks to Elppa, although there is still one a little smaller than the others, but she is healthy all the same."

He couldn't hide the pride he felt as he spoke. The other clans regarded them well for their care and skill as parents, because of their success with their clutches for the past eight seasons.

"Good to hear, mate. If she's anything like the one I have, she'll only know one bloody word, hey, and use it incessantly, 'food, food, food'. I'll tell ya she's driving me spare."

Corzell understood how demanding young birds could be in their need to be constantly fed. "But you only have one, don't you? I have three to look after and while I'm glad of Corselia's and Corhelia's help, it is still constant and demanding work with three to feed."

"One's enough, I reckon, mate," the kookaburra replied.

They sat on the branch together, for a moment in silence. Corzell watched his kookaburra friend casually out of the corner of one eye. In many places, the kookaburra will opportunistically take and eat young magpies, but Corzell and this kookaburra had struck up an informal alliance or friendship and Corzell felt confident that Bill, at least, could be trusted to leave his chicks or young alone. *But still...* he thought as he watched the visitor carefully.

"You've been busy then," Bill asked. "Too busy to look beyond your territory for trouble I guess."

"Trouble?" Corzell asked, suddenly concerned.

The kookaburra looked briefly at Corzell and then began to preen the feathers on his right wing. The kookaburra's beak was thick and powerful and like the mytre's its tip ended in a powerful point. Bill then spread his wing showing the brown, light brown, and pale blue feathers of its powerful wing. His head turned and tucking it under the wing, he began to delicately clean and twitch his beak along each individual feather. Without warning the kookaburra stopped and looked across at Corzell.

Suddenly, Bill said in a whisper, "Sometins' goin' on, I can feel it, mate. I was flying over the norzela park yesterday and something was definitely not right." Bill looked up briefly at Corzell, blinked and then returned to preening his wing.

"What wasn't right?" Corzell asked suspiciously. The norzela park was an area on the eastern flank of the valley. It was beyond Corzell's territory, and he had only ever seen it from a distance. To reach it, would mean flying over the Kar clan's territory to the far side of the valley or to cross the sealed road and trespass on both the Wayt and the Dart clans' lands, actions which Corzell knew were strictly forbidden and carried a significant risk of attack.

Each clan knew to keep to their own territory, and each clan vigorously defended their territory from other clans of the valley, or even invaders from beyond the valley's bouncary. Corzell knew the boundaries did not apply to kookaburra and Bill was safe flying over the valley, unless he'd come to take their young. Corzell waited intently for what Bill was about to say.

The kookaburra ignored him for a moment longer as he continued to pluck and pull at the feathers under his wing.

Corzell became impatient. "Did you see something?" Corzell asked insistently, feeling his impatience grow. "At the norzela park … did you see something?" he asked again.

Suddenly distracted, Bill looked down. He saw something on the ground below them, something slithering or crawling through the leaf litter at the base of the gum tree. He stopped his preening and focused intently on the movement on the leaf-strewn ground.

"Dead mate, two of them were dead, two mytre, by the tall line of pine trees. You know… south of the sealed road."

The kookaburra spoke in a matter-of-fact way, his focus now shifted completely to his potential prey. His eyes never moving from the shuffling in the leaves below him.

Corzell didn't understand and turned his head sideways at the visitor. "Who was dead?" he asked, with growing concern and frustration. "Which clan were the birds from?" Although, he knew that the pine trees south of the road were on the Dart clan lands, so he assumed the dead mytres were from that clan.

"Dunno," Bill replied as he shifted his weight from one claw to the other and folded his wings in tightly to his flanks.

"And how did they die?" Corzell asked, becoming more worried.

"Dunno mate. But it was a horrible sight."

Corzell wanted to know more, but the kookaburra was now completely focused on whatever was in the underbrush below them.

However, before launching himself off the branch he simply said, "It was horrible, two mytre dead. But I can see yer flat out like a lizard drinking here, so I'll be off, mate. You take care… and good luck with the young'uns."

"But… what else can you tell me?" Corzell called after Bill, but it was too late. The kookaburra had already dropped off the branch.

Corzell watched him dive toward his prey and saw the stocky bird land and swiftly snatch up a small lizard in his thick straight beak and lift off into the air. He flew low at first, then higher, east towards the climbing Elppa and the norzela park in the near distance.

He watched his friend Bill fly away swiftly to find a private place to consume his prey. His sense of foreboding returned, and a shiver ran down his back. Then thinking of the two mytre who were now gone, he spoke softly, to himself, almost like a prayer, "May they find flight in the Great flock of Elppa."

4

Fledgling Flight

And so here we go, bluebird
Back to the sky on your own.

Oh, let him go, bluebird
Ready to fly, you and I
Here we go
Here we go.

Sara Bareilles - 'Bluebird'' (2010)

BRINGING UP YOUNG chicks is a time-consuming activity. From nwad to ksud, Corzell, Corhelia and now, Corselia flew back and forth from the orchard, or from the branches of other trees, from the creek bank or from the lawn in front of the norzela's nest, back up to the nest tree with food, loaded in their beaks. Corselia and Corhelia's help was invaluable and between them they formed an efficient trio of hunters and gatherers.

The chicks were about to fledge and as the hour for the chicks' first flight grew near, Corzell's anxiety increased. Lately, to help grow the chicks' strength more quickly Corzell had taken to stealing food placed out for the norzela's old, lazy golden labrador dog. The labrador had lived in the valley almost as long as Corzell and he didn't seem to mind the familiar magpie taking dried dog food from his bowl. So, with the fledglings about to fly the nest, Corzell's full interest was in feeding his young and building their courage. His conversation with Bill, from the day before troubled him still, but he had other more pressing and altogether more practical concerns to address. The first flight of a new brood was a stressful time for all birds, but high up in the Spotted Gum tree, high above the ground, the risk of encouraging a chick to fly too soon meant a sudden fall and the risk of death.

"Maybe we should wait another day?" Corselia said, feeling uncertain.

She looked at the smallest chick. Her daughter had remained smaller than her brothers and she could see that while healthy, Cordelia looked more fragile, even with the tuft of feathers that made a small horn like protrusion on her forehead.

"Another day will allow the little one to grow stronger," Corselia said.

"No, it's time," Corzell said with certainty.

"We've seen Egnaro rise and fall, grow and diminish. It's time now. They have to fly at some point, and the time is now."

Corzell was eager to clear the nest as soon as possible. His feelings of unease had returned. His sense that something dreadful was coming to the valley clans had grown with the kookaburra's news about the two dead mytres near the line of pine trees on the Dart clan's territory.

He'd tried to explain how he felt to Corselia but with nothing more to go on than a 'feeling' she had listened but dismissed his concerns. She had other more pressing and practical concerns too. She was worried about the impending young birds' first flight and about the risks and work involved in bringing up three chicks after their fledge. She was exhausted.

They all were, even Corhelia had said how tired she was from the constant work of flying in and out of the nest tree with food for the chicks.

"That's why we need to get the chicks to fledge," Corzell said. "Once they can fly, we can take them to the food rather than bring the food up to the nest tree for them to feed there."

"But they're not ready," Corselia insisted.

"Ready or not, they will fly or fall today," Corzell asserted.

This is not like my partner, Corselia thought. *Maybe he really is sure that something terrible is coming.* She pondered his need to hurry the chicks out of the nest and into flight. *Maybe he is right. Maybe it is time and their rush to fledge is important.*

"Can we at least fledge the boys first?" Corselia begged, as a concession.

Corzell nuzzled up to his partner and placed his head beside hers. Their beaks clicked as they sat next to each other. For a moment all was calm. Their acute hearing meant they could hear each other's rapidly beating hearts. It allowed them a moment of comfort and reassurance and the sound of their combined heart beats gave them confidence and joy.

"Boys first... as you wish, my dear," Corzell conceded kindly.

"Gather about, boys," Corselia said to the two bigger birds of her brood. "Cordelia, you watch for now, dear."

The boys had bold black wing feathers, but their chest plumage was still a mottled grey colour. Their primary wing and tail feathers looked to have grown strong and thick with grey-white patches showing on the underside of each wing where the secondary wing feathers grew. The two young birds had partially white tail feathers, although, Coruell had a much more pronounced patch of white on his upper tail, while Corxell had a darker upper tail. Both young birds looked eager to fly and came boldly to the rim of the nest.

"Wait," said their father from a branch opposite the nest. "You look strong and ready to fly. That I am sure will be easy for you, but I know from experience that the real test of your first flight will be landing. I will fly down with you and be there when you land. Stay near me on the ground, near the tree roots at the bottom of the nest tree, then we will fly back up and land on this branch. Now watch me as I show you what I mean."

Corzell dropped from the branch and mostly glided to the tree roots near the base of the nest tree. He touched down for a moment then, flapping his strong wings, took off almost vertically and flew back to the branch he had left, where he landed delicately.

"Easy," said Corxell, adding excitedly, "Can I go first?"

"Okay, follow me," Corzell said as he again dropped off the branch and glided down to the ground.

Corxell had no hesitation and almost leapt from the nest, diving after his father in a reckless and foolhardy way. Within moments the two birds were on the ground. Corxell had glided easily down, only needing to correct his inflight pitch once or twice as he adjusted to the wind closer to the ground. To Corzell's surprise his son also found the landing on the ground uncomplicated.

"There, I told you it would be easy," Corxell called up to his brother as he lightly touched down on the soil.

"Now we'll fly back up to the branch," his father said as he took off.

Corxell struggled at first to generate enough lift to rise into the air, but after a few rapid flaps of his growing wings he rose slowly skyward. With each down beat he flew higher and within moments he had risen to the height of the branch opposite the nest. His father had landed and was encouraging him to land next to him.

"Come on, son, come in easy, don't hurry at the branch."

They were wasted words, Corxell flapped and fidgeted over the branch as he struggled to bring his claws onto the wood. Three times he tried to grip the branch and three times he flapped up as he tried to put his feet down. He just couldn't coordinate the landing.

"Not as easy as you thought," Coruell said mockingly.

In the end, Corxell stopped flapping his wings and simply slumped onto the branch and tried mightily to hang on with his claws. He slipped once then found his grip on the branch. Taking a deep breath, he settled, finally, on the tree branch. He was down, but it was a most ungraceful landing. Cordelia watched carefully, learning from her brother's efforts.

"Well, you made it back in one piece," Corzell said encouragingly. "I'm sure with a little more practice you'll master the landing soon enough."

"My turn," said Coruell playfully.

Corzell gave the same instructions, and the father and son flew down to the roots of the nest tree and back up again. Coruell was no more graceful than his brother, and he too struggled with the landing.

The two male birds then set off from the branch opposite the nest again and again so that by the tenth attempt at landing high on the branch they had mastered the art of landing. Their flying and landing practice continued until Elppa was high in the sky.

They had mastered flight easily but each of the boys had landed awkwardly in bushes or on limbs that didn't hold their weight so they each sported dusty wings or loosened feathers by the end of their initial fledging.

All the while, Cordelia had been watching her brothers, learning as they flew and landed, and noting the delicate wing adjustments that were needed in high winds, or when coming close to the ground.

"Come on, Sis," Corxell called, "Your turn."

"Are you ready?" Corselia asked her daughter, still concerned.

"I'll be fine, Mum. Dad did you want to fly down with me and watch me land before I come back up into the nest tree?"

"No dear, I'm sure you'll be fine. I saw you watching your brothers." As he spoke, he suppressed his anxiety. He briefly looked across at his partner and Corhelia perched next to the nest. He tilted his head as if to say, here goes nothing.

Cordelia hopped up to the rim of the nest and looked out over the valley. It was only in that moment that she saw how high up they were and how big and beautiful the valley was. She looked around at the other trees, at the creek line, at the norzela's nest and at the vast powder-blue sky above them.

Then without a care in the world, she dropped into the void and glided down towards the tree roots. She corrected her yaw, pitch and roll perfectly as she descended, however, instead of landing, she swooped low over the ground, centimetres above the leaf litter and tree roots, then darted away from the tree in a direct line toward the gravel road. There, she turned swiftly and flapped vigorously high into the sky between the nest tree and the line of Port Jackson Pines.

Corselia and Corzell gasped as their youngest and the smallest of the brood raced along the narrow gap between the trees and easily switched direction, flying around the northern end of the nest tree before coming into land perfectly on the branch next to her father. Both parents looked worried and concerned, but each secretly felt the pride that comes from knowing their child is gifted and would be safe.

"Show off," said Corxell.

"I can do better than that," said Coruell before dropping off the branch and flying up into the sky near their nest tree.

"Come back at once," Corselia shouted after him. Coruell ignored his mother and flapped vigorously, labouring up above the height of the tall tree before swooping down toward the line of the creek. His parents continued to call him back squawking at him vigorously.

Coruell continued to ignore them and stayed out, flying between the pines and the eucalypts, twisting, and turning in flight and swooping low before flapping with all his might to climb high over the valley. Seeing Cordelia's flight had made him envious, and he couldn't help himself as he continued to show off to impress his parents and siblings. All birds love to fly and to have come from the confines of the nest into the zephyr and sunshine of the sky was a wonder only birds and some insects ever feel.

Although upset with the liberty he had taken, as his family watched, their joyful delight grew seeing the freedom and happiness Coruell exhibited. He was living the dream all birds have before fledging. The dream to be free and unhindered on the wing.

"Tell him to come back," Cordelia called out suddenly. Shouting, "Tell him to come back, now!" Her voice sounded urgent and insistent.

"Don't spoil his fun," her brother said, misunderstanding her cry as envy.

"Father, tell him to come back now! Something isn't right, something else is flying today."

Cordelia's voice had become deep and sinister, her words came almost from another's voice. Her parents looked at her aghast as if she had been possessed. Corhelia froze where she was perched, and her brother now afraid, cowered low on his branch. Was this the fear, the terror, Corzell had foreseen weeks before? Could his daughter also read the signs, hear the voices, and feel the vibrations that foretold the future. Corzell called at once, urgently, to his son.

"Coruell come back to the nest tree." Then he braced himself for flight and was about to launch himself into the air when it struck.

Coruell had just dived down between the small trees near the creek line and was struggling to climb higher, making ready to dive back into the nest tree when the Wedge-tailed eagle crashed into him. Coruell didn't stand a chance. The eagle's talons gripped onto the smaller bird's body and wing, tearing it from the sky and making off with it held tightly in its grip.

Corzell took to the wing to chase the big bird and to try and save his son, but it was too late. The eagle rose swiftly into the clear powder-blue sky, higher than Corzell could fly, and was soon lost in the glare of Elppa's rays to the west. In a flash, their newest, eldest son was gone. Taken on the wing by a Wedge-tailed eagle.

Corselia was in tears, but with Corhelia's help she ushered the two young mytre back into the nest.

Corzell returned to the nest tree and joined the others of his family in their grief. "I haven't seen an eagle near the valley in six seasons," he said, his voice laced with remorse, anger, and sadness. "Why did one have to pass by today?"

Corselia and her young lay in the nest, in shock. Corhelia sat stunned and quivering on her branch perch. No one spoke for a long time as they came to grips with the eagle's attack. Eventually, Corzell spoke to Cordelia.

"You saw it coming didn't you, Cordelia?" her father asked, solemnly.

"I felt something, Father. I didn't know what it was. But I felt something keere (evil) coming."

Her two parents looked at each other. "She has the gift of foresight," Corselia said in a soft voice. "Your gift, my dear," she added talking low and directly to her partner, reminding Corzell that he also had the gift to sense the future.

"Maybe," Corzell conceded, whispering back, disappointed. "But I didn't see the eagle coming. Foresight without knowledge and wisdom is still blind. We must keep her power quiet until we, and she, can learn the full extent of the gift she has."

"This has been the first fledgling we have lost in eight seasons," Corselia said sadly.

"It was Elppa's will," Corzell said. "The Gods give, and the Gods take away. It has ever been thus."

"Then the Gods are fools," said Corselia bitterly. The two adult birds sat outside the nest close together on one of the broad limbs that supported the nest.

"He has joined the Great flock of Elppa," Corzell said sadly.

"Then our son flies with the best of the mytre," Corselia added.

The loss of their son cut them deeply, but after a short time of reflection and mourning, they returned to the only duty they had that made any sense, feeding their two remaining fledgelings.

Trying to understand what Cordelia's gift might mean for our clan's future is a challenge for another time, Corzell thought.

5

An Invitation

Talking to the songbird yesterday
Flew me to a past not far away
She's a little pirate in my mind

Singing songs of love to pass the time...
Talk of better days that have yet to come
Never felt this love from anyone.

She's not anyone...

A man can never dream these kind of things
Especially when she came and spread her wings
Whispered in my ear the things I'd like
Then she flew away into the night.

Oasis – 'Songbird' (2002)

THE COR CLAN gathered on the lawn near the norzela nest. They stood amongst a slew of discarded toys, spread about the lawn by thoughtless or lazy norzela children, who had left them, abandoned after their play. Toy trucks and toy alien creatures with long necks and wide mouths with white teeth. They looked to have come from another world or another time, as they were not creatures any of the Cor clan had seen before. They proved harmless and stood or lay like statues amongst the grass.

Corselia explained to Cordelia that they were norzela things, harmless and foolish things, "toys" she called them.

The birds ignored them as they gathered. Even the birds from other nest trees, the sisters, and brothers of Cordelia and Corxell from previous broods, came to sing in recognition of their loss.

The birds were all related to Cordelia's parents as either offspring or the sons and daughters of their offspring. As a successful mated couple, Corzell and Corselia's broods that had stayed in the valley had made homes in the trees in the Cor clan's territory. Word spread of their loss and while the two small fledglings needed feeding constantly, there was still time to gather and sing as Elppa reached his zenith.

The birds didn't stay long, gathered on the lawn. But their short warbling carol brought the woman norzela out from the nearby house to listen.

"Look at the magpies," she called back into the house to her two boys. "Come on... I've never seen this many in one place before," she said with surprise and delight. "There must be twelve magpies here all in one place... come on boys come and look at them."

The boys stayed inside, engrossed in their video game, and still smarting from the big magpie chasing them away from the nest tree weeks before.

"This is remarkable," the female norzela said to herself. She watched for a moment longer then went inside to bring the birds some scraps of food as a reward for their vocalisation. The birds carolling was a lament that she had no understanding of and while the human heard a melodic, coordinated, joyful chorus of almost continuous hums and warbles, the birds were singing of their loss, of their sadness, and of their grief at Coruell's parting.

"May he find a place in the Great flock of Elppa," they sang as one. Then, they stood silently on the lawn with their heads bowed and their wings tucked in solemnly.

Only Corzell hadn't sung. His loss was too recent and his grief too raw. Instead, he held his head high and scanned the sky in case the wedgie should return. He half hoped it would so he could fly up and challenge the vile creature. If it returned, he vowed to fly up and fight his enemy and release his grief in what would surely be a one-sided and pointless suicidal battle. *Then*, he thought, *I can be beside my son in the Great flock of Elppa.*

But the Wedge-tailed eagle did not show itself, and before the woman had returned, the circle of mytre's had finished their song and flown away.

"Where have they gone?" she asked herself when she came outside, pieces of bread in her hand. "Silly birds," she said, as she cast the scraps of stale bread onto the lawn for them in case they came back.

Corzell and Corselia returned to the work of feeding the two-remaining offspring. Each took one of the children and began the work of teaching them what to eat, where to find food and how best to get the most succulent snacks from their territory.

Corzell took his daughter, in the hope of learning more about her gift. They flew away after the gathering on the lawn to the fruit tree orchard near the sealed road. There was always food to find; beetles, bugs, ants, small flying insects, bees, or even fallen fruit. Corzell wanted to ask his daughter some questions while they searched and ate in the orchard. They walked slowly under the fruit trees lined up before them in rows and Corzell asked in a whisper between his search for worms.

"How did you know the eagle would take your brother?"

"I didn't... I mean... I don't think that was what I felt coming."

"In the nest, almost from before I could see with my eyes, I felt I could see beyond the nest. I could feel you coming back to the nest. I could feel the wind in the branches above and I could sense if you were tense or relaxed."

"'How?" Corzell asked quizzically.

"I don't know... they were just... feelings. But yesterday I felt something dark, like a cloud sliding across Egnaro. Something slid across my mind's eye. But it wasn't the Wedge-tailed eagle, I'm sure of that. There is some other tragedy coming, some other calamity, but I can't see it clearly."

Corzell plucked a beetle from the short grass under a fruit tree and dropped it into Cordelia's open beak as she squawked at his side. She gulped it down without hesitation and instantly began to beg for more food.

"I can sometimes sense when things are turning ill," Corzell said. "It seems to be a gift we share. Before you hatched, I had a sense of impending doom. That some shadow or foul net were about to be cast over the valley. But I couldn't see it clearly. I wondered if the Wedge-tailed eagle was the manifestation of the shadow. But I still feel there is something else, something..."

"Dark and oppressive..." Cordelia finished.

"Exactly... " Corzell said quickly. "But I can't see it all, just glimpses of some illness, or keere that will come to the valley."

He snapped at a grasshopper and missed. Then he stood still, listening for a grub moving underground. Cordelia followed behind him, listening as he did and only moving, only stepping forward, when her father strode slowly forward one step at a time. He pushed his beak into the soft moist soil near a fence post and withdrew a thick white grub. Cordelia again opened her mouth wide and swallowed the juicy grub in one gulp as her father dropped it in.

Slowly, looking constantly for food, he paced over to the side of the sealed road. Before them was the bridge and the Cor clan side of the creek.

"This is a corner of our territory," Corzell said solemnly. "Our lands and skies extend back from here on this side of the road and in this direction," He pointed with a wing. "And along the creek line to the north." Cordelia looked back to where her father was pointing in through the trees and bushes beyond the orchard. Then she looked along the sealed road, towards the east.

"What's up there?" she asked casually.

"On this side of the road." He pointed left. "Are the Kar clan lands. On the other side of the road are the Wayt, and further up by the norzela thing, is the start of the Dart clan lands."

The norzela thing was a road sign that indicated that the turn off to the Westland's Golf Course was 500 metres ahead.

TURN OFF TO THE WESTLAND'S

GOLF COURSE 500 METRES

(ON THE RIGHT)

Cordelia looked at the sign. None of it made any sense. But something made her consider it in detail. Something odd or dreamlike gripped her as she considered it.

Her father went on, "The land directly opposite us here across the sealed road belongs to the Yat clan. We're closely related to them, but still, it is against our custom to trespass on another clan's land or sky without permission or consent."

As they stood near the bridge, Elppa dropped lower, toward the western rim of the valley casting much of the valley in shadow.

"Time to go," Corzell said, as he, then his daughter, took to the wing and returned to the nest tree to prepare for the coming ksud chorus.

Corzell though was troubled and still grief stricken, and back at the nest he spoke with Corselia. "I need some time alone... to think, to... just to be alone with my thoughts," he told his partner.

She could see the stress of the fledglings' flight, the shock of losing their son to the eagle and at discovering that Cordelia may have the gift of foresight had all taken their toll on his sense of wellbeing.

"We'll be here when you get back," she reassured him. Corhelia was still with her and together she knew they would be able to settle the distressed, tired, and excited young birds down for the looming night. The valley shadows had grown but she knew they had time yet before the ksud carolling so she encouraged him on his way.

He knew the creek with its gentle flowing water and the lush rich green river plants and shrubs was the right place to go now and he flew off in search of the solitude he sought. He landed near some large boulders and scratched about in the moss beside the rocks for worms and even small frogs. The air was always cooler at the creek, and he immediately felt more comfortable. However, he'd not been there long when he heard another mytre call his name.

"Corzell!"

He looked with a start, across to the further bank of the creek and saw Karbett and Kardelia, from the Kar clan, a short hop away. He knew them well, but they still caught him off guard, so focused had he been on his ongoing search for meaning in his loss.

"Elppa's greeting," Corzell said, after a moment. Though his love of Elppa was waning.

"Elppa's greeting to you too," Karbett offered formally.

"Are you foraging for your clutch?" Corzell asked politely, respectfully, not knowing if they had even had eggs this season.

"We had two eggs hatch, but the norzela's cat took them when they were still blind," Karbett said sadly.

Corzell knew about the cat. It lived at one of the two norzela nests in the Kar clan's territory, and it had been terrorizing the Kar clan's nests for the past few years. This was not the first time Corzell had heard of the cat's keere doing.

"I'm sorry to hear of your loss," Corzell said solemnly, remembering his own recent loss to the eagle.

"But that isn't why we've come to talk with you, Corzell," Kardelia said abruptly. She paused, then said quickly, "There's going to be an elpitlum," (*community meeting*).

Corzell looked shocked. "There hasn't been an elpitlum in ages, and it's hatching time, nestling time, feeding time, fledgling time. This is no time to talk, to meet."

"It's not nestling time, feeding time, or fledgling time for us," Kardelia said sharply and bitterly, reminding Corzell of their loss.

"We have lost a fledgling too," Corzell said softly. "A Wedge-tailed eagle took him on the wing, yesterday, on the day of his first flight." Saying it aloud brought it all back and he paused and dropped his head with renewed grief.

"It's important," Karbett said in a softer tone. Adding, "Karmann has sent us to call all the clan leaders and their partners to the elpitlum. After ksud tonight."

"Tonight!" Corzell said, sounding shocked, before he relaxed his tone as he realised it must indeed be important.

"I can come, although Corselia will want to stay with the young." He paused, then added, "In fact I want her to stay with our offspring if the cat is about. It has been a troubling time without more worry."

"How many young do you have?" Karbett asked, kindly.

"Three… no… two, bless Elppa," he found himself saying in spite of himself. Before adding, "We have one male and one female. She's small, but a fighter. We called her Cordelia," Corzell said respectfully.

"Cordelia… like the mytre from legend," Kardelia scoffed incredulously.

"Yes, she has spirit, and like the Cordelia from our stories, she will be a proud leader one day, I'm sure," Corzell spoke proudly, but drew in his tone to a humbler aspect.

Quickly deciding to change the subject he asked, "Why is the elpitlum so important?"

As he spoke, he walked over to the creek bank and then hopped up, onto a large bolder at the base of a grey and mottled tree. A Bronze Rambler Grevillia bush grew near the bolder and as some of the leaves and toothbrush like flowers cascaded over part of the rock, he pecked at one of the flowers.

Kardelia took a few steps and leapt onto a bolder on the opposite bank. The two birds faced each other from their own territories seemingly challenging the other to cross the line of the creek between them.

"We'll explain it all at the elpitlum," Kardelia said abruptly.

"Come on, Kardelia," Karbett said trying to split the tension, "We have to talk with the other clan leaders about the elpitlum, we don't have time for any more trouble. I'm sorry for your loss," he added solemnly to Corzell,

"As I am for yours," said Corzell, genuinely, bowing his head low as he spoke.

Kardelia's amber eyes blazed with grief and bitterness and although she knew it hadn't been Corzell's fault, and that he had also suffered, her clutch had been destroyed and she felt the loss and envy tear at her soul. She suddenly turned and sprang into the air, flying for the briefest of moments across the territory boundary and flapping past Corzell's head in a cynical mock challenge and trespass, before turning back into Kar territory and disappearing toward the orchard.

Corzell stooped to avoid the mock attack and was ready in a flash to respond.

Karbett spoke quickly, saying, "It's been a difficult few weeks for her and, well, for all of us really." He spoke softly, "You'll learn more tonight. After the ksud chorus." Then, he too sprang into the air and flew, speedily after his partner towards the orchard.

6

The Story of Cordelia's

Strength and Wisdom

Say! Everyone's talking 'bout chicken;
Chicken's a popular bird;
Anywhere you go, you're bound to find,
A chicken ain't nothin' but a bird.

Some folks call it a fowl,
That's the story I heard,
But let 'em call it this and let 'em call it that,
A chicken ain't nothin' but a bird.

Louis Jordan and His Tympany Five – 'A Chicken Ain't Nothing but a Bird' (1932).

CORZELL RETURNED to the nest tree and told Corselia about the urgent elpitlum. She could see he was upset and agitated, distracted and uncomfortable.

"Something isn't right," he kept saying. She could see he'd had no time to process the recent events, his conversation with the kookaburra, his feeling of disquiet and unease, the loss of his son and the attack by the cat on the Kar clan's brood. She could see he was troubled.

Corzell knew too, that it seemed as if everything pointed to a more significant calamity. He could feel it, but he couldn't see it. His frustration grew.

"Something isn't right," he said again.

"I can come with you to the elpitlum if you want. Corhelia can look after the children," Corselia offered.

"No... no, I'll go alone, whatever it is that I feel coming may be revealed tonight, and I feel it will be best if you stay away, here with the brood.

"Do you want me to come with you, father?" Cordelia offered.

Corzell looked upon his youngest chick with compassion and sympathy. He wished he could take her. She would be a comfort, he was sure.

"No, dear," he replied. "The elpitlum is an important meeting of the senior clan members of the valley. It wouldn't be appropriate. But thank you for offering your wing in support." He looked kindly at Cordelia.

The family sang their kusd chorus, but it resonated with uncertainty and doubt and lacked the lustre of their usual carolling. As soon as they had finished, Corzell said abruptly, and sadly, "I have to go now. But your mother will stay with you." Cheering a little he added, "...and I think your mother has a story for you all." The two chicks squawked with glee as Corzell looked over at his partner and whispered, "Tell them one of your happy nest-time stories. They have had a few difficult days." He wished he could stay and hear one himself. A happy story might settle his mind and calm his anxiety. But he had to leave and fly to the elpitlum, or he would be late.

"Take care, my dear," Corselia called to her partner as he mounted the rim of their nest and dived into the growing gloom of late evening. She watched him go.

"He'll be back," Cordelia said from behind her in the nest with the assurance of a sage. Corselia cocked her head in wonder, and spreading her wings she ushered her children, including Corhelia into the belly of the nest for her story.

"Cordelia," she said. "You are named after a mytre hero from myth. All mother mytres know the story of Cordelia's strength and wisdom, and it is this story I'm sure your father wanted me to tell you tonight. Now are you all nesting comfortably?"

The two young birds and Corhelia nodded their heads and focused intently on their mother's beak in eager anticipation.

"Then I shall begin… in the beginning there was no night or day. The animals lived on land, the birds in the air and the fish in the water, all in a state of constant twilight. The two Gods; Elppa and Egnaro lived in harmony. Peace, joy, and happiness reigned. All the creatures of the world, the animals, the fish, and the birds, shared the world and lived without need in complete happiness. The world was quiet, the only sound was the wind and rain, and none of the creatures had language. There were no songs, and no colours, other than pale, pallid grey. The world was dull, light, and dark grey, but all was in harmony.

"One day the Gods argued. Elppa wanted there to be more light, more colour, and more noise in the world. Egnaro, fearing Elppa's power, wanted more darkness, more blackness and even more quiet. The Gods fought in the heavens and the animals of the earth, the fish of the water, and birds of the air hid to avoid their wrath. When the battle was over, the land was scarred by gorges, and valleys, rivers, and creeks; hills and mountains had formed and broken down, and oceans divided the continents of the earth.

"Neither God had won the battle. Instead, exhausted, each agreed to stop fighting. When they saw the damage, they had caused across the world, they agreed to share the earth and heavens, with each reigning for half of every day, for the sake of all living things, and they agreed never to argue or fight again.

"Elppa became the day, the sun, the bringer of light, of warmth. Egnaro became the night, the moon, the darkness, and the bringer of cold, and frost. Many of the creatures of the world had been destroyed in the battle, and the remaining animals, fish, and birds were distressed and felt abandoned by their Gods. To satisfy and reassure the creatures of the earth, the sun, Elppa, and the moon, Egnaro agreed to reach out to each other momentarily, twice each day. Once at nwad and once at ksud where they would kiss briefly in memory of their past love, before handing over the care of the world to the other God.

"Most animals, hurt and upset turned their back on the Gods and vowed to cope with the extremes of night and day, light and darkness forced upon them in their own way.

"When the war between Elppa and Egnaro was over and they agreed to split the world into night and day, light and dark, they also changed the appearance of all things from placid and pallid grey; to colourful, bright, and bold. Elppa loved colour and it was he who saw to the allocation of colour for all the creatures of the world. In one flash of his power all the animals were coloured in bright reds, blues, and yellows.

"Every animal from the smallest to the largest, from bird to bee was changed into all the colours of the rainbow. Animals and birds with legs all had red legs. Every animal, bird, and fish's head were suddenly bright blue. Every animal, fish, and bird stood out with bold yellow bodies, and all animals with tails, had tails of bright green. Birds, animals, and fish glowed with their new fur, feathers, or scales of red, blue, yellow, and green. Elppa was pleased and he looked down on his creations with pleasure and joy. But the animals, birds, and fish were again confused and afraid.

"Egnaro loved the dark and she saw to the allocation of colour to the land, the earth, the sky, and the plants. As such, all plants were dark grey, all hills and mountains were brown and tan, the sky became a pale-grey and the waters of the earth became as black as the moonless night sky. Even the shallow rivers ran black. Egnaro loved the darkness, and she was pleased with her contribution to the new world.

"Many animals grew fur to keep warm at night or learnt to sweat or pant to lose heat during the day, but none were happy with the gift of such bright colours. The fish too, hated their uniform bold colours and they turned their backs on the Gods. They vowed to stay in the water and while the moon sent the tides to affect their habits, the fish lost their love for the sun and moon and stayed wet and away from their influence. Only the birds, glad to see the end of the quarrel saw the compromise between Elppa and Egnaro as a blessing.

"At every nwad and ksud when Elppa and Egnaro kissed briefly, they rejoiced with a loud vocal chorus to celebrate and remember Elppa and Egnaro's lost love. Of all the birds, the mytre celebrated the most joyfully and loudly, even singing when Elppa is at his highest during the day, so that as a result, when hearing their song, Elppa blessed the brightly coloured mytre with intelligence, a keen eye, swift wings, and the skill to harmonise with a beautiful voice.

"The animals, fish, and birds were soon very conspicuous and stood out in the trees, or on the land, against the pale sky and they glowed iridescently in the dark waters. Even on land, the animals' and birds' bright colours made them stand out against their monotone environment. No animal could hide, many struggled to hunt, or caught their own kind in confusion. Many began to starve, and no animal, fish or bird was happy. Elppa and Egnaro, high in the heavens, lived in peaceful ignorance of the pitiable state the world was in. Though unhappy, every animal was too afraid to complain to the Gods for fear of retribution or punishment.

"The birds, the descendants of the dinosaurs and the oldest and most noble of Elppa and Egnaro's creations, decided to meet and discuss what was to be done. Water birds, night hunters, great flocks of starling, large lone high-sky hunters, darting swallows, gliding ducks, and graceful swans, large birds and small birds met to discuss their plight.

"After much discussion they decided that someone must approach the Gods and ask that their colours and those of all creatures be returned to the pale grey of before, or changed in ways they might choose themselves. This way, they reasoned, they could at least hide and survive in the strange new world. But which bird was to take the message to the Gods?

"The birds selected the Wedge-tailed eagle because he was the strongest and bravest of all the birds. But fearful of the Gods' wrath, he refused to go. 'I like my new colours,' he lied. 'I look handsome, and I can see prey clearly, colourfully below me as I hunt. I will not upset the Gods.' The birds argued and discussed their plight long into the night.

"Finally, one bird stepped forward and spoke. 'I am not the biggest or strongest of birds, but I am willing to speak with the Gods and plead our case for new colours for all the creatures and the world.' It was the shrill, small voice of the willie-wagtail. All the birds were shocked. 'This bird is too puny to go,' said the eagle gruffly. 'Then I will fly with him,' said the magpie-lark quietly and firmly. 'You are too lowly, too tiny, to represent us, even if you go together,' said the mighty *emu*. 'But they can fly, and we can try,' spoke the mytre. 'I am Cordelia, and I will fly and try with them. Together we three, the willie-wagtail, the magpie-lark and I will go and talk to the Gods. No bird should have to stand alone and we three will speak with the Gods on behalf of all the animals, the fish, and birds'.

"All the birds chorused as one in agreement, and while many were fearful and many more had little faith in the attempt to talk to the Gods, every bird finally agreed to let them try. The willie-wagtail was called Tnim, the magpie-lark was called Tcap, and together with Cordelia, they set off to find and talk to the Gods. They flew up into the grey pale sky.

"The willie-wagtail was soon tired. 'Rest on my back, Tnim, I will carry you,' Cordelia offered, and although it was a burden Cordelia struggled on upward into the sky. 'Keep going,' encouraged Tcap. 'We'll reach the Gods soon'.

"But soon, even the magpie-lark, Tcap, was tired, and Cordelia allowed Tcap to rest next to Tnim on her back, as she alone flew on. The weight of the two smaller birds added considerably to Cordelia's task, but she laboured on, climbing further into the sky.

"After a long, tiring journey, Cordelia found Elppa sitting above them looking down on all the world, with Egnaro resting far off behind him in the sky. Cordelia was exhausted and short of breath, but kept flying up towards the Gods, thus it was the magpie-lark, Tnim who spoke first. 'Elppa, Lord of brilliance and of the day. Can we speak with you?'

"With Tnim and Tcap on Cordelia's back, Elppa saw only the mytre flying before him. 'Who would dare to approach me so?' Elppa demanded angrily. 'It is I, Lord, Tnim, the willie-wagtail,' Tnim said courteously, peeking out from behind Cordelia's head. 'And I, Lord, Tcap, the magpie-lark,' said Tcap, respectfu ly, also looking over Cordelia's head. 'And I lord, Cordelia... the mytre and friend of... Tnim and Tcap,' Cordelia said between breaths as she struggled upward. Elppa called to attract the attention of the other God, Egnaro, before asking Cordelia, 'What do you want and why are you here?'

"Tnim spoke first. 'Lord... we have come to ask for an opportunity to speak with you. With you both. We know Lord Elppa that you love all the creatures of the world and that you delight in bright light and colour. We know Lady Egnaro that you love the dark and the night and love the land and the waters of the world, but we have a concern to put to you.' Tnim spoke calmly and politely as Cordelia flew, hovering before the Gods. 'A proposal, a request, oh Lords of the world and heavens," Cordelia added quickly. 'Speak,' said Elppa intrigued by their courage and boldness. 'You, Lord Elppa have blessed all the animals, fish, and birds of the world with colours of wonder and glory,' Tnim said. 'True,' said the Lord of day and sun.

"And you, Lord Egnaro, have blessed all the land and the waters with a dimness that makes our colour sparkle and flash against the earth, sky, and sea,' said Tcap, respectfully. 'Also true,' put in the Lord of night and the moon. 'You have made us all beautiful and colourful, but you have made us all the same and because of this we cannot hide or hunt or blend into the colourless, beautiful world of the land, the black of the water or the pale sky,' said Tnim. 'Many birds and animals are starving because they cannot hunt or live in fear because they can't hide from predators,' added Cordelia. 'Then what do you want?' Elppa asked in a booming voice like thunder.

"Tnim and Tcap took cover behind Cordelia's head, but Cordelia remained firm, and while tired, she said calmly. 'We ask that you allow all the animals, fish, and birds of the world to choose the colours that best reflect their place and purpose in the world. We also ask that you work together to re-colour the plants, the land and the seas, and waters of the world to help the animals find their rightful place amongst your creation.'

"You claimed to have a proposal, this is a demand. Surely you cannot expect to demand a gift like this from the Gods without some sort of compensation, punishment, or retribution?' 'On no, Lord Elppa," said Cordelia still holding her two smaller friends on her back as she flew before the Gods. 'We ourselves ask for nothing. We will forsake our choice of colour if you grant our request on behalf of all the other birds, animals, and fish.'

"The two Gods whispered together for a long time. They could see Cordelia's strength as she continued to carry her friends, they could see how brave they all had been to approach them, and they could see that they clearly risked their own lives to act on behalf of all creatures. As they waited, Cordelia became more and more tired, and she was not sure how much longer she could hold her two friends on her back.

"Eventually, Elppa spoke, 'You have all spoken well and respectfully before us. We have decided that we will work together to re-colour all the land, deserts, hills, mountains, valleys, seas, rivers, and other waters of the earth. Although apart, we Gods should work together for the wellbeing of the earth and all its creatures. Also, we will grant the power of choice for all animals, fish, and birds, to select their own colours, be they feathers, skin, hide, fur, or scale. Every animal, fish, and bird can now choose.'

"Elppa paused, "Except you three. We can see that you love the Gods. We can see that you faithfully worship us each nwad and each ksud with your songs of faith and devotion. Therefore, to add to your celebration of your enduring love for us, you three will be granted no colours, only black and white. This will remind all other creatures that you carry with pride the symbols of the Gods; light and dark, night and day, black and white. In this way you will honour us with your feathers too. It also shows all creatures of the world that there is a price for disturbing the Gods.' 'Lords,' cried, Cordelia. 'You are wise and powerful.'

"However, at that moment, Cordelia's strength was spent. She could no longer hold up her wings and she tumbled from the sky with Tnim and Tcap on her back. She, and they crashed down to the earth a far distance below. In their fall they each became unconscious and when they woke safe on the earth, they saw that all the world was brightly coloured. Bright green trees covered the hills, flowering plants had a multitude of coloured petals, wattle shone yellow and all about them the colours of the land shone, while the sky was a beautiful pale blue. Soft white clouds drifted above them merging and drawing apart with the breezes of the afternoon.

"They saw that all the animals and birds were now different colours and the Gods had kept their word to allow all creatures to choose their own colours. 'And look at our feathers,' Tnim said with delight. We are no longer red, or green, yellow, or blue, but simply black and white.' 'We all three are," said Tcap, with joy. 'Even you Cordelia.' 'We are night and day, dark and light. We are the union and difference that shows the love of the Gods,' said Cordelia.

"And to this day, as before, the mytre sing at nwad and ksud and even more at nwod (*Noon*), to celebrate the grace and benevolence of the Gods, the courage of Tnim, the tenacity of Tcap, and the strength and wisdom of Cordelia."

Cordelia's eyes sparkled in the moonlight as her mother finished the story. "And I am your Cordelia," she said softly to her mother.

"'You are. As soon as I saw you, I knew that you would be special. Your father agrees. He could see it. You are our little Cordelia." At that moment there was an ear-splitting screech that rose from the vicinity of the bridge over the creek near the sealed road.

Cordelia looked at her mother with fear and dread. "Father?" she cried.

7

The Elpitlum

Pack up all my cares and woes
Here I go, singing low
Bye, bye, blackbird

Where somebody waits for me
Sugar is sweet, so is she
Bye-bye, blackbird.

No one here can love and understand me
Oh, what hard luck stories they all hand me

Make my bed and light the light
I'll arrive late tonight
Blackbird, bye-bye.

Ringo Starr – 'Bye Bye Blackbird' (1970)

THE ELPITLUM WAS an ancient tradition among the mytre, and even amongst some other types of birds. Mytre held these regular ceremonial gatherings as either celebrations or welcomes, or to gather information and share news. This meeting of the five valley clans was not new, but its timing during the main hatching, nesting and fledgling time was unusual.

They met by the sealed road bridge over the creek with the birds gathering on the northeastern side of the road, by the driveway to one of the norzela properties on the Kar clan territory. Although the territory belonged to the Kar clan, a truce existed for the envoys from each clan. The moon, Egnaro, was almost full and as it grew into the sky Egnaro spread her shadowed light across the valley.

The Yat clan sent their most senior leaders, a mated pair called Yatdoll and Yatnolia. Each had been raised in the valley and each had a long association and connection with the Kar and Cor clan. Yatnolia was an offspring of Corzell and Corselia and had partnered with a member of the Yat clan. She still met her parents occasionally at the place where the creek and the sealed road met, or at the roadside near the orchard. They had no young this hatching season and they were both able to come to the elpitlum without leaving any chicks unprotected. Yatdoll and Yatnolia were the first to arrive. They perched on a horizontal fallen log that overlooked a lawned area, to await the others.

Corzell was the next to arrive, and as he had indicated to Kardelia and Karbett, he came alone. He joined the first birds and perched beside them on the log. All three chortled their greetings and waited for the others. While they waited, Corzell asked if they knew why the meeting had been called and why it was so urgent. But neither Yatdoll nor Yatnolia knew the reason.

Yatdoll speculated that what had occurred on the Dart territory had prompted the meeting, but other than a vague hunch about this he couldn't say more.

The two mytre from the Wayt clan arrived next. Waytjulia and Waytbill flew into the gathering in the growing darkness, each with a flurry of feathers. They came to rest on the short grass in front of the log and each burst into a song of welcome and greetings directed toward the other birds. The three mytres on the log responded with their own welcomes and soon the post-ksud elpitlum was a cacophony of chortles and chirps as the birds sang out their reassuring greeting chorus.

"Elppa's greeting," Waytbill said, as he strode about the grass before the others tapping the ground for worms. Then he looked up and asked, "Do you know why we are here and why the meeting is so important?"

None of the others knew and although Yatdoll offered his previous speculation, he admitted that he really didn't know. As he finished talking, the remaining members of the elpitlum arrived and flew into the small clearing near the road bridge to join in a chorus of welcomes and greetings.

The final birds to arrive were three members of the Kar clan, Karmann, the elder statesman and leader of the largest clan in the valley and his most trusted lieutenants Kardelia and Karbett, who had flown about the valley inviting and informing the others of the elpitlum, earlier that day.

Karmann had lived in the valley all his long life. He was known to every clan and respected by everyone. He was large and strong, but his years had thinned his head feathers and slowed his flight. As the leader of the largest clan, he commanded instant respect. He had shown wise leadership over the years, and it was more than his age that defined him as the valley's primary mytre. In his youth he had led the combined clans in their war against the infiltration of a fox into the valley and they had managed to chase it away.

More recently he had led his own clan in a battle to see off the potential invasion of a rogue mytre, that had flown in from the north looking to establish a colony of his own in the valley. Karmann was a successful mate and father, and it was he who had been calling and running the elpitlum of the valley for over thirteen seasons. All the mytre listened when he spoke.

Just one bird represented the Dart clan, Dartkull, who arrived with the Kar clan. None of the other birds had met him before and they were all surprised by his presence at the elpitlum. He was a small, lowly ranked bird and Corzell wasn't sure he was old enough or experienced enough to have joined with a mate or raised a brood. To Corzell he looked as shy as a sparrow in winter. There was still the faint marking of grey feathers on the bird's underbelly and shoulders. Corzell's unease grew.

It was Waytbill, from the Wayt clan who spoke though, "Who is this mytre? Where are the senior members of the Dart clan to represent them?"

Dartkull looked embarrassed and hung his head in silence.

"I invited him," said Karmann, of the Kar clan. He spoke with authority and power. His voice was rich and deep and instantly every other mytre fell silent as he spoke. "He is here because he has important news to share, and I wanted you all to hear it from him. I have invited him, and you will treat him and regard him as the new leader of the Dart clan."

This stunned the mytre present and a rumble of disapproval spread between the birds.

Then Corzell asked, boldly, "Does this have anything to do with the two dead mytres that the kookaburra told me about?"

"The kookaburra!" exclaimed Karmann, scoffing. "What did he say?"

"Only that he had seen two dead mytre near the line of pine at the norzela park place."

"Had he now," Karmann said, as he looked around at the two members of his own clan and the new young, quiet 'leader' of the Dart clan, with concern and disapproval. Karmann spoke again, "Tell them what you know, Dartkull."

All the mytre present watched as the aging bird strode over to the log and sprang awkwardly up to take a perch next to Corzell. Karmann lowered himself into a sitting position and squatted down on the log.

Karbett spread his wings and half hopped, half flew over to his clan elder and sat next to him, forcing Corzell to move slightly out of the way.

The Wayt clan birds flew to a low branch that stretched out at right angles to the log and perched there so they too could hear and see what was to unfold.

Once everyone was settled and quiet, the insignificant, young mytre of the Dart clan stood alone in the small lawned area surrounded by the others and began his explanation.

"I am Dartkull of the Dart clan, my parents were our clan leaders and seniors, Dartvada and Dartspadd."

"Were?" said Yatdoll emphasizing the 'past' nature of the word 'were'.

"Were," confirmed Dartkull. "They're dead now, killed on the norzela park thing on our territory two rising of Elppa ago."

"What do you mean killed?" Corzell asked.

"Killed… I found them… dead, near the water hole on the norzela park on our territory.

"Killed by who," asked Waytbill

"Or by what," said Karmann in a sinister tone.

"What do you mean?" asked Corzell, "We have many enemies, the eagle, the cat, the dog, the lizard any one of them could have killed our friends."

"Or even the norzela in their cars," added Yatnolia, before others in the gathering mentioned a chorus of mytre enemies.

"It wasn't any of these," said Dartkull quietly, his head lowered.

"What…" asked Corzell above the noise.

"It wasn't any of these…" he repeated, earnestly. The group of mytre had begun to chatter loudly so that Dartkull had to shout above the chatter.

"It wasn't any of the usual enemies…" Dartkull shouted above the din. "I saw what happened…" He waited until they had all quietened down and were focused on him, then Dartkull said at last, "I saw it all, it wasn't any of our enemies. It was a group of mytres that killed them."

Every bird was suddenly quiet, before Karmann said, "So you can see now why we have called the elpitlum."

"But you don't think any of us would leave our territory to kill anyone of the clans in the valley, do you?" Corzell asked.

Karmann shook his head.

"It wasn't any of the valley clans," Dartkull said. "They were from across the norzela park. I think they came out from the eucalyptus forest to the south. I was with my parents, Dartvada and Dartspadd when they saw a lone mytre fly across our territory and land near the pines on the edge of the norzela park.

"They told me to stay hidden and they flew off to challenge the invader. But I followed silently and carefully. Flying or hopping from branch to branch or bush to bush. I hid on the inner branch of one of the tall pine trees and I saw them approach the stranger. They exchanged greetings as is our way then asked the stranger to state his business or leave their lands. I was far off, and it was difficult to hear everything said.

"The invader looked very relaxed; even calm as he strode about on the lawn at the end of the green circle near the norzela park hole. This mytre looked to be huge, and I thought it was a raven, but it had a white nape and white feathers under its wing and on its tail. It also had a strange, small white fleck of feathers on its brow that looked like a star, very un-mytre like."

"It could have been a pied currawong," suggested Waytbill urgently.

"No, he said it had white nape feathers. Now don't interrupt," Karmann said sternly, becoming impatient.

"No," agreed Dartkull, "I thought that, but its tail was too short, and it walked too easily. I was soon sure it was a mytre, and it loomed over my parents. I was too far away to hear exactly what they said, but Dartvada and Dartspadd started to become angry and began arguing with the new mytre.

"Suddenly, a strange bird landed next to me on my branch. I was taken by surprise and froze. An instant later, another landed next to me, on my other side. They were not like any mytre I had seen before. They looked like ghoulish ghosts of birds, with grey feathers and with huge, bright yellow eyes. They had short goshawk like beaks and a tuft of feathers above their beak. One of the strange birds said in a voice that sounded like it came from a long way away, 'You, stay still...stay silent, you not hurt.'

"I dared not move and fear's talon gripped me. They looked vicious and tough, but also menacing in an otherworldly way. I was transfixed by the three birds near the edge of the norzela park green and continued to watch them. The bigger, new mytre seemed to continue to disregard my parent's loud protests and simply strode about with the strut of a clan leader.

"I could see Dartvada flapping her wings and it looked like Dartspadd was trying to get her to calm down, when I saw four more birds alight on the flat green area beside the first big, strange mytre, with the white brow feathers. The intruders flew in from the east and all looked like the first bird, but not quite as big, and without the flash of small white feathers on their heads.

"My parents looked shocked and embraced each other in the face of the invasion. I was sure now this was what it was, and I remained still and silent on my branch as the two birds beside me shuffled in closer, pressing their wing feathers into mine. I dare not move.

"On the green, by the pines, the big bird was talking calmly and confidently with my parents. The wind shifted a little and came from the east. It meant I could just hear what they were saying. 'You have no right to be on our territory without our consent,' Dartvada was shouting.

"Still the big bird looked unconcerned and seemed to ignore her as he strode about. 'I have come to take your territory,' the big mytre said. 'I don't need your consent for that.'

'You can't have it," Dartvada said in protest. 'It's ours and the valley clans will come out to help defend it.'

'I'm asking you to give me your territory, and live... or...' the big mytre left the last word hanging as he said calmly, dispassionately but forcefully, 'you can join my clan. Live with me or die for your own territory. Either way, I'll have this territory.'

'Who do you think you are to come onto our lands and make demands and threats?' Dartvada said angrily, incredulously, repeating, 'who do you think you are?'

'I'm sorry, how rude of me,' he announced, 'I am Captain Kratt, and this is my clan.'

As he spoke, he spread his wings wide signalling to a few other birds hidden in the high pines. Given this signal, they flew down to the green lawn and landed surrounding Dartvada and Dartspadd. Shocked, they turned their heads as these other mytre dropped down, silently to the green, smooth lawn.

"Two of the birds who had initially arrived shortly after the captain, stepped toward the Krat clan leader, and bowed their heads low. Neither spoke nor made any sound. 'These are my loyal and faithful lieutenants; Krattac and Kratatora,' The captain announced. 'These others you see about you are my clan warriors; clan Krat.' Kratt waited a moment while the two mytre they had surrounded grasped the reality of their situation. 'It's your choice... join clan Krat or die. It's simple really.'

"The two stunned and surrounded mytre, my parents, looked at each other. Dartvada looked forlornly at her partner before a look of spirited defiance flashed on her face. I saw mother whisper to Dartspadd, I was far off but I thought it was a warning. To warn Karmann or something. He looked worried but nodded slightly in approval and agreement. Dartspadd braced himself for flight and was about to launch into the night sky when he felt the weight of one of the Krat lieutenants force him to the ground.

"Within a moment, Krattac had pushed him onto his back with his legs flailing in the air and pinned him to the ground. Dartvada suffered the same indignity as the other Krat officer, Kratatora, held the second Dart leader firmly to the ground with her wings splayed out at her side.

"I stayed in the pine tree guarded by the two strange birds and could do nothing. I dare not cry out or flee, so I watched, hoping my parents would be alright. As I watched, I heard Captain Kratt say coldly, 'You had your chance. You've made your choice.' Then he stepped over to the captives, my parents. 'My clan know they only get one chance. Loyalty is everything in Krat clan.'

"With that, the clan leader stepped over to Dartvada and stabbed her in the head with his beak."

Dartkull became incoherent at this point and started to mumble, "He just stabbed her... right there while his lieutenant held her down... just stabbed her in the head... stabbed her."

"What about Dartspadd?" Karbett asked in shock.

"He stabbed him with his beak too, in the chest. But they weren't dead, I could see them struggling and trying to get up." He stalled again with the terror of what he'd witnessed clearly audible in his voice and in his trembling wings.

Corzell gasped and realized this was the terror he'd had a glimpse of in his thoughts and what Bill had spoken of.

Dartkull went on, "Then he stepped back, and each bird of his clan stepped up to strike at my parents. Some stabbed once, others, expressing some perverse loyalty, or desire to show greater allegiance to the captain, stabbed multiple times. Soon Dartvada and Dartspadd only moved under the stark strike of a Krat clan member's beak or when a bird tore at my captured parents' wounds with their claws."

Dartkull could not go on. He was in tears and broken in his retelling of the story. Kardelia and Waytjulia flew down to the centre of the lawn where Dartkull was slumped, and they offered their support and sympathy by spreading a wing over the distraught bird. The gathered elpitlum members had never heard such a sorry story.

Dartkull began to sob, "They just kept pecking and plucking. One after the other, while the leader... the captain, watched on, satisfied with his power. I couldn't believe how savage and sudden the attack was."

"But how did you get away?" Corzell asked.

"Oh," said Dartkull, as if caught off guard. "Oh, they let me go. After my parents were dead, I guess they didn't see me as a threat. The two strange birds flew away as silently as they had come. Then the Krat flock flew back to the eucalyptus forest to the south or away over the norzela park. Once they'd gone, I flew down to my parents. They left them bleeding and dying next to the green lawn. My mother was still alive, and I dragged her to a bush, a short distance away from the smooth green lawn for shelter. My father was dead, but I dragged him to the bush so scavengers wouldn't take him. My mother died soon after the attack, but she told me to tell Karmann what had happened. I did, and now I'm telling you."

There was silence all about the gathered mytre clans as they considered what they'd heard, what the tragedy might mean for their valley, for their peaceful life and for the safety of their own clutches of young.

"They let you go," said Corzell incredulously as he hopped down from the log and strode over to the whimpering mytre in the middle of the lawn before him.

All the other mytre, apart from Karmann and one of his lieutenants, Karbett, flew or hopped over to Dartkull and stood in a circle around him. Karmann sat on the log with Karbett beside him and surveyed the sad elpitlum.

"Will they come back?" Yatnolia asked.

"They'd better not try," said Kardelia defiantly.

"They let you go after they had made you witness your parents' murder? And flew to the south? I thought you said they came from the east, over the norzela park, or was it the south?" Corzell's amber eyes blazed red with rage and confusion. "You said, they came from over the norzela park, not out of the great gum forest?" Corzell asked insistently, "Well, which was it?"

"Give the child some air," Karmann said, "he's been through a lot. Let him breathe."

Karbett jumped down from the log and walked over to the small gaggle of birds in the lawned area. "Give him space, Corzell. He's witnessed enough," Karbett insisted as he joined the mytre circle.

"But…" Corzell began to protest.

"Step back," Karbett cried pushing Corzell back.

Dartkull looked at the squabbling birds, tilted his head skywards for a moment then grinning, stepped back from the centre of the grassed area, towards the opposite side of the gathering and away from the log. Suddenly, there was a flurry of feathers and wings beating in the small space beside the road bridge. About eight black and white mytre descended into the middle of the elpitlum.

Startled, Corzell tried to take flight but two of the intruders instantly knocked him to the ground and within a moment, were standing on and over him. Krattac and Kratatora pinned Corzell down on the lawn at the foot of the log. Other intruders landed and held the other mytre's at the elpitlum. Soon, they guarded Yatnolia and Yatdoll. They forced Waytbill and Waytjulia to lie down on the lawned area as if they were about to be arrested or searched. They were held next to Corzell and his captors.

The old leader of the elpitlum was in shock, so sudden had the intrusion been. Before he could squark out a warning or protest, the biggest of the intruders landed next to Karmann. Karmann drew up a claw in defence, but before the older bird could respond further, the intruder pushed the valley leader and flung him down, sprawling across the log as the big mytre crashed into him. Within a second, the huge intruder was standing with a large-clawed foot at the old bird's neck.

Kardelia and Karbett immediately tried to fly to their elder's aid but were both knocked to the ground and soon had two of the intruding mytre standing on each wing or had a claw forced into the black feathers of their neck. None of the other birds, surrounded or overpowered as they were, moved, as other intruders landed next to them in the tree branch, at right angles to the log.

Without needing instructions, all of the elpitlum mytre, apart from Karmann, were forced into the centre of the lawned area while some of the intruders assumed positions on the log next to their leader or stayed above the group in the branches of the low tree. All birds know that holding the higher ground or branch was a distinct advantage in any fight and all the members of the elpitlum knew at once they were in no position to fight back or defend themselves without considerable loss.

Oddly, Dartkull was not being held and he simply bobbed down to one side of the lawned area, cowering in fright.

Only Corzell and Waytbill tried stubbornly to resist, but Corzell had been overpowered quickly in the shock of the initial attack, and while Waytbill had some initial success against his attacker, their struggle, with each mytre pecking and flapping or striking out wildly with their claws to hold off the other's strikes, ended abruptly, when the large mytre with the strange star of white feathers on his brow called out loudly, "Enough."

"Stop now, you're outnumbered and beaten. Stop or I'll kill this old bird." As he spoke, he raised his clawed foot into the air to strike at Karmann. The struggling stopped. Waytbill stepped away from the mytre he was fighting with and two of the invaders from the log flew down and pinned Waytbill to the ground by standing one on each of his out-stretched wings. Finally, with their leader, the elderly Karmann, pinned under Kratt's claws, all the valley mytre were subdued.

The captain spoke. "I'm Captain Kratt, of clan Krat. You have lived for too long in this peaceful and beautiful valley and it is time to share. We don't want to take it from you, but we do want to share it with you and as you can see, we have the numbers to take it all if we wanted. However, I would rather live in harmony as your leader, with you in your sub-clans helping my clan to prosper."

Corzell knew it was a lie, but he was powerless to fightback.

"Never," hissed Karmann as he struggled under Kratt's claws.

"Let me put this another way," Kratt said. He raised his foot slightly then forced his claw down into the old mytre's neck.

Within a moment Karmann was struggling for breath. His eyes began to bulge, and his face puffed out as he struggled for air. The old mytre tried to bring his beak around to peck at Kratt's leg but he couldn't get any strength into the strike, and he soon gave up.

Two of Karmann's offspring and faithful lieutenants, Kardelia and Karbett, tugged at the mytre holding them back but could not break free to help their elder, their father, their clan leader. As they struggled to escape the grip of the intruders holding them back, Karmann struggled for breath under Captain Kratt's massive, clawed foot. Soon the battle for air was over. Karmann's limp form was struggling no longer. He had died under the pressure of Kratt's claw, and his head fell to one side, limp.

"Shall we try again," Kratt said without a hint of emotion.

"This is our valley now, but we're willing to share it, if you pay a toll, a tribute to clan Krat. Do this and you can live here… in peace. Do not and… and well… we'll take it all for ourselves and force you all out. It will be law by claw."

"That is what you are doing anyway," said Corzell, as he continued to struggle with the two Krat mytre holding him down. "We have young to feed, to care for, this has been our valley since before Elppa and Egnaro's first kiss and you have no right to come here and just take it."

"You lead the Cor clan, right?" Captain Kratt said.

"I am Corzell, and yes, I am the leader of the Cor clan," Corzell replied defiantly and with dignity.

Captain Kratt spoke cheerfully. "Then you can keep doing so, but a quarter of all the food you find is now mine. You can go on being your clan leader, but only if you pay tribute to the Krat clan. You can even keep your territories, although, with this old mytre's death, clan Kar territories are now clan Krat lands and skies, and anyone of my clan mytre can wander with impunity on any of your territories whenever they wish.

Therefore, as well as the Kar lands, the whole valley is really mine and while I will allow you to live here, you must submit to my rule and live under my protection and leadership. And pay rent or a tribute as long as I am in charge."

Kratt pushed the dead body of Karmann off the elpitlum log, and it slipped and slithered slowly down the curve of the log's surface and slumped onto the grass at its base. His eyes now black, dead, his body unmoving. He lay just a short distance from where Corzell was being held.

Kardelia and Karbett each let out a long high-pitched shriek and dropped to their chests with their wings wide before them on the ground. Prostrate in mourning and in grief, but also in submission to the new Lord of the valley.

"I'll break my beak on your head if you try," cried Corzell. Still struggling with the two birds holding him. "He was our leader. You're not welcome here," Corzell shouted.

"You misunderstand," said Captain Kratt, coldly. "I already am your leader, and I'll give you the same choice I gave brave Dartvada and Dartspadd. Join me and live or stand against me and die."

Corzell looked at the prostrate Kar clan lieutenants, quivering and distraught at the base of the log. *Now is not the time, we have been surprised and caught off guard. This is not the time*, he reflected. He said softly, "Cor clan will join you." Then he too bowed low to the intruder.

"Good," said Captain Kratt, "Good."

8

Kratt's Valley

When I was a little girl
With clay horses and lambs on the shelf
I caught frogs in ditches, listened for elves.
My friends and I had a world unto ourselves

No grownups could find us when we
Made our plans so secretly
To run away and fly to be
With the two birds of paradise...

Come into my dream with me and dream.

The Pretenders – 'Birds of Paradice' (1981)

ALL COULD SEE THAT resistance at this time was useless. Captain Kratt stood on the log, towering over the gathered mytre, his original clan members and his new 'subjects.' No one spoke for a long moment as they each took in the gravity of the situation. The captain gazed around at the captives and his clan members. Seeing them all subdued, Kratt said coldly, "Before we send you back to your territories and families, I'd like to thank Dartkull for his help in setting up this elpitlum." Kratt specifically watched for Corzell's response. He was not disappointed.

"You traitor," Corzell roared at Dartkull forgetting his pledge to be loyal.

"It wasn't all lies and betrayal," Kratt suggested as he strode about confidently on the top of the log. "Was it, Dartkull?" Kratt said confidently.

Dartkull hesitated and looked cowed before Kratt and his former elpitlum leaders.

"Well, answer, youngling," Kratt shouted.

Dartkull quivered and replied meekly, "Yes, Lord. I mean, No, Lord." His quivering squark betrayed his fear and as he spoke, he bowed low.

"Tell them what really happened the day your parents died."

"Yes, Lord," Dartkull said quietly, still bowing low.

"I did see the Krat flock swoop in, and I watched from the pine tree as Captain Kratt and his clan killed Dartvada and Dartspadd, as I said. But they did not let me go as I said. Two strange birds of the Krat clan held me hostage."

"As you lied, youngling," Captain Kratt suggested.

"As I lied, my Lord," Dartkull repeated feebly.

"What did happen?" the captain asked.

"I was not let go… I did not escape… I was offered my life if I served the Krat clan. They took me down to the smooth green lawn and made to stand next to the mutilated bodies of my kin. There, the captain asked me, if I would serve him… or if I wanted to die like my parents. I was afraid. I agreed to help. The captain wanted to know about the valley, about our community, and about the other clans in the valley. How many of us there were and how, where and when the elpitlum met. I didn't want to tell them, but they had just killed my parents and I was afraid." Dartkull paused and looked around at Corzell. "He said Dart clan would be safe, that I would be a hero and I could… save the valley." Dartkull began to sob as he spoke.

"You, foolish feather-brained mytre," Corzell said in rebuke as he again struggled vainly with the two Krat mytre that held him.

"I'm sorry," the young mytre sniffed, "I didn't know they would kill Karmann. I didn't know Krat clan would want to take a quarter of everything." Dartkull became angry as his tears ebbed. "He lied to me… he killed my parents, and he fooled me too."

Dartkull's fear turned to rage as he spoke. He looked at the lifeless form of the old mytre at the foot of the log. Something snapped, something had reached its limit and it just snapped in him. He lifted his head, his eyes blazed with anger and hatred. Suddenly, the young mytre, who was not being held or guarded, flew at Kratt and in that moment of surprise, in the sudden attack, he knocked the older, bigger bird off the log and the two birds tumbled into the bush behind it.

Dartkull had the upper wing at first, flailing wildly at the older bird's head with his wings and pecking viciously at the broad chest of Kratt. But the Boronia Floribunda bush behind the log hindered his assault as the pinnate leaves and pink star-shaped flowers meant the smaller bird's blows floundered and he soon tired. It took only a moment longer before Kratt's power and strength began to show.

Dartkull was also overcome with emotion, and this too diminished his accuracy and the potency of his striking power.

Kratt pecked at Dartkull's wings and flipped the younger bird on his back against the bush's foliage. Krattac, one of Kratt's lieutenants flew up into the air and landed near the brawl poised to join in the battle. But Kratt waved him off saying, "Leave this youngling to me."

Kratt returned to pecking savagely at the smaller bird's wings and soon Dartkull was unable to raise his wings to defend his head and face. Then the bigger bird switched to make repeated blows at his attacker's head. Within minutes, Dartkull was almost unconscious, and blood poured from multiple small wounds on his head and body.

"He's had enough," Corzell shouted. "There's been enough killing for one day," he added. "He's little more than a fledgling. Let him be." Corzell felt sick. Sick of the killing, of the loss of their valley and sick with worry for their future. "Let him be," he shouted again.

Dartkull was unable to raise a wing in defence and Kratt could see he'd won. He stopped pecking at the younger bird and hopped back up onto the log. He had hardly been injured in the clash and apart from the initial shock of the attack he had not suffered at all. But his pride was injured.

"That attack has cost you all. The price of my tribute is now half of everything. Obey or be punished," Kratt reminded them. "And there is one other tribute I will take tonight. He nodded to the two mytre holding Corzell and the two birds roughly shuffled and pushed the Cor clan leader over to the base of the log, directly under where Kratt was standing.

"This is my valley now. You can all stay in your territories, you can keep your clan names and your clan leaders, but you will all need to pay me half of all the food you find, every day. I will now demonstrate the price of defiance. Kratt looked around at the group of terrified, cowed valley dwellers. He jumped lightly from the log with his wings extended and stood over the prostrate Corzell laying on his back. Corzell looked at the captain with defiance.

"I sense you're a strong leader, Corzell. Your clan is lucky to have you." Kratt strode around Corzell. As he did, he looked at the captured and restrained valley clan leaders that watched him. Corzell looked with disgust at the invader.

"This is a brave leader," Kratt said. "But I'm your leader now. I have killed the Dart clan leaders and taken the Dart clan territory for my own. I have killed the leader of the Kar clan and claim their territory as is my right. This is law by claw," he bellowed.

Suddenly and without warning, his head flashed forward and he buried his beak in Corzell's right eye. In an instant Kratt had plucked the eye from its socket and it was dangling on the end of Captain Kratt's beak. Corzell rolled away and with his right wing snatched from the grasp of one of his guards, he used it to cover his face, in a futile and late defence. The cry he made split the valley air.

Kratt flicked the plucked-out eye away and asked, "Are there any others who will defy my lordship of this valley?"

The two members of the Kar clan Kardelia and Karbett remained prostrate before their new Lord. Yatnolia and Yatdoll did the same, lowering themselves to the ground with their wings out wide.

Waytbill and Waytjulia hesitated for a moment, then also fell on their chests with their wings splayed in subservience.

Corzell rolled from his back and shuffled to his feet, still with his right wing covering his injured eye and stood for a moment to confront the captain. The captain sniggered in puzzlement. *Surely this bird could see he was beaten*, he thought. Then Corzell moved his head so he could see with his good eye the submission of his elpitlum members. Realizing all was lost, he slowly lowered himself to the ground and spread his wings upon the ground in subservience to their new Lord.

With all the senior birds of the elpitlum offering to agree to his rule, Captain Kratt waited for a second to allow the moment to sink in. Then he said, "Now go back to your clan territories and tell your fellow mytres what you have seen. Tell them that Captain Kratt is their lord, and that my lieutenants will come to them each day for their tribute." Kratt looked at Corzell and added, "do this and no further harm will come to any clan territory or clan member. As long as you pay the tribute on time and in full and show no disrespect and do no harm to my clan brothers, all will be well. Do not test me. I have taken one eye. I will not hesitate to take more if I am provoked. Now…" he shouted magnanimously, "go with Elppa's love and peace."

Corzell rose last. He could hear the other captive birds take to the wing and return to their nest trees. As he staggered slowly to his claws, he felt the presence of the captain above him. Kratt had jumped up onto the log and was looking down at the injured Cor clan leader. He was wondering about his future. About the trouble Corzell might cause. Kratt nodded to one of his lieutenants. Krattac understood and stepped over to Corzell. As the injured bird became steady on his feet, he felt a sharp peck to the right side of his head. Unable to see the blow coming he was taken completely by surprise. Corzell dropped down onto one knee and raised his right wing to deflect a second blow.

It didn't come.

"We will be watching you and your clan, Corzell," Krattac said snidely. "You won't see us coming. You won't see us watching you, but we will always be there. So, pay up and keep your beak clean." Krattac pushed the kneeling mytre over and Corzell tumbled to the ground, taken again by surprise at the blow.

"Yes, Sir," Corzell said as he tried to rise again.

"Leave him, he will pay or die," the captain said as he lifted from the log into the sky. The other Krat clan members did likewise and Corzell was finally left alone in the clearing before the log.

He took a moment to stand, and he turned a full circle to ensure he was now alone. He was. A wave of relief came over him as he considered the events of the elpitlum. "All I have lost for now is an eye. It could have been far worse," he told himself as he gathered his wits. He was glad Corselia had not come to witness their betrayal or the death of old Karmann. He looked around at the dead former Kar clan leader. His body was not mutilated, but he had died savagely all the same.

Corzell dragged the body to the creek line with difficulty and placed it under the overhanging branches of a Fishbone Water-Fern plant. The small fern was old, and the light green fronds created a wide floral curtain that hid the dead clan leader's body. Corzell then returned to the flat lawned area in front of the log. He jumped with difficulty over the log, stumbling as he adjusted to his altered depth perception.

He found Dartkull still prostrate on the Boronia Floribunda bush's leaves. Kneeling at his side, he lifted his head with a wing. "Dartkull," he whispered, "are you alive?"

"Yes," came the weak reply, "But I'm hurt, and I'm sorry. I... should have warned you."

"Too late for that now," Corzell said softly, kindly, "You were afraid, I know, we would all have done the same faced with such keere, but listen, can you fly, youngling? There is hope yet."

"No... I'm sorry, my wing and my head are both hurt," the young mytre replied.

"Then, I will help you walk, I can hide you while you recover, but we must move quickly." Corzell was weak himself, but he managed to get the young strong bird to his feet and support him as they struggled away from the elpitlum place and down to the sealed road bridge. They walked with difficulty, Corzell continued to have trouble with depth perception, and he frequently mistook the distance of objects or obstacles and stumbled or fell.

Dartkull struggled too, as his wounds hindered his progress and limited his energy. Under the bridge, Corzell lay Dartkull down on the creek bank, behind the margin of a Hibbertia Sericea plant whose bright yellow flowers and hair-like leaves covered the small round shrub and hid Dartkull from casual observation.

"I'll come back tomorrow with food for you, youngling," Corzell whispered as he lowered the injured Dart clan member to the ground.

"There is something I must tell you, Corzell. The two strange birds that looked like ghosts were working with the Krat clan... they are not mytre. They were..." Dartkull's energy was failing, and he struggled to complete his sentence. "They were..." he couldn't go on and slumped into a deep sleep.

"I know," Corzell said to himself softly. "I have heard of these birds before. They might be tawny frogmouth, night spies. Very sneaky, nasty birds. But they are not owls." As he spoke, he turned his head to look about at the tree branches overhanging the creek. *They may be watching us now*, he thought. *Time will tell.*

9

The Emissary

I look up to the little bird
That glides across the sky

He sings the clearest melody
It makes me want to cry

It makes me want to sit right down
And cry, cry, cry, yeah.

Annie Lennox – 'Little Bird' (1992)

EACH OF THE CLAN leaders returned to their nest trees to spread the news about the Dart clan tragedy, Karmann's death, Corzell's mutilation, the clash with the Krat clan and their invasion of the elpitlum, heralding a new order that was taking over the valley.

In the Dart clan territory, concern at the death of Dartvada and Dartspadd, and the apparent death of their offspring; Dartkull had caused outright panic. The arrival of an emissary from the Krat clan to tell everyone in the Dart clan what had happened caused even greater panic. They were only a small clan to begin with, and losing their leaders left the few remaining mytre there with little choice. They could stay and become part of the Krat clan or leave the valley and risk finding a new place to make a nest tree.

The emissary gave them the remainder of the night to decide which options they wanted to pursue.

Only one mated pair had a recently fledged brood. They couldn't see any reason not to accept Kratt as their new leader. After all, they reasoned that they could only bring up their chicks safely if they stayed in the valley and they needed leadership to help keep them safe.

One pair of mated mytre without a brood chose to leave the valley and start a new life somewhere new. They reasoned that they could fly over the eucalypt forest and find a new nest tree, and new territory to the south, though none had made the journey before, and they didn't know what they'd find.

All mytre are afraid and unsure without leaders, and the remnants of the Dart clan were no exception. While each pair had said what they would do. The two who planned to leave hesitated and delayed, unsure of their future.

None of the Dart clan mytre that night heard the arrival of a strange dappled-grey bird with yellow eyes that perched stealthily a few branches away from the remaining Dart clan and listened to their debate, discussion, and the decision they made. None of them heard the tawny frogmouth depart silently and report what she had heard to Captain Kratt. Although shortly after the pair of Dart mytre who had decided to go, flew away over the eucalypt forest, the remaining Dart clan members heard the dreadful cries and screeches of two birds in distress to the south.

-0-

After the elpitlum, Kratt and his clan followed Karbett and Kardelia back to the Kar clan's nest tree. A few Kar clan members had broods, but most had either lost them like Karbett and Karelia to the cat or they had already fledged and were now out of the nest. Kratt brought the members of the Kar and Krat clans together in a mini-elpitlum for both clans. They met in the branches of the Kar clan's nest tree, although the night was growing old and cold.

This meant the Kar clan members could not see the full size of the Krat clan's numbers, for if they could, they would have been shocked. The impression the original clan leaders had at the elpitlum was that the invaders significantly outnumbered them. Certainly, Dartkull had given the impression of the invaders having a dozen or more adult birds. The reality was that they only had enough adult birds to kill the two Dart clan leaders effectively and speedily. For the rest of their plan, they relied on bravado and bluff.

Kratt had instructed Dartkull to embellish the numbers of the attacking birds in his story and when the Krat clan attacked the elpitlum, they used every bird of their clan including some fledglings that were hard to identify as such in the dark. Had Corzell and the others been prepared they would have been able to call upon many more mytre from the combined clans than the Krat clan could set to wing. Even now, while Kratt explained the new order in the valley the two Kar lieutenants, Kardelia and Karbett could not get a sense of the number of Krat mytre perched in the nest tree about them.

They knew their flock size and both Kardelia and Karbett suspected that the Kar clan alone outnumbered the invaders. But in the dark, between the branches of the tree, it was impossible to see all the invaders and possible that their 'guests' had other mytres that they held back in reserve in case they were needed later. Only Dartkull knew the true size of the invader's clan and Karbett thought he was likely dead under a shrub near the elpitlum.

Kratt had also worried about his numbers. Had it not been for the drought, he would be leading a much larger invasion force than he was now, and he had trusted deception, and the darkness to mask his force's true size. As he sat before the dejected and cowed Kar clan, he was confident his plan had worked.

The whole of Kar clan listened bleakly to Captain Kratt as he explained the new order of things. Most Kar clan members were in deep shock, without warning, they were unprepared for the arrival of a rival clan, but while sullen, they listened attentively to how the new system would work.

"You can all stay here in your former territory, you can keep your nest trees and you can raise your fledglings and young as you always have, but from now on you will be members of the Krat clan, for the Kar clan is dead."

Many of the listening mytre crowed and squawked their disapproval and displeasure with Kratt's message.

It was a short protest and once they were silent, he continued, "Or you can leave…" He paused. "The choice is yours… stay and live as Krat or leave. Or you can fight me and trust to the strength of your beak, claws, and wings. Law by claw. I have killed your former clan leader, and I will not hesitate to kill anyone who defies my rule."

In the gloom of night, only the orb of Egnaro illuminated the shadows of the nest tree.

With their elderly leader dead and with his two children, Karbett and Kardelia cowed after the elpitlum, few of the mytre dared speak out in protest.

Only one of the Kar clan parents, with fledgling chicks spoke. "Where will your nest tree be located, Sir?"

A lieutenant from the Krat clan moved toward her to admonish the outspoken mother. Kratt though signalled for them to hold off. "A good question," he replied, sounding pleased to have received the enquiry. "Tonight, we Krat will leave you to your nest trees. We will fly away and roost in the high pines on the western flank of the norzela park. Tomorrow, we will move into more formal nest sites here on your former territory, and onto the territory of the Dart clan, who have invited us to join them, or rather they have agreed to join Krat clan."

He sounds so smug, Karbett thought.

Although, there was no response from the defeated Kar assembled in their nest tree, Kratt tried to guess the Kar clan's mood. *Would they fight? Would they rebel? Would they surrender and give in? Would they accept him as their new leader?* His mind quickly considered each question. *It won't matter*, he told himself. *Either way I will take their territory and destroy any mytre that stands in my way.*

"You have until nwad. Then I shall have your answer or your lives, and your territory." He sounded confident. This approach had worked for him in the past and he was confident it would work again. "I will return at nwad, with Elppa," he said gruffly. "Leave them to talk," Captain Kratt called out.

With that, the Krat clan rose as one and flew east, into the night. As Kratt flew up he nodded to a strange bird hidden in the branches. He meant for the spy to stay and listen to their discussion.

The second of his tawny frogmouth strained her head, stretching her long neck, into the night sky, so that anyone looking without intent would see only a broken tree branch pointing upwards. Her camouflage was perfect and even the mytre who had lived all their lives in the same nest tree didn't notice the intruder and spy in their midst. Their grief also helped hide the spy for almost all the clan were bereft and lost without their leader, Karmann.

Once the Krat clan had departed, Karbett said coldly, "You should accept the captain's offer. But I cannot. I saw that keere choke and kill Karmann and I cannot stay here under his yolk."

Karcelia, the mother who had spoken earlier, said angrily. "You and Kardelia have no young, you can fly, we must stay, we have young fledglings who cannot fly far and who need constant attention. How can you leave us alone to our fate?"

"How can we stay? We will have no peace, no freedom, no law that is not from the Kratt's mouth... how can we stay?" Karbett, snapped back.

"Then the clan is dead," said another of the Kar clan throng gathered in the gloom of the nest tree. The darkness closed in on the spaces between them in the nest tree, and no breeze moved between the branches.

"There may be hope yet," said a small bird in a soft twittery voice close to Karbett's head. Only he heard it. The voice said, "He has spies in the tree. He has spies everywhere. Do not acknowledge me." The soft twittery voice belonged to the willie-wagtail, who lived near the norzela nest on the Cor clan land.

"Don't lose hope, Corzell is making a plan to save the valley." The small bird said as he settled on a slender branch near Karbett and waited for a sign in response.

Karbett hesitated as he considered the news. Finally, he said, "My heart was cold and dark when I spoke before."

Karbett looked at the mytre gathered about him in the nest tree. Then said boldly, "I will not leave you to your fate. Karmann would not have wanted his kin to run, to hide or to cower. We are the Kar clan, we have long been here, and longer still will we stay."

Karcelia and Kardelia looked with astonishment at the lieutenant. Pride swelled in them, and their spirits rose.

He winked briefly at Kardelia and then in a loud voice he added, "We are proud, we are strong, we will stay where we belong."

As one, but almost in a whisper, the Kar clan mytre replied, "We are proud, we are strong, we will stay where we belong."

The willie-wagtail understood and flew quickly away to report back to Corzell.

The tawny frogmouth saw him go, and although she had not overheard anything the willie-wagtail had said, she made a mental note to report the tiny visitor's departure, and the defiant chant to Kratt. For now, she had heard enough, and she flew silently from the tree branch above the Kar clan gathering. *Kratt will want to know that they plan to stay,* the tawny frogmouth thought, as she glided and flew unobserved, east, into the night.

-0-

In the Wayt clan territory, some of the clan members had overheard the cries and squawks from the elpitlum and all were eagerly awaiting their clan leader's return. Waytbill tried to explain everything as quickly and as accurately as he could. Like the Dart clan, their clan was small and feeble with only six members, and he knew the stronger Krat clan would soon overrun them. He reasoned that if Captain Kratt decided to take the Wayt territory, as he suspected he would, they would be unable to resist.

Waytjulia and Waytbill had only been a mated pair for two seasons and clan leaders for just one. But they knew they needed to act fast if their clan was to survive the coming storm.

"We have to leave and leave now!" Waytbill said quietly and earnestly.

"Where will we go?" asked one of the other clan members fearfully.

"First, into the eucalypt forest, we can hide there, regroup, and make a proper plan. But what we can't do is stay here any longer," Waytbill said, clearly and with conviction.

"I agree," put in Waytjulia sternly. "I was there. I saw how they were. How cruel they were and how they killed Karmann and plucked out Corzell's eye. They have no compassion. They will take all the valley before long. We have to leave now!"

As she finished speaking, one of the other clan members said, "Who's this?" As he spoke, he thrust a wing in the direction of a strange bird that flew into the Wayt territory and landed at the base of their nest tree. All the clan members were suddenly silent and Waytbill and Waytjulia flew down to the ground to confront the invader.

"You have no right in our territory without an invitation or prior arrangement." Waytbill spoke forcefully and rightfully.

"Leave at once," Waytbill demanded angrily. The strange mytre was shocked at the reception. But he didn't show it. Instead, he remained silent and gathered his thoughts while looking confident and stately.

"Who are you and what do you want with us?" Waytjulia said sternly to the strange mytre who ignored their law and seemed rude to boot. As she spoke, two other Wayt clan mytre descended to the ground beside her.

"I have come from the Krat clan, Captain Kratt sent me, and I speak with his voice. I am Kratthood and I am one of Captain Kratt's emissaries." He spoke confidently, as if on a high wire and with an air of arrogance.

"You're not welcome here," Waytbill shouted. "Leave!" Usually, the mention of Captain Kratt instilled respect or at least fear in his audience, but Kratthood began to feel his entreaty was having little impact.

"I speak on behalf of Captain Kratt. Some of you have met him I know, and I am here to…" Kratthood began.

"You're mistaken, Sir," said Waytbill his blood rising with his rage, "We're not here to treat with you, or to listen to you. Go now…" he looked at Waytjulia and the other Wayt clan members and added, "or you die."

The two remaining Wayt clan mytres flew in behind Kratthood and started to walk slowly toward him. All the Wayt clan mytre did likewise, slowly edging in, to surround the emissary.

"Don't do anything you'll regret," Kratthood said, in a stern, commanding voice. However, he had hardly finished speaking when Waytbill flew at the intruder, claws high. Kratthood took off in the same instant and avoided the initial blow.

Waytbill knew that the emissary must not escape, and he shouted to the others, "Bring him back, bring him down."

But Kratthood was fast, and he rose speedily into the air and began to circle east around the nest tree. Two of the Wayt clan mytres flew in the opposite direction and approached Kratthood as he flew around the tree, forcing the Krat bird to dive low. As he flew on, he dodged under the two approaching Wayt birds.

Suddenly, the blinding light of a massive vehicle approaching along the road, travelling east assaulted him. The keere was massive with the brightest array of lights Kratthood had ever seen. Even Elppa's light seemed dim in comparison. He tried to fly up and over it, but Waytbill had caught up with him and forced him to fly low. Waytbill was also in danger and in an instant, both birds twisted in flight and climbed up and away from the truck.

Because the Wayt clan lived near the sealed road they had seen the lights and heard the sound of these keere all their lives, but even Waytbill had never come this close to colliding with one. As the birds spun in the air as it passed, the bright blazing lights passed too, and the valley road was in darkness again as the truck thundered away into the distance. Half blind and tossed by the turbulent backdraft of the truck, the invader and Waytbill were firstly, sucked into the truck's wake and then tossed about in the air like leaves in autumn, as it moved away.

The invader was the first to recover and look about, but Waytjullia crashed into him as he regained his senses. Her beak struck Kratthood on the side of the head, before another of the Wayt clan birds, struck him almost immediately, sending the Krat bird to the roadway.

"Bring him down, bring him down," Waytbill shouted as he too recovered his senses.

Fearing for his life and terrorised by the lights and wind from the massive vehicle, Kratthood decided his best chance of escape was to fly low across the valley floor and twist and turn between the trees along the creek line. He looked quickly about and could see two Wayt clan birds approaching rapidly along the black surface of the road from the west. They were coming right at him. *Escape!* was all Kratthood could think. He waited for the two birds to attack, but they overshot him. They had anticipated he would leap into the air to fly off. Instead, he bobbed low and let them pass a feathers width above his head. Then he took rapidly to the wing, flying into the former Kar territory, where he knew he would be safe, if they didn't follow.

It was a mistake that cost him his life. Not knowing the lay of the land, the way the Wayt or Kar clan did, Kratthood flew fast and low across the road, skimming the low shrubs at the side of the road and then dropping low as he entered the area of the orchard. He began to feel the relief he imagined the orchard would provide when something stopped him dead in flight.

None of the Wayt clan had followed him, for they knew it would have been unwise to stray into another clan's territory. They also knew that flying low into the orchard meant flying directly into a low open weave wire fence, strung out to keep fruit hungry animals from the fruit and to delineate the norzela's property from the road. Waytbill had flown closely behind his foe for a short while before he came to rest in the long grass at the foot of the wire fence. Looking up he could see that the fence still held Kratthood, with his head caught, twisted and limp on one side, in a rectangle loop of the open weave wire fence, and his body and wings hanging limply on the other.

Broken neck, Waytbill thought, *serves him right.* Within a moment, the five other Wayt clan birds, including Waytjulia were at his side in the long grass. All looked at the dangling carcase of the Krat clan emissary.

"That settles it then," Waytjulia said solemnly. "We leave tonight, follow me."

-0-

Earlier, Kratthood had waited for Yatnolia to respond. "We can keep our clan territory?" she clarified. "Our leader, and Captain Kratt will not interfere with our lands or young or make more territorial claims?

"Of course, you will need to pay a tribute, 'er half of all you find, I believe it was." He spoke as if he was their lord and master. An arrogant tone clung to every word. Yatnolia and Yatdoll knew, as surely as Elppa's appearance each day, that he couldn't be trusted.

"What shall we do?" Yatnolia whispered to her mate.

"We accept," Yatdoll said suddenly. "We are not a large clan, and we don't want any further trouble. We can pay your price and as long as you hold up your end of the bargain, we will respect your terms. The emissary looked shocked. Yatdoll was pleased, he had hoped to tilt him off guard.

"I have only one request, and that is that you respect our territorial boundary and that we bring the tribute to you, say, near the sealed road bridge each day." Yatdoll spoke quickly and confidently, inviting no argument with his proposal.

"I… I will need to speak with Captain Kratt 'er… before I can agree to these terms," Kratthood stammered.

"I thought you were Kratt's voice," Yatnolia snapped immediately. "Or is that not so, perhaps we should wait and speak with Captain Kratt himself."

"I am his voice, it's just that I can't change the treaty terms without his permission."

"We have agreed to your terms… all we are discussing is the location of the tribute payment," Yatdoll put in.

"Yes, I see, but I will still need to…"

"He said he was the 'voice' of Kratt, now he's not sure," Yatdoll said in a condescending tone.

"Well, now I'm confused," added Yatnolia snidely.

"Alright, I can agree to this, I'll tell Captain Kratt, but can I have your assurance that you will stay in the valley and pay the tribute."

"On the life of our young and the wings of Cordelia the courageous," said Yatdoll sincerely.

Every mytre knew the story of Cordelia's courage and wisdom and the value each mated pair placed on their young's life. Kratthood had no choice other than to accept that a deal had been made.

He nodded and bowed low, then said, "I am flying now to the Wayt clan, I hope they will be more accommodating."

I'm sure they will not, Yatdoll thought as he too bowed low before the Krat emissary. Yatdoll and Yatnolia watched Kratthood fly away.

"We must get a message to Corzell," Yatnolia said, earnestly. "He will have a solution to this mess."

-O-

Corzell had finally arrived back at the nest tree, he was exhausted and in pain. His missing eye meant he had to walk part of the way back and he was overcome with the effort of moving on the ground at night, of moving Karmann's body and hiding Dartkull. He was also slow to adjust or to become accustomed to having lost half his vision. He tried to fly twice and each time he flew into a stand of bushes that appeared unseen on the side of his blind eye. It took a while although he eventually learnt that he needed to swivel his head from side to side to see obstacles and objects about him.

When he arrived back, Corselia was shocked and distraught at his physical appearance, but relieved and glad he was alive. As she examined his eye socket she said quickly, "An emissary was here. He was asking for you. I told him you had gone to the elpitlum and that I was wondering when you would return. What's happened to you, what's going on?" Cordilia and Corxell looked on anxiously as their father appeared wounded and bloody before them.

"I'll... tell all... shortly," Corzell said between panted breaths. "First... Cordelia... I have a... mission for you." Corzell looked into his young daughter's eyes and held her small grey body between his wings.

"This is important, go to the line of shrubs near the norzela nest and seek out the willie-wagtail. Ask him to take this message to Karbett of the Kar clan. Tell him that he must speak with no one else and that there will be spies watching him. Tell him to say that they must not give up hope and that I have a plan to save the valley clans."

"No..." cried her mother, "she's too small, too young."

"That is her advantage," Corzell said firmly. "It is because you are small that our enemies may not see you. Then come back right away."

Cordelia understood at once and repeated, "Find the willie-wagtail, tell him to find Karbett, of the Kar clan, and say that you have a plan and that there is hope."

"And come straight home to the nest," Corzell added. "Go quickly, girl."

Cordelia stepped to the edge of the nest and dropped into the dark night air.

"What's happened, dear?" Corselia asked with concern. "Look at you, you have been fighting and you're injured…"

"We must act quickly. There is no time to waste," Corzell said sharply, then he asked, "What did the emissary want?"

"He was called Kratthood, and he said, he spoke with the voice of… Captain Kratt. I didn't understand, and he asked where you were and why you hadn't returned to the nest? I was so worried. He said we had to decide to stay or leave, accept Kratt or find another home." Corselia sounded anxious as she spoke, but she had not panicked. "I was worried sick but knew you would be alright. Cordelia said you would come back."

"It was an ambush," Corzell said quickly. "A new clan, the Krat clan has invaded the valley and destroyed or taken over the Dart clan, they injured Dartkull a young mytre whom I have hidden. Their leader is… this Captain Kratt, he took my eye as a warning to the other clan leaders, and I believe they are moving into the Kar clan territory soon. They killed Karmann," he concluded, drained.

Corselia was shocked and became immediately anxious before asking, "What about the other clans?"

"I don't know. Maybe this emissary is going about asking for their allegiance to Captain Kratt as he did here." Corzell sounded tired, worn, beaten.

"Will they give it?" Corselia asked with concern.

"I don't know… I don't know. I hope some will resist… but I don't know. I can't think straight with this pain in my eye. I have a plan, but I'll need to know more about what the other clans do before it will work."

The news stunned Corselia and finally, she looked closely at her partner's eye. Blood and dirt had obscured the depth of his eye injury and she finally saw the extent of his wound. His right eye was completely gone.

"Corxell," she called, "quickly, fetch me some sap from the nest tree trunk." Her son didn't hesitate, and he quickly jumped out of the nest and began searching for sweet, sticky sap, where it leaked from the tree. Within a short time, he was back at his mother's side, and she took the sap and dripped it into the open eye socket of her partner, sealing the wound and stopping the bleeding. She also plucked at the sand and dirt on his face and as she finished cleaning her partner's wound, and sealed his eye socket with sap, Cordelia flew up to the nest tree and came to rest on the lip of the nest.

Excitedly she said, "I found him, the willie-wagtail... I found him and he's gone to speak with Karbett." Corzell sighed with relief, his eye felt better too, and he slumped into the nest himself, displacing both chicks as he sank into a deep sleep.

-0-

The next day, Corzell returned to search for Dartkull. He had left him hiding under the bridge, under the cover of a drooping Hibbertia Sericea plant near the creek's bank. He'd wanted to come back sooner, but he was tired and injured himself. He contemplated sending Corselia but knew the risks of being discovered were too high. When he did get away, it was after ksud and darkness added to the dappled light by the creek, and to the shadows under the bridge.

Corzell took care to look for any sign that Dartkull, had been found, and he approached the hiding place with caution. He could see no sign of any others being in the area, but he felt uncomfortable with the stillness and quiet as he approached. He hesitated and held back while he listened for any sign of life or for an ambush. Eventually, his courage rose, and he crept under the bridge and lifted the skirt of the plant.

He found Dartkull where he'd left him. Sadly, he had passed over to the Great flock of Elppa sometime in the night. Corzell looked at the young mytre, still with grey and blood-tinged feathers on his chest and shoulders. It had been almost a single passage of Elppa since the tragedy at the elpitlum had occurred.

Corzell sat and contemplated the events of the recent past. The Dart clan had been destroyed and subsumed into the new Krat clan, Karmann had been killed and the Kar clan had been overrun, he had lost an eye and now, Dartkull had died. All at the wing and beak of this new Captain Kratt. Corzell would normally chortle and chorus at a death, especially one as tragic as Dartkull's. But he couldn't, he wouldn't dare to make any sound that might draw the Krat clan spies or warriors down around his beak. Instead, he said a silent prayer and vowed to find a way to avenge this fallen Dart clan member.

As he gathered his thoughts and flew away back to his nest tree, he didn't see a ghostly grey bird laying still and lost amongst the grey bark of a nearby Rose Apple tree, Syzygium Moorei. As Corzell left, the ghostly silent night hunter slipped from her hiding place and followed the Cor clan leader back to his home tree. She was sure there would be more to hear and see in the coming nights and she set up a listening position, unnoticed, close to Corzell's nest in the Cor clan home tree.

10

The Plan

Patti Smith – 'China Bird' (2000)

KRATT WOKE WITH a start. His dreams had been dark and bleak. He was sure he was doing the right thing. The few of his clan that remained needed to live in the lush valley, and he was the mytre to lead them in their attempt to take it over. However, thoughts of hardship and struggle flooded his mind and, as he had slept, the trials of his early life and recent misfortune crowded into his dreams. Now awake, he reflected briefly on his and his clan's struggle to survive. This recent invasion was just part of a larger struggle, and he was determined to see it through, but his tragic past was never far from his thoughts.

His parents had lived on the outskirts of a clan a long way from the valley and once he'd fledged, he'd needed to scavenge and fight alongside his family to find food as they lived in constant fear of their bigger, neighbouring clan. One day, a brown goshawk killed his father and he and his mother begged to join the bigger clan, for protection and the security of the family networks the larger clan offered.

They refused and forced him and his mother to leave even the outskirts of the clan area. On their flight to find a new home and clan area, a norzela with a gun killed his mother. On his own, he had to fight to survive. From an early age, he'd learnt that he'd have to fight for everything he wanted, and he grew into a strong bird with a skill for taking and giving powerful blows.

Alone and mature, he decided to take over the clan that had rejected him and his mother, and he returned to the area where he'd been born to challenge the clan leader. In the fight that followed he defeated the old clan leader and asserted himself as the new head of the clan. He was surprised at how easy it was. Once the clan leader was gone, the remainder of the clan simply fell in behind him passively. He was soon a powerful and feared leader.

Then the norzela began to build more nests in the area, digging up the trees, and land, laying tubes under the ground, putting up thick poles and joining them with wires and cables. More cars and vehicles came to the clan territory and the norzelas destroyed their nest trees. Soon his clan were starting to die, as the number of cars increased and began to kill more of the clan's mytre. Their once quiet, lightly forested hillside soon became a norzela nest site with hundreds of new norzela coming to live in the area where he and his clan once flew free.

The stress diminished chick numbers and as more cats came into the area, more chicks were killed, and families destroyed. The clan soon became broken, as numbers and their hope for survival dropped. Kratt decided to move the whole clan away to a new site, with more nest trees and fewer norzela and their cats.

They flew a long way. But the journey cost them many lives as vehicles, goshawk, wedge-tailed eagle, and hunger killed his clan mytre. The young suffered the most, and their mothers soon perished from despair and heartbreak, as much as from the hardships of the journey and their many enemies. They found a home near an open parkland, with numerous potential nest trees, on the edge of a large grain silo facility and norzela rail siding.

Kratt thought this would be an ideal location and the clan settled into their new home without opposition, although Kratt thought it odd that there were no other mytre in the area. Still, he welcomed the new site because of the rich concentration of food in the area and the many possible nest trees.

Soon though, more of his clan began to die. Within a short time, over half of the clan were dead. Enemies did not kill them and Kratt didn't know what did. The remaining clan members became disillusioned with their powerful leader. Many wanted to leave and return to their former home, and although Kratt had the power to stop them, he could see they were already broken.

Belatedly, he explored the silo area himself and noticed trays of corn distributed about the area. Surrounding each tray, were dead mice and it occurred to Kratt that his clan were dying from the ingested poison in the corn, or after eating the dead mice who had also been poisoned. By the time he'd discovered this, only a handful of mytre were left, and it was these few he led away to find a safer home in the valley.

As he considered the events that had led them to the valley, he called for one of his lieutenants, Krattac, to summon the tawny frogmouth for a report. Kratt knew there was still a lot to do to secure the valley for the Kart clan.

-0-

Corzell woke with a start. His dreams had been dark and bleak. A norzela vehicle had driven through his thoughts with its lights blazing in the darkness. He felt tired and thin, like a mist on the valley floor in spring. His head hurt and, as he came to his senses, he was aware that half of his world was still dark. In the light of Elppa, he was even more aware that he had lost part of his eyesight and that hunting and gathering were going to become greater challenges in the future. Then he remembered there was an even more pressing danger that needed his attention – he must challenge Captain Kratt.

The nest was empty. Corselia and Corhelia had taken the two young fledglings for breakfast. He'd missed the nwad chorus and realized for the first time how hungry he was. He swivelled his head about, looking over the rim of the nest, trying to see if he could see his family. He thought he could hear them and lifted himself so he might see further. Looking to the north he could see the norzela nest and the lawned area in front of it. He thought he could see two mytre walking slowly across the grass, listening, and pecking at the ground for bugs, worms, or grubs. One was definitely Corselia, he would recognize her plumage anywhere. He was about to fly down to her when he was aware of the sound of a bird flying into the nest tree and settling on a branch near-by.

Kratt didn't bother with the usual 'Elppa' greeting. He just said, "So you are still alive, Corzell."

Stunned, Corzell turned so that he could see the visitor.

Kratt said simply, "I've come for your reply."

"Reply?" Corzell said, confused and still groggy from his disturbed sleep.

"Don't play the fool," Kratt said annoyed. "Will your clan stay or go? Will you pay the tribute or die?"

Corzell suddenly realised what he was asking. "Captain Kratt, my apologies. I was injured as you know and am still recovering." *You will pay for my eye,* Corzell thought, bitterly, while remaining polite.

"I hope you've learnt your lesson. Now your answer," Kratt demanded abruptly.

Corzell hesitated. His senses having returned, they brought back his anger and disgust for the invaders. His anguish from events of the night before, returned with his wakefulness.

Suddenly, Corselia appeared at his wing with Cordelia and Yatnolia at her side. "You must be Captain Kratt," Corselia said without introducing herself. "You took my partner's eye. We gave your emissary our reply, last night. What else have you come to take?"

"Do you have permission to be on Cor clan territory," Cordelia added.

Captain Kratt, stunned by the onslaught, turned to face the young bird. He saw she was a youngling, who had a strange horn like feather protruding from her forehead. He was initially taken aback, shocked by the appearance of her deformity, as it reminded him of his own white forehead feather. But seeing in her no threat, he recovered, quickly. He snapped, "I sent an emissary here last night. He has not returned so I don't know what your response was."

"It was the same as the one the Yat clan gave," Yatdoll said. "We agreed to your terms, but it was agreed that we would place your tribute near the sealed road bridge at the end of each day and that no Krat clan mytre can trespass on our clan territory."

"Who agreed to these terms," Kratt demanded, angrily.

"Your emissary, Kratthood," Yatdoll replied firmly.

"We made the same agreement. We will stay and pay, but you must collect your tribute by the bridge and your clan can not cross on to our territories without prior consent," Corselia confirmed.

"I made no such agreement," Kratt snapped back quickly.

"Your emissary said he spoke with your voice, and this was the agreement we made with him," Yatdoll said.

"This may be, although as he didn't come back last night, I have no knowledge of this agreement."

Corzell and Yatdoll looked concerned and confused.

"Kratthood said he was going to talk with the Wayt clan when he left the Yat clan," Yatdoll said insistently.

There was a strained silence for a moment, although before anyone could speak, a Krat mytre landed at Kratt's side. It was Kratatora. She landed quickly and began to whisper into Captain Kratt's ear. "We found Kratthood's body. It was near the Krat clan orchard, his neck had been broken." She hesitated and then said, "He was hanging on a fence."

Kratt looked at the gathered subjects with suspicion. It all sounded too convenient. He was doubtful of the cause of death and watched the other mytre for a clue to their involvement. Then he said, "We have just found Kratthood's body... on a fence." The gathered mytre all appeared genuinely shocked and there was nothing in their response that convinced Kratt that they had been involved, though he remained sceptical.

Kratatora lent towards Captain Kratt and whispered again. "We also found no sign of the Wayt clan. All of them are gone," Kratatora said gravely.

Kratt looked around at Kratatora, surprised. "All gone," he said.

Corzell knew what the whispered conversation meant. Wayt clan had gone, and the emissary was dead. Now there was no way to verify their claims of a new agreement.

Kratt looked disturbed, and hesitated before he added, solemnly, "Kratthood was a faithful servant and will be greatly missed."

"We had nothing to do with his death," Corzell said, honestly. Adding, "May he find flight with the Great flock of Elppa."

"He was well and of good wing when he left the Yat clan," Yatdoll confirmed, also adding, "May he find a place in the Great flock of Elppa..." Then she said, "Anyway, why would we kill an emissary who was carrying our new terms to you?"

Kratt thought that they had a point but couldn't show any weakness. Then Krattac landed next to him and Kratatora on the branch, and announced, "It seems it was the fence wire that killed Kratthood. It also appears that the Wayt clan lands are completely empty."

"Then," Kratt called, "I claim the Wayt lands as my own." Captain Kratt moved along the branch and came closer to the Cor clan nest. The other birds watched him as he took in the new information and contemplated his options. He'd been fortunate that the small size of his clan had not been detected, and that none of the larger clans had been made aware of their coming. His surprise attack had been executed perfectly, and he was now in possession of half of the valley. There was time yet to take more territory if it was needed, but Kratt thought his best option was to consolidate his victories and to negotiate a peace, at least until he was ready to strike out for the rest of the valley.

He looked at Corzell, Corselia, their two chicks in their nest, and the Yat clan leader, Yatdoll. He regarded them as 'pathetic.' And knew they would be little further trouble.

Magnanimously, Captain Kratt announced, "I will honour my emissary's agreement."

Stunned, Corzell thought, *What's going on?*

"I now have possession of the former Kar ard Dart territories and now, it appears that I have the Wayt clan land and sky too. So it seems that I control all the territories east of the creek." This was far more than Kratt had hoped for when he had launched his invasion, and it had cost him only one of his clan, the unfortunate Kratthood, who it seems, had flown into a fence. By all accounts, it was a stunning victory. He reasoned that he could afford some magnanimity, some grace, some generosity of spirit, a sign that the invasion was over, and their peace could begin.

"Will you stay on your side of the creek?" Corzell asked.

"Will you release us from having to pay a tribute?" Corselia enquired, hopefully.

"You have more territory than you can use, if the Wayt clan are gone," she added.

Kratt knew that a small bird had visited the former Kar clan last night. He thought he was going to have his wings full, dealing with dissent in the former Kar clan. His small numbers meant he would need all the mytre he could muster to manage and control what he had, let alone, deal with these organised and motivated western neighbours. *My spies will watch them,* he thought, *while I take hold of the lands and skies I have.*

"Agreed, you can keep your territories, none of my clan will trespass, and I will forgo the tribute. But only if you also stay on your side of the creek and do not spread unrest or discontent within my clan."

Kratt seems to be reasonable after all, thought Yatdoll. But she didn't know his plans, and she'd not learnt not to trust him. Then Yatdoll looked at Corzell's eye, where the sap had hardened amber in the socket. It looked like Corzell's eye had grown back, but it was a falsehood, a trick that foretold more deception to come, especially if they remained blind to Captain Kratt's tricks. *No*, thought Yatdoll, *he can't be trusted*.

"Come, Kratatora," Kratt said suddenly as he took to the air, calling back, disingenuously, "Elppa's blessing to you all."

-0-

"I was told nothing I swear," Karbett said.

"Hit him again, Kratatora," Captain Kratt said coldly as the obedient lieutenant scratched the hapless former Kar clan leader's son across the head.

"Leave him alone, please. Have pity. We have agreed to all your demands. We will become faithful Krat clan members and will report any rumblings of dissent or subversion. Please... he knows nothing," Kardelia pleaded passionately as they held and beat her partner.

"He knows something. Our spy saw the willie-wagtail here last night, talking with him," Kratatora said angrily as he slashed her claw across the poor bird's head again. Karbett could hardly hold his head up and whimpered pathetically in response to the strike.

"You want to speak?" Kratatora said, "finally some sense."

"I was told to have hope..." he said as he gasped for breath. Then he spat blood into Kratatora's face before turning to Kratt and adding, lying, "I'm to wait for a great bird to come and scratch out your eyes and tear your tail from your body."

"Take his flight feathers," Captain Kratt cried. "If he won't talk, he will only walk! Let's see how that brings him down to earth."

Immediately two Krat clan birds set to work ripping the vital flight feathers from the dejected bird's wings.

"Take his tail feathers too," Kratt called, adding, "are there others who were told to have hope of salvation?"

None of the former Kar clan spoke and only a few dared to watch as Karbett was horribly mutilated. Kardelia watched through a blanket of tears that seemed to hide only the superficial aspects of her partner's agonies.

Captain Kratt waited until the de-feathering was complete. He looked on the bedraggled mytre, stripped of his proud feathers and beautiful plumage. This was an insult on two levels, without, flight feathers, he could no longer fly or hunt, only scavenge on the earth where his enemies, the lizard, cat, or the dog could easily catch and kill him. The other insult, although less fatal, was an insult to his mytreship. Without his true colours he was no longer seen to wear the badge of honour that the mythical Cordelia had won for them from the Gods.

Blood ran down his face and dried on his beak. The whole Kar clan had seen him humiliated and beaten. But his pride remained unbowed, and he held onto the hope the willie-wagtail had promised him the night before.

"This bird is now banished. Any bird seen talking with him will also be banished. This is the will of Lord Kratt. Lord of the eastern valley, captain of the Krat and noble giver of law." Krattac spoke clearly and with purpose, then he turned and bowed low to his Lord.

As he did, the quicker and wiser mytre dic likewise, before even the slower birds picked up on the cue. Before long, every mytre, Kar or Krat bowed before the Lord of their world. Kardelia tried hard to slow her sobbing and to put the torture and banishment of her partner from her mind, although, while she had her head low, her rage burned within her.

Lord Kratt, he liked the title. He stood tall and let out a clear choral sound that rang about the valley. Then he called the two sly tawny frogmouths over to him. Both dark and pale grey creatures, with yellow eyes landed silently at his side.

"Suca and Traps, I have a mission for you. Serve me well and I will reward you greatly," Kratt whispered. The two female tawny frogmouths had been Kratt's allies for years. They had helped him defeat enemies and take over previous clan territories in the past. They were an unusual pair, both female and both loyal to a fault.

"Yes, Lord," they replied in unison, adding, "as you command." They also bowed low before leaning in to listen to Kratt's plan.

All the while the gathered mytre remained bowing low, too afraid to rise or move. Eventually the tawny frogmouth flew away and Kratt signalled for the audience to rise.

"Fellow Krat clan," he said as he spread his wings. "I will take this splendid tree as my own nest tree. You are free to find new nest trees within what were the former Kar, Dart and Wayt clans. You can choose new mates and you can mate with any member of your previous or new clans." He knew this would settle any initial conflict as male mytre tried to assert their claim over mates new and old. Then he turned his attention to Karbett. "Take this fallen bird to the sealed road and cast him out. I never want to see his face again."

With that Krattac and Kratatora marched and pushed the bedraggled and blood splattered bird along the gravel driveway that led past the former Kar nest tree and down toward the sealed road. Once there, they forced him to the east and made the now tired and defeated mytre march toward the norzela park. Karbett's despair and disappointment grew, as his energy dwindled.

-0-

In the Cor clan, as soon as the wicked Captain Kratt had gone, Corzell began his plans to free the former eastern mytre clans and secure a safer future for his own and the remaining Yat clan. Corselia and Corhelia took over the task of feeding and teaching Cordelia and Corxell. Corzell was still having trouble with flight and while he practiced at every opportunity, unseen branches or leaves often brushed him as he flew through the nest tree and further afield. Still, with Yatdoll's help a plan began to formulate.

He called the willie-wagtail to the nest tree. There, Corzell thanked him for his bravery in going into the Kar nest tree and asked if he was willing to help further. "It will not be easy," Corzell admitted, "but you are vital to the plan's success." The willie-wagtail said he was proud to help but wasn't sure what more he could do.

"You will be our secret messenger," Corzell explained. "Here is what I want you to do."

-0-

Between the Cor and Yat clans they had over a dozen mytre, although they also had a few younglings that would be of little use in a fight. With this in mind Corzell and Corsela realised they would need allies and tricks to overcome the invaders. Stealth and wits were worth more than a host of beaks and claws, they knew. They also knew they needed time to build their plans and to gather the resources needed. The first part of their plan involved stalling and playing for time. It meant cooperating without seeming weak.

Yatdoll was not impressed. He wanted action. Their friends in the east would be losing heart each day as they waited to retaliate, and the Krat clan would be growing stronger.

"The time to act is now," Yatdoll insisted.

Corzell disagreed saying, "We'll lose everything if we act too rashly. Time is our only ally, and we can't waste any advantage we have on impetuous, reactionary folly." Although Yatdoll was still upset and eager to fight he listened and pondered Corzell's advice. "We'll lose it all in a fight. We're too few and too weak. I can still only fly with caution. And anger is no defence against seasoned fighters," Corzell said.

"Be reasonable, Yatdoll," his partner Yatnolia offered, soundly. "Plans need time to develop. We need time to contact our allies and to build up our strength," Yatnolia added.

"Time is all we have now. Wait friend," Corzell said calmly. "Our time will come."

-0-

Weeks passed. Cordelia and Corxell grew, their fledging and feeding skills grew more competent and their interest in their territory and clan history grew in parallel to their size. Cordelia was still small. "She always will be," her mother said, "but there is something special about her, something I can't understand or see." Cordelia's feather pattern was like her fathers, and apart from the small 'horn' like protrusion of dark, black feathers on her forehead, she too had developed a white band of feathers that stretched from the nape of her neck to join at her throat.

The plan to free the valley of Captain Kratt had also developed. The willie-wagtail had flown almost every day with messages from their potential allies and they were approaching the day when they could launch their plan.

Corzell and Corselia were in their nest tree, they had sung the nwad chorus and they were enjoying the residual warmth of Elppa. The spring was passing, and the first signs of summer were everywhere. The grass had turned blond and long. The dams were low, with lines about the rim where Elppa had drunk from them each day. The leaves in the nest tree rustled more with the wind as they too became crisp and dry and turned from rich glossy deep green to the pale sallow green of summer. In spite of their troubles and the plans being made, they both felt the joy of a warm nest and the happiness of sleeping chicks.

"Corzell."

It was only a whispered sound, like sand blown over a corrugated iron roof, and at first, he'd thought it was the wind playing tricks in the high branches of the nest tree. "Did you hear that?" he asked Corselia. They both listened as the wind blew through the tree.

"Corzell."

There was no mistake this time. It was a fleeting raspy sound, and it wasn't from near them in the tree. It was coming from below them near the ground.

"I'll go down and look about," Corzell said. "My sight is no better, but I have learnt to adjust to my disability." With that reassurance to Corselia, he stepped carefully over the nest, so as not to wake the chicks, then glided down to the base of the tree and landed gracefully on an exposed tree root.

"Is someone there?" Corzell asked softly.

"I'm here, Corzell. I have come a long hard way to find you." Karbett's voice sounded course, like he needed a drink to unsettle the dust from his throat.

Corzell didn't recognise the bird as a mytre at first. He was covered in filth, had no tail feathers, and clearly couldn't fly. What was it... he didn't know, and trepidation initially filled him. Then when the creature spoke again, he remembered immediately who the wretched form was before him... Karbett.

"Corzell, I'm so glad to find you. I've come for help. Friend, will you forgive my pride and foolishness, will you help me?"

Pity overcame Corzell as he looked on the injured bird, and he was at once at Karbett's side.

"Can you come to the nest?" Corzell asked, half knowing the answer.

"No, I cannot fly. But I must talk with you," Karbett said, sounding sad, tired, and drained. To the left of the tree trunk was an overgrown Crimson Bottle Brush with the beginning of its distinctive crimson-red brushes starting to bloom. This was where Corzell took the tired traveller. Together they scraped a nest amongst the leaves and bark fallen from the tree, and from the other plants nearby.

11

The Story of Cordelia's

Cunning and Wit

You tell me that you've got everything you want
And your bird can sing, but you don't get me
You don't get me.
You say you've seen seven wonders
And your bird is green, but you can't see me
You can't see me.

The Beetles – 'And Your Bird Can Sing' (1966)

CORDELIA WOKE AFTER a dream. "Where's father," she asked almost immediately. "I saw him in my dream." Then she said, afraid, "I saw a car."

"Why, whatever would you see one of those for?" her mother asked confused.

"I saw one in my dream, I felt like I was riding in one, and I saw father too, but he was all white light and so bright. He looked like a star. Where's father?" Cordelia asked again.

"He is talking with someone below the nest tree," Corselia explained, "Go back to sleep."

"I can't, not now… will you tell me a story. One about the Cordelia of myth."

Corselia was worried, Corzell had been gone a long time and although he had come to tell her he was talking with Karbett, this had not reassured her, and she had little sleep. "Alright, young one, just one story." She thought for a moment, got comfy and said, "This is the story of Cordelia's cunning and wit."

"Once upon a time, Cordelia was in the middle of a long wet and cold winter. Her clan were freezing, and they had little to eat. The ground was too hard to get at worms and grubs and even the wind seemed to always be blowing in their face, making flying harder. Many of her clan were suffering and they asked her to help them find warmth. Cordelia also felt the cold and rain and came up with a plan to bring more warmth to her clan.

"First, she approached the God of rain, Xervinu, to ask if he would make the rain stop. 'Please,' she asked, 'we are cold and wet, and the rain has been falling for a long time. Can you stop the winter rain so we can be dry and warm, even for a short while?' 'Oh no,' said Xervinu. 'This is the time of rain and the time for rivers to be replenished, for creeks to flow and for the lakes to drink in my gift of rain. I could not stop on behalf of some cold wet birds, without the wit to stay dry.'

"Cordelia was disappointed but understood that the birds also needed to take responsibility for finding a dry place out of the rain. Rather than give up, she went to Korzela, the God of wind, to ask him to blow some warm breezes, or to stop the cold wind altogether. 'Please,' she asked, 'we are cold and wet, and the wind is blowing through our nest trees and adding greatly to our discomfort. Can you stop the winter wind so we can be dry and warm, even for a short while?'

"'Oh no,' Korzela replied. 'This is the time of winter wind. It is the time for boughs to fall and branches to break. It is a time for sweeping wind to clean the land. I could not stop on behalf of some cold wet birds who feel a chill, and who don't have the wit to stay out of the wind.'

Cordelia was again disappointed, but in her heart, she knew that the Gods had no reason to listen to her request. However, she soon conceived an idea for how to solve their problem of staying warm and out of the wind and rain.

"Cordelia set off to see the God of the sun and the day, Elppa. It was a long journey, but she was glad that he remembered her from before, and he asked her what she wanted. 'Oh Lord of the sun and the sky and the day, I want nothing but to sing in your honour and I have come to let you know that myself and my clan, who love you so much, want nothing more than for you to listen to our celebration of rejoicing in your power.'

"Pleased and delighted, Elppa agreed to listen to the concert. Cordelia knew that with the rain falling, and the wind blowing, very little of their celebration would reach Elppa's ears. However, Cordelia still called all her clan together in the branches of their nest tree. Then she instructed them to sing in praise of Elppa. 'Sing with all your might,' she implored. 'Sing with resounding chorus,' she called. 'Sing as you have never sung before,' she shouted.

"However, the wind blew through the home tree and the rain tumbled down on their heads, beaks, and backs and little of the celebration reached Elppa's ears. The next day Cordelia though still cold and wet, went on another long journey to see Elppa. 'Did you enjoy our singing, Lord Elppa?' she asked. 'I could hear no singing,' he said. 'I'm sorry, Lord Elppa,' Cordelia lamented. 'We did sing, but Xervinu, the Lord of the rain, and Korzela, the Lord of the wind, were clearly jealous of our love for you, and they threw rain clouds between us and blew away our voices in the blustery wind. We will try again tomorrow.' Again, Cordelia implored her faithful clan to sing as loudly as they could. As before, the rain and the wind hindered their performance and cut the songs they sang from the sky. Again, Elppa could hear nothing of the concert.

"Cordelia approached the Lord of the sun, and the sky, and the day again. 'Did you hear the rejoicing chorus of our love for you, Lord?' Cordelia asked. 'No, I did not,' Lord Elppa said, angrily. 'Do not be angry, Lord. It was the same as before,' Cordelia explained. 'Xervinu, the Lord of the rain, and Korzela, the Lord of the wind are jealous of our love for you and placed high winds and thick rain clouds between us to block our voices.' Then Cordelia said, 'You are surely the greatest Lord of all and if you can ask the Lord of the wind and the Lord of the rain to stop, you will be able to hear our voices celebrate our love for you.'

"The Lord of the sun, and day, and the sky knew the trick that Cordelia was trying to play. He was indeed wise and great. But he could see she and her kin loved him and he considered her suggestion carefully. 'I can see you love me, Cordelia, and I can see your clan wish to celebrate their love for me… so I will grant your wish.'

"The next day when Cordelia and her clan gathered to sing their chorus to Elppa, the sun shone down upon them. The wind was still, and Xervinu and her rain clouds were gone from the sky. Soon the ground softened, and they could easily find and pull worms and grubs from the soil, and every bird rejoiced in the sun's glory. Cordelia and her fellow mytre sang as they had never done before. Lifting their voices in thanks to the Lord of the sun as He shone down upon them. As he did, it warmed their faces and dried their wings.

"Cordelia's cunning and wit had saved her clan and helped them find warmth and keep dry in the dead of winter. Even now, Corselia explained, all mytre, in memory of Cordelia's cunning and wit, will sing not just at nwad and at ksud, when Elppa and Egnaro kiss, but also at nwod when Elppa is at his mightiest and highest, so that Elppa will see and hear the mytre's love for the Lord of day, the sky and the sun."

12

Karbett's Journey

If I leave here tomorrow
Would you still remember me?
For I must be traveling on now
'Cause there's too many places I've got to see.

But if I stay here with you, girl
Things just couldn't be the same
'Cause I'm as free as a bird now
And this bird you cannot change...
Won't you fly high, free bird, yeah.

Lynyrd Skynyrd – 'Free Bird' (1973)

Once Corzell had settled Karbett under the bottle brush, he brought him some water and dribbled it from his own beak into the injured bird's beak, as if Karbett was an infant.

"Thank you, friend," the grateful mytre said, his voice a little less raspy.

"What has become of you? We heard from a willie-wagtail in the Krat territory that you had been banished and then killed."

"I had been," Karbett said, cryptically. "At least I have been banished. My death is somewhat exaggerated, although I have nearly died since leaving the clan. But I need to talk with you. I have come a long way."

"And I need to talk with you," said Corzell, "but tell me how you came to be here tonight? You look like you have been caught flying in a whirlwind."

"I have, my friend," Karbett agreed. "A whirlwind that the Krat clan and their leader Lord Kratt started."

"He's Lord Kratt now?" Corzell said, shocked. *Why have our spies not reported this.* He wondered.

Karbett went on, "His name was changed but he remains insufferably arrogant... Lord indeed." Karbett sounded and looked both frustrated and anxious as he spoke of the invader.

"But how is it that you are alive and here now," Corzell asked, sympathetically.

"When Lord Kratt banished me, two of his lieutenants marched me off the former Kar territory. They took my flight and tail feathers as a punishment for my stubbornness, and the same thugs that walked me off 'their' lands beat me. They led me to the sealed road, and I hoped I could go west, towards your territory. However, they walked me east toward the norzela park. I was sure they were going to kill me, but they soon lost interest in me once we reached the line of pine trees near the park. They cuffed me about the head a few times with their wings, as we walked. Then they pointed to the east and said, 'Just keep walking and don't come back.' As I walked on, , I heard one say to the other, 'Come on, I'm bored with this walking lark, let's fly over to the Dart clan lands and see what mischief we can cause there.'

"I hopped and stepped off the sealed road and hid under the tall pines. There I thought about a plan to make my way back into my old clan territory and kill Kratt. Although, before I could act, Kardelia flew low over the road and called out to me. I squawked and called for Kardelia to land.

'Kratt wants you dead, he is sending a group of his warriors to find and kill you, he was furious with the two lieutenants who walked you out. He said they should have known to kill you and not let you go. You must leave and hide, and don't come back. I can't stay, he'll miss me. My love, go now, hide, and stay safe.'

"Her heart was broken, and her spirit dimmed, but she didn't want me to risk my life further and she begged me to stay alive and stay away. 'Go to the Cor clan,' she advised through her tears. Then she flew off quickly back to the old Kar nest tree before she was missed.

"With no time to waste I hopped and flapped as best I could and as quickly as I could, along the line of the tall pines heading south. I was soon exhausted and looked for a place to hide. A small mob of kangaroo rested in the shade of a tree, and I asked if they knew a place I could hide. 'There is a rabbit hole over there,' one of the big male kangaroos explained, pointing laconically to a warren near the edge of the norzela park's long grass. 'It's empty now, the foxy cleared them out a few weeks ago. He comes back every few nights in case others are still hiding here, or more have moved in. But they are all dead now. Nasty business.'

"The kangaroo chewed a mouth full of grass as he spoke and looked to be half asleep with his eye lids only just open. 'Nasty creatures these foxy. They don't belong here you know, the norzela brought them. My ancestors never had to deal with such evil.'

"Mytre have a long standing, deep respect for kangaroo, having lived alongside each other since the beginning of Elppa and Egnaro's reign. 'Thank you, your majesty,' I replied. I had lost a lot of blood by now, but I managed to find the warren and got into the opening. I thought of going deeper, but it felt fowl and rank, the smell of death still hung about the tunnels. I almost left but felt something sinister coming, so I crawled into the opening of the warren and fell asleep exhausted.

"I don't know how much time passed. But I awoke to the sound of cries and squawks nearby. Lord Kratt's hunters were after me. My instinct was to fly, and I was half out of the hole before I recalled my wings were useless. I could hear their voices close by, calling out for me to show myself.

"I had no choice but to slither back into the tunnel as far as my courage would allow. As you know, a hole is nct a natural place for a mytre. All our life we are in the open, under Elppa's hot rays and even when Egnaro shines, we are in the open under the stars or cloud. A hole is never a place of security or comfort for a mytre. But unable to fly, I had no choice, and I suppressed my urge to fly.

"After a few moments one of Kratt's lieutenants appeared in the light at the end of the tunnel." 'There is some blood here, and a black feather.' 'Oh yes, 'e was definitely 'ere,' said another of Kratt's hunters. 'The foxy took him,' one of the kangaroos said. It was the big grey that had instructed Karbett to hide. The kangaroo sat back on its tail with its head high and hopping legs spread wide. It scratched its belly with a long fore-paw claw and chewed grass it had pulled from a tussock from the ground before it.

"The two hunter birds looked deep into the hole. 'What did you say?' one of the Kratt acolytes asked. 'The foxy took the bird you're looking for, just as he did all the rabbits who lived here. Very sad,' the kangaroo concluded.

"He reached down and pulled up another clump of soft, moist, green grass to chew. 'A what? A foxy, what's this dopey sac of bones on about,' said one of the Krat clan birds rudely. 'He means a 'fox' has killed the rabbits and I think he is saying that Karbett was also killed.'

"The second of Kratt's servants turned to the big grey kangaroo and said in a loud voice, 'Dead, you say,' still unsure what to believe. 'Dead as the heart of a norzela vehicle that the... norzela ride in. Horrible heartless things.' 'Does he mean the norzela or the vehicle?' the first Krat hunter clarified with his offsider.

"The big kangaroo lifted the bulk of its body onto its hind legs and tail and shuffled forward across the lawned area towards the two mytre at the opening to the warren. 'I saw it all, dreadful thing to see.' The two mytre looked at each other confused. Then they looked at the big kangaroo and shrugged. 'Jcb done then, I guess,' said the first Krat hunter, dismissively, looking pleased. The second looked into the rabbit hole a moment longer, listening intently for sounds of movement in the underground shadows. 'Come on… he's a fox's meal now,' said the first Krat hunter, 'let's go home.' 'Okay, it's getting close to ksud anyway, we'd better get back,' the second bird agreed, a little reluctantly.

"I watched them strut about at the opening to the warren a moment longer, then they flew off, north, back towards the nest tree. I couldn't stay a moment longer in the hole, it stank of blood and death, and I was sure there were other creatures in the recesses of the warren, altogether as deadly as the Kratt hunters. Still, I waited until Egnaro was high, and darkness loomed in the shadows of Egnaro.

"When I came out, the big grey kangaroo was gone, as were the others in his mob. They had saved my life. But my journey to find you had only just begun. That night, I decided on a plan to find you and the Cor clan. I would walk or hop, for I had no other choice, south across the creek and travel through the great gum forest. Then I would turn north and find you in the Cor clan territory. Had I known then, as I made the plan, what was in store on the journey I had set myself, I would rather that a fox had indeed found me in the hole.

"I limped out of the dark hole and began my trek south. I walked all night along the boundary of the norzela park and the creek, with the great eucalyptus forest standing ever more imposing on the far bank of the creek. I came to a fallen tree trunk spanning the creek and decided to cross. The forest was dark even when Elppa was at his highest.

"Dappled light only just reached the forest floor and the branches and leaves seemed to close in about me as I hopped and stepped carefully through the undergrowth. There was no wind on the forest floor, and rank smells and strange creatures stalked my imagination as I walked on.

"Ferns and shrubs grew thick all about and I was soon lost. The creek was some way behind me but without Elppa's light to guide me I became confused. East, west, north, south, every direction became the same as the other. I had travelled two or three days when I found two dead mytre. They were lying mutilated on a narrow track that ran across my path. I was shocked to realise I knew them. These had been members of the Dart clan. They must have been the two who chose to leave their clan lands and fly off to find a new life and a new nest tree. Clearly, Kratt's hunters had pursued and caught them and made them pay for their desertion.

"They had been dead only a few passages of Egnaro and the way they had died was evident on their feathers and bodies. I dragged their carcasses into the undergrowth and sang a short lament in their honour. I realised then that I was still very close to the valley clan territories and decided to travel further south to escape the Krat clan's reach. The path the two dead mytre were on ran north-south and I chose to walk and hop south along it. Away from the valley.

"The eucalypt forest is immense, and for a long time I saw Elppa and Egnaro only briefly as they reached their zenith above me as I moved down the path. On the fifth day the forest thinned and opened into a large swamp. The air was thick with the sound of flying insects and great winged bugs. Moisture lay across the path and soon I was walking through small puddles and mossy patches of mud. The canopy of thin branches allowed greater light through, and I saw Elppa's bright rays light my path. I was so taken with wonder at the multitude of life and light about me that I didn't see the snake rise before me until it was too late.

"There was no trap, I was simply too tired and too awe struck by my surroundings to see the creature in time. As I stepped onward, it slithered right across my path and rose ready to strike. Suddenly, it was gone. Snatched and taken before my eyes, an instant, a second before it was about to kill me. At first, I thought Elppa himself had sent a flash of his light to kill the terror, but as I crouched in fear, I could hear the woosh of wings near me. I knew then that the snake had been lifted into the sky. The kookaburra had taken the terror in its beak and lifted it off into the blue and out of my path.

"It all happened in a flash. I was too fearful to move, and I sat crouched where I was for a long time before I began to look about again. As I began to look around, I could see the kookaburra high on a tree limb, slapping the snake's body on the tree branch, stunning and killing it before he was ready to eat. 'Thank you,' I called with relief. 'You should watch where you walk next time, mate,' the kookaburra called with a cackle. Then he called back, 'Are you lost, mate? You're a long way from the valley.'

"'Actually, I am lost,' I said, 'can you help me?' I walked over to the kookaburra and was under his tree by the time he had finished his lunch. I introduced myself and then asked how he knew about the valley? He said he had lived there once and that he knew a mytre there called Corzell. He said you and he were mates.

"I told him I was on a journey to find you. I told him about the invasion by Kratt and his clan and that you were in danger. That the whole valley was in danger. He explained that was why he'd left. He said he'd seen the bodies of the two Dart clan mytre and sensed that some evil thing, some keere was coming. I stayed with him for a few days resting and growing stronger again. Then I set off to find my way back to the Cor lands and sky.

"The kookaburra gave me directions and I started to move northwest through the middle of the eucalypt forest and back toward the valley. After I left the kookaburra, I walked for almost half an Egnaro cycle. Again, the forest closed in, and low shrubs and bush, some of it almost impassable, hampered my journey, but I struggled on each day finding new obstacles to overcome.

"I was soon lost again. I thought of trying to get back to the kookaburra, but I became even more lost. As I couldn't fly, I had no way of getting my bearings and I staggered on, completely confused about which direction to take. Then I met the strangest bird. I'd never seen anything like it in my life. I could hear something scratching in the bush ahead of me and I hid for a long time before I had the courage to approach and investigate. As I did, I walked quietly, closer. Soon I could hear a loud nasal *gok* noise, and the bird was continually scratching in the bush.

"Then I could hear the bird start to grunt and cluck with what sounded like satisfaction. I thought it might be safe to approach and eventually I stepped into the dappled light on the forest floor and introduced myself. 'Excuse me,' I said. The bird I saw before me was huge, with a red head, a yellow throat, a round, black body and massive claws. I wasn't sure that I had made the right decision, and was regretting my boldness, when the strange bird looked at me, stopped scratching in the forest, turned and fled, darting away into the undergrowth.

A few moments later it returned, but it kept its distance and a thick tree trunk between us. 'What do you want?' it asked, shyly.

"'I am Karbett,' I said, 'I'm lost. Can you help me?' 'Lost? How can you be lost in a forest,' the bird said in a low voice sounding confused. 'I… I don't know,' I said, 'but I am… can you help me?' 'I was building a nest,' the strange bird said, in a low deep voice. 'I'm busy.' 'I'm sorry to disturb you,' I said, and I was about to leave the bird to its building, when it said, 'Maybe I can help you, if you can help me?'

"'I'd be happy to help,' I said, 'if you can tell me who and what you are.' 'I'm an Australian Brush Turkey, my name is Terry. I'm building a nest mound for my partner. But she said it's not big enough,' Terry said, sounding deflated. 'Size, she said, is everything, and no matter what I do I just can't seem to get my mound to rise.'

"'A nest mound?" Karbett repeated confused. Terry gestured to a small conical pile of leaves and soil to his right. 'Here I have started, and I thought I was making headway, but I think she'll still say it's too small.'

"I looked at the low mound of leaf litter. *It doesn't look very impressive*, I thought, *but what do I know.* Terry sighed. 'I build the nest and my partner will come and lay eggs in the top of the mound, where the eggs will be kept warm and safe. My job is to add leaves or take leaves away to keep the eggs at the perfect temperature. But she said the mound is too small and will not heat the eggs enough.' Terry sounded depressed and almost resigned to failure.

"'I think I can help you, Terry,' Karbett said, cheerfully as he looked about, adding, 'if you can lead me out of this forest.' 'Agreed,' Terry said immediately, before adding, 'how can you help?'

"I showed Terry that he could get a better structure for the base of his mound if he built it wider at the bottom, and in the space between a number of tree trunks. This way the tree trunks would help hold the base together and support a taller conical dome, making the nest larger. Terry had tried to build his nest in a small clearing, but he agreed that moving to a location surrounded by tree trunks might give him a greater chance of building the nest upwards and having the trunks support it. 'I can help scrape leaves for you,' I offered.

"We set to work immediately, and in a short time, thanks to Terry's massive claws, we moved the smaller nest to a space between the trees and it grew quickly. Terry found and scraped the leaf-litter, and I helped scrape or place the leaves and twigs higher up the mound, adding greatly to its height. We'd soon completed a gigantic nest, that even impressed Terry. 'This is terrific,' Terry said as we both sat back to admire our construction. *I've never seen such a massive structure. She's sure to be satisfied when she sees this,* Terry thought. With that he climbed to the top and let out a booming call. '*Gok, gok,*' he called at the top of his lungs. 'She's gunna' love this,' he said, confidently.

"I hop-flapped over to a low branch and waited to see what his partner might think of his nest mound. I can tell you she really was impressed. She clucked and crowed, saying that his was the biggest nest she'd ever seen and that he should be the proudest bird in the forest.

"The nest mound we'd created really was something, but I was getting impatient to be away. I waited two days, watching Terry and Sherry, his partner, tidy the area around the nest and I watched as she dug a deep hole in the top of the conical mound, before laying eggs and then covering them with leaf-litter. Then she laid even more eggs, before again covering them up. This went on for a few hours, before she left.

"Terry said, 'My job is to make sure the eggs stay at the right temperature,' but he sounded sorrowful. When I asked why, he said that she wouldn't be coming back to help raise them. He sounded sad, and lonely. But added, 'It's our way, but I still wish she would spend time here, with me and the young, before they hatch.'

"While he waited and monitored the nest temperature, Terry said he had time to show me the way north-west. He said it wasn't far. We travelled for only one passage of Elppa, then he left me on the edge of a more open part of the forest. He thanked me for helping him and we parted. He really was a strange bird, but he was a very proud father-to-be.

"I walked on for a few more Elppa. On the third Elppa after leaving Terry, I was surprised to meet a small clan of mytre. They found me before I saw them, and they were about to attack me before they recognised me from the valley. I could hardly explain my relief when I saw it was the Wayt clan. Waytbill, his partner, Waytjullia and four others of their clan were hiding in a more open glade of the forest, where they'd established a new nest site of sorts.

"They were still afraid of the Krat clan and the likely retribution for their leaving. They hid each day, only coming out at night to hunt and forage and never straying far from their new nest site. They told me how Kratthood, the emissary, had died and how they had fled immediately to hide in the eucalypt forest. Fear lived with them, as they waited for Kratt to find their new home and destroy them.

"They said they had only seen one of the Krat clan, flying high above the forest, a few Elppa's after they had gone, and had seen nothing since. Still, they were careful to watch throughout the day and hide, only coming out at night, always ready to attack at a moment's notice. They also helped me find the right direction, and after I stayed with them for three passages of Elppa, I again went on my way, still moving northwest through the forest."

"I crossed the tracks of a fox, wombat, and lizard, but never met them, and once had to fight a young raven who mistook me for a magpie-lark. I was lucky as he was an inexperienced fighter, and I got the better of him when he landed to attack. I had been walking and hopping along, with my damaged wings out for balance, for miles from nwad to ksud. Each night I slept in the spaces between the roots of a tree or between rocks or under bushes draped with a curtain of foliage and flowers to hide my scent.

"As I walked, my fear grew less, my strength grew more, and my determination rose. My wings are still unable to carry my weight, but I can hop-fly into the low branches of a small tree and these last few nights I have slept off the ground and out of reach of most keere.

"Hope carried me on. Hope that I would find you and hope that together we can defeat the Krat clan and return the valley to peace. But the forest seemed unending, and I started to lose hope. I wandered on, feeling lost again, feeling tired and feeling foolish, forever trying to get through to you. I wondered if I would ever find you or even reach the end of the great forest. But yesterday I stumbled out of the forest near the old derelict norzela nest on the Yat clan land.

"Fear gripped me again. I didn't know if the Yat clan were still alive. If they had left or been turned into servants of the Krat. Again, I had to travel with great care, hiding and moving only when it was safe, while Egnaro was hidden behind the clouds. I knew that Kratt had sent out spies and I also wanted to avoid them if possible. Even once I had crossed the sealed road and was on Cor land, I wasn't sure what had happened to you, or if you too had stayed faithful to your promise of hope."

Corzell said softly, "You are safe here. We are preparing to be rid of Lord Kratt and his clan of vile keere who poison the very word mytre. They have brought our valley nothing but misery and soon I hope it will end."

Karbett let out a sigh of relief and Corzell could see the tension in Karbett's body lessen as he finished the story. But he looked truly spent with the effort of retelling his adventures, of the journey itself, and of the dangers he'd faced.

"Rest now, friend," Corzell said in a whisper. "We can talk more tomorrow."

-0-

The next day, Karbett was feeling more rested. Corhelia had been sent to him with food; grasshoppers, and beetles, and one large juicy white grub, that she had contemplated eating herself. But when she saw him, she felt only pity and sadness and gladly offered him the food. She told him that Corzell was out searching for food with Corselia and their two offspring Cordelia and Corxell, but he would be back to see him later that day.

Corzell came back after nwod and settled in next to Karbett under the bottle brush shrub where the feather depleted Karbett had remained hidden.

"I have a plan. It was set before your return and now, because of the information you provided, I have sent messengers to find the kookaburra, Bill, and the Wayt clan in the eucalypt forest. Their numbers, if they come, will help swing a battle in our favour, if it comes to a fight. Corzell explained that his plan was to wait until Lord Kratt called an elpitlum and then strike as he had done, with an ambush.

"He will only have some of his clan with him and we can undertake an ambush and force him to leave the valley."

"Or die," added Karbett.

"Or die," agreed Corzell. "My strategy is to get there first with the most birds and overwhelm his elpitlum group. His lieutenants Kratatora and Krattac, will most likely come with him to the elpitlum, and we can easily overpower these few. It is very unlikely that many others from his clan will come. If they do, we will force them out too. Once we defeat this Kratt and his two lieutenants, we can force the rest of the Krat clan out as they will be leaderless and lost." Corzell spoke with determination as he explained his plan.

"But when will there be an elpitlum?" Karbett asked, concerned about having to wait in hiding for too long, extending his risk and making their plan easier to discover.

Corzell said quietly, "There is one tomorrow night after the ksud chorus. My plan is to gather everyone in an ambush and use our superior numbers to take them by surprise."

"If Bill, the kookaburra, and the Wayt clan can join us, all the better, if not we will still have Cor and Yat clan to overcome the leader of the Krat clan. You can wait in hiding here until we have been successful." Corzell sounded confident, but he thought, *All we have to do is keep our nerve and hope Kratt's spies don't find out about our plan.*

"Tomorrow after the ksud chorus," Karbett confirmed with a nod. *Hope*, he thought, *'was what had kept him walking and hopping through the forest.* Hope now had a plan and he felt reassured that his efforts were not wasted.

-0-

Suca stayed still and unflinching as she held onto the branch low on the Cor nest tree. It was only when she watched Corzell fly back up to the nest, higher in the tree, and after she heard the soft sleepful breathing of Karbett as he drifted into a warm afternoon sleep, deeper than he had had in a full cycle of Egnaro, that she dropped unseen and unheard off the branch and flew swiftly and silently back to her Lord, Lord Kratt.

13

The Battle Under the Bush

And when He come descending from Heaven
On a cloud like He said in His word
I'll be joyfully carried to meet Him
On the wings of the great speckled bird

Jonny Cash – 'Great Speckled Bird' (1959)

CORZELL WAS ANXIOUS all day, although he tried hard to hide his misgivings from Cordelia and Corxell. He flew with them, play-fighting, twisting, and diving, looping, and turning in mock pursuits above the Cor clan territory. Corxell had grown strong and even though he was still a young fledgling with grey downy feathers on his breast, Corzell could see he would grow into a proud and powerful mytre. Cordelia was still small, but she had learnt to fly with great skill and her small size meant she seemed even more manoeuvrable in flight than he was.

Corzell thought at first that the loss of his eye hindered his flight, but he soon realized that his daughter was simply a gifted flyer. It stunned him that she had mastered the art of close aerial combat, to the point where she was frequently able to dive low and swoop back in an arc to appear above her adversary, usually her older brother, who hated being so often caught in her aerial traps.

Corselia knew Corzell was on edge. His messenger, the willie-wagtail, had not returned and he had no idea if the kookaburra or the Wayt clan would be coming to support their revolt. It had been an addition to his plan and although they were not vital, something told him that they might be needed before the day was done.

Before the after-nwod grew long, he flew over to the sealed road to look out for Yatnolia or Yatdoll. He wanted to make sure all was ready before the elpitlum, but they were nowhere to be seen. His anxiety grew a little, but it wasn't uncommon for his neighbours to be away at the far end of their territory. He was disappointed but not concerned. Instead, he flew around to the nest trees in the Cor territory, visiting his clan brothers and sisters. He found all was well, and each mated pair were ready to join him and Corselia at the elpitlum.

The ksud chorus was as beautiful as any Corzell could recall. It lifted his spirits, and he grew confident that his plans were sound and that before Egnaro climbed into the sky, his worry about Kratt's invasion would be past him.

"Your mother and I will be back after the elpitlum," he reassured the two younglings. "Stay here with Corhelia. She will take care of you until we're back."

"But father, why can't we come?" Corxell asked petulantly.

"Next time... maybe," his father said. "Now look after the two girls, you are the man of the nest until I come back," Corzell joked.

The three young mytre knew the gravity of the events about to unfold, but could only conceptualize it as a game, as a mock chase in the sky, or a lesson about the hunt. None of them really knew the seriousness of the elpitlum about to unfold.

Corselia was about to take off and fly to the next nest tree to collect her clan members there, when Corzell said, "I'll meet you at the elpitlum." Adding, "Be brave, we will be rid of the invaders before the next glow of Elppa I am sure." They hugged, briefly placing their wings around each other in a show of support and love.

"Fly true," Corselia said.

"And you, my love," Corzell said, resolutely.

As she took to flight, Corzell found himself caught in a net of doubt. *I wish I knew why the messengers had not returned,* he thought. He dropped from the nest tree and approached Karbett's hiding place. As he lifted the curtain of the bottle brush, he said, "We are about to go to the elpitlum now…" Adding, "wish us luck…"

As he finished speaking, he saw before him, sitting next to a subdued Karbett… Lord Kratt.

"Lord Corzell, is it?" Kratt said mockingly. "I hear you had plans for some sort of revolt, to overthrow my rule."

Corzell couldn't speak. He simply didn't know what to say.

"Cat got your tongue?" Lord Kratt asked.

"No… how?" Corzell stammered in disbelief.

"My spies have eyes and ears, and it seems yours are blind and dumb. I will explain all at the elpitlum I have arranged. We can all go there now. Well, you and I and my two lieutenants will go there. I am afraid this pathetic, foolish, featherless bird will be staying here. With my two faithful servants, Suca and Traps. They'll make sure he gets the end he deserves." With that, Lord Kratt nodded to the two tawny frogmouth and stepped out from under the bottle brush bush, leading Corzell with Krattac and Kratatora close at his side.

Corzell's single eye throbbed, his chest heaved, and he felt flat, defeated, his plans were in ruins and his hope was squashed under the bottle brush.

Karbett watched them leave, for him, hope had also died, crushed by Kratt's spies. Outside the bush, Corzell thought of flight, of simply taking to the wing and leaving, but his partner and children still lived, and he wanted to do all he could to make sure they at least were safe. For he kept no hope for himself, or Karbett. The three birds escorting Corzell and himself, rose swiftly into the darkening early Egnaro sky and flew to join the throng gathered at the elpitlum site.

-0-

Lord Kratt flew down into the centre of the lawned area of the elpitlum, accompanied by his two lieutenants and Corzell. As they landed, a host of other birds stepped back to the edge of the lawn or flew to perch on nearby branches with a good view of the gathering about to take place. Already, a great many mytre perched on branches or sat along the fallen tree trunk, and every bird flapped or fluttered excitedly or anxiously as the captive Corzell was escorted in.

Corselia, who had arrived ahead of them stood silently and sadly, as she watched them land. She already knew the revolt was over, what she was worried about was what their revolt would now cost them, now it had been killed before it had begun. Other members of the Cor clan gathered at the edges of the lawn, and Yatnolia and Yatdoll from the Yat clan were standing next to Corselia. All the traitorous clan leaders gathered on the ground, while a host of Krat clan, Dart clan and ex-Kar mytre looked down from their perches on the hapless Cor and Yat clan mytre.

-0-

"You should have stayed away," Suca said, teasing the wing and tail featherless Karbett.

"You'll die now, foolish bird," Traps said, with a cruel lisp.

When Kratt and his acolytes had turned up a short while before Corzell had come to speak with him, Karbett had been completely caught off guard. Before he could raise himself to confront his nemesis, they had subdued him and made him keep silent. With Lord Kratt, his two spies and his two lieutenants, Karbett knew he had no chance if he fought.

"Well, you came back," Kratt had said, "you were warned not to return to the valley. Some birds have no sense. Some birds can't see when they're beaten and when they should give up and die." He then instructed the tawny frogmouth to hold him still and silent so he could surprise Corzell, who he was sure would come to say farewell before the elpitlum.

"You won't win," Karbett had managed to whisper before Suca struck him to remind him to be silent. It was only moments later that Corzell had come to the bottle brush hide away and he too was captured.

Now the two tawny frogmouths were about to kill him, one of whom he knew must have overheard their plan and reported it to Kratt.

Both tawny frogmouths had dealt with 'lesser' birds before and their opinion of the tattered, feather and tailless mytre gave them no clue about his tenacity. Suca had heard his story about crossing the eucalypt forest and fighting with a young raven, but she failed to hear the desperation in his voice as he had struggled to survive.

As Karbett waited for the struggle for his life to start he knew they would not find him an easy victim.

"Let me kill him," Traps said again with a pronounced lisp.

"Be my guest," Suca offered, stepping wide to allow Traps to set upon the mytre.

We are all on the ground, Karbett thought, *The ground has become my home now and I'm master of wingless fighting. Let them try and kill me.*

Each bird struggled for dominance as they pecked and clawed the other viciously. Traps was soon exhausted and in spite of her hooked beak and sharp claws, the flightless mytre appeared to have the upper wing. Karbett had clearly done well parrying her blows and beak, replying with scratches of his own sharp hooked claw, and striking a few well aimed pecks at the tawny frogmouth's head.

Soon each bird was worn out and bleeding from various head and body wounds.

"He's a tough old bird," Traps said, with a lisp. As he panted from the effort to beat the mytre down.

"Let me finish him off," Suca offered gleefully. "You catch your breath."

With that, Traps slumped to the ground and huffed heavily as Suca stepped forward. Fresh from simply watching the fight, Suca landed a number of powerful head blows and Karbett began to tire as his energy fell. But he also landed a few of his own scratches with his claws, sharpened as they were from his long journey. Soon even Suca began to slow and became less willing to close with the mytre, striking only if Karbett overextended his reach and exposed his head and neck.

"You might have to help, mate," Suca said, panting with her excursions. *This is taking far longer than I had anticipated*, the tired tawny frogmouth thought.

Suddenly, Suca's legs were pulled from under her, and she disappeared under the hanging curtain of the bottle brush bush and away from the hide away. Stunned, Traps looked about before she too was savagely dragged under the foliage and into the night beyond the bush.

Karbett was unsure what was happening. One moment he was about to face the prospect of fighting on, although exhausted, with two tawny frogmouths about to resume their battle. Now they had gone, snatched away from under the bush. He could hear them crying and pleading beyond the hem of the bush but had no idea what had occurred.

Quickly, although with some difficulty due to his wounds, Karbett stepped out from under his hiding place in the bush. There he saw Cordelia, Corhelia, and Corxell pecking and scratching at the two tawny frogmouths. Each, having already suffered grievously from their initial battle with Karbett, the young energetic mytre now pummelled them.

"Leave them," Karbett shouted, seeing the tawny frogmouth were all but done in. "Leave them to me."

"We came when we heard the fighting," Corxell said, pleased with himself.

"Thank you," Karbett said, "but you must go back to your nest. You can't be seen or implicated in this battle. Leave these two keere to me."

"But..." Cordelia began to protest.

"Go now," Karbett insisted.

"No..." Cordelia cried, "we have to find father."

Karbett had no time to argue. "Wait here he demanded," before dragging first Suca and then Traps back under the hem of leaves and branches of the bottle brush shrub. Hidden again, the three young mytre didn't witness Karbett kill each tawny frogmouth and leave their bodies out of sight. When he returned from under the bush, Karbett said defiantly, "I am going to help your father."

Instantly all three mytre, Corhelia, Cordelia, and Corxell, said eagerly, "We'll come too."

"No, stay away, it's too dangerous," Karbett insisted.

"He's our father," Cordelia cried, "we have to come."

Karbett hesitated. There really was no time to argue, he knew time was against them.

"Okay," he said finally. "You can come, but we are going on foot. They'll be looking out for an air attack. They'll be looking up and we need the element of surprise if we're going to have any impact on them."

Cordelia and Corxell set off at once hopping across the ground past their nest tree and toward the orchard and the creek, where they crossed to the elpitlum place.

Corhelia was slower and unused to walking or hopping at such pace, she soon fell behind. But Karbett tired and bloody from his battle under the bush with the tawny frogmouth, led them all the way, striding and hopping along, flapping as he went with the remnants of his wings, and with his strong, powerful legs, at a fantastic pace.

-0-

Lord Kratt waited for the collection of mytre clans to settle to a hush. "We are gathered here to discuss treason." He emphasized the word raising his voice as he said it. "Treason," he repeated as if the very word were some sort of curse on Corzell. The birds on the branches cried and squawked for an instant disapprovingly. Some at the suggestion of treason and others, in the Krat clan, at the likely consequences of it.

"This bird," Lord Kratt said in a deep, commanding voice, "plotted to overthrow my reign. He plotted to have me killed and to take the Krat territories, the Krat sky and the Krat land, all for his own profit, for his own clan." He paused for effect as the assembled birds crowed and cried disapprovingly. Then he went on, "While these charges are despicable, he was also planning to use outsiders to help him and had made an alliance with the Yat clan for support." Lord Kratt allowed what he had said to resonate about the confined space of the elpitlum, as birds on branches hissed and scratched their beaks on the branches of their perch in derision.

The Lord went on, "My spies intercepted a message this mytre sent. This dull beak." As he spoke, he lent forward and while leering, he pointed a wing at Corzell. "To invite the fighting support of a kookaburra, no less, and a clan who had left the valley in disgrace..." He paused again, while the Krat clan birds knocked their beaks on their branches in disgust. "The Wayt clan." There was an outcry of clicks and whistles, and more beaks knocked on wood in protest at the shame of Corzell's actions.

"He has no ears to hear worms," one of the Krat birds shouted in insult.

Corselia glanced carefully at the birds spread about her. She could see that many of the former Kar birds didn't have their heart in the protests, and only made half-hearted responses. She could also see that mixed throughout the gathered mytre were hard core Krat clan members who gave a rousing response whenever Lord Kratt spoke.

All through the speech, Corzell tried to look skyward, in case Bill might arrive, or in case the Wayt clan would somehow still come to save the day.

Then Lord Kratt said, "Here is my proof." As he spoke, he pushed a tiny, quivering willie-wagtail out from the edge of the grassed area and into the centre of the lawn. Even Corzell gasped.

The smaller bird didn't wait to be asked to speak, he simply began to blurt out, "He made me go, he asked me to find the kookaburra called Bill, and the Wayt clan and invite them to this war, but I didn't find them, I was caught before I coul…"

"That's enough," Kratt said interrupting the bird and brushing it aside with a wing.

They didn't get my message, Corzell thought, disappointed, but also relieved that they had not discovered his friends' locations.

"Can there be any doubt about his treasonous acts?" Lord Kratt demanded of the crowd.

"No… kill him now," most of the mob of angry birds replied as one.

"More than this, he conspired with an exile of the Kar clan to unite the Yat and Cor clans in an attempt not just on my life, but also to unite the valley under his rule." Lord Kratt could feel the crowd behind him.

Lies, thought, Corzell, *'but the mob has no ears.'*

"Kill the traitor, kill the usurper," many Krat clan started to chant. Lord Kratt allowed the mob to have its head and he lifted his wings to encourage the chant.

"Kill the traitor, kill the traitor," they demanded.

Corselia felt helpless, they would surely kill her partner and she could do nothing. Their carefully laid plans were in tatters at the feet of Lord Kratt.

"Wait…" Kratt shouted teasingly, "what about mercy, compassion, forgiveness?"

In the branches all about the elpitlum, the chant grew, "No… kill the traitor, kill the traitor."

Corzell began to lose the little hope that remained. Hope that he might be saved or rescued or even, let go.

Above them on the trees that grew high over the elpitlum place, a few watchful Krat clan mytre had sat as lookouts in case there were other surprises that even Lord Kratt hadn't heard of or anticipated. The lookout mytre also began to join the chant and soon, even former Kar clan birds, overcome with the mob mentality, were cheering as loudly as the Krat clan mytre for Corzell's life.

The elpitlum was a cacophony of sound, with long low crows, short, chorused chortles, and deep base cries for Corzell's murder. Afraid, the willie-wagtail suddenly took flight rising above the throng and climbing with a piercing, sharp, high cry into the night.

"Let him go," Lord Kratt shouted, "he's of no consequence."

As the willie-wagtail flew into the air, the assembled birds, apart from those on trial, Corzell, Corselia, Yatnolia, and Yatdoll, who's heads were bowed low, watched him leave, lifting their heads as he travelled aloft.

It was at this moment that Karbett struck.

14

The Attack

Baby, say it isn't true
You were never there
It wasn't you
It's more than I can do
To try and keep it shiny new

The gap just opens up
Between the words we like to use
And the thing that's seen
Seen through your eyes now darling
In blue distances calling
Like the birds of the high arctic.

David Gray – 'Birds of the High Arctic' (2014)

FLAPPING WILDLY, Karbett dived into the elːitlum, with his beak aimed directly at Kratt's neck. Corxell followed, surging low at one of the Krat clan mytres guarding his mother. Cordelia came up behind her brother and flew savagely at one of her father's guards. Corhelia was less sure of herself and flew behind Corxell as he rolled into a tussle with his adversary.

Taken completely by surprise, Kratt was stunned to see a very much alive Karbett dive quickly towards him.

Krattac and Kratatora left their posts next to the prisoners and flew instantly to their Lord's aid. Lord Kratt flew into the air a moment before his attacker closed with him, meaning Karbett's beak only caught Kratt's tailfeathers as he surged past. Pivoting quickly and flapping his damaged wings, he tried to fly after the Lord of the Krat clan. But he couldn't generate any effective lift and he flapped wildly as he fell and tumbled back to the surface of the log.

Krattac and Kratatora almost instantly set upon him and began to peck repeatedly at his head and body.

Karbett fell to the ground and raised his claws pirouetting as he fell. His claws still bloody from his previous fight, caught the Krat mytre, Krattac across the face, taking out one of his enemy's eyes. Krattac fell, injured to the grass. With no time to steady himself, Karbett fell to the lawn too.

Kratt didn't fly away, instead he turned and dived right back into the fight crashing brutally into Karbett's flank, just as he was beginning to regain his footing. With the knock, he fell and found himself pinned under the claws of Kratt, his wings splayed wide across the lawn.

I have you now, Kratt thought as he positioned himself ready to strike.

Corxell was still a young, light bird and with nothing but play fighting experience, he was no match for the tried and tested Krat warrior who guarded his mother. But the impact of his assault had forced the bigger Krat guard back and they both rolled a few times across the lawn.

But it was the Krat guard who was on his feet more quickly. Almost instinctively, he lashed out with his beak at Corxell catching him twice on the shoulder.

Corxell pulled back in pain and then surged again, claws up as he tried to fend off his attacker's blows. Then the blows stopped, and he realised a second bird had come to his aid and distracted his attacker.

Corhelia had seen the attack on her younger brother and dived into the fight without further hesitation. She slashed with her beak and claws, tearing feathers and flesh from the hapless Krat sentry.

But this was Kratjoa, a long-time member of Lord Kratt's personal guard and she'd fought in more fights than Corhelia had had juicy grubs. At first Kratjoa was forced on the defensive, but she soon got the upper wing, forcing Corhelia back and driving her to the ground under her relentless thrusts and slashes with her beak. Corxell was about to rejoin the fight when his mother pulled him back, saying, "Escape now. Fly, there are too many of them."

As she spoke Kratt and Karbett rolled between them, across the lawned elpitlum area, locked in mortal combat. She could see Lord Kratt, the bigger mytre, was slowly getting the upper wing and she knew their chance of success or even survival was low. Time seemed to go slow. She could see Cordelia fighting with a Krat guard to her right, Corhelia struggling with Kratjoa to her front and the two Yat clan leaders being held firmly by their Krat clan sentries. *But where is Corzell?* she wondered.

At the start of the assault, Corzell had pushed one of his guards away, while Cordelia crashed into the second guard. Free, he had taken to the air. Flapping frantically to rise above the melee, he could see Karbett fighting with Krattac and Kratt, he could see Corxell and Corhelia fighting the Krat guard, and he could see Cordelia tumbling and fighting with one of his previous guards. Then he saw Corselia jump into the thick of the fighting to extract Corxell. Corzell could see he needed to help Karbett, who was tiring, and Lord Kratt was getting the upper wing. He was about to dive down and strike Kratt when Cordelia let out a loud desperate cry. Quickly, he changed direction and dived to support his young daughter.

Kratjoa pushed Corhelia back and she took a number of savage blows to her body and head. Her beak had never been used for war and she soon tired as the Krat warrior forced her to use her wings only in defence. Using them like an umbrella, Corhelia deflected and parried each of her attacker's strikes.

Then, as she stumbled and fell onto her back, her wings splayed wide to arrest her backwards fall, as they did, she allowed her protagonist to lunge forward and peck savagely at her head.

It only took one well directed blow, landed in the centre of her forehead above her beak and she died before she had even fallen onto her back.

Corselia saw the strike and watched as her child fell dead. "Fly," she called to Corxell, "fly…" She too took to the wing, and before anyone of the Krat clan could respond, Corselia and Corxell lifted into the air and escaped the battle.

As they departed, Corzell dived back to the lawn and began to strike and tear at the Krat guard fighting with Cordelia. Corzell soon overpowered the guard, taking him from behind, and he took to the sky in an effort to escape Corzell's onslaught.

Corzell quickly embraced his daughter, "Why did you come here?" he asked.

"To save… you father," Cordelia stammered still dazed. Adding, "Karbett killed the two tawny frogmouths, and he wanted to come to help you." As she spoke, they both looked to the centre of the elpitlum lawn. Kratt had managed to flip Karbett onto his back and while Karbett kicked and scratched with his claws, even Cordelia, with no experience of war, could see he was defeated. His strikes had lost their force. His previous fight with the tawny frogmouths had clearly worn him out. Now, after struggling with the large Krat leader, and Krattac, Karbett was spent.

Lord Kratt stood over the exhausted mytre at his feet, claws pressed into his neck and chest. It reminded Corzell of how the Kar clan leader Karmann had died just over a cycle of Egnaro ago. Lord Kratt was breathing heavily too but he felt supreme as he looked down at the defeated Karbett.

"You should have stayed away," he panted bitterly as he pressed his claws more firmly into his victim's neck. Karbett choked and coughed, fighting for air.

"Leave him alone," a mytre cried from the branches above his head. Kardelia had watched on from her perch in the tree branch above as the fight unfolded. At first, she was amazed to see her partner had returned, and then she grew increasingly fearful as the battle with Lord Kratt turned in the Lord's favour. She wanted to join in and fight, to help her partner, but her previous experience under Krat law had dimmed her will to fight. As she watched the fight progress towards its conclusion, she realised she had lost all hope and a light that had burned so brightly dimmed in her soul. Now as her partner was finally back, she could only watch on as Lord Kratt held his life in his clawed foot.

"Let him live," she pleaded. "Let me have him back. Let me be with him again."

"Come here. Come and be with your partner," Lord Kratt said, softly. Kardelia, her face a sea of tears, glided down, and stooped next to her partner's side. Kratt kept his claw on Karbett's neck and the bloody, defeated mytre began to cry as his partner landed next to him.

"I'm so sorry," he murmured as she came close to his face. "I tried, to come back, my dear." His voice was only just audible to Kardelia, and listening to his sobbing lament, broke her heart all over again.

Corzell watching on could see the Lord was only tormenting the Kar clan to reinforce his power over them. He'd killed their leader, taken their territory, banished Karbett and was about to kill and break the two most senior remaining Kar members.

Kratt pressed his foot into Karbett's throat. Karbett began to suffocate. His breathing grew shallow, and he gurgled as air and blood collected in his airways.

Kardelia cried a long piercing cawr as she dropped her head, sure Karbett was now gone. Inconsolable, she lifted her head to take a breath, determined to fight Lord Kratt for killing her partner. She looked up under the rim of her grief and was about to shriek again, and braced herself to fly at Lord Kratt, when Kratt struck Kardelia on the side of the head with his beak. Knocking her unconscious and ending her pitiable life in one blow.

Kratt stood over both their bodies and shouted, "This is my valley now. Now I'll make this valley great. Now you can both fly with Elppa's flock."

Corzell and Cordelia huddled to one side of the elpitlum lawn watching silently as Kratt dealt a fatal blow to the life of the Kar clan. In the drama of Karbett and Kardelia's deaths, none of the Kar clan had pressed on with their fight.

"Come on," whispered Corzell as he helped Cordelia to her feet and then braced to take wing.

Lord Kratt saw them lift off and turning sharply cried, "Kill or capture those birds."

Corzell and Cordelia had a momentary head start and took to the night sky. Several Krat clan mytre stretched their wings and took off after them.

The father and daughter flew together almost wing tip to wing tip as they flew frantically in the direction of the norzela park. *Clan boundaries seemed to matter little now,* Corzell thought, as he raced away. *Where have Corselia and Corxell gone?'* he wondered as he flew rapidly away from his pursuers. "Split up, go back to the nest tree, find your mother," Corzell shouted to Cordelia.

15

Flight of the Star

And when I awoke, I was alone
This bird had flown
So I lit a fire
Isn't it good, Norwegian wood?

The Beatles – 'Norwegian Wood (This Bird has Flown)' – (1965)

CORDELIA TURNED sharply and flew high and speedily away to the west, back down the ribbon of the dark sealed road. Corzell turned south, low toward the eucalyptus forest. *I'll find the kookaburra and Wayt clan,'* he thought, *they might still be able to help.*

Two of the Krat clan guards were tailing Cordelia, while three had gone in search of Corzell. The chasing birds were soon on the tail feathers of both escapees.

Cordelia had great speed and could manoeuvre and turn as well as birds much older than herself, but her followers were much older birds, and they were able to match and follow her closely. She used all dimensions of the air space she could, diving low and flying high, dipping, and twisting, rolling, and pitching, in an effort to avoid the Krat birds behind her.

They soon saw they were not going to catch her in a direct chase, so they divided their efforts. If Cordelia flew left and down, one of her followers, would fly left and down and the other left and up, cutting off options and forcing Cordelia to continually alter her flight path.

As she flew, she scanned the way ahead in case she saw her father or oncoming Krat birds to trap her or cut off her escape. Her energy soon fell, and she began to tire. Her breathing increased too as she contemplated the consequences of her capture. The thought of being held, beaten, or killed drove her on and she found energy to fly harder, at least for a short while longer.

Corzell also struggled to lose his pursuers as they tailed him closely, one behind and one on each wing. He soon recognised he had nowhere to go. He couldn't fly into the forest looking for the Wayt clan or kookaburra without leading the chasing birds to his friends. Running out of options, Corzell decided to head back to his nest tree in the hope that the following birds would not come into the Cor territory. Turning, he flew high and dropped back in a loop that took him back in the direction of the Cor clan lands.

One of the Krat chasers came at him from below as he looped back, and Corzell was able to strike out at the unfortunate bird. Corzell's claws struck the chasing mytre on the wing and forced it into a spiralling dive. The injured bird looked to be out of the hunt, and Corzell thought, *One down.*

Cordelia picked up her pace, twisting and turning as she flew into the orchard on the Cor clan territory, but she only managed to attract more Krat clan guards as she flew close to the elpitlum site. Soon these too joined the chase. Now five Krat birds were swooping and turning trying to bring her down. However, their number impeded their manoeuvrability and two of the chasing birds clipped each other, with one tumbling down on to the ground while the other careered off and fell into the low branches of a tree, before tumbling, wing over wing, into the shrubs near the creek.

Suddenly, Corzell appeared at her side, adding his two Krat pursuers to the host of birds chasing the two Cor fugitives. Cordelia could now feel herself starting to tire.

Clearly the Cor territory is no longer going to be the sanctuary I imagined it would be, Corzell thought. "Follow me," Corzell shouted to his daughter as he turned left, back towards the sealed road.

They both rose above the trees as she followed close to his side, and they continued to avoid the hunters. The following birds struggled to make the turn speedily and Cordelia and Corzell managed to open a small gap between them and their pursuers. *The dark night might be our friend*, Corzell thought, racing toward the sealed road.

"Here," he cried for Cordelia to follow him, diving for the dark space under the bridge that crossed the creek at the sealed road. Cordelia followed and they were soon together in the dark, under the road bridge. Although it was close to the elpitlum, it offered a sanctuary at least for a moment. The Kar clan pursuers flew over the road and up towards the norzela park.

"We can't… stay here… long," Corzell said, as he struggled for breath. "They'll… be… back." Then he added quickly, "Go… back to the nest tree… your mother will be waiting there… I'll lead them north… away to the escarpment and I'll come back when it's safe… Wait until I draw them off, then you go." He hugged his daughter again, tightly, and smiled, somehow, he knew she'd be safe.

They both looked along the road to see where the Krat clan chasers were, then seeing nothing to the east, Corzell took to the air. As he did, he swung low across the road and for a moment he became a bright light, like the brilliant blazing white star Cordelia had seen in her vision. Cordelia couldn't believe how bright her father had become, like the light of Elppa come to earth, *Though brighter and more radiant,*' she thought.

Then he and the light were gone. The sound of the collision was not loud, a thump, a thud. She hardly heard it, as the light consumed all her senses. A car struck Corzell, and his limp body was tossed back to the side of the road where he rolled, as if in a bundle tied with string, to be caught in the long grass. Cordelia saw it all. His initial flight toward the road, the blinding bright white lights from the car, her father's body plunging to the roadside. She also felt the wind race by in the wake of the car, then she felt the anguish of loss that swept over her with the realisation of her father's collision.

Cordelia reacted quickly and flew to her father's side. She knelt beside him with his head in her wing, hope filling her mind. He was still breathing.

"Go," he said in a shallow whisper.

"No," she cried, as grief overpowered her emotions. She jettisoned all thoughts of escape. *"This can't be…unhappy that I am, I cannot leave, my heart is in my mouth, I love you, father." She sang clearly and loudly, a precise and haunting lament. Cordelia sang between sobs and deep chest heaving breaths.

Corzell lifted his head ever so slightly and opened his remaining eye and said softly with the last of his strength and a fairy-flies meek breath, "Go." He coughed slightly and repeated, "Go… fly my love."

She had to lean in to hear him. As she leant back, she could see his eye closed and his head roll to one side as he died, cupped in Cordelia's wing. Cordelia was suddenly aware that other birds were landing near her. The Krat hunting pack had found her.

Her world became black again. The wind from the car had gone, the lights that had consumed her father were gone with it. With his passing, stillness and silence surrounded her, broken only by the arrival of Krat hunters at her side. She was still holding his head in her wing when the first Krat bird tried to pull her away.

"Enough," she cried, fighting back.

*(*Paraphrased from Willian Shakespear's King Lear, 1.1 90-92*).

16

The Reckoning

I'm like a bird, I only fly away
I don't know where my soul is (soul is)
I don't know where my home is
And baby, all I need for you to know is
I'm like a bird, I'll always fly away.

Nelly Furtado - 'I'm Like a Bird' (2000)

CORSELIA AND CORXELL waited in the nest tree for the others to return.

"'I saw that bird kill Corhelia," Corxell said sorrowfully, still panting and breathing heavily with the effort and emotion of their escape.

"We can't stay here," Corselia said softly. "They'll soon come for us all. We have to go!" she sounded insistent, even desperate.

"We have to wait for father, and Cordelia," Corxell said, earnestly.

"We can't, we have to fly now." Corselia knew her partner would fight on if he could and if not, he'd flee. Most likely toward the Wayt clan territories in the forest.

"We'll go into the forest," she said, "but we have to go now." She was surprised none of the Krat clan had come to find them already, but she hadn't realised that they were nearly all, at that moment, out chasing her partner and daughter. Without knowing it, Cordelia and Corzell were giving them time to gather their wits and escape.

"We'll fly west and then come back to the forest from the other direction," Corselia suggested.

"But if we leave the valley, will we lose the valley?" Corxell questioned, sounding confused.

"We'll find another home, another valley," Corselia replied solemnly, "To survive we need to leave." Corselia wasn't sure what they would find in the eucalyptus forest. She had never been there and when she remembered the state of Karbett after his journey through the forest, she shivered involuntarily. *But we have to go… now*, she thought.

"Can you fly with me?" she asked Corxell. "Will you fly with me, son?" she asked again. "This is our only hope now."

He hesitated and looked at the bottle brush bush at the base of the nest tree where the two dead tawny frogmouths were hidden. Then he looked out over the space between the nest tree and the creek, orchard and the elpitlum site beyond. The valley had been all he'd known. His world. The thought of leaving saddened him more than he could say. But he agreed, nodding once to affirm his willingness to leave with his mother.

She threw her wings about her child in delight and support. Then she too looked over to the elpitlum area. She could hear a commotion and imagined some other mytre were being tormented and chased. But she knew she couldn't help them. "Come on, son," she said firmly, with hope still teasing the edges of her words. Then, they both dropped from the nest tree and flew west away from the valley.

-0-

Lord Kratt stood over the bodies of Karbett and Kardelia. He could hear his faithful Krat clan warriors rising to chase the escaping Cor clan leader, the rebel Corzell, and the other Cor fledgling. With him gone, Lord Kratt knew the valley was now his. He raised his wings encouraging the gathered mytre to celebrate his victory.

Soon even the remnants of the Kar clan had joined in celebration of his victory. Mytre all about the elpitlum site cried out in recognition of 'The Great Lord Kratt.' All the mytre about the branches of the trees near the elpitlum site took up the chant.

Lord Kratt, or as he was now, 'The Great Lord Kratt,' basked in his glory. As he did, he reflected upon his considerable triumph. In just over a cycle of Egnaro he had killed the leaders of the Dart clan, and the Kar clan, he had driven off the Wayt clan and taken all their territories. He had banished then killed the traitors Karbett and Kardelia. He had the leaders of the Yat clan at his feet and was sure the troublesome Cor clan leaders, while they had escaped for now, would soon be in his claws or dead. Either way the valley was surely his.

Held too firmly, Yatdoll and Yatnolia had not been able to escape their captor's grip. Both had been on their knees when Karbett made his surprise attack, and they were both unable to help Corzell or Corselia escape. They tried to struggle but gave up once they had seen Corhelia killed. They were both on the lawned area in the centre of the elpitlum and seeing the jubilation of the Krat clan and their supporters, both lay prostrate with their wings wide to their sides, splayed out low in submission.

The Great Lord Kratt looked at the two Yat clan leaders and considered his next move. "You Yats conspired against me, didn't you?"

"We were misled, Lord," Yatdoll replied, respectfully.

"We are sorry, Lord... forgive us, The Great Lord Kratt," Yatnolia said, hoping her flattery would go well when he considered their fate.

"Kill them both," The Great Lord Kratt cried. Instantly, two former Kar mytre, looking to win his favour, fell and glided down from a branch above them ready to carry out The Great Lord Kratt's orders.

As they landed and were about to strike, Lord Kratt called out, "Wait." The two former-Kar birds froze moments before their attack began.

"Your lives for your lands," Lord Kratt said coldly. "You can choose to live under my rule or die under the beaks of these loyal birds."

Yatdoll looked across at his partner. She was crying, as was he. "Our lands and skies are not great, Lord… but if you see fit to pardon us for our misguided part in this revolt, you can have our lands and skies and we will gladly serve you faithfully and be pleased to call you, The Great Lord Kratt." Yatdoll paused as he closed his eyes risking a future without his own territory to call home. Then he said, with great reverence, "The choice is yours, Lord, we ask for nothing ourselves."

The Great Lord Kratt signalled for the two mytre poised above the prostrate supplicants to withdraw. They looked crestfallen as they flew back to their places on the branches above the elpitlum site.

"There has been too much killing in the valley," Lord Kratt said, ignoring that he had been the reason for much of it. Then he added, "You spoke well, Sir and I will grant you your lives." Lord Kratt hopped down from the log and used his wing to lift Yatdoll's head from the lawn. "Go now, your land and sky are now my land and sky. Forfeit for your lives." As he spoke, he smiled at the bird beneath him feeling himself every bit, "The Great Lord Kratt of the Valley."

Yatnolia and Yatdoll rose slowly, their eyes fixed on The Great Lord Kratt as he stepped away. Their clan was gone, their lands, their sky, their nest trees… all gone. Rage burnt in their hearts, but seeing the gathered mytre rejoicing and celebrating, their fear and revulsion doused the flames of hate.

After a brief glance at each other, they knew they could no longer fight, or stay. Yatdoll smiled briefly at Yatnolia, reassuring her, and confirming his desire to stay at her side. Without a word, they backed away from the centre of the elpitlum, before both birds turned and fled the valley, the reign of The Great Lord Kratt, and his Krat clan. Though defeated and down hearted, they flew with all their might, north and away from the valley.

Hopping back onto the log, Lord Kratt raised his black wing feathers, with the white tips high at his side. Then in a booming voice he chorused, "I am The Great Lord Kratt of the Valley." All the gathered mytre cheered and chortled in response. He waited until the noise settled down then went on, "All the valley is now mine and you are all members of the clan Krat. All clans that existed before are now banished and anyone using a clan name other than clan Krat will be driven from the valley or killed."

There was a more muted response and only the Krat clan mytre really rejoiced enthusiastically. Kratt noticed the diminished response. "Stay or go, it is your choice. If you stay you will be clan Krat, if you stay and cause any disruption, you will be stripped of your feathers and banished."

No one cheered, although a few Krat die-hards, chortled a few short, whistled notes.

Suddenly, a Krat bird that had been chasing the escaped mytre returned and landed in the middle of the lawn before the elpitlum.

"Lord Kratt," he said, commandingly. There was a low rumble of disapproval around the gathering. A Krat mytre who had previously been guarding Yatdoll lent in and whispered to the messenger.

"Forgive me," the newly arrived bird said, "The Great Lord Kratt. I have news about the escaping birds." The messenger bowed low before going on.

"Yes, go on," Kratt said, impatiently.

"The leader of the Cor clan is dead sir. Killed by a car. The other mytre," he hesitated, "She has..."

"Well?" demanded The Great Lord Kratt.

"We had her, Sir, but she seems to have... she has... she has..." The mytre's voice quivered as the bird spoke. "Disappeared, Sir."

-0-

Another Krat chaser tried to lift Cordelia to her feet. She struggled, fighting with them and her grief. Finally, two strong birds took her between them and lifted her to her feet.

148

Cordelia was blind with grief and could hardly see the six mytre from the Krat clan gathered about her.

"You," said Kratjoa, "Go back to Lord Kratt with the news of the rebel's death." "You two, take her back to Lord Kratt."

"Come on you," said one of the birds at her side. "He's dead, the old, half-blind fool, he's had it, come on, you."

With that, something in Cordelia broke. She was suddenly beyond grief. She felt numb, but also, she felt her loss like an electric charge surging through her body. Her loss demanded action. She looked at the birds gathered around her. Some were looking at her father's body by the roadside.

Few, even the two who had lifted her from her place by her father, felt she was a genuine flight risk; they could all see how broken she had been when they landed. Still fly she did. Within a second, she had pushed both birds at her side away and crashed into the bird designated as the messenger, knocking him to the ground, before taking to flight.

She flew directly into the air and took off east, along the sealed road. She could just see the lights of a car in the distance. Believing it to be the one that killed her father, she thought, *I could ask why it had killed my father.* Remembering the size and speed of the car, she thought. *I can see why these norzela things kill and destroy without being harmed.'* She flew low and fast. She flew past the strange sign, with the norzela hieroglyphics that loomed large on her right.

It took the Krat clan hunters only a moment to realise she had escaped again, and again they were after her, this time with renewed vim.

She was exhausted from her earlier efforts at evasion and seeing her vision of her father's death come so violently to fruition had drained her. But she drove herself on. She was almost level with the back of the car.

Suddenly, she was aware of a bird right at her side. *Father,* she thought as she glanced at the black and white shape at her wing tip. Instead, she saw it was Kratjoa.

Cordelia had almost reached the cab of the strange car with an open back end. This one had a tray with sides and a tail gate at the back, with a black tarpaulin stretched out over the back part. Clips were holding the tarp all along one side and most of the other side. But the tarp was loose in one corner creating an opening to the body of the tray, with part of the lose tarp flapping in the wind.

Suddenly, the Krat bird at Cordelia's side struck out at her. Kratjoa had slipped into her wind stream and was able to get right alongside her before she could react. Kratjoa's beak was well directed, and she struck Cordelia directly at the back of her skull.

Instantly knocked unconscious, Cordelia dropped like a stone onto the top of the tarpaulin covering the tail of the ute. She bounced and skipped lightly towards the open corner of the tarpaulin above the ute's tray. Without a sound, she dropped, still unconscious, into the body of the tray, under the tarp. The pursuing birds had no idea where she had gone, she seemed to have simply dropped from the sky and disappeared.

The ute sped along the road heading east, its headlights piercing the night, and blazing a path along the sealed road. After a short while, it turned at the foot of a vast escarpment, as the road sloped down and ran west, into the vast Australian central planes.

PART TWO

CORDELIA'S FLIGHT

17

Lost and Found

When you see me fly away without you
Shadow on the things you know
Feathers fall around you
And show you the way to go

It's over, it's over.
Nestle in your wings my little one
A special morning brings another sun
Tomorrow, see the things that never come today
When you see me fly away without you
It's over, it's over.

Linda Ronstadt – ''Birds' (1972)

THE UTE PULLED off the road at the roadhouse and drove up next to a diesel pump, where it came to a stop. The norzela who drove it was called Chris. He was dressed in a red-pink checked flannel shirt, dark blue jeans, and tan ankle high leather boots. He left his dusty, oil-stained dark-brown Akubra on the dashboard and made his way over to the diesel pump and withdrew the bowser nozzle.

"Get uz a cool drink, Lilly love," he called to his daughter as she left the passenger seat and stretched. She was about to walk over to the petrol station when she noticed the tarp covering the back of the ute was loose at one corner.

"Dad, I thought you'd tied this down," she exclaimed. She didn't wait for a reply but shook her head. *He's always doing things like this*, she thought. She quickly pulled on the cords attached to the tarp and looped the slack of the cord over some studs at the side of the ute. "That'll keep the load secure," she said to herself, before turning and going into the servo to buy a drink for herself, and her dad.

Lilly was in her late teens. She had dusky-blonde hair and wore light blue jeans and tan boots like her father's, but her shirt was a Matilda's soccer top, a souvenir from a recent trip to watch her heroes play soccer in a 'friendly'. She'd been at boarding school for the last two years and she was delighted to be finally on her way home. Now her high school studies were over she was looking forward to getting to grips with station work and station life again. Although she was tired from the long trip, she couldn't have been happier.

"How far do we have left to go before we get home?" Lilly asked her dad, as she buckled up her seat belt.

"Oh, still a few hours yet. I'll have to go a bit slower than I'd like. The bloody roos are all over the road between here and the front gate." He started the engine, slipped the four by four into gear, turned on the spotlights and set off again. He had an ache at the back of his eyes and his forehead throbbed. Since leaving Sydney, he'd hardly stopped, but he wanted to be home as soon as possible. *Stations don't run themselves*, he told himself. He rubbed his eyes and looked into the tunnel of light on the road ahead. *Soon be home,* he thought, pleased with their progress.

-O-

They arrived not long before dawn. The sun was low in the east behind them, and they could feel it was going to be a warm day.

"I'll get my bag from under the tarp," Lilly said feeling suddenly soporific. As she undid the cord from the studs, she thought she heard something moving in the ute's tray. She lifted the loosened tarp cautiously and tried to look under the cover. It was dark underneath and she struggled to see anything. Suddenly, something moved and caught her eye. A bird of some sort was flapping frantically about between her sports bag and the two bags of clothes she'd brought from town. She jumped back, startled. She let go of the tarp and let it fall back over the bags and whatever was in the tray.

"Look at this, Dad," she called as she dropped the tarp back down over the tray.

Her dad was stretching his back, and he walked over towards her slowly. "What's the matter?" he asked casually.

"Look at this," she said again, lifting the tarp, gingerly. The bird began to flap and hop about in the tray, trying to fly.

Her father jumped back as she had done. "How the bloody hell did that get in there?" he exclaimed.

"It looks like it's injured," Lilly observed. "It must have come in when the tarp was open back at the roadhouse, but I can't see how."

"I'll get a stick," her father said, as he looked about on the ground for a branch or some sort of weapon.

"No, don't hurt it," Lilly cried. "Catch it, it doesn't look like it can fly, and it'll only die if we don't help it."

"It won't thank you," her dad said. "'Wild things should be free and left in the wild."

"I know, but it can't fly. Come on, Dad, help me catch it."

He shrugged and scratched his head. His leather jacket was in the ute's cab, and he reached in and brought it back. Lilly lifted the tarp, and in one motion, Chris threw his jacket over the injured bird, stopping it from flapping or trying to escape. He then scooped up the jacket and bird and holding them both firmly, he carried the bird over to the house.

"Put it in here," Lilly suggested, pointing at an old wire-barred, dog cage near the back door. It was big enough for a large dog and more than large enough to hold the captured bird securely and safely. She opened the wire door, and her father placed his jacket and the bird it contained into the cage. Lilly closed the door and they both stepped back as the bird slowly pushed its way out from under the jacket.

"It's a young magpie," her father said. "It still has grey breast feathers and a dark beak. It looks like its wing is injured, and I can see some blood on its head, near that strange horned feather above its beak." He scratched his own head again. It was a habit he'd developed. Lilly knew it meant he was thinking.

"It could have been attacked by a hawk or some other big predator and crashed into the ute or it could have injured its wing travelling in the ute's tray," he speculated.

"I'll look after it," Lilly said as she bent down to get a better look at the small bird. "I'll get it some water and food."

"Better get a vet to look at that wing too," her father said, "Or it might not fly again."

"What's this?" Lilly's mother said as she came out through the back door and onto the back veranda to greet them both.

Lilly sprang up, and smiling she gave her mum a big hug. "Look what we've found," she said while still in the embrace, "an injured magpie."

"You don't see many of those around here, it's too dry. What are you going to do with it?" her mother asked, sceptically.

"First, I'm gunna help get it better," Lilly asserted.

"Well, I can tell the money we spent on your boarding school education was well worth it, luv," her mother joked. Adding, "'Gunna', really?" She walked over to her husband and gave him a tight hug, then said, "Come on, I'll put some breakfast on, and you can both have a sleep before you fall over."

Lilly went to collect her bags from the back of the ute while her mum and dad hugged again.

"Good to see you safely back, luv'," she said to her husband, adding as she pointed at Lilly, "She hasn't been home for 5 minutes and she's already rescuing wild animals... what'll we do with her?"

"It's good to have her home though. I didn't half miss her." Her father loved his wife and his two sons, but he'd always had a soft spot for his youngest, his daughter. *Yep*, he thought, *it's good to have her home.*

-0-

Cordelia had been unconscious for a long time. While she was in the ute's covered tray, one of Lilly's bags had moved in transit and caught her right wing. When Cordelia woke, she was suddenly aware of a pain in her wing. Then she felt a stabbing pain in her head. She couldn't see anything around her, and for a long time, she lay in pain, unable to get her bearings or even move. The motion of the ute as it rolled along the road meant she was frequently tossed from one side to the other. Each roll causing her excruciating pain in her head and wing.

The space felt like a large hollow tree nest. The smells were something she'd not smelt before, but one of them was something rank and it made her stomach turn as a wave of nausea swept over her.

The smells were leather, dust, and diesel.

As she tried to focus on where she was, and what had happened, a thought came to her, *Who was she?* She struggled to get to her feet but couldn't stand. Every time she tried, she fell, tossed, and rocked by the movement of the ute as it drove along. She tried to recall what had happened. But her mind was blank. Consumed by pain, she thought, *Maybe I'll know more when Elppa comes up. When I can see what sort of hollow, I'm in.*

In the dark and in pain, she'd lost all sense of time. The rolling, unsteady, unbalanced feeling, and the nausea just seemed to go on and on. Resigned to being unable to stand, Cordelia lay as best she could between the strange objects around her.

Suddenly, it all stopped. She could hear norzela voices close by. At first, she froze. *In the dark,* she thought, *they might not see me.* Then, a wind blew her feathers as the roof of her hollow lifted. A dim light appeared and a dark silhouette of a norzela loomed before her. *They've found me,* she thought. She tried to lift in flight and began to flap wildly and although her head still hurt and her wing was excruciating, her only thought was of flight. But no matter what she did, her wing would not respond. All she cou d manage were short hops in the limited space of the hollow of the ute's tray before the pain made it impossible to go further or try again.

Exhausted, confused, and afraid, all Cordel a could think was that she was about to join the Great flock of Elppa. Suddenly, her world went completely black again. She was awake, but the light around her had disappeared in an instant. Then a strong force lifted her. She could feel herself flying without using her wings, she was sure she was ascending into the Great flock of Elppa; dead. She allowed herself to feel the peace that comes with the certainty of death. '*So,*' she thought, *this is how it ends. This is what it feels like.*

But something didn't feel right. Pain… she still felt pain and she thought, '*Surely in the Great flock there wouldn't be pain and suffering, unless this was the opposite of being in the Great flock?*' Fear consumed her. *Am I in some other place, where all birds go who are not worthy of the Great flock?* A wave of panic came over her and she tried to struggle, but she couldn't move. Then, she was released. She was still in darkness but the force that held her was gone.

I'm here, she thought, *The Great… the Great… what!*' Then pain gripped her mind. It was the pain that brought her back to her senses. She struggled and found she could move, that the grip on her had really gone and she could see shards of light about her. *Maybe I'm not dead,* she thought. She could move and Elppa's light grew around her. '*But am I free?*'

Cordelia peaked out from under the thing that covered her. A young norzela stood looking at her. She drew her head back under the covering. She'd never been this close to norzelas before and she shuffled as best she could away from them, back under cover. She soon realised she couldn't go far as some sort of norzela box held her captive still. Fear pulsed through her body. Nothing made sense. She couldn't recall how she arrived where she was, where she had come from, and worst of all, who she was. Her fear multiplied when the thing covering her was snatched away.

She found herself alone, in the middle of a cage. It was made of black painted wire, and it smelt like young dog. There were several norzela looking at her through the bars. She froze, petrified, not knowing what else to do.

18

A New Home

Right now, I feel like a bird
Caged without a key
Everyone comes to stare at me
With so much joy and revelry.

They don't know how I feel inside
Through my smile, I cry
They don't know what they're doin' to me
Keepin' me from flyin'

Alicia Keys - 'Caged Bird' (2001)

LILLY HADN'T VISITED the station in over a year, and she was eager to reacquaint herself with the property. Her family had owned and run the station for over 140 years, and she was keen to get out and about on the land she knew so well. She rose and dressed quickly, it was late afternoon and she'd slept longer than she'd planned. After checking up on the magpie in the cage on the back veranda, she went outside into the bright afternoon sun. It was warm and a light breeze was all that made the heat bearable.

It was early summer, and the pale blue sky offered a splendid canopy in contrast to the iron red dirt and thin yellow-gold grass on the flat, open terrain that surrounded the homestead and station buildings. A four-rail ironbark fence that her grandfather had built in the late 1880s surrounded the house. The original homestead building had been replaced in the early 1930s and further added to in the late 1990s, but the fence still stood as a testament to her grandfather's hard work and determination.

The house had a wide veranda that ran all the way around the building and offered shade and a place to sit on the warm evenings when their work was done. Surrounded by a stretch of lawn that struggled to hold on in the thin red soil, the driveway ran right up to the front steps. Most of the lawn was pale and thin, but around the water taps, and where the sprinkler lay each day as it was moved about the lawn, patches of darker green grass clung to life.

Lilly noticed that the outside of the house had recently been painted, *A sort of welcome home gesture*, she thought. But even so, she could see where the corrugated iron roof was showing signs that it was starting to rust in places. The house had two chimneys, one from the open fire in the living room, and the other from the old log stove in the kitchen. Lilly couldn't remember when it had last been used, but she could recall her mother using it to make cakes and biscuits, when she and her brothers were kids.

As she walked across the home paddock now, she could almost remember the smell of wood fire smoke as it dropped from the smokestack, and the sweet smell of Anzac biscuits her mum had made for them, on their return from school. These were happy smells, comfortable smells that reminded her of her childhood and the joy of family. The station had other smells too that reminded her that the sheep and cattle were never far from the homestead buildings. The smell of dust also returned quickly to her nostrils as she kicked it up with her boots as she walked. Clearly the spring rains had been poor, and she could feel the telltale signs of another hot summer looming.

As she strode over to the shearing shed, she called out to her brothers. She knew they would be there, preparing for dipping, delousing, worming, or sorting sheep, or playing with some machine or other, and she wanted to say g'day, after not having seen them for so long.

Her two brothers were older and had already committed to continuing their life on the property. They knew she was home and had stayed away from the house, so they didn't wake her after her long journey. She found them tinkering with some farm machinery on the shearing shed floor.

"What hav' yer broken now?" she said, coming up beside them.

"Sis," said one, affectionately.

"Lilly, mate," said the other with a chortle, as they both tried to embrace her in a hug.

"Whooo," she said, pulling back from their grease and oil-stained hands and fingers. "Good to see ya, boys," Lilly said. "But you'll need to wash up before you come near me with those hands."

The boys looked at each other with cheeky smiles and an evil twinkle in their eyes. They both reached out and pulled her into a tight embrace, while rubbing their dirty fingers through her hair and across her face.

"You buggers," she exclaimed feigning disgust. She knew farm life was often dirty work and getting dirty was almost a relief after months of clean, city living at boarding school. *Anyway,* she thought, *I half expected them to do exactly that, and I only have myself to blame.* She wrestled with them for a moment, then pulled back as they each began to giggle, hiding the small discomfort they felt, now they were all a little older than the children they had been when they last played.

"Now you look like a proper farm girl," said one of her older siblings, laughing.

Lilly's face was a canvas of black and dark brown streaks and her tidy hair had been ruffled into a crumpled, haystack mess.

"What yer doin'?" she asked, brushing her hair back into place with her hands.

"Fixing the quad bike," said the older one, "we thought we'd do some roo shoot'n tonight."

"Der yer wan'a come?" asked the younger of the two.

"Nar, bin a long day already, un' I'll need to rest for tomorra." Lilly was conscious that she had instantly fallen into the station drawl that she had taken years to shake off in Sydney. Catching herself speaking like a country girl again, she felt a sort of personal distain, although she was also glad she'd not lost her inner country spirit. She smiled to herself. "It's great to see you, boys, we can catch up again at dinner time," she said, with more care and closer attention to her diction.

Her brothers watched her walk away and the older said to the other, "Looks like sis is all grown up now, bro."

"She'll always still be me littl' sis though, bro," said her other brother, as he returned to the engine of the quad bike.

Lilly walked through the shearing shed and came out near the station slaughterhouse. It was behind a set of old wooden doors. She was glad they were locked. She'd always hated the slaughter room. It was where her dad and brothers butchered sheep, cattle, or roos, if they'd shot any, and where her dad prepared the meals for the yard dogs. She could smell the blood and stench of death even through the closed doors. It was her least favourite place on the station and she walked on quickly across to a set of stock holding yards and a large vehicle storage shed.

The four yard dogs lived there, away from the house and away from the sheep. They were all tied up on the end of strong metal chains, all in a line and each with their chains attached by a hook to their own little kennel.

When Lilly approached, the dogs began to bark frantically and wagged their tails joyfully. Lilly whistled once, a short sharp whistle made by putting two fingers in the corner of her mouth and blowing hard. Immediately the four yard dogs fell to the ground and went silent. Again, she couldn't resist a sly smile, *This is my place*, she thought.

From the stock yard near the yard dog kennels she could see an old dysfunctional windmill about 300 metres to the west and beyond that... nothing... nothing but endless, flat, red, dusty, sparsely grassed plain, with a few slim, leaf-bare, struggling trees. In the far, far distance were some low rolling hills before some very far away mountains. *This is home,* she thought, and she loved it.

-0-

Exhausted, Cordelia had slept longer than she had since she'd been in the egg. When she awoke there was a slow drip water feeder attached to the side of the metal cage, for her to drink from. As well, a few scraps of food, hardened pieces of dry mincemeat and stale bread, had been left on the cage floor. She noticed something else too. Her injured wing had been strapped firmly to her body and she squirmed in discomfort, but she was unable to stretch or extend it. She had no memory of anyone doing anything to her, but she was grateful that at least in her right wing, the pain seemed less. However, her head still throbbed, and she struggled at times to lift it and look around.

Sometime later, Cordelia finally managed to look about. She was alone in the cage, but she had no memory of being there before. A thick covering, some sort of norzela cloth thing, draped across the top of the cage, warmed her. She felt warmer than she had ever felt before. It was the atmosphere that was strange. It was dry and warm, the very air felt parched, close, almost crisp and something told her she'd never experienced the warmth that surrounded her like this before. There was something else that felt strange. For the first time in her life, she couldn't see or smell trees.

Then she saw the male norzela looking at her from a seat, across the covered space of the veranda. He looked almost as tired as she felt, despite her long rest.

Cordelia looked around to see if the norzela girl she had briefly seen before her capture was there.

She saw an older woman sitting near, and she looked at her closely. She looked old, weathered. Her face was wrinkled, and she looked weather worn, and tough. Still Cordelia thought she had a sort of dignity, her hair was going grey, but well styled and tidy, and she noticed something she'd not seen at first. The norzela's eyes still shone brightly and she couldn't see any weariness in them. Cordelia hadn't seen anything like this norzela before and she thought, after a long look at the norzela's eyes, that she looked kind.

She couldn't understand what they said but watched them as they communicated.

-0-

"The vet said, there was no point coming all this way for a wild bird. He said, if the wing is broken, I may as well put it out of its misery, but he would have no way of knowing without an X-ray," Chris said.

"You can't just kill it, luv," Lilly's mum, Mary replied. She was sitting across from him on another casual chair on the veranda "Lilly seems to think the bird is some sort of welcome home present."

"A bloody mystery more like," her dad said. "I still can't understand how it got into the back of the ute. Very strange," he added before taking a sip of his tea.

"You probably didn't tie the tarp down properly, and it flew in," Mary said. Adding, "you're always doing things like that."

He looked hurt, but went on regardless, "The vet said, I should just strap its injured wing and see what happens in a day or two. If it's a sprain, the bird should respond well and start to flap and try and fly in a little while, but if it's a break, it may set out of place and the poor thing may never fly again. I've strapped it now, so we'll know more in a few days. Then I'll decide what to do with it."

-0-

Cordelia had only seen norzela from a distance and she didn't understand their song and she listened, confused, and baffled by their strange chirping chatter. She was also confused by their plumage. She was sure the male norzela had different head feathers when she had first seen him. Now he had a round, flat brimmed, brown set of feathers on his head.

Cordelia's head hurt, from her injury and from trying to understand the odd, unfamiliar changed world she found herself in. She called out to the norzela, "Elppa's greeting to you both," to be

163

polite, although she wasn't expecting a reply. She felt safe though and while in an unfamiliar place, her sense of gratitude compelled her to sing. She sat up then stood on her legs, she threw her head back and began a long chorus, carolling and warbling loudly and melodically for the two norzela.

"She's got a beautiful song, doesn't she, luv," Mary said.

Cordelia didn't understand a word of the response, but something told her she was unlikely to come to harm from these norzela, at least in the short term. *Otherwise*, she thought, *Why would they feed me and make sure I have water to drink*. Content that she was safe and cared for and that her song was being appreciated, if not enjoyed, she sang on. Suddenly she was interrupted, and her singing stopped abruptly.

"I know what you're thinking, you're wondering why they haven't killed you yet, aren't you bird?"

Cordelia looked around and saw a small dog sitting near the back door.

It had silently come out through a small dog flap in the screen door and was looking at her curiously.

Cordelia dared not move or make a sound. She had heard of a dog and seen one once before, she was sure, but her mind was cloudy, and she couldn't recall where. Something deep in her mind said, *Dogs are sleepy and lazy, but they'll kill you if they can catch you.*

The strange dog spoke with a playful snarl, "They're going to fatten you up and when you are good an' fat, they'll eat you, or feed you to the yard dogs."

Cordelia understood little of what it said but she understood the outcome for her was not going to be pleasant. Fear gripped her again, her head throbbed, and she was still unsure who she was or what had happened to her.

Still, she decided to risk some sort of conversation with the strange little dog. If only she knew it's language.

"I… am…" she couldn't remember. *'Who am I?'* she thought. *I wish I had the courage and wisdom of Cordelia from the myth,* she thought, as she pondered her situation. The story she'd heard came back to her mind slowly, and as if a cloud had been blown from the face of Egnaro, she was suddenly sure of who she was.

"I'm Cor… d… e… lia," she said slowly, emphasizing each syllable and turning her head to look squarely at the dog as she spoke. This was the first memory that she was confident about, sure about. She was Cordelia. She looked at the small dog again. She'd been initially afraid, but there was something comical about the torment and the size of her tormenter, and anyway, she thought, *I'm safe behind the bars of the norzela's cage.* But her main source of courage came from remembering who she was. "Cordelia," she said, over and over to herself as she looked at the strange looking dog.

-0-

The dog was a chihuahua, with massive bulging, dark eyes, a black nose, black upper body, and tail. He had a white and light brown underbelly and tan inner ears. His ears were pointing like two large leaves into the air. *The creature looks like a toy,* Cordelia thought, then she frowned in concentration. *A toy, where have I heard of toys before? How do I know what a toy is?* She racked her brain, surprised by another recollection so quickly after the first. *A toy! I know the shape of toys, and the way norzela children leave them on the lawn, uncared-for, outside.* Then she paused. *The 'lawn',* she thought. *I know that too, there must be a lawn near here somewhere.* But her mind was still fuzzy and the pathways to her memory remained locked to her. She gave up thinking about the toy. The dog looked young, like herself, and she hoped she could establish some sort of alliance with it.

"Cor…d… e…lia," she repeated. The dog turned its head to the side with a quizzical expression.

"Cor… d… e… lia," the chihuahua stammered in a low growl.

"I'm Bruce," the young chihuahua barked back while putting its head on its fore paws, then jumping playfully backwards. "I'm sorry to have teased you. They won't eat you and I'm sure they'll look after you. I was in that same cage myself when I first came to the station. And they gave me food and water." He paused and came up to the cage. "I'm sure they will care for you," Bruce reassured the new arrival.

"Bruce…" Cordelia repeated slowly, "Elppa's greetings to you. You're a very fine-looking dog," she said hoping praise and complements might help break down the barr ers between them.

"Bruce don't do that, the bird is injured, the last thing it wants is you barking in its face," the lady norzela, Mary, said.

"Leave him, Mary," Chris said softly, in mock rebuke. "He has to learn about what we want to be warned about, and what not to bark at, and I'd say a bird poking about out here should be something Bruce should alert us about." He then said in a commanding voice, "Here, Bruce, up."

"But he shouldn't bark at the injured bird in a cage," Mary scoffed at Chris.

Chris shrugged and turning to the dog, he called again, "Here, Bruce, up."

Bruce looked at Chris, wagged his tail and jumped up on Mary's lap. She laughed and said, "One word from you and he does exactly what he wants."

"Traitor," Chris said, stretching across to offer the small dog a remnant of biscuit, despite his betrayal.

"Bloody hell, I'm tired. Might have to go to bed early tonight I think," Chris said sitting back and stretching.

Just then, Lilly came over from the paddock near the homestead to join them on the veranda. "How's the bird?" she asked, cheerily.

"Looks like it's bin talking with Bruce here," Mary suggested, with a chuckle.

Lilly looked doubtful. "Did you call the vet?" she asked her dad as she took a seat in one of the other veranda chairs.

"Yep, luv," her dad replied. He said, "If the bird can't use its wing in a few days, I should put it down."

"No…" Lilly cried, distraught. "I'll look after it, it won't be in the way I promise."

"Honey," her mum said kindly, "it'll be for the best."

"It's a wild bird, luv," her dad said calmly, "If it can't fly, it can't hunt or find food, it'll die. It's the way things are here." He knew she would understand, she was from the country, off the land, and she'd seen the highs and lows of drought, floods and the way nature could be cruel and unkind. She'd know what the right thing was, and when it was the right time to act.

The chihuahua, Bruce, looked down at Cordelia from his resting place on his mistress's lap and flopped his tongue out of his mouth as if it had died. *She's had it,* he thought. But he called down to the resting bird in the wire cage, and shouted cheerily, "You'll be fine, mate. Chin up."

Cordelia lay in her cage, resting. All she really knew was that her wing was useless, her head still throbbed and her name. She was Cordelia and knowing this gave her the courage to go on.

19

OTHERS

Well, I was wondering how long
this could go on, on and on
Well I thought I could never be surprised

But could it be that I bit my own tongue
Oh yeah, it's so hard to swallow when you're wrong.
A bird of paradise
The sunrise in her eyes

John Lennon – 'Surprise, Surprise (Sweet Bird of Paradox)' (1974)

CORDELIA SPENT HER time resting and sleeping. Her dreams had been strange, and often repeated in her mind, influenced, she was sure by her trauma. In her dream, she could see a massive eagle gliding high above her. She wasn't afraid, and it seemed to give her strength. The wedgie was high, but lost to her vision in a fog, or mist. *Like smoke,* she thought. It was as if an angel, shrouded in cloud was watching over her. Oddly, she felt uplifted and when she woke, she felt light, buoyant almost.

Cordelia couldn't explain her dream. Wedge-tailed eagles were not friends, they were enemies. Why would she dream about one watching over her? Or was it stalking her? A few times now, the vision of an eagle gliding high above her had filled her dreams, yet on waking, she felt unafraid.

Apart from sleep, the only other things she could do in her cage were eat and walk about, although even this was restricted by the size of the wire cage and a sense that she might lose her balance

168

with her injured wing still strapped. While she recovered, she watched the norzela and talked occasionally with Bruce.

Bruce was only six months old, and he'd been brought to the station as a house dog, unlike the working or yard dogs that were tied up near the sheep pens and machine shed. They each struggled to understand the other at first, although, the more they talked, the more comprehensible they became to the other. But Bruce rarely came outside when his masters were in the house.

"Sometimes they 'accidentally' drop food, or if I ask nicely, they feed me biscuits and cake. The yard dogs never get the treats I do," Bruce explained, feeling very privileged. "I even get to sleep inside," he added, proudly. Bruce jumped up onto one of the outside chairs to sleep in the warm afternoon sun, and although he'd only been living at the station a short time, he'd already settled into country life.

"What do you do here?" Cordelia asked as he dozed.

Sleepily, Bruce replied, "My job is to protect the family here in the house."

"From what?" she asked.

Bruce thought for a moment and yawned before he spoke. He'd never really thought about it. *What was it he could protect them from?* After a moment he said, "Mice. Mice," Bruce repeated with conviction. "They sometimes get mice here and I think my job is to chase them away."

Cordelia accepted this explanation, after all, what else could such a small dog chase from the house? *If anything,* she thought, *the small creature is at risk of being taken by a larger one.*

"Have you remembered where you come from?" Bruce asked, sympathetically as he stepped in a circle before settling down to rest on another, cooler chair.

Cordelia could not recall anything more from before waking in the tray of the ute and being captured and put in the wire cage.

Apart from having known what a dog, and toy were, and of course, remembering her name. It was starting to frustrate her no end.

"No, I still can't recall," she said, sadly. "I think I come from a cooler place than here though. The heat here is something I cannot recall experiencing before, and the openness is new to me too." She stretched her neck and looked past the outdoor furniture on the veranda. "Trees, I am sure I am from a place with lots of trees. There are hardly any trees around here and it feels wrong."

"Trees are good," Bruce said. "But if there are no trees nearby, I can manage with fence posts and car wheel hubs. Anything can be useful for leaving a sign for the other animals to stay away and let them know this is my territory."

Cordelia laughed. "No, the trees were for… were for…" she struggled to concentrate. She looked about her cage, the girl norzela had put some newspaper on the floor of the cage and Cordelia was sitting on it, like she was in a… in a… nest… that was it. Suddenly Cordelia said, "I remember now, the trees were for nests. My parents built a nest, and I was born and raised in a nest, high in a tree."

The thought stunned Cordelia. *Parents? Did she have any? And where are they if she did?* She'd solved one quandary and was left with another. Her frustrations grew.

The girl norzela, Lilly, came out through the back door, and stepped over to the wire cage. She dropped some mincemeat through the wire and sat down to watch Cordelia peck at the treats. Cordelia devoured the delicious food quickly, looking up at both the chihuahua and norzela between pecking at the meat.

Bruce jumped down from his place on a chair and came over to the cage in the hope that Cordelia would accidently flick some of the food out through the bars for him.

Instead, she deliberately picked up a piece of the mincemeat and dropped it through the cage bars for Bruce to take. Lilly was amazed and although she'd seen it, she sat back and blinked, unsure if she had indeed seen the bird feed her father's house dog. She jumped up and went back inside for more mincemeat.

She was soon back, with a small amount of mince that she again dropped into the cage for Cordelia. Cordelia did the same thing. She ate a few pieces of the mince herself, then she deliberately picked up a piece of the meat and dropped it through the wire bars of the cage. She retreated as Bruce stepped over and picked it up to eat.

"Bloody hell," Lilly said, stunned.

Then Cordelia began to sing. Her carolling was clear and melodious, soft, and sweet.

Lilly had heard magpies in the city, while she had been at school, but they had always sounded disconsolate, like they were lamenting a loss, or their songs were far off and lost in the background of the city sounds. Now with Cordelia singing almost as if it was just for her, the beauty and majesty of her song captured Lilly.

Lilly's mum, Mary, came around from the side of the house where she had been putting washing on a line. "That's beautiful, isn't it?" Mary said.

"We can't put her down," Lilly said, "not if she can sing like this, and you should see how cute the bird and Bruce are together," Lilly added in an excited tone. "I can keep her in the cage and look after her here on the veranda," Lilly pleaded.

"It's up to your dad, luv," Mary replied, vehemently. "But it's a lovely sound to have here at the station, that's for sure."

Cordelia kept singing, thanking Lilly for her food, and rejoicing in her friendship with Bruce. Suddenly, two large black and white birds landed on the dying lawn opposite the veranda. Cordelia was suddenly afraid. She watched them closely as they strode about, pecking awkwardly at the grass roots in the soil or at small insects hidden between the blades of pale-dry grass. They had bright yellow eyes and a slightly curved beak, their feathers seemed to be more black than white, and they looked uncomfortable as they stepped about the lawn.

Bruce turned to look at them, then casually jumped back up on to the seat cushion, disinterested. *These were not creatures he was meant to warn his master about,* he thought.

The black and white birds seemed not to notice Cordelia and strode about casually ignoring everyone and everything about them. Heat rose from the ground and as it did it cast the two birds in a type of quivering mirage.

Cordelia found herself recalling two similar birds. As she looked at the strange black and white birds, her mind was dragged to a more distant recollection. Suddenly, the name 'Krat' came into her mind, and she remembered the evil invaders who had come to their valley.

The valley, it came to her consciousness like an egg falling from the nest and cracking on the ground. The valley that had been home. The creek, the line of pine trees leading to the norzela nest and the lawn, with the toys left out after play. The sealed road, the orchard, the dam above the norzela nest, the nest tree.

As if shaken by a wild wind, she was now truly awake. The nest tree, she thought. *I'd learnt to fly there. Home was in a valley.* Then fear gripped her again, *The Krat… why were they there?* She squawked and called loudly in terror and alarm.

Bruce responded first, jumping from the seat he'd been resting on, and suddenly barking wildly at the two strange birds.

Lilly had no idea what was happening. She turned and saw the two black and white birds behind her. She recognised them as Pied Currawong but didn't understand what the commotion was about.

"What's going on?" she asked her mum.

"I don't know, these currawongs often come here to strut about the lawn. I have no idea what's gotten into the magpie or Bruce though," Mary replied.

"Oh, do stop that racket, darling," one of the currawongs said scornfully, lifting a wing to its head as if it hurt, as it paced about the lawn.

"Oh yes, please, dears, my ears hurt with all that squawking and barking," the second said. The noise stopped and both birds continued to strut about the lawn, paying no further attention to the norzela, dog, or mytre on the veranda.

Cordelia looked at them more closely. They were not Krat clan come to kill or capture her, they were an altogether different type of bird. Her mother had told her about them one day when they had watched two similar birds over fly the valley. 'They are pied currawong,' her mother had explained, 'They are not an enemy.'

Her mother, she thought. *Where is she now? Her mother had been with her from birth, but why was she not with her now?* Her mind clouded over again, and confusion came to roost in her mind like a stone bird.

"We've not seen you here before, sweety," one of the pied currawongs said softly.

"Where are you from, darling?" the other asked as it tossed its head as if flicking a feather from its face. Cordelia was still in shock from realising she was from a place called the 'valley', and remembering her mother, that she couldn't answer.

Bruce answered on her behalf, "She's an injured mytre, but she's not from around here." As he spoke, he skipped over to the edge of the veranda to get a better look at the birds.

"I'm from the valley," Cordelia said quietly, as she remembered more about her valley home. She strode over to the bars on the side of the cage near the veranda edge, and asked boldly and hopefully, "Can you help me get back there?"

"Very forward, isn't she," one of the pied currawongs said, sounding aloof or snobby.

"Yes, darling," replied the other, "Very." Both ignored the new bird and strange little dog for a moment longer, then, one introduced himself, "I'm Trev," before saying politely, "and this is Sid," indicating his partner. "We've lived here for a long time now. We're from much further east, but the wind blew us out here one day and well, we like the dry air and the solitude, so we thought…"

"…we'd stay," interjected Sid.

"We did, yes," giggled Trev. As they both turned to the other and clicked their beaks together, affectionately.

"Do you know the valley?" Cordelia asked, "I need to get back there."

The two birds looked at each other. They shook their heads and Sid said, "Sorry, darling, never heard of it. How would you get there anyway? By the look of that wing, I'd say you can't even fly," Sid suggested, coldly.

"Or get out of the wire nest," Trev added, as he flew up to the veranda balcony railing and looked into the cage. Sid followed and they both sat on the railing chorusing for Cordelia, Bruce and the norzela.

"Can you fly?" Sid asked, sounding sceptical.

"I think I could once," Cordelia replied, "but I won't know until I am free of this cage."

"When will that be?" asked Trev.

"Oh, how insensitive of you, darling. Can't you see she's a captive. A prisoner, doomed to a life in a cage. Don't worry, we'll sing a lament for you each day, so you'll not be held captive alone," Sid said.

"I'm not a captive," Cordelia replied, "just injured. I'm sure the norzela will let me go when I'm better. Or at least I hope they will." Cordelia sounded forlorn as she spoke. She really didn't know and while her wing was feeling less painful, she was starting to resent the wire cage and how it restricted her to only walking.

"Oh, my poor dear," said Sid, "it breaks my heart to see you treated this way. It's tragic."

"Oh, the utter cruelty of the norzela," Trev cried.

"Vile beasts... vile," put in Sid. Then Sid and Trev said together, "We'll stay here and watch vigil over your incarceration... you'll not die alone, sweet child."

"Die?" Cordelia said, shocked. "Die?"

"Oh, I'm sorry, how insensitive," Trev said, "But you are a wild bird. You'll not last long in a cage... I thought you'd know."

He looked embarrassed and dejected to show Cordelia he understood and empathised with her plight.

Bruce gave the two perched birds a sharp disapproving bark. "You'll be fine in a few days," Bruce said, trying to cheer Cordelia up. "I'm sure they'll let you go."

Cordelia thought about the valley, the nest tree, and her mother. Her mother had been with her in the nest, she'd taught her how to hunt and supported her when she'd learnt to fly. As she pondered her past, she recalled more. The tall spotted gum, the pine trees leading to the norzela nest, the creek, and the other birds in the bushes near the dam and the norzela house. She suddenly felt alone, she missed her home, and she began to feel desperately morose.

Bruce saw her mood turn and again tried to cheer her. "I'm sure they'll set you free once you're better, Cordelia." Bruce tried to believe what he'd said, but he couldn't hide the doubt he felt.

"Oh dear," said Trev, "what a cruel situation you're in dear." As he spoke, he dropped his head and placed a wing across his breast.

"Agreed," said Sid, adding, "don't worry dear, we're here to comfort you now."

Cordelia was glad they were not Krat clan mytre come to kill her, but she wondered about her future and if she ever would see the outside of the cage, or indeed, the far-off valley again. *Hope is hard to grasp with an injured wing and sore head,* she thought, *but it's all I have.*

"Bruce, you might be right," Cordelia said after a moment. "Even in this cage I have many blessings, and I'm sure my song doesn't end with me in a cage."

"That's the spirit, darling," Trev called out.

"Chin up, old bean," Sid added as both birds flapped their wings with joy on the veranda banister railing.

Bruce jumped up on a chair cushion to add his barking to the celebration, of hope. Lilly and her mother couldn't understand the racket the chihuahua or the birds were making, and they decided to go inside and start the evening meal.

"Strange animals," Mary said as they went indoors. She looked at Cordelia oddly, *That one,* she thought, *There's something special about that bird.* But she let the thought take flight, and as she turned to go inside, the idea drifted into the dry, parched air and heat that smothered the station.

-0-

"The bird is looking better," Lilly said, "you know... stronger. Dad, do yer think we can put her wing to the test soon?"

As she spoke, her dad looked past her into the cage. He put his cup of tea down and considered his daughter's question carefully. It had been a week since Lilly had come home. Lilly had fed the bird each day, often on multiple occasions. She'd cleaned the cage and made sure there was plenty of water, especially as the summer temperatures had started to climb. Its grey breast feathers were still evident, but the bird had started to almost dance about the cage whenever anyone approached, and it regularly sang in appreciation of a handful of mincemeat.

"We can let it out tomorrow. Although, if it can fly, it is likely to just fly away, and you'll never see it again." He thought it best to be frank. "It's a wild bird and it's unlikely to stay here. It probably has a family to go home to." Then he paused. "On the other hand, if it can't fly, the best thing to do would be to put it down. It can't be much of a life locked in a cage all night and day."

"But, Dad..." Lilly began.

He held up his hand. It was calloused, and strong, big, and scarred from multiple cuts and knocks, with scabs still on three of the four knuckles on his right fingers. "We discussed this the other day. The vet agreed, if the bird can't fly, we'll have to do what's right and not extend its misery."

He was right and she knew it. *He always is,* Lilly thought. "Okay," she said, with bitter resignation. "I guess we'll see tomorrow."

20

Recovery

Blackbird singing in the dead of night.
Take these broken wings and learn to fly.

All your life.
You were only waiting for this moment to arrive.

The Beatles - 'Blackbird' (1968)

A FLOCK OF SULPHUR-Crested Cockatoo lifted from the dry paddock surface. Having picked the seeds and grasses clear of provisions, they suddenly lifted as one into the air. Instantly, as if a magician had flicked a magic sheet, the air turned white, with flashes of yellow. The noise was terrific, like a jet plane lifting from the paddock, and every other bird within earshot was catapulted into flight and fright by the cacophony of sound. The flock turned as if it was one bird and after circling over the feeding place, landed a few hundred metres away to continue their search for seed.

It was a spectacular display and as the flock settled back to earth to feed, Lilly was amazed at their wild beauty, the sheer volume of their cries, and the uniquely Australian behaviour of the majestic birds.

At the sound of the birds, Bruce had come outside to watch. He saw them settle then observed the two strange currawongs land before strutting about the pale lawn.

Lilly's attention also turned to the two strange birds. She thought they looked like they were waiting, like the rest of her family, to see

177

if the magpie would or could fly. Lilly opened the cage and tried to reassure the magpie. "You'll be fine", and "it's okay," she said over and over.

Cordelia couldn't understand the words, but she felt the kind sympathy in her tone, and it relaxed her. Lilly's mum and dad stood behind her on the veranda, eager to support her whatever the outcome. Her brothers stayed inside and watched through the full-length window, from the kitchen.

Her older brother looked at the bird with contempt. *Should put it out of its misery,* he thought. *Stupid looking bird, what magpie has a feathered horn on its head?* He loved the station, but he knew he'd rather spend time with guns and dirt-bikes, motors, and machinery, than animals. *Sis is just wasting her time with a stupid bird*, he thought.

Cordelia had been fed and she felt rested. Sid and Trev flew off and perched on the roof of the shearing shed and looked on from a distance. Bruce moved to the cage and watched from the end of the cage opposite the door, while Lilly was in the process of opening it. Ever playful, even young, scatty Bruce could feel the tension in the air.

Lilly put on some thick gardening gloves and reached into the cage. Cordelia awkwardly moved back in trepidation, but she had nowhere to go. Lilly gently held the bird before carefully removing the strapping from Cordelia's wing. Then Lilly tossed away the strapping, removed her gloves and stepped back. The door was fully open before Cordelia realised she had a path to freedom. Lilly and her parents stood back. Her mum picked up Bruce in case he decided to run at the bird. The two pied currawong began to chant in the background, "Fly, run, flee, take to the sky, be free, escape, be free."

Cordelia didn't know what to do. Lily had placed a line of mincemeat that formed a path from just inside the cage to the veranda, a metre outside the cage door. Corcelia wasn't especially hungry, but she couldn't resist the food.

Before she looked about again, she was standing outside her cage, having followed, and eaten the food.

Cordelia stretched her wings. There was no pain at all in her left wing, but her right felt stiff and sore. She tried to preen it as best she could but even this caused her to wince as she stretched her beak into the feathers and their quill attachments. She was in no hurry to go. The cage was safe, the food was nutritious and plentiful, and the company was... charming. *Yes, 'charming' was the right word*, she told herself, despite Bruce's banal jokes and tricks.

She wasn't sure how she would have coped alone, without Bruce, Sid, and Trev. *But what now?* she pondered. *Fly and flee or stay and... and... and what?* She stretched her wings again. *A small flight,* she thought. *Best to start small, as I did on my first flight, not that many passages of Egnaro ago.* She flew up onto the top of the cage. Flapping with a little difficulty. *But still, it was flight*, she reassured herself. She landed well and began to sing.

"She flew, look she flew," Lilly cried out excitedly.

"Come on, that was hardly a flight for the ages," her father replied.

"Pathetic effort," Bruce barked. "I could fly that far."

"It's a start," Mary said, with relief. "And a start was all we need. Wouldn't you say, dear?"

Lilly hugged her mum, then kissed her dad on his cheek. "She's better," Lilly cried with relief.

Cordelia unconcerned and unimpressed with the excitement about her, settled down to perch on top of the cage. Lilly placed some mincemeat on the veranda banister rail and stepped back to see what the bird would do. Cordelia, sensing the food was hers to take, flapped three times and was soon on the banister rail. She ate the mincemeat and flew back to the top of the cage.

"She'll take a while yet," her father said, "but it looks like its wing is mending well."

Cordelia began to preen her wings again. Taking a lipoid sebaceous fluid from her uropygial gland near the upper tip of her tail with her beak, she used her beak to spread the fluid across and over her wings. Then she stretched, and tidied her damaged wing feathers, preening them in turn. Before she knew more and could remember where she was from and what had happened to her, Cordelia determined to stay near the metal nest, at least until she knew where to go next, and until her wing strength recovered.

21

Too Soon, Too Hot

Skybird – Make your soul
And every heart will know
Of the tale
Skybird – Make your tune
For none may sing it
Just as you do.

Look at the way I glide
Caught on the wind's lazy tide
Sweetly how it sings
Rally each heart at the sight
Of your silver wings.
Skybird.

Niel Dimond – 'Skybird' (1973)

CORDELIA STAYED CLOSE to the cage, only flying a short distance each day. Her wing was not strong enough yet for more than brief journeys and she felt safer if she could easily reach the wire nest without difficulty. Sid and Trev came by each day to see how her flying skills were progressing and to offer moral support, the sort that young Bruce was simply incapable of providing. It was Bruce though who was starting to become Cordelia's true friend. Their friendship grew as their respect for each other developed, and as they recognised that they were both aliens in a strange place.

It was Bruce who was always waiting for Cordelia to come out to play, and he was always there with a reassuring word or boost of encouragement. Most days they played on the veranda, near the cage or on the lawn, from Elppa to Egnaro.

Sometimes, Cordelia would find food or treats for Bruce on a plate left absent-mindedly by an outside seat or some scraps that had dropped down the back of the cushions of the outdoor furniture.

Bruce was careful not to re-injure Cordelia's wing and they only played a primitive form of chasing game that Cordelia would always win by flapping up to a perch Bruce couldn't reach. If she was up high, she would swoop down and peck Bruce on the backside when he wasn't watching. Bruce always yelped but the game was great fun and each day, the dog and the mytre teased and played with each other and as they played their games, Cordelia could feel her wings getting stronger and stronger.

Sid and Trev didn't approve of their playful high jinks, and while they liked Cordelia's company, they found the energy and excitement of Bruce rather tiresome.

"Come and fly with us, Dear," Sid said, inviting Cordelia on a longer flight. "We'll go out to the low hills and back. It's a lovely journey."

"It'll do you a world of good, Dear," Trev added. "It's not too far."

Cordelia was unsure, but she agreed to give the flight a go. The three birds set off just after nwod and Cordelia immediately found the going difficult. Sid and Trev flew higher than she was used to, and they had a more loping gait in flight, flapping and dropping down before flapping their wings and rising again, all the while traveling in one direction. As they flew, they chatted merrily away about other birds they'd known and places they been.

Their flight technique was employed to save energy and take advantage of the strong dry outback updrafts, common in the area.

Cordelia though was a more traditional straight track flyer, and she flapped her wings more often and with greater purpose than the pied currawongs. Flapping more frequently while flying in a straight line, lower to the ground, she tired more quickly and used more energy in flight. Cordelia had not gone halfway to the hills when she realised she could not go further.

"I'll wait here," she called to the two pied currawong flying a few wing lengths ahead. She glided to a tree branch and waited for the two older birds to return. Behind her a long way off, she could see the station buildings shimmering in the heat haze. She'd not flown far, but her energy was gone. Her strength was sapped, and it was all she could do to hold on to the tree branch with her still weak claws.

Sid and Trev flew on, enjoying their flight, but they failed to recognise how exhausted Cordelia was. As she waited the sun blazed down on her, and she began to feel weak and dizzy. Her breathing rate increased, and her beak was open constantly as she tried desperately to cool down. She tried to fluff out her feathers and bring more blood to the surface of her skin. But still she began to boil under the heat of Elppa.

"I've gone and done too much too soon," she told herself. She felt a deep thirst and her head began to swim and swoon. She could see the two pied currawong disappearing into the distance. They looked small, like the flies that buzzed around Bruce's food dish. But were they going away, or coming back towards her? Even the thought of this choice seemed to have taxed her more than she could afford, and without another thought, her world went black.

-0-

Cordelia awoke with a bright light shining in her eyes. Brighter than anything she had seen before. *Or was it?* She recalled a thought or was it a dream when she'd seen a light like this. Her mind strained to grasp the memory. *It wasn't her*, she thought, *that was in the dream, it was another mytre who had been consumed by the bright light, brighter than Elppa. It had been her...* She struggled to see clearly in her mind. *It had a light like a star that surrounded her... father.*

In a flash as the bright light burnt into her mind, she recalled it all. She had been on the run, flying away from a mob of chasing mytre, the Krat clan, who wanted to kill her. Her father was helping by leading the vile Kratt hunters away, when a vehicle trapped him in its light and injured him with a thud. She remembered kneeling over his body. Holding his head in her wing as he said, 'Fly, go, fly!'

Suddenly she remembered to fly, but it was now too late. The bright light had trapped her, and she couldn't struggle against its power. The light held her too tightly and she couldn't move. Then the world went dark again. She was free but in darkness. She was back in the hollow of a tree or in a large black nest with high soft walls and a top.

Confused, she tried again to flap her wings, but the effort was too much, and she collapsed into a lying position, with her wings tucked into her flank, and her claws tucked under her belly. It didn't matter anymore, her father was dead, she was exhausted again and captured by the light. *The same light*, she thought, *that had killed my father*. Overcome with despair, grief and utter exhaustion, Cordelia was soon asleep.

-0-

"Your bird's not back," Mary said, concerned.

"I saw it flying off towards the west earlier today, with those strange currawong birds," her father said.

"Might have been taken by a wedgey," her mum said.

"Oh, don't say that!" Lilly exclaimed, distraught and on the brink of tears.

"Yer, it could be…" her dad agreed.

Lilly began to cry softly.

"But if yer want, we can go for a drive and look for it," her dad offered kindly.

Lilly dried her eyes and after going to fetch her torch she came to join her father in the ute.

Before he turned on the engine he said, "You know I did say she might just fly away, she's a wild bird after all."

"I know, Dad," Lilly replied, "'But I'm sure the bird hasn't gone yet."

They drove west a dozen kilometres. Her father had no hope that they would find the bird, but he felt obliged to do something to help his daughter and lessen her grief. The sky had turned bright red as the sun prepared to set and Lilly scanned the red, dust covered plain for any sign of life.

They had been driving slowly through the scrub and grass when Lilly cried out, "There!" She pointed to a scrawny tree almost devoid of leaves. "Those two stupid currawong things are there. Let's look there."

They pulled up a few metres from the tree and could clearly hear the two birds squawking and calling from the upper branches of the near-naked tree.

"She's over here, dears," Sid was calling.

"Down here, loves," Trev was shouting at the approaching Norzela.

"I do hope they've come in time," Sid said as the ksud light dimmed behind them, turning from bright red to soft crimson and finally darker red to black. "Thank goodness the norzela came," Sid squawked.

"I think we might have gone too far on her first flight," Trev cried, distraught.

This is very odd, Chris thought, scratching his head as he alighted from the ute. The sun had almost set before them, and the twilight made the scene by the barren tree most eerie. The two currawongs looked like carrion hunters waiting for something to die, before flying down to devour it, but having found their prey at their mercy they were too lazy to finish-off their victim. *I hope this isn't some sort of wicked bird trap,* Chris thought, remembering an old film he'd seen as a child.

"Take care, luv, we don't know what's happen here yet," he said to Lilly who was about to approach the tree with her torch on.

She scanned the ground near the tree, shining the thin torch beam across the scrub. She shone the torch light up at the two currawongs, who flew off as she approached.

"The light, the keere light," Trev shouted in fear, before the two birds took flight.

Then she shone her torch at the base of the tree trunk. There she saw a black and white bird, lying still on the ground. "Found something," she called excitedly over to her dad as she followed her torch light beam to the unmoving form on the ground. As she approached her worst fears filled her mind. *The bird is dead*, she thought, *Killed by a wedgy or attacked by the two strange currawong birds*. Tears formed in her eyes as she gently picked up the bird and cradled it to her breast. "It's still breathing, Dad," she said with relief.

Her dad was more relieved than she knew, or than he would ever admit, and he quickly wiped a tear away before his daughter saw it fall. "Come on," he said kindly, breathing a sigh, "let's get it back to the house."

-O-

When Cordelia woke, she was back in the cage. There was water in the drip feed system and mincemeat near her on the newspaper floor. She didn't notice but the cage door was still open. Her breath was not dry or parched and she could feel moisture on her pallet and throat.

Bruce was lying next to the cage, with his head pressed close to the bars as it rested on his forepaws. He had been distraught all night and hadn't left the side of the cage in case Cordelia woke. As she stirred, he smiled and sighed with relief. "Thank, El... pp... a, is that right?" he said a little unsure of the correct blessing.

Cordelia nodded her head slowly, as she regained consciousness. "I saw the light that took my father," she said, "It nearly took me too."

"The young norzela dripped water into your beak," Bruce said. "You had heat stroke," he added. "That's the second time this norzela has saved your life. You really are a blessed bird."

Cordelia rose to her feet. She felt weak, and feeble, but she took a few steps and even managed to eat some of the mincemeat. "I'm not blessed," Cordelia said bitterly. "Tomorrow, when I am feeling better, I have something important to tell you, Sid, and Trev. Something I remembered in a dream." Then she walked into a corner of the cage and sat down to rest. She was soon asleep, dreaming and recalling the events at the valley before she left.

Her sleep was not settled, and Bruce who watched her all night, could see her twitch and flinch as she relived the flight to escape with her father in her dreams.

In her dreams, she also saw a large mytre with one of Egnaro's stars on his forehead. She couldn't breathe and she was at his mercy. But she didn't feel afraid. She'd seen the bird before. *Kratt,* she thought, as her dreams rose and fell in her wakeless mind. Kratt was standing over her, but she felt strangely calm and unafraid. Then in a flash he was gone, and she could breathe again.

22

Butcher's Block

I saw a beggar leaning on his wooden crutch
He said to me, "You must not ask for so much."

And a pretty woman leaning in her darkened door
She cried to me, "Hey, why not ask for more?"

Oh, like a bird on the wire
Like a drunk in a midnight choir
I have tried in my way to be free.

Leonard Cohen – 'Bird on a Wire' (1969)

CORDELIA TOLD BRUCE, Sid, and Trev all about the valley, the elpitlum, the invasion, the Kratt clan, the mutilation of Karbett, their flight from the chasing Krat hunters and her father's death in the lights of a vehicle.

The savage world outside the homestead stunned Bruce, who had only ever known life as a pup with his litter and life on the station as a house dog.

"I'm glad I don't live there," Bruce said at the end of Cordelia's terrible tale. "It's far safer here," he decided. Then he added, almost as an afterthought, "I'm sorry to hear about your clan lands and your father being lost though."

Sid and Trev agreed that she had been lucky to escape and survive, but that she was safer here at the station with her new friends.

Emotions cut Cordelia. She was pleased and relieved that she'd finally recalled much of what she knew about her life before coming to the station, but she was also sad and bitter about recalling the events that led up to her flight and fall. "No, you don't understand," Cordelia cried, despondently, "I have to get back. I have to find my mother, my brother and kill Kratt and retake my clan lands."

"But you don't even know how to get to the valley," Bruce said abjectly.

"I'm sorry too, but I'm sure it's a long way from here," said Sid offering his condolences.

"Best to forget it all," Trev suggested, dismissively.

"No… no," Cordelia cried, "My home is in the valley. My mother may still be alive. I have to try and get back." Cordelia began to sob.

"But you're still too weak to try. You collapsed after only a short flight and your speed and agility in the air need considerable improvement," Sid reminded her.

Cordelia knew he was right. She could only just fly, and weakly at that. She had no idea which direction to take, and she couldn't make a long journey even if she did know the way.

Bruce pawed her wing gently, with concern. "Don't go, it's too far, too risky… stay here… stay with us here… it's safer here."

Cordelia could see he meant well. She stretched a wing out over his head. *Where would I go? What direction should I take?* she thought. Cordelia had no choice really. At this point all she could do was stay at the station. But sadness overwhelmed her at the thought. After a while of contemplating her situation, Cordelia declared, "I guess you're stuck with me at least until I am stronger."

"A wise choice, dear," said Sid, relieved.

"Capital decision, sweet," Trev agreed.

Cordelia really could do little else without any idea where the valley was or how far it was from the station. Although, having finally remembered her early life with her family and relatives in the Cor clan, she was determined to find a way home, somehow, one day.

Cordelia perched on the veranda railing, looking out across the station. She'd resigned herself, at least for now, to life on the station. Bruce was right, it was safe and comfortable. She had no territory to defend or siblings to squabble with. Clearly, she was as blessed as the Cordelia from myth, but she still found herself feeling disconsolate. A deep sadness rose within her that she couldn't keep down. It ate at her sense of calm and gnawed at her soul. Or was it something else.

She decided to sing out in the nwod chorus to Elppa thinking this might help. As she began, the sound of something that also seemed to gnaw at her sense of calm distracted her. *The yard-dogs,* she thought, suddenly. She could hear the yard-dogs barking beyond the shearing shed and near the vehicle store shed. *I wonder what is the matter,* she thought. Curious as always, she took off to investigate. Cordelia was far more confident conversing with dogs after days of practice with Bruce and she landed on top of one of the kennels to make enquiries.

"Elppa's greeting to you all," Cordelia began.

"Piss off, mate," said one of the yard-dog rudely.

Cordelia was taken aback but responded kindly, "You seem upset or agitated and I thought I'd come to see if I can help."

"You're right, but you can't help. Now piss off," the disgruntled dog said.

"I can try… if you'll tell me what's the matter," Cordelia persisted.

A second yard-dog responded. "He's forgotten again. He sometimes forgets, but it's been a long time since we were fed, and we're getting hungry."

Anticipating Cordelia's next question, the oldest of the yard-dogs, who was not barking loudly, said, "The master's oldest son, he means well, but he gets distracted, and he's forgotten to feed us. It's been a full day and we've not been fed. The big master, his dad… he was the same, always forgetting to feed us."

"That's terrible," Cordelia said, sympathetically. "I can fly and tell him," she offered.

"It's no use, he's out shooting roos or something. He won't be back until tonight."

"Or even tomorrow," the smallest yard-dogs added. "All we can do is protest and hope a norzela comes to feed us."

Cordelia recognised this as an opportunity to build favour with the yard-dogs and she pondered what she could do to help them. She was also glad to be thinking about something other than how she might get to the valley. She thought for a moment then said, as she took to the wing, "I'll be back soon."

When she'd flown above the station a few days earlier, she had been aware of a rotten smell coming from a building behind the shearing shed. Although she hadn't been there herself, she knew it must contain some sort of food storage or preparation area that was used to prepare food for the yard dogs. *I'll begin my search there,* she thought.

She flew the short distance to the room at the back of the shearing shed. The door was locked with a chain and bolt, but a square of wood was missing from one of the upright planks of the door. It was down low and looked like it was big enough for her or even Bruce to bob through. Cordelia landed near the hole in the door and walked about for a moment, exploring the area for danger or predators.

Bruce had said there were wedge-tailed eagles and snakes in that area of the property, but he'd never seen one. Sid and Trev had said there was a large eagle that flew by every so often, but that they were mainly interested in the fat lambs, rather than old birds like them, and it always flew too high to worry them.

Cordelia looked about one last time and seeing that the area was clear, she ducked under the broken plank and into the darkness of the room. She hesitated a moment while her eyes adjusted to the dim light about her.

The room had a large, tall, round wooden block in its centre with a smaller wooden block, full of silver metal norzela things, sitting on it. She flew up and perched on the large wooden block. On one side of the room, she saw a row of hooks up high and from one, the fleshy carcass of a kangaroo hung. Stripped of its fur, the skin and muscle were visible. It hung upside down, hooked by its leg's sinews. Blood had run down the kangaroo's body and had dripped from its nose to the concrete floor. A small pool of congealed blood lay below it.

Cordelia felt a wave of nausea rush over her. She looked away and could see parts of other slaughtered animals on hooks or in trays around the room. Everything looked far too heavy for her to carry or fly with. She told herself, *I might be able to drag a small amount of meat out through the hole in the door, but I couldn't drag enough to feed the four yard-dogs.* Cordelia felt frustrated and considered what her other options might be. *Maybe Bruce would help?* She thought.

Quickly, she flew to the hole in the door and walked out into the bright afternoon Elppa. She flew over to the homestead veranda and called for Bruce to come outside.

Bruce was asleep on his bed in the kitchen, and he woke slowly and stretched before padding over to the dog-door in the flyscreen. "What is it?" he asked, with a yawn.

"Will you help me?" Cordelia asked, "I need a thief."

Bruce was still half asleep. He agreed without knowing what he was required to do, thinking it might be a game. Then Cordelia explained what it was she wanted him to do.

This shocked Bruce into wakefulness. "Go across the yard?" Bruce said in response to Cordelia's instructions. "No way, I'm a housedog, a lap-dog, not an adventurous do or die work in the hot sun-dog. No… I'm not going."

Cordelia pleaded with him, "You'll be a hero, you'll save the day and win the respect of the yard-dogs forever." Bruce wasn't sure. "You said it yourself, the house is a safe place. Come on let's have an adventure. You only live once," Cordelia told him, adding, "There's no one there, and the food is just waiting to be taken." She nudged him with her wing and said, "Come on, be brave and adventurous with me. It'll be fun."

"Can I get some of the food?" he asked.

"All you want… after the yard-dogs get their share," Cordelia confirmed.

"Okay," Bruce said reluctantly, with a half wag of his tail.

Cordelia flew over to the slaughterhouse door and waited for Bruce to arrive. He sprinted across the station yard, and panting, appeared at Cordelia's side. His fear had diminished as his excitement grew and he was now keen for the sport.

"I'll go in first," Cordelia said, "then you come in. I'll push the meat tray off the bench, and you take pieces of meat to the yard-dogs, one at a time."

Bruce nodded and yapped excitedly. Cordelia bobbed into the room through the small hole in the lower part of the door. She waited for her eyes to adjust to the light again, but Bruce bounded in behind her and pushed forward into the room. His eyes darted about as he surveyed the room. All he could smell was flesh. Meat of every sort assaulted his senses, and his nose began to twitch and sniff in every direction.

Cordelia flew up onto the bench on one side of the room and slowly began to nuzzle a tray of cut meat toward the edge of the bench. A thin layer of cling film covered it to keep it fresh, however a small horde of flies had settled on the surface of the film. These buzzed into the air as soon as Cordelia pushed the tray forward.

Below her, Bruce wagged his tail and panted in delight and anticipation as he watched the meat tray slide slowly in his direction.

"It's too heavy," Cordelia called, out of breath. Without a second thought, other than for the prospect of food, Bruce leapt in one go onto a stool and then up, onto the bench top. His sudden arrival startled Cordelia, but within a moment they were both eagerly pushing and sliding the meat tray forward towards the edge of the bench.

Bruce was almost crazed with delight with his nose so close to the meat. It took all their strength, but soon, the tray was about to topple. In anticipation of the fall, Bruce jumped back down to the shed floor.

Cordelia gave it one last push and it crashed with a clang to the concrete floor.

Bruce pulled back, frightened by the noise, then gingerly approached the meat tray sniffing wildly as he did. The cling film had lifted on impact, and he could reach a few of the pieces of meat that had fallen from the tray.

"Take them to the yard-dogs," Cordelia reminded him, commandingly.

"Can I try a piece first?" Bruce asked as he sniffed the meat.

"No," Cordelia called sternly, "feed your hungry fellows first."

Bruce looked chastened but understood. He took a large piece of meat into his jaws. It tasted wonderful. Bruce, as the house-dog, had always been spoilt. He'd had the best treats, dog and norzela biscuits, the finest foods, and been treated with great care. But this meat, this raw untreated kangaroo meat, it was... he could hardly describe it, tender, sweet, delicious. He could have been in dog heaven. Still, he pushed through the hole in the door and with tremendous self-control, he strode over to the yard-dogs' kennels.

"This is from Cordelia and I," he said proudly as he placed the piece of meat on the ground, just beyond the reach of the oldest yard-dogs. He then turned and with his hind legs, he flicked the meat toward the still barking old yard-dog, who caught it and swallowed it in one gulp.

"Where's ours," the other yard-dog barked loudly.

"Coming," Bruce said as he ran back, excitedly, to the meat store.

Cordelia walked about the butcher's chopping block, picking at the scraps of dry meat left on the wooden surface or wedged into cracks where the knife had pushed the meat into the wood.

Bruce came in quickly through the hole in the door, his tail wagging and his tongue lolling foolishly out of the side of his mouth. Without hesitation, he chomped onto another piece of meat. This one was far too big for him to carry, and he dragged it as he walked backwards towards the door. It took a number of tugs and pulls to get the meat through the hole in the door.

Dirt covered the meat, but the yard-dog who received it – the youngest and smallest of them – was pleased non-the-less and barked her thanks as Bruce ran off for another meal. After several trips back and forth, all the yard-dogs had been served a small amount of the stolen meat.

Cordelia was busy exploring the meat store when something caught her eye. The room was cool and dark, but near the ceiling, a beam of Elppa's light shone on a high narrow roof beam. Cordelia had to look for a long time before she was sure something was there. *It couldn't be mice or rats,* she thought, *they are small and fast.* She turned her neck to get a better look.

Bruce came in and went directly to the fallen tray. He moved some of the residual cling film and took another piece of meat in his mouth. Without looking at Cordelia, whose eyes were transfixed by the creature, he darted out through the hole and was gone, back to the yard-dogs for another fast-food delivery.

The creature moved slowly, as it uncoiled. "What are you?" the creature asked with a hiss.

"I'm Cordelia," she responded, trembling, "a mytre of clan Cor. Elppa's greetings to you," she added politely.

"Elppa…" the creature scoffed. "Elppa is the light, I am a creature of the night, of dark holes and the hidden places. I am Egnaro's child. I am called Yrarbil… I am death. Lightning that strikes the slow; coils that strangle the small and weak."

Cordelia froze. She had been told that night creatures like this existed, all mytre tell their chicks the tale of snakes, the deceiver, the taker of light, the dark lightning strike, the strangler.

Cordelia's mother had told her about how snakes would steal the eggs and chicks from unguarded nests.

"This is my place, my home," Yrarbil hissed. Then in a deep emotionless accusation, it hissed, "You're trespassing."

"I'm sorry," Cordelia said, "forgive our intrusion." Cordelia bowed low and was about to fly to the hole in the door and leave when Bruce charged in through the door and started sniffing about the fallen tray of kangaroo meat.

"This stuff is the best," Bruce barked excitedly before starting to eat some of the pieces of meat that had fallen clear of the tray.

"We came for food for the yard-dogs. Their master had neglected to feed them, and we were..." Cordelia began to explain.

"Yard-dogs," the snake hissed angrily. "We hate them. We hate their teeth, their barking; they're fools."

"Bruce," Cordelia called, urgently, "we have to go."

"No, you said I could eat some once the yard-dogs were fed... well they are and now it's my turn." He could hardly get the words out his mouth was so full of food. Just then a massive thing fell between him and the door. He jumped back from the meat tray and looked through the dim light in the slaughter room as the creature curled into a tower before him.

Yrarbil was ready to strike at Bruce, when Cordelia flew down and flapped between her friend and the gaping, fang filled mouth of the snake. As she left the butcher's block, she clipped the knife block and the knifes it held tumbled to the concrete floor of the room. Bruce jumped again and started to panic.

"Run," Cordelia called to her friend.

Bruce, unsure what to do, first ran behind the butcher's block while Cordelia darted about, wing feathers flashing in front of Yrarbil so she couldn't see her target.

Bruce, still with a mouth full of tender, succulent kangaroo meat, made a dash for the hole in the slaughterhouse door. He dodged and weaved past the snake as he tried to reach the door.

Yrarbil hissed at Cordelia, "Out of my way, bat," as an insult.

Bruce jumped quickly across the snake's curled body and then dived for the hole in the door.

He skidded through just as Yrarbil saw him go and struck out at his rump. She missed. Disappointed, she slithered toward the hole and blocked it with her body.

Bruce, safely outside, ran all the way back to the homestead.

"Now… you're stuck, bat," Yrarbil's tone was evil, dark, and malicious.

Cordelia flew back up to the butcher's block and perched there a moment as she considered her options.

The snake slowly uncurled leaving her tail quivering near the small opening low in the door. "You have nowhere to run, do you, bat?"

The snake is right, but I don't run, thought Cordelia. Yrarbil was about to climb the leg of the butcher's block and reach Cordelia when Cordelia looked up and saw the ray of Elppa's light shining above her. *The light,* she thought. "Thank you, Elppa," she cried as she took flight, flying up to the top of the room.

Part of the corrugated tin roof had come lose, and it allowed both a shaft of light into the room, and provided a small, bird sized hole, for Cordelia to scramble and fidget through, most ungracefully. Once out of the meat store, she flew over the yard-dogs, where they all barked with gratitude and joy as she passed over head.

"'There's a snake in the meat room," Cordelia shouted to them, above the sound of their barking. "I'm sorry we can't bring you more food."

The dogs barked their thanks and Cordelia flew back to the homestead where Bruce crouched behind one of the veranda chairs.

"That was close," Cordelia said as she landed on the veranda railing.

"That's why I don't leave the house," Bruce said, out of breath and still chewing on the remnants of the kangaroo meat.

Cordelia burst into song. Praising Elppa and his help with her escape from the keere snake.

In the meat store, Yrarbil slithered toward the hole in the door and following the scent of the tiny chihuahua, it moved away under the foundations of the shearing shed, across from the homestead. Its long quivering tongue searched the air for the dog's scent as its body curled and slid forward so that it was completely hidden in the dark, cool, dry foundations under the shearing shed. "We'll meet again," Yrarbil said to herself, as she curled into a coil, waiting for nightfall.

23

Stars

Hear me now and understand
He's gonna find me some piece of mind.
And if that piece of mind won't stay
I'm gonna find myself a better way.

Carly Simon – 'Mockingbird' (1974)

THE THREE BIRDS; Cordelia, Sid, and Trev, were sitting on the veranda railing late one evening. The norzela family were all inside watching the *picture window-box but Cordelia had grown tired of the flashing blue light and the noise. Sid and Trev were in a relaxed mood, and they all looked out over the night sky.

"Do you know all their names?" Trev asked Sid looking at the stars.

"No, not all of them," he replied. "Most of them though," Trev bragged, proudly.

Cordelia was impressed. "I don't know any of them," she said feeling a little uneducated and ignorant.

"Oh well, you wouldn't, would you – if you serve Elppa." Trev looked scornfully at Cordelia. "Elppa's not interested in the sky of Egnaro. Just the bright blue Elppa sky."

"But Egnaro's sky is beautiful too," Cordelia suggested. "Especially here, in the wide-open outback."

**The mytre words for a TV.*

"Some birds say you can fly at night if you know how to read the stars," Trev said.

"Only the boobook owl says that," Sid said mockingly. "All he knows is, "Boo book, boo book.""

"No, all birds," Trev asserted, "All birds can follow the stars and find their way if they know how."

Cordelia didn't care, she just enjoyed watching them twinkle and sparkle in the great black beyond.

"All birds should know about the stars," Trev insisted. "You can find your way, north, south, west, and east, if you know the stars to follow. They're part of us all. They are the eggs all birds come from."

"Here we go," said Sid, "Now you've got him started."

Trev pointed with a wing into the inky blackness at a line of stars that sat distinctively in the sky. "For example, look at Orion's belt, there, they are the only three bright stars that form a short straight line in the whole night sky and they rise very close to due east, and set very close to due west," Trevor explained.

"I warned you not to get him started, Darling," Sid said with a sigh.

"Have I ever told you the story about how the stars came to be?" Trev began.

Cordelia hadn't heard the story and flew over to the blanket on top of her cage to settle and listen to his story.

Sid joined her, as Trevor began his explanation.

"Once," Trevor began, "there were no stars. Elppa and Egnaro lived in either the complete brightness of Elppa's light, or partial darkness of Egnaro's glow alone in the sky. Elppa was happy with his light, his colour and the life that grew about him in the day. Egnaro though was unhappy in darkness, she felt alone in the night sky and asked Elppa for children to keep her company

"Elppa loved Egnaro, but he didn't want children to steal his glory and brightness. He could see Egnaro was lonely, and he asked his friend, the mytre, Cordelia to help him trick Egnaro.

"Cordelia was very afraid to help, not wanting to incur the wrath of Egnaro, or displeasure of Elppa, but she agreed to help if she could. Elppa asked Cordelia to take a message to Egnaro on his behalf. She agreed, reluctantly, and listened to his message with great care. 'Tell Egnaro, I cannot give her the children she seeks. I am sorry she is lonely, but I do not want children other than the children I have on the earth; the animals, the fish, and the birds.'

"Cordelia was full of trepidation as she flew to Egnaro to give her the message. But she was too afraid to give Egnaro bad news, so she said, 'Faithfully, my lord Elppa knows you are lonely, he also knows that you will be unable to care for children without giving up your cycle, and he hopes you will accept eggs, for you to incubate and keep safe. One day they may hatch and become your children.' Egnaro thought about the message for a moment and replied, 'Thank you mytre, I will accept Elppa's eggs and care for them as best I can.'

"Cordelia flew back to Elppa and said, 'Lord there is a way you can give Egnaro what she wants without giving her children. My lord, Egnaro doesn't want children, she's just lonely and wants company through the long dark night.' She paused and took a breath before saying, 'Can I suggest you send her eggs filled with your light so that she can have some company in her dark cold world.'

"Elppa was at first angry that Cordelia had not passed on his original message, but he soon saw the value in Cordelia's idea. 'Eggs, you suggest, filled with my light?' Instead of punishing Cordelia, he ordered her to return to Egnaro with the first egg that night.

"Cordelia flew to the Lady Egnaro and said, 'My Lord Elppa asks that I give you this egg for you to incubate.' Egnaro replied, 'But I cannot sit on an egg as you know, how will I incubate an egg if I am on the move all night?' 'I have a suggestion," Cordelia said, 'You could hang the egg in the heavens, where you can see it and where the darkness and emptiness of space will keep it safe and protected. Lord Elppa has blessed the egg with light so that each night you can see the egg shining in your honour.'

"Delighted, Egnaro agreed, and Cordelia flew into the heavens and placed the egg that became a star, high in the night sky. The next night Cordelia returned with another egg and Egnaro instructed that she do the same. This occurred for the next thousand nights. Each night, Cordelia would bring a new egg and Egnaro instructed her to hang it in the heavens as a star.

"Cordelia soon realised that as the number of eggs grew, and became stars, she was starting to lose track of all the stars, and she was afraid she would lose her way in the night sky. To help find her way, Cordelia began to arrange the stars into constellations and shapes so that they would guide her on her journeys. To point south, she made the Southern Cross, to find north, she placed the north star, and arranged the constellations so she could find her way and they would help with her nightly navigation.

"Cordelia placed eggs that became stars with the influence of Elppa's light and Egnaro was delighted with the light and company they gave. Soon there were many thousands of stars blinking and twinkling whenever Egnaro appeared, and the stars shone every night and were a constant source of company for Egnaro. She soon forgot about wanting children and was happy with her lover's light for company. Cordelia was rewarded by Elppa with the wisdom to navigate the night sky, knowledge she passed on to all birds, although many have forgotten the gift."

Cordelia thought about Trevor's story. "So, I could find my way home if I knew the way, while being guided by the stars?"

"In theory," Trevor said grudgingly.

"So, the mythical Cordelia helped place the stars as a map to guide her at night?" Cordelia confirmed.

"And because they gave pleasure to Egnaro and helped brighten the night sky," Sid put in, to show he'd been listening too.

Cordelia had never heard this story before, and as the three birds continued to gaze upon the bright, twinkling lights in the far-off night sky, Cordelia began to ponder what value Trev's story might have in her own search for a way home.

24

Gary

White bird, dreams of the aspen trees
With their dying leaves, turning gold.
But the white bird, just sits in her cage.
Growing old
The sunsets come, the sunsets go
The clouds roll by, and the earth turns old
And the young bird's eyes, do always glow.
White bird must fly, or she will die.

It's a Beautiful Day – 'White Bird" (1969)

CORDELIA WOKE TO the sound of a *shotgun* going off. She'd heard the sound before, although this one sounded closer to the homestead than the others she'd heard. The yard-dogs had told Cordelia that it was the norzela who made the sound as they hunted kangaroo in the night. They were always excited by the noise as it usually meant a big feed of kangaroo for them. But the sound today, as well as being closer to the norzela's nest, rang out in the early light, near nwad.

Startled by the noise, she was prompted to begin her nwad chorus early. To do so, she hopped out of the cage that had now become her nest, and she perched on top of the blanket that covered the roof of the cage.

"Shut that bloody bird up," someone called from inside the norzela nest.

Lilly shouted, "Well, tell those boys to wa t until after breakfast before shooting at the bloody roos."

Cordelia, who didn't understand the norzela conversation continued her rejoicing of Elppa as usual. Cordelia liked sitting on top of her cage. She could see across the station's pale, thin lawn, to the shearing shed. She could see what was going on, and about the veranda, and see the norzela when they sat outside.

She could also see the pictures on the strange colourful picture window-box across the open-plan kitchen to the living room, where the picture window-box sat. After chorusing for nwad each day, Cordelia liked nothing more than to watch the big colourful picture window-box from her place on top of her cage. It was sometimes alive at night, after ksud, when the family of norzela's would sit about and laugh or cry or smile as they watched it.

She didn't like it then. It disturbed her sleep and gave off an eery blue glow in the half dark of the house. But she did like it in the morning. In the morning, the colourful picture window-box was always on, and it flashed and blinked with what she thought looked like stories and information. An unusual sort of norzela elpitlum, she assumed.

She couldn't understand the stories or information, or what the norzela were saying as they talked or shouted at the picture window-box, but it seemed to hold a vital place in the norzela nest and in the family structure. Sometimes she just liked the hum and noise it gave off. At other times she liked the flashing images and pictures. They seemed real and she longed to get into the norzela nest to have a closer look at the strange picture window-box of light and sound.

Sometime after Elppa was rising in the sky, Cordelia was still watching the picture window-box, while the norzela family ate their breakfast. Lilly's brothers returned to the homestead for breakfast. They both appeared excited and vaulted up the veranda steps and in through the back door, with gusto. Lilly's older brother kicked at the cage as he passed, causing it to rock and Cordelia to flap her wings to keep her balance. "Stupid bird," he said as they went inside.

"I think I hit it, Dad," the older brother said, his excitement barely contained.

"Yer missed, I reckon," said the younger brother. "You've always been a piss weak shot."

"Have not," protested the older brother.

"Have so... piss weak."

They faced off across the table as their mother said, "Enough, now... eat your bacon and eggs. You've a lot to do today. The sheep are ready for drenching, and you and Lilly are gunna help yer dad."

"Arr, Mum, I just shot that bloody eagle that's bin carryin' off the lambs."

"No," cried Lilly, "they're protected."

"They are if yer dickhead brother here is shootin'," said the younger brother. "He couldn't hit an elephant if it was ten feet away."

"I got it, I said," the older brother protested loudly.

"Eat yer breaky, boys," their dad said. "And stop shootin' at the bloody eagles. You know you aren't meant to." But he winked at the older boy as he spoke. He knew they took too many of his lambs and he would welcome the bird's destruction.

-0-

Cordelia sat on the blanket, on top of the wire cage watching the picture window-box and gazing across the station. The open cage had become a safe place in the alien land she'd found herself in, unless Lilly's older brother was passing unobserved. Then he'd stretch out a boot and kick at the cage, and usually say, 'Stupid bird'.

Today, as the norzela workers walked past Cordelia's cage, most threw a scrap of food onto the cage's blanket for Cordelia. Lilly's younger brother threw a scrap of bacon. Lilly threw a half-eaten crust off some toast, and her father Chris, threw a quarter slice of toast covered with vegemite.

However, Lilly's older brother who followed them out, showed Cordelia a slice of toast, waved it between his fingers, then ate it himself. Then he kicked the cage and said, "Stupid bird," as he walked away.

Cordelia had started to sing and carol in gratitude of the gifts but stopped once he kicked her cage.

"Geezes that's a bloody happy bird," said Lilly's younger brother as he crossed the yard.

"It doesn't have to spend all day dip'n bloody sheep, does it? I'd sing too if I just had to sit about, get fed, and sing all day," her oldest brother suggested as he caught them up.

"God help us, you can't sing, can you?" Lilly exclaimed.

"Can't shoot either," added her younger brother.

"I tell you I got it," the older brother protested again.

"Come on, you lot," their dad said, "let's get this mob of sheep wet."

Cordelia ate the offerings as quickly as she could. She especially liked the dark brown sticky covering on the bread. When she'd finished, she watched the four workers walk over to the shearing shed and the sheep holding pens beyond. *What is wrong with Lilly's older brother,* she thought.

Well recovered from her heat stroke, Cordelia had started to fly about the property again. The day before this, she had flown back to the tree where she had collapsed and made the journey there and back without trouble. She had rested for a while at the tree, before returning, but she was feeling stronger and stronger with each flight.

Today, she planned to undertake some smaller flights and test her speed. Flying itself was not the issue. What she really needed to develop was her speed and aerial acrobatic ability. Today, she thought she'd start with speed. A dilapidated windmill and water trough stood about 300 metres behind the shearing shed, and Cordelia's plan was to time herself flying between the shearing shed and the old windmill tower. She made sure to stretch before she left for her trial, and she flew only slowly out to the shearing shed. She perched on the apex of the iron roof and looked about the station.

Lilly, her father and two brothers were busily herding sheep into pens before guiding them through a set of fenced paths that led to a long water trough. There they pushed and cajoled the sheep into the water where chemicals, mixed with the water treated lice and other sheep related infestations. Cordelia didn't really understand it.

It had been the yard-dogs who'd told her about the process and while it seemed barbaric to her at first, the dog said it was a norzela way of keeping the sheep healthy and growing more wool. The dogs were there today running about and nipping at the sheep as they helped guide and push them through the maze of fences and gates. Cordelia was impressed with the way the yard-dogs jumped over and walked on the sheep's back as they kept the drenching process moving.

Cordelia looked west, out over the unending grass plain, toward the low hills and mountains in the distance. Triodia Scariosa grass grew in individual tussocks and clumps between the low shrubs and weedy gums. She could see no Spotted Gums or tall trees suitable as nest trees. She wondered though if that way, west, was the way to the valley. If that was where she would find her mother and brother, if they were still alive, and where she would find the evil Lord Kratt and his clan of thieves and murderers.

Then she looked east. Elppa was already gaining height in the sky, and she could feel it would be another hot day. She saw the road to the property came in from the east and disappeared into the distance, near a clump of low scrubby Eucalyptus Gracilis trees and Scribbly Gums that sprouted from a trunk low to the ground. It made the trees look like big shrubs or bushes and Cordelia knew this was not her home or country. North, south, east, or west, Cordelia had no idea which way to go to find her home. All she could do was prepare for the flight whenever it came.

She could see the broken windmill standing alone in one of the dry, barren paddocks a short distance from the shearing shed.

A water trough sat at its base and a few clumps of the long Triodia Scariosa grass or some weeds sprouted from the foot of each of the four struts that held the windmill aloft. Cordelia braced herself for flight.

Slowly at first, she told herself. She took off, lifting herself into the air gracefully. As she gained height, she turned and sped up, aiming for the windmill. The sails were made of metal, and she kept a wide birth to avoid the risk of a collision. As she looped around the tower like structure, she lifted her head and rose into the sky, almost gliding gracefully upwards. Then gaining speed she dived back down and gathered pace. She felt comfortable, confident, and sure that she was ready to stretch herself in a greater test of speed. Within a moment, she landed back on the shearing shed's tin roof.

Again... this time faster, she told herself. Cordelia spread her wings wide and shot off from the tin roof, she could feel her speed grow as she neared the windmill. Then she turned to loop about it. This time she dived down under the wind sails as she looped around the structure. She was about to sprint away when something odd caught her eye. Something was blended into the red brown soil but didn't belong amongst the grasses or weeds at the base of one of the windmill legs. She pulled up suddenly using her tail feathers and pivoted back toward the windmill. She came to rest on one of the windmill cross struts.

Cordelia looked down at the strange shape of what looked like a massive, feathered creature. She hopped down onto another metal strut and took a closer look. *It looks to be injured*, she thought. The creature was still breathing, she could see that, but she could also see that it was wounded. Blood lay on the ground and over the brown, hazel, and dusty feathers. Its wings were spread wide, and one looked to be at an unusual angle. *Broken*, Cordelia thought.

Worse than this, one of the creature's feet was horribly deformed, blood and dirt hid the true extent of its injuries, for its left talon looked to have been almost completely blown off and the leg lay with its useless talon half-hooked on the branch of a scrubby bush.

The creature's eyes were closed, but as Cordelia dropped onto a lower metal strut to get a closer look, one of its eyes opened slowly.

"I'm not dead yet," the bird said in a deep low voice as it eyed the smaller bird with suspicion.

"Thank Elppa," Cordelia said, compassionately.

"Piss off," the wedgie snapped. "Elppa can't help me, and neither can you. Can't you see what the norzela did to me."

"The norzela did this?" Cordelia replied, shocked and unsure if she could believe the creature. *They're so nice to me*, she thought remembering everything Lilly and her family had done for her. Apart from her oldest brother, he seemed cruel, or at least negligent.

"Yes... now go and... let me die... in peace." The eagle became breathless as he spoke, and his eyes closed again.

"I can help you," Cordelia said. The great bird didn't respond, although she could hear the big bird's deep raspy breaths and quiet moans as it tried to get comfortable. Cordelia hopped closer to the bird. *What sort of bird is it?* she wondered. Bruce had talked about a massive bird called an emu. Cordelia's mother had told her about them, she was sure. They had grown too fat to fly and she had called them emu as well. But this bird had beautiful plumage and did not seem too fat to fly.

"Who are you?" Cordelia asked, gently, suddenly afraid of the answer.

The bird opened its eyes and looked directly at Cordelia. "I... I'm Gary, son of Garth, grandson of Graham, great grandson of George, and descendant of the Great Gus, from the western mountain cliffs." He paused to allow his lineage to settle on the smaller bird and to catch his breath after his elaborate explanation. Then he added, "I'm a wedge-tailed eagle."

Cordelia was stunned. *An eagle,* she thought. She'd heard this name before. Her mind reeled as the memory slowly came to the fore. *An eagle... an eagle had killed her brother, hadn't it?*

"Killer!" she screamed and flew back to the top of the windmill. *How could I have forgotten?* she asked herself. *Coruell was killed on his first flight. Taken by a wedge-tailed eagle on the wing. And here I am with one before me dying, wounded by a norzela. I can just go... just leave this bird to its deserved fate*, she thought, *But... I'd be dead now if not for the help of strangers.* Her mind tugged between thoughts of revenge and retribution, and forgiveness and kindness.

She looked back at the injured bird. It looked pathetic and weak, a threat to no one. Still a wave of hate for the large bird that killed her young brother swept over her. *I could watch this one die, I could sing at its death, and rejoice at its demise,* she pondered. Her thoughts caught her off guard. *'Is this who I am now?'* she thought. The wave passed. *'I could live with hate in my heart,* she thought, *but to truly fly free, hate is too great a burden to carry. I will fly higher and further, with love and forgiveness as my guide.* Her mind was now clear. Cordelia flapped down to the ground and landed near the prostrate, injured eagle. He immediately opened his eyes.

"I thought I told you to leave," the bigger bird demanded in a deep voice that broke into a low cough with the effort of his demand and left him exhausted.

"I'm going to help you," Cordelia said, "even if you don't want me too." She could see the eagle was too weak to resist and she set to work helping the bird. She looked at his injured foot. It was in a dreadful state, *I'll deal with that last,* she thought. She could see small black stones embedded in his wing and flank. *These must be the cause of the injury*, she assumed.

Without stopping to consult Gary further, Cordelia began to peck at the black stones. They were easy to reach, and hard, harder than any seed she had tried to eat. Gary lay back and endured the bird's pecking until Cordelia finally said, "I think that's all of them." A small pile of blood-soaked black pellets that she had removed lay beside her. "I need to cover the wounds, I'll be back in a short while," Cordelia said, as she rose into the sky.

She was gone only a short while. She'd flown quickly to the working windmill near the sheep pens and scooped up some moss from the surface of the water. Carrying it in her beak she returned with it to Gary and started to drape lines of the moss across the injured parts of his abdomen, chest, and wing. *Now the foot,* she thought. It looked very badly injured with the lower leg only being held on by a slender tendon. The claw looked to be black and necrotic, as if it had already died.

"Can you move your injured claw?" Cordelia asked, suspecting he could not.

Gary tried, but he was in such pain he gave up almost immediately. "How was that?"' he asked, breathing heavily. Cordelia's face said it all. Her eyes were open wide, and her dark face took on a pale tinge.

"That bad, hey?" Gary said as he looked at her. "I've got another talon, so all is not lost," he said calmly. "Best to take it off now," Gary said. "It'll be useless like it is now."

Cordelia looked at Gary's large, curved beak and the other still functional talon. Suddenly, Cordelia felt vulnerable next to the massive hunter.

Gary sensed her trepidation. "You need not worry, friend," he said softly, in a deep voice, almost kindly, as if it was he who was helping her. "I'll not harm you. You have the word of Gary, son of Garth, grandson of Graham, great grandson of George, and descendant of the Great Gus from the western mountain cliffs."

Cordelia nodded in response, acknowledging his pledge. She swallowed and stepped forward towards his injured leg. Gary laid his head back and closed his eyes.

25

Thief

Late at night when the wind is still.
I'll come flying through your door.
And you'll know what love is for
I'm a bluebird.

Paul McCartney and Wings – 'Bluebird' (1973)

CORDELIA FLEW BACK to the homestead. Only Mary was at home, cooking dinner for the four workers who were still at work with the sheep. She knew they would return soon as ksud was approaching. Cordelia landed on the blanket on top of the cage and began to sing. She lifted her voice in celebration of the approaching ksud and also in the hope that Mary would come from the house with a reward for her chorus. She sang beautifully as usual, but Mary seemed unimpressed. *Maybe she is too busy,* Cordelia thought.

Cordelia hopped down from the cage and walked up to the hole Bruce used to go in and out of the norzela nest. She poked the flap with her beak. It swung away from her a little. She tapped it again. It swung a little further away from her. She pushed it this time and popped her head into the norzela nest. It was warm inside and she could see the female norzela preparing fooc on a bench top and stove. Cordelia bobbed through the dog hole and stood inside the kitchen door, on a black rubber mat. *I'll sing again,* she thought and began to carol at the top of her voice.

"What the... how did you get in here?" Mary cried with surprise. "Cheeky bird... out you go." Mary approached the back door to open it and let the intruder out, but the magpie flew over to the kitchen bench and started to peck at the lamb roast she'd just taken from the oven.

"Hey, get away," Mary cried as she pushed the screen door wide and propped it open with an outside chair. Then she returned to the kitchen where she started to chase Cordelia toward the open door, with a tea towel flapping in her hand. "Out you, crazy bird... out."

Cordelia had what she wanted. With a large piece of lamb roast that had been cut from the bone in her beak, she darted out from the open back door and away, into the growing darkness around the station. She flew over the returning workers who ducked as she skimmed low over their heads.

"Crazy bird," Lilly's oldest brother said, as he made a mock rifle with his hands and arms as if he was pretending to shoot Cordelia. "I might have to shoot that one, one day," he said, before softly saying, "Bang," as Cordelia flew away towards the old windmill tower.

"Over my dead body," Lilly said, adding, "look at her go. She's amazing."

Cordelia dropped the cooked lamb so that the injured bird could reach it easily. He lent forward and picked it up with his beak, swallowing it in one gulp.

"Thanks, mate," he said, in a deep, drawn voice, "but I'll need more than this if I'm gunna heal."

Cordelia thought, *If his appetite is back, he must be getting better.*

"I know," Cordelia said, "but I have a plan." The moss on Gary's wounds had dried and Cordelia flew back to find fresh moss from the water trough. Gary was comfortable and resting when she returned. She decided to sleep near him that night and roosted, a few struts up on the windmill structure. *If a fox came past, Gary would have no hope of defending himself*, she reasoned. The cool breeze that rolled over the flat plain to the east of the shearing shed would likely carry the scent of his blood far.

Cordelia could see the claw and part of his lower leg that she had pecked away. It was laying on the dirt a mytre's wing width away from the windmill tower. She'd hated taking his leg and powerful talon off, but she knew if she left it on, he would likely die.

Gary knew it too, and as he drifted into a fitful sleep, he pondered what would have happened to the only son of Garth, grandson of Graham, great grandson of George, and descendant of the Great Gus from the western mountain cliffs, if this strange bird had not come to his aid. Dead he knew, he would have been the last in his line and died at the foot of the windmill. His pain had settled, and he slept on, while Cordelia watched from above.

-O-

Cordelia returned to check on Gary each day. Sid and Trev offered to fly with her, but she refused their support, saying she needed to build her confidence on her own. Really, she just didn't want them to discover Gary's hiding place.

Fortunately, the two pied currawong left her to it. They had their own business to attend too. They'd learnt that staying near the homestead lawn meant greater prospects of finding insects and to their delight, berries from the norzela's garden. They were respectful, and didn't eat all the fruit, but the dark coloured berries proved to be a special and unlooked for treat in the well maintained norzela garden.

Gary was recovering slowly, he'd been seriously wounded and if Cordelia hadn't removed the pellets from the shotgun, embedded in his wing and body, he would surely have died. He'd lost his left foot and talon, but this was a small price to pay for his life. Cordelia brought him meat scraps from the kitchen when she could get them, and from her own foraging. But the big bird needed far more food than she could find. She dared not go back to the slaughterhouse after her encounter with the snake and even Bruce refused to set foot off the veranda.

Cordelia spoke with the yard-dogs and was able to get them to donate a few scraps from their meals each day. Cordelia knew it was never going to be enough, because, as he healed, Gary's appetite was almost insatiable.

Each day, Cordelia tried to find time to stretch her wings and fly away from the station in search of clues about which way she needed to fly to get home. On one of these trips, she discovered a dead creature decomposing at the side of a track. She decided it must be an emu. She'd heard of these creatures, from her mother and in stories, but this was the first one she'd seen. She knew it was a bird because it was covered with feathers, but it was even larger than Gary and its feet looked like they had never left the ground. She pulled strips of flesh off it and flew them back to Gary.

She did this for most of the day and although she was very tired, she reasoned that the flights were a good way to help build up her chest and flight muscles. Gary, who still couldn't move, remained hidden, at the base of the windmill. With each trip Cordelia found the task of taking flesh off the emu most distasteful, but she knew it was the only way to help her injured friend, so she pressed on. As she flew, she was sure even this food source would not last long and she'd need to find a way to supply Gary with a more constant supply of food, or at least a supply that didn't require her to fly all over the station searching and carrying.

Cordelia returned to the norzela nest hoping to speak with Bruce. When she arrived, little corellas infested Mary's small fruit and vegetable garden. A small flock of about 50 or 60 were pulling fruit off the trees, tearing at the roots of the vegetables, and causing havoc in her precious garden. Mary had placed white plastic nets over the trees to protect them as best she could from the occasional fruit pilferers, like Sid and Trev, but the corellas were making a terrible mess and noise as they pulled at the netting and tore randomly at the fruit, searching for seeds and berries.

Mary, desperate to protect her garden, was outside with a straw bristled sweeping brush trying as best she could to shoo the birds away, but each time she moved one group away, another would land and start their destruction behind her. Sweat was beading on her brow as her energy and patience dropped.

The Little Corellas were in heaven. They'd not seen a feast like this in a long while and it was well worth even the risk of an occasional brush sweeping near them. Soon, the birds had settled into the garden like a plague of locus on a ripe corn crop.

Cordelia could see that the norzela was in a losing battle and she called loudly for Sid and Trev to come and help. They flew over from the shearing shed where they had been sitting, watching their delicious berries become corella food, and settled on the veranda balcony railing.

"Follow me, and shout like me," Cordelia called to them as she took off toward the garden. The pied currawong pair followed Cordelia closely as the three black and white birds swept over the garden.

"Wedge-tailed eagle, wedgie, wedgie," Cordelia called at the top of her lungs. Sid was at first confused, but Trev understood immediately.

"I say, darlings there's a wedge-tailed eagle coming," he said politely.

Sid, finally catching on, began to screech, "Wedge-tailed eagle, eagle," in an alarming way.

"Get away, it's coming, fly, fly, wedge-tailed eagle, eagle," Cordelia was shouting as she flew low over the little corellas causing additional alarm with her swooping flight.

Mary was shocked and was at first terrified by the three birds' low diving arrival and ear-piercing screeches. *Now I have to deal with these too*, she thought as she braced to sweep the brush at the new invaders. But with each pass of the three black and white birds, more and more of the little corella took to the air and seemed to be circling above the garden. Soon the whole flock had taken to flight and were circling above Mary's head.

Cordelia flew in amongst them and between the white birds and kept up her false warning about an approaching killer bird.

Trev flew behind her shouting and crying as if a massive wedge-tailed eagle were almost upon them. So successfully had he played up his fear, that within a minute the corellas had all taken to the wing and followed Cordelia away towards the east of the station.

The pied currawong pair flew back and settled on a fence near the garden, and each began to preen their feathers in triumph.

Cordelia arrived back a few moments later and joined them on their perch.

Mary, her hair a mess and dripping with sweat, blew a strand of hair off her face and lent on the broom as she regarded the three birds.

"Was that your doing?" Mary asked the birds.

They didn't understand and just kept on preening their underwing feathers. Mary shook her head, looked at Cordelia, and said to no one, "Well I can't really believe it, but maybe you really are a clever bird."

Cordelia, Sid, and Trevor began to sing in celebration of Cordelia's cunning. "I knew at once what you were doing," Sid said sounding proud of himself. Cordelia and Trev looked at each other doubtfully but sang with joy anyway.

Once the little corellas had gone and Sid and Trev had finished celebrating their part in the plan to scare off the fruit and vegetable thieves, Cordelia spoke with Bruce and asked if he would help with her plan to steal food from the kitchen. She explained about Gary and told him what she had been doing to keep the large bird safe and alive. Bruce was amazed and said quickly that he'd help.

"Great," Cordelia said, "but you can't tell anyone else and remember if this doesn't work," she paused, "we might have to go back to the slaughterhouse."

"Oh no, I'm not goin' near there again," Bruce cried, before asking, "What does your kitchen plan involve?"

"I'll explain it all later, I have to talk to the yard-dogs first. Can we meet back here after nwod?" Cordelia asked, before flying away to talk to the yard-dogs.

Cordelia returned just before ksud and explained her plan carefully.

"But we have to start the plan now," she said with a sense of urgency. Cordelia had noticed as she watched through the large kitchen window that looked out onto the veranda and her cage perch, that at least once every few passages of Egnaro the older female norzela would prepare and cook a roast meal. Sometimes it was chicken, or lamb or beef, but at least once each quarter cycle, there was a roast meal being prepared. Bruce knew this too because, as Cordelia had noticed, Bruce was always somewhere near the kitchen table to collect fallen food or beg for scraps of meat.

"I have noticed that not long after Elppa's rise, the older female norzela takes some meat from the white box and places it on the kitchen table to stand before it's cooked." Bruce nodded to show he understood. "Well, today is another roast day," Cordelia said, pointing a wing in through the glass at the kitchen bench. The roast lamb sat on the kitchen bench top defrosting, covered by a tea towel. Bruce was gobsmacked, but he still wasn't sure how they would get the meal. "We'll never get that out of the house." Bruce declared. Adding, "it's too big for you or me to carry."

"I know, but I think I can get the norzela to bring it out, and to give it to us. If I can get into the norzela nest unseen." Cordelia spoke quietly, with a twinkle in her eyes as she explained her plan. Finally, she said, "You keep a lookout and stand guard, and distract the norzela? I'll sneak in and do my part, but you have to keep them away from the kitchen bench while I work." Cordelia was most insistent.

Bruce thought for a moment and began to wag his tail and nod vigorously.

"Wait here," Cordelia said, as she flew off, leaving Bruce on the veranda. She was back in only a few moments. There was brown soil on her beak, as well, in her beak she was holding four small worms she'd taken from some rotten fruit near the norzela rubbish bins. Cordelia put them on the veranda decking and watched them squirm and roll about.

"Yuck," Bruce exclaimed as he curled up his nose. "What are they for?" he asked, a little disgusted.

"I'll show you. Are you ready with your distraction?" she asked.

Bruce nodded and wagged his tail in delight.

"Off you go then," Cordelia instructed.

With that, Bruce rushed in through the dog-door in the screen and darted into the area where the norzelas were watching the brightly flashing picture window-box.

Cordelia picked up the four small wriggling worms carefully in her beak. She pushed through the dog-door and made her way over to the kitchen bench top. Meanwhile, Bruce began to bark and yap at the top of his voice.

"What's this silly dog want?" Mary said.

"I don't know, have you forgotten to feed it," her oldest son asked.

"No, I fed it after breakfast and dinner. I'm sure I did," Mary said, unsure.

"Well can you put the noisy thing out or something, I'm trying to watch Farmer wants a wife," her husband said, getting frustrated.

"Bruce come…" he called, "settle down, or you'll go out with the yard-dogs." The thought of spending a single night in a yard kennel silenced Bruce almost immediately. Instantly, he stopped yapping and jumped onto his master's lap. But he'd done enough. As he watched, behind him he could see Cordelia slipping out through the pet flap, her mission to place the four worms under the tea towel and on top of the meat a success.

Once Cordelia was back outside, sitting on the blanket, on top of the wire cage, Bruce began part two of their plan. He jumped down from his master's lap and ran over to the kitchen bench and started barking at the meat.

"Now what is it," Lilly said, getting annoyed. Mary looked over and could see the small dog scratching at the kitchen bench and trying to climb up to the defrosting roast.

"What's got into this bloody dog tonight," Mary said, standing and going over to the kitchen to chase Bruce away.

Bruce kept up his barking as Mary approached.

Cordelia was watching through the window and could see Mary looking confused as she noticed the tablecloth had been pulled back off the roast a little. She removed it completely and looked at the semi-defrosted meat. Then she drew back in horror. Four small fruit worms were wriggling across the surface of the meat. "Oh no, the meat's spoiled," she cried disappointed. "Look at this, Lilly, there are worms coming from the meat, it's horrible."

Lilly stepped over briskly and examined the meat. "Oh, gross, Mum, we can't eat that," Lilly exclaimed, turn ng up her nose. "And I thought boarding school food was bad," she added, in disgust.

"I'll have to throw this away, dear," Mary said to her husband.

"No wait, I'll give it to the yard-dogs, in the morning," her husband suggested.

"Lilly luv, will you carry it over to the butcher's shed for me. This bloke on telly is about to choose who he'll take back to his farm with him."

"Now, Dad?" Lilly said in protest.

"Well, you weren't really watching it were you, luv?" her dad suggested. He refocused on the TV.

Mary looked at Lilly, shrugged her shoulders, and handed her the roast, still on the large metal serving plate it had been resting on. She picked it up and carried it outside. She noticed that the bird was not in the cage. *'Must be off feeding,'* she thought. She descended the veranda steps and began to walk across the station yard. She walked over the pale thin grass and onto the dry dusty soil that lay before the shearing shed. As she strode across the open space there was a sudden rush of feathers and a woosh in the air.

Lilly looked up and around then seeing the bird preparing to swoop again, she ducked and bobbed to avoid the onslaught. As she did, the plate she was carrying tipped, and the weight of the meat shifted. The meat slid to one side of the plate. She corrected the slide immediately, but her over correction sent the meat sliding in the other direction across the plate. This time her correction meant the semi-defrosted and slippery meat simply did a summersault into the air and landed with a thud onto the dusty ground. In a flash the bird was back making another dive at Lilly. She ducked and covered her head with the now empty plate and shouted as she tried to defend herself.

"Bird, bloody, ungrateful bird," she cried.

At that moment, one of the yard-dogs dashed from its hiding place near the foundation of the shearing shed, snatched up the leg of lamb from the ground and darted away with it around the back of the shearing shed.

Cordelia followed the dog closely and together, the dog, bird, and leg of lamb, vanished from Lilly's sight.

Lilly stood from her stooped position and lowered the plate to her side. *That was odd*, she thought. But without the meat there was no point going on and she returned to the family, who were still watching TV.

"How'd yer go, luv?" her dad asked.

"One of the yard-dogs is off the chain. It stole the whole bloody thing, after the bird attacked me. I'll swear they were working together," Lilly claimed.

"The bird... the magpie? That's unusual," Mary said. "I'll bet it was one of these cunning currawong things. They have been getting into my garden too, bloody things, eating my fruit," Mary proposed.

"Could have bin, Mum," Lilly admitted feeling a little confused, and still in shock from the attack. "Anyway, meat's gone, and the dogs'll be happy tonight."

"Shush luv, the show's still on," her dad said. Adding quickly, "I'll put Bruce out tonight, he can sleep in his old cage with that bird after all the racket he made this evening."

-0-

Behind the shearing shed, Cordelia watched for any sign that they would be chased. As she kept watch, the yard-dog, chewed a part of the leg of lamb free.

"I'll take the smaller part," the yard-dog said graciously, "it was your plan."

"Now where shall I take the meat?" the dog asked.

Cordelia led the dog to the base of the windmill. But she didn't let the yard-dog see Gary. Cordelia was sure she could drag the roast the short distance further.

"Thank you, Martin," Cordelia said, as she flew down and sat next to the smallest of the yard-dogs. Earlier in the day, Cordelia had explained what she had wanted from the yard-dogs. They were all excited to take part, but only the chain of the smallest of the dogs was held in place by a narrow hook. And Cordelia was only just able to lift the chain loop over the hook to free Martin.

The oldest yard-dog advised against going. 'Loyalty is everything on the station,' he'd explained, adding, 'Our master will be angry.' But Martin was eager to be free at least for a short while, and he'd agreed to be involved in the adventure.

"Enjoy your share of the meat," Cordelia said, as Martin left to make his way back to the kennels. "I'll come by later and make sure all is well," Cordelia said as Martin disappeared into the dimming light of ksud.

Cordelia struggled to pull the piece of lamb over to Gary. But after a short time, she had the meat close enough for him to reach out his beak and pull it towards him.

Gary tore into the meat as if he'd never been fed before. "Lamb," he said between gulps of meat torn off the bone, "delicious."

Cordelia had other things to do before the plan was concluded but she promised she'd be back in a short while. She was glad the plan had worked, but she couldn't watch the wedge-tailed eagle eat, it reminded her too much of what she imagined must have happened to her brother.

She flew to the kennels and tried to reattach Martin's chain back onto the hook at the side of his kennel. It took a lot longer than it had taken to lift the hook off, but she finally managed to re-hook Martin.

-0-

When Chris came the next day to see which dog had been set free, he was gobsmacked to find all the dogs chained as he'd left them. Although Martin was sleeping, the others were awake ready for work. Chris bent down and picked up a small black feather from the ground near Martin's kennel. He took off his hat and scratched his head.

"He's thinking," one of the dogs said.

"He always scratches his head when he thinks," the oldest yard-dog agreed. He barked with pleasure. "He'll never figure it out though."

-0-

After Cordelia had secured Martin back into his kennel chain, she returned to check on Gary. The eagle was sitting with the leg of lamb bone before him, still picking over the tufts of meat in the crevasses of the lamb joint.

"That was delicious, young Cordelia, I don't know how I will ever repay you."

"There's no need, Gary," she said softly. She remembered her dream, about a wedge-tailed eagle gliding over her, giving her strength. "Helping you was the right thing to do. The young norzela

223

girl, Bruce, Trev, and Sid helped me, and Martin did today. Kratt gave us nothing, he just took. Giving is better for everyone."

She wondered now if her vision of a high-flying eagle was a sign that she should help this bird. Whatever it was, she was sure that helping him now was the right thing to do.

Gary spoke slowly, graciously, in a deep voice, "I owe you, my life. I will soon recover and return to my life of hunting and supporting my family… if I ever get one."

"Are you saying you don't have a family?" Cordelia asked, surprised.

"I have a friend; someone I have asked to be my partner…" Gary hesitated. "She is still thinking about it… I was going to present a small lamb to her as a gift for when she said 'yes'," Gary admitted. Then he looked forlorn, and tears formed in his eyes. "But I was brought down when I was out hunting. Who would want me now? Now I have just one talon, and I don't even know if I will ever fly again…"

"You'll fly, you'll be fine I am sure of it," Cordelia said, remembering her dream.

I have seen it, she wanted to say, but she kept her vision to herself.

"I'd better go and see how Bruce is getting on," Cordelia said as she raised herself to her feet. "I'll come back tomorrow," she reassured him. "Rest and heal, Gary," Cordelia said as she rose into the sky.

"Egnaro's greeting," he called after her.

She rose into the darkening sky. Egnaro was indeed high in the air above all. Her glow dimmed the stars, even the strongest stars struggled to compete with the reflection on Egnaro's face. Cordelia flew back to the veranda and settled on the blanket, on top of the cage. The picture window-box was off and the norzela nest rang to the sound of the occupants sleeping soundly.

"Bruce," she called softly. There was no reply. "Bruce," she called again, a little more loudly. There was no bark or snappy, yelped reply. Cordelia looked about the veranda. The light was poor, and she could see nothing. She thought it odd, but assumed Bruce must be asleep on a blanket, in the norzela nest. Cordelia flew down to the opening to her cage. It was then she saw Bruce. He was lying at the far end of the cage, he looked to be asleep, still, and unmoving. Cordelia thought, *It's odd he didn't respond to my calls.*

She couldn't see him breathing, he wasn't moving, and he'd not responded to her soft calls. She rushed into the cage and knelt beside him.

"Bruce, wake up," she called. She had no response.

26

Bruce

Johnny is a joker (He's a bird)
A very funny joker (He's a bird)
But when he jokes, my honey (He's a dog)
His jokin' ain't so funny (What a dog)
Johnny is a joker that's a-tryin' to
steal my baby (He's a bird dog)

Johnny sings a love song (Like a bird)
Sings the sweetest love song (Ya ever heard)
But when he sings to my gal (What a howl)
To me he's just a wolf dog (On the prowl)
Johnny wants to fly away
and puppy-love my baby (He's a bird dog)

The Everly Brothers – 'Bird Dog' (1959)

OUTSIDE THE CAGE, beyond the black wires, the snake rose over Bruce. Its eyes transfixed on Cordelia as its head slid and darted back and forth, its tongue flickering in and out as it tasted the air. "You're too late for your friend," the keere hissed. "I wanted to kill you too, but at least I have the dog. Snappy little thing. but too slow for me. And now it's your turn."

Cordelia stepped out of the cage door and flew up to the blanket on top of the cage. She rested there briefly, waiting for the snake to move.

Yrarbil rose higher, coming up to meet her. It slithered and twisted, urging its slender body up so that it rose between Cordelia and the back door, and the dog-flap that led to the kitchen.

Cordelia knew she had no weapons to defeat the snake, but she stood ready to fight anyway. As the snake drew level with Cordelia, she took to the air and flashing her feathers she tried to confuse her attacker.

Yrarbil struck out ferociously at Cordelia and caught her by her tail feather. Her attacker's fangs went right through the barbs on the feather near the rachis and pulled the feather out, shaft, calamus, quill and all, as Cordelia flapped and flew to escape its grasp.

"You coward," Yrarbil hissed with difficulty, "stay and fight, don't turn to flight."

"Oh, I will fight you alright," Cordelia said. *In my own way,* she thought. She hated leaving Bruce, but she needed to draw the vile creature away and alert the norzela.

Cordelia's extracted tail feather had stuck in the snake's fangs and for a moment her attacker was distracted as it tried to free it from her mouth. Cordelia saw her chance and hopped past the snake down to the veranda surface. Although she'd lost one tail feather, Cordelia had not absorbed any of Yrarbil's venom, and she bobbed in through the dog-door, into the norzela nest.

Yrarbil used her tail to extract the feather stuck on her fangs, and as she tossed it aside, she turned to see where Cordelia had gone. Fury rose in the snake, and she slithered quickly after her prey. She had seen Cordelia poke her way through the dog-flap and disappear through the screen door. Without hesitation, she used her nose to push the flap up and move through into the norzela nest, in pursuit. The inside of the house was an unfamiliar place for Yrarbil and once inside, she hesitated and looked about to get her bearings.

Cordelia flew up to the kitchen bench and started to sing and cry out at the top of her lungs. She also began to flap her wings frantically to try and attract Yrarbil's attention, and alert the norzela, asleep in their nest.

"'Here Yrarbil, you vile creature," she shouted. "Can you fly? I think not." As she flapped her wings over the kitchen sink, she knocked a plate from the drying rack and it crashed to the floor, with a clatter before it broke. The snake slithered and twisted quickly towards Cordelia and tried to stretch up to reach her, but the bench top was too high.

"Coward," Yrarbil hissed as a taunt. "Come down and fight me." Cordelia flew over to the open fireplace on the opposite side of the room, crying and shouting her alarm call with all her lungs. She landed on the fire hearth and waited as the keere charged on its belly across the room, slithering and twisting beneath the lounge furniture and over to Cordelia. As the snake approached, the room was suddenly full of light. Cordelia flew into the air just as Yrarbil struck and this time the fangs closed without touching Cordelia.

"Stay still, you coward," the frustrated snake said, hissing after the hovering mytre.

Suddenly, Yrarbil's head was slammed to the surface of the hearth, as an iron fire poker was thrust into its skull. Cordelia flew over to the kitchen bench and settled there to catch her breath.

"'Got yer, yer bastard," Chris said as he hit the snake a second time.

Cordelia's noise had woken Chris who had come to the kitchen and open plan living room to see what the racket was. He'd turned on the lights and immediately saw Cordelia by the fire, with a large snake trying to bite her. Without hesitation he'd grabbed the fire poker from a stand near the hearth. Because the snake was so focused on Cordelia, he was able to smash the snake in the head, before it had seen him.

The snake's body writhed and contorted spontaneously, but the life had gone from the reptile. The hook on the fire poker had penetrated the snake's skull with the second blow and as Chris lifted the poker up, the snake hung from its hook. He held it at arm's length and marched quickly over to the back door. Once outside, he carried the dead snake over to a rubbish bin, lifted the lid, and dropped it inside. It landed with a solid thud at the bottom of the bin and Chris closed the lid.

Inside, Lilly and Mary had come into the kitchen area to find Cordelia perched on the kitchen bench. "What's been going on?" Mary asked as she brushed the sleepiness from her eyes.

"And why is the bird in the house?" Lilly asked.

"I'll ask your father to get rid of it I think, it caused a real racket in here tonight," Mary said through a yawn. "And look at this mess," Mary exclaimed, pointing at the broken plate on the kitchen floor. "No way," she said, disappointed, "this bird has to go."

Just then, Chris came back into the kitchen. He was carrying a fire poker and carrying the limp body of Bruce in his arms.

"It was a bloody snake," he said angrily, "It got Bruce and if your magpie hadn't warned us, it might well have come for one of us in the night."

"So, the noise was to try and warn us?" Lilly exclaimed.

"Yer, I think it was," Chris declared.

After her initial annoyance Mary, sounding surprised said, "What a clever, brave bird."

"But it looks like the snake got Bruce before I could kill it," Chris said as he lay the poisoned dog on the family couch.

Cordelia flew over to the couch and perched on the headrest, so she could look down on her chihuahua friend. She could see in the light that he was still breathing, but only just.

"I'll call the vet," Chris said as he rushed to find his mobile phone.

"I'll put the kettle on," Mary said.

While Lilly said, "And I'll get this clever magpie out of the house."

Chris spoke with the vet. His view was that Bruce had little chance of surviving, being such a small dog and getting a high venom load. "But will you see the dog?" Chris insisted. The vet agreed, and Chris and Lilly made the car ready for the long drive to the vets.

Lilly's brothers woke up just as they were leaving, having slept through the racket and drama of the night. Mary made up a small plate with mincemeat and a few small strips of beef, from the replacement roast they'd had that night, and left them just inside the cage for the heroic and brave magpie.

Cordelia was too distressed to eat. She watched as Chris loaded Bruce into the front seat of the ute, on Lilly's lap. The ute turned in the driveway and quickly sped off towards the nwad. She had no concept of where they were going or what might happen to Bruce, only that she had seen her friend on the brink of death and the look on the norzela faces confirmed that Bruce was destined to die. Unsure of what to do, Cordelia settled on the blanket that sat on top of the cage. She suddenly looked up and saw Lilly's older brother looking intently at her through the kitchen window above his cage.

"You made a bloody racket last night bird. I'd watch your neck if I were you." The older brother drew his thumb across his neck as if cutting it with a knife. Then he said, malicious y, "if that dog dies, so do you." He turned and left and although Cordelia didn't understand a word he'd said, she knew it sounded menacing.

Confused and hurt, Cordelia bowed her head, and although Elppa was rising in the east, she had no heart for the celebration chorus and instead, remained silent.

Sid and Trev flew over to the veranda and perched on the railing. They had come when they hadn't heard her sing. Indeed, even the yard-dogs, were surprised that for once their day hadn't started with her song, and they too wondered what had happened in the night.

Mary was also suddenly aware of the unusual silence of the morning and recognised how lucky they had been because of Cordilia's warning. She stood at the kitchen window and said, "Clever bird," before noticing that none of the mincemeat had been eaten. *Strange,* she thought.

Cordelia was in tears, heartbroken and distressed as she explained to Sid and Trevor about the snake's attack, about it biting Bruce and the norzela taking him, about how the norzela had killed

Bruce's attacker, and about the strange behaviour of Lilly's older brother. Nothing Sid or Trevor said gave her comfort and after a long silence Cordelia asked if she could have some time alone.

Sid and Trev respectfully agreed and flew away to the far side of the station so that Cordelia could mourn and worry in her own way. They also said they would tell the yard-dogs what had happened and explain the reason for the absent morning song.

-0-

Unable to find an appetite and unable to settle at the cage where Bruce had been attacked, Cordelia decided to fly with the food she'd been gifted, over to Gary. She was sure he'd appreciate it. She found him trying to balance on one leg.

He had wrapped his strong right talon around one of the low windmill tower struts and spread his wings out to either side as he tried to balance on his one foot.

"Are you sure you're ready for this?" Cordelia asked as she landed nearby on the ground.

"I feel much better," Gary said, "and I can't just sit about waiting for you to bring me food all day." As he spoke his attention on his balance was broken, and he toppled forward, and fell with a 'flap' to the ground. He lay there a moment as the dust about him settled.

Cordelia couldn't help but laugh. The tension of the previous night needed a release, and watching the mighty Gary fall flat on his face was too much for her, even in her sadness, it just exploded from her.

"There's no need for that," Gary cried, sounding embarrassed.

"But you didn't see yourself fall," Cordelia explained, "You were like an eagle ninja one moment, then you were just sprawled out on your face the next. It was funny."

But Gary struggled to see the funny side of his fall. He huffed, "Not for me." Although, as he watched Cordelia's giggles subside, he accepted that it probably was funny from her point of view.

Cordelia was feeling a little better, and she told Gary about the snake, Bruce being bitten and about how she had led Bruce's attacker into the norzela nest so the norzela could kill it.

Gary was very impressed but concerned too that the snake had bitten her friend, Bruce. He wished he'd been able to help. "Snake can be a good meal if you can catch them before they bite you," he said.

"Well, I never want to go near one of them again," Cordelia asserted. She hopped over to Gary and helped him back on to his foot. It was difficult to help such a large bird regain his balance and although it was a struggle, soon Gary was back on his foot and managing to hold his balance again.

Gary was surprised at how well he felt, his wing and chest were healing, and he was sure he'd soon be ready to fly. "Tomorrow," he said, "I'll try and fly tomorrow." They sat next to each other in the dust at the base of the tower. Gary ate the food Cordelia had brought and as she sat there, she was suddenly aware of how large he was, compared to her. She looked at his massive-hooked beak and although he now only had one, his talon was a powerful weapon. His body was also considerably larger than Cordelia's and she was dwarfed by the size and girth of his chest and wings. *He is at least six or seven times my size*, she thought.

As he finished eating, he noticed her sensing his power for the first time. On previous occasions he'd been laying on the ground, crippled and twisted by his injuries. Now he was recovering, he could see she was aware of his prowess as a lethal hunting bird. He felt it himself, his energy and power were returning, and he could feel how much larger and imposing he was again. "You don't have to worry, Cordelia," Gary said softly. "I owe you my life, I will never hurt you and you can count on me to help you if I can."

"I know," she replied. Then correcting herself, she added, "I mean, I don't expect anything from you. It was the right thing to do to help you. Anyway," she said, joking, "I reckon I could take a one footed wedgie if I had to." They both laughed, Gary in his big deep voice and Cordelia, only a little as thoughts of Bruce and her fight with the snake, Yrarbil returned.

"Why are you here, on this station?" Gary asked. "I've flown over here for a while now and never seen you before, not before you appeared to help me."

Cordelia told Gary about how she came to the station in the back of the ute, and about what had happened in the valley before she'd arrived. She explained that her father had died in the lights of a car and that she was fleeing the evil Krat clan and their leader Lord Kratt.

Gary was horrified and stunned that she'd been through so much, and still had the decency to help him when he'd been injured. He knew that one of his kind had killed her brother and that she had most likely lost her dog friend, Bruce. *Yet after all she'd suffered,* he thought, *she is still willing to risk her life to help me.* "I'll be strong enough to fly tomorrow, I think. Will you come back and help me once more?" Gary asked, kindly.

Cordelia nodded and looking up at the powerful bird, she said, "I'd be glad to."

27

Practice Makes Perfect

We will fly, way up high
Where the cold wind blows.
Or in the sun laughing having fun
With the people that she knows.

And if the situation should keep us separated
You know the world won't fall apart.
And you will free the beautiful bird
That's caught inside your heart.

Daryl Braithwait - 'Horses' (1990).

CORDELIA HAD BEEN given an extra helping of mincemeat and she sang cheerfully and loudly at her nwad chorus. The norzela's had returned in the ute later the previous day, but Bruce was not with them. Cordelia could only imagine the worst. Sid and Trev said it didn't mean Bruce was dead and proposed that he might just be recovering, and that she should have hope, that he'd be back soon. Cordelia had seen how her father's hope had been dashed when Kratt had taken over the valley and Karbett had been killed. *Hope,* she thought, *'is for fools and the desperate.* All she had now, was now, and she planned to make the most of her time by finding a way back to the valley. First though, she'd help Gary get back in the air.

Gary was ready when she arrived at the windmill. Cordelia had brought a portion of her mincemeat and once he'd finished his breakfast, he prepared to fly. Cordelia took up a perch on a high run of the windmill tower and watched as he steadied himself on the ground to take to the air. She could see he was nervous.

He stretched out his wings and fanned his tail a few more times before he called out, "Here I go." Then he hopped along with his wings spread and his one powerful leg pushing him off the ground. He flapped a few times and rose slowly a small distance off the ground, but he couldn't gain any height. After a few more hoppy steps and wild flaps of his wings he stopped and hopped back over to the windmill.

"It's… no… use," he said, out of breath, "I… can't… get any lift… I can't hop into the air high enough." Breathing heavily, he collapsed to the ground.

"Come on," Cordelia said. "Don't give up, its only your first attempt."

Gary tried again, hopping, and jumping as best he could with his one leg and trying to generate lift with his massive wings. He failed again.

Cordelia started to worry, *What if he couldn't get any lift. If he lost his ability to fly, he'd be forced to hop everywhere, and he'd soon die or become snake prey, or worse, be shot at by the norzela boy with the shotgun again.*

"Try a longer run up," Cordelia shouted as he returned to the base of the windmill.

Gary looked up at her with a frown of exasperation. "Maybe I… should wait… another… day," Garry shouted, still panting.

"You just need some lift," Cordelia called down to him. She thought about her first flight from the nest tree. She'd been up high and glided before her wings caught the air. Her first flight was more like a controlled drop. It was only once she'd felt the zephyr in her wings that she learnt how to use her wings to gain lift.

"Gary," Cordelia called, "you need to be up higher."

He looked up at her. "Easy for you to say, but until I can fly, I can't get higher." He was getting very frustrated and tired, and his patience was beginning to fray as he contemplated a life without flight.

"I have an idea," Cordelia shouted down to him. "Have you ever seen a corella eating fruit?" she asked. Gary looked confused and wondered what she was going on about. Cordelia, seeing his expression flew down to explain her plan clearly.

"Little corellas," she explained, "use their beak and claws to climb." Gary looked none the wiser. Cordelia explained further, "If you can use your powerful beak and talon to climb the windmill tower's ladder, you could launch yourself off and use the updraft from your fall to generate lift."

Gary considered the idea as he looked at the tower. It had struts that meant he could potentially climb all the way to the top, but he was not sure about the 'launch yourself off at the top' part. If he simply fell, he'd be even worse off and likely injured a second time.

"It's basically how I learnt to fly," Cordelia reassured him.

Gary was tired from repeated failures at ground level and although he could see how Cordelia's plan might work, he wasn't sure he could master the art of corella-climbing. He took a few deep breaths, "Okay," he said, "let's try." He hopped over to the tower and used his beak to grasp the first run of the ladder. It was metal and difficult to grasp, but he soon found a firm grip. He pulled himself up one run. Then he flipped his body over in a sort of summersault and gripped the next run with his talon. He found he could get a better grip with his talon and quickly flipped himself over again as he stretched for the next run with his beak. He missed.

Cordelia's heart flew into her mouth as she closed her eyes and waited for the inevitable fall and crash. She heard nothing. When she looked again, Gary was still holding on with his talon, having regripped the run he had just let go of.

Try to grab them cleanly, Gary told himself. He flipped around again and used his beak to grip the next run. He grabbed it and held on, and quickly swung through to reach up with his talon again. This hold held, and he swung through again, quickly building momentum.

Before long, he was five rungs up the ladder and well on his way to the top. His beak was ideal for gripping the ladder rungs and although he'd never climbed like this before, as he advanced higher his confidence grew. After a short time, he was at the final rung. He held on with his beak, and flicked his body, wings flapping, up to the small platform under the windmill sails. Exhausted, he lay panting, but triumphant as he caught his breath.

Cordelia flew up and landed next to him on the plank of wood at the apex of the tower. She looked at Gary who was still breathing heavily and said, "Well done, that bird."

"I can see why we fly now," Garry said, between gasps for air. They each rested and looked out over the view. Gary looked west toward his home in the mountains and hills. He'd missed them, and before he was sure he'd recover, he thought he'd never see them again. But there they were, looking more inviting and beautiful than he could remember.

Cordelia looked east, toward the homestead and the buildings of the station. It was therefore Cordelia who saw them first. Lilly's brothers were standing near the shearing shed and one was pointing in their direction. *That was troubling enough,* Cordelia thought, but more worrying was the fact that one of them was carrying a shotgun.

"Gary, you need to fly now," she said in and excited tone. "The norzela hunters are back."

Gary turned and looked at the two norzela as they approached the windmill. He saw that as they were walking, one was loading the shotgun while the other pointed toward the top of the windmill tower.

"You have to fly now," Cordelia repeated. "It's the only way you'll escape."

"But I'm worn out, I can't do it," Gary said defeated and tired.

"You have to, there is no time to waste… fly." As Cordelia shouted, she took to the wing and dived low to the ground, skimming the grass and scrub of the paddock in a low dart like flight. She flew away to the north hoping to distract the hunters.

"I told yer, yer missed," the younger brother said scornfully.

"Nar, I hit it alright. This must be another one. Bloody eagles," said the older brother. "And I'll get this one too." As he spoke, he raised the gun and took aim at the tower top about 150 metres away.

Gary could see he had no choice, fly, or fall. That was it. He raised himself on his one talon and hopped towards the edge of the high tower plank. Spreading his wings, he dove off the top of the windmill. As he did a hundred little pellets peppered the windmill sails and the high metal structure, clattering about him. The older brother had missed.

Gary plummeted towards the ground. His balance was off as he struggled to come to grips with so long a rest from the air. The ground seemed to rush up at him and he closed his eyes in anticipation of a base tone thud into the soi . Then within a tiny-dog's height he spread his wings, his pinions spread wide, splayed out like tiny yacht spinnaker sails as he caught an updraft that lifted his body into the air. He could feel the stems of grass in the paddock brush against his chest before he arced back into the sky. As he did another blast from the shotgun tore up the soi under his flight path. Gary swivelled in flight and arched around the back of the windmill, away from the brothers. Away from their aim.

Cordelia had flown a short way north but was soon returning to where the norzelas stood, with the aim of distracting Gary's attackers.

"That was shit shoot'n'" The younger brother shouted, as both his older brother's shots had missed their mark. "Give uz the bloodly gun, let an expert shot have a go," he cried snatching the gun from his older brother. The older brother resisted briefly, but his younger brother soon snatched the weapon away into nis grasp.

Gun in hand the younger brother, loaded both barrels and searched the sky for the eagle. "There it is," he said as he coolly took aim at Gary who was flying slowly as he tried to gain height. "I never miss," the younger brother said taking careful aim at the large bird.

Cordelia was just about upon them, and she flew in low, almost skimming the ground, before diving up, aiming right at the younger brother's head. As she struck him, the shotgun discharged, and she feared she had been too late to save Gary.

Her timing could not have been better. The gun had been fired, but her collision with the younger brother's head meant he pulled the barrel low and discharged both barrels into the ground and into the backside and legs of his older brother.

"You bastard," the older brother cried in pain. "Yer've only gone and shot me." He was soon on the ground, writhing in the dust and grass of the paddock, shouting, and crying and swearing like a trooper. "You bastard, you shot me," he kept repeating at the top of his lungs, between cries of pain and anguish.

His younger brother was at first horrified, although, seeing his older brother alive and shouting blue murder, he decided it was more funny than fatal. "I said I never miss, bro," he cried, struggling to hold in his laughter.

"You bastard..." the older brother cried again.

"I didn't mean it, Bro. It was that bloody bird that swooped me," the younger brother said in his defence. "I'm sorry mate, 'ere I'll give yer a hand." The shooter laid the shotgun down in the dust and rushed to help his brother to his feet. They slowly hobbled across the home paddock and back to the homestead.

Cordelia flew back to the top of the windmill and waited for Gary to join her.

"You saved my life again," Gary said as he landed gently next to the mytre.

"That brother has been asking for it for a while," Cordelia said, with a smirk. "Are you hurt?" she asked, hoping he'd say he was fine.

Gary took a breath and replied, "Na, he missed me. I'm good, and better for being able to fly at last."

"I don't think we have to worry about the norzela brothers for a while," Cordelia suggested suppressing a chuckle.

"Come on," Gary said, exhilarated at escaping his ground bound state and at surviving the gun shots. "Let's go for a short flight, I need to get my strength and agility back, if I'm going to get home to the mountains."

-0-

A few days later, after carolling for Elppa in the nawd light, Cordelia flew to the top of the windmill and watched as Gary flew high above her.

Gary saw her and came into land next to her a short while later. He was able to fly well now and was catching his own food. Sometimes he'd bring back a small lizard or a rabbit that he would share with Cordelia. Mostly though, he'd hunt and eat when she was back at the norzela nest so she could warn him about the brothers' movements and give him the peak-up in case they were going to hunt again.

Neither Gary nor Cordelia knew that their father had banned them from using the shotgun again. He'd said that he'd shoot them both himself if he found them shooting anything at all, including each other.

Their mother had been very upset and rather than threatening the boys she simply found the shotgun and locked it in a gun safe, before hiding the key. "You're both a couple of fools; you for shooting him and you for getting shot; but I don't doubt this isn't karma paying you back," His mum said to her oldest child.

"Fetch some towels from the bathroom," she called to her younger son, before whispering to her older boy, "I've seen you kick the bird cage. This is what you get, I suppose."

"But I might die," her foolish older son said indignantly.

"I very much doubt that. Although you'll have nasty scars on your backside and leg for the rest of your life. Now if you get any blood on my new couch, I'll shoot you again. And don't think I haven't seen you tormenting that bird. Serves you right if you ask me, you're a bloody fool." Still his mother gave her boy some pain killers with a drink of water and stroked the fair hair off his forehead.

Cordelia settled on top of the cage to watch the drama unfolding in the norzela nest. The older female norzela seemed to be fussing over her injured son, and the older male was talking into a small picture window-box in his hand.

"I'll be there in an hour and a half. I'll bring him myself," he said into the phone.

"Come on, you," Chris said to his younger son, "Help me get him into the back of the ute, I'll drive him to hospital. You roll out the swag for him to lay on." With that the younger son, ran outside and began preparing the ute, while Lilly and her father helped the injured and crying older brother out of the house, down the steps and into the now ready, back of the ute.

Cordelia watched as they passed and began to carol with joy.

"Bloody bird," the older brother said as he was helped past.

"Clever bird," Mary said as she watched them leave. *I wonder what's really going on in that head of yours. It can't all be songs and mincemeat.* "Drive carefully," she called after her husband as Lilly came back to stand next to her on the veranda. The three of them, Lilly, Mary, and Cordelia watched as Chris drove away with the two boys in the back of the ute.

"He'll be fine," Mary said, as she looked at Cordelia.

Cordelia had no idea what had really happened. But she felt suddenly safe, and she carolled clearly with joy.

"Clever bird," Mary said with a smile.

-O-

Days later, Gary was getting stronger, and he told Cordelia that he felt able to return to his mountains the next day.

She was sad, but glad too that he would be able to make his journey home. "Before you go," Cordelia asked. "Will you teach me how to fight. How to fight and defend myself, so that if I do get home to the valley, I will be able to kill Lord Kratt?"

"But you're not a fighter, Cordelia," Gary said. "You're a general, a strategist, a thinker, a leader. Your skills lay in tactics and strategy, cunning and wit. I think you'll beat that Kratt fellow with your cunning, not your claws or beak."

"But I still need to know how to fight. My father was wise, and he was still beaten. Please teach me," Cordelia pleaded.

Gary owed her his life and he soon agreed, but he added, "Fighting is not the only way. Sometimes being brave, having confidence, and a sound plan will overcome bullies and evil. I can see you're brave, but, I agree, being brave is sometimes not enough." Having agreed, they both flew away as he explained the first lesson.

"Sometimes I attack from above and out of Elppa. This way your adversary doesn't know you're coming, or can't see you coming, and they have no defence from an attack on their back and shoulders... I'll show you," he said. Gary flew off and climbed higher.

Cordelia flew lower and waited for his approach. She told herself she would surely see or hear him coming and be able to respond, but as she was thinking this, Gary was on her. His strong talon had lightly gripped her shoulder for a moment and then let go. It sent her tumbling toward the ground. She quickly recovered and flew back up to him. "I had no idea you were upon me," she said, sounding surprised.

"It's an old Wedge-tailed eagle trick," he explained, "but all hunting birds will use it if they can."

"How can I combat it?" Cordelia asked.

Gary paused for a moment and wondered if he should pass on his hunting secrets, then he remembered how she had saved his life, twice, and his doubt disappeared. "There are three things you can do," Gary explained as they flew along. "You try and attack me from above and I'll show you."

Cordelia thought, *I'll show him*, and she flew as high as she could before turning and diving down like an arrow for the lower flying Gary. She was just about to collide and take him in her claws when suddenly Gary twisted in flight and veered out of her way. As he did, she went spearing past him. Then he was on her, with his talon, resting on her back. It had all happened in an instant, one moment she was about to sink her claws into his shoulders, the next he'd twisted so she passed him, and he was then diving after her.

"That was sneaky," Cordelia said, as she flew back alongside him.

"Not really, I was just aware of your approach, and I was able to turn your speed to my advantage." Cordelia was impressed, then Gary said, "Here I'll show you another defence, but don't be afraid, I won't hurt you."

Cordelia again flew up high. *I'll make sure I come out of Elppa's light this time*, she thought as she prepared to dive. She flew directly at Gary's back, trying to stay as silent as possible. However, as she was within striking distance of Gary, and on her final approach, Gary flipped over onto his back and Cordelia found herself facing the terrifying sight of Gary's massive sharp and powerful talon. She tried to twist away, and pull up, but as she passed, Gary was able to stretch out and practically pull Cordelia from the sky. He released her almost immediately and called out an apology in case he'd hurt or scared her.

Cordelia was shaken and took a few moments to return to flying alongside her instructor.

"What was that?" Cordelia asked still shaken.

"Your back and neck are your weakest parts, if you can flip mid-flight and face your enemy with your talons or claws, you'll have the advantage even if they come from above."

Cordelia pondered what he had said. She understood now why fighting may not always be the best or only option, but at least she could learn how to defend herself if attacked mid-flight from above. "There is another defensive technique," Gary said, "but you'll need to practice this one on your own. My wings are still too weak to do it now. It's called the corkscrew defence." He explained it to Cordelia and watched while she practiced a few times.

They also repeated some of the other manoeuvres with Cordelia attacking or defending until Gary was too tired to go on and he returned to the windmill tower to rest before his long flight the next day. Cordelia though, stayed in the sky twisting and tumbling, diving, and dodging as she continued to practice her attacking and defensive manoeuvres.

-0-

Cordilia woke with a start. She'd had a disturbed night. Visions of Gary fighting her tormented her sleep. His talon loomed large in her mind, and she imagined it crushing the black and white feathers around her neck. She woke several times in the night, with a feeling of being suffocated or strangled. Each time it had been Gary's talon that had featured deadly in her dreams. She tried to return to sleep, but her mind was alive with the possibility of going home. *If Gary was going, and Bruce was gone, what was there for her at the station?* She pondered her own future and was sure she was urgently needed back in the valley. Her dreams had also involved a chase, flight from a pursuer and cries for help. She was sure it meant she needed to get home soon.

She was tired and drained but knew she had to see Gary off. She flew over to the windmill as soon as she had finished her Elppa chorus. He was waiting, perched high atop the windmill, on the upper most platform. He looked well, strong, and proud. As he sat, balanced on his one talon, she landed next to him and both birds were silent for a few moments before Gary spoke, sombrely.

"I owe you my life, young Cordelia," he said solemnly, in his deep voice. He looked at her sincerely then said, "You are Cordelia the brave, friend of Gary the wedge-tailed eagle, only son of Garth, grandson of Graham, great grandson of George, and descendant of the Great Gus from the western mountain cliffs. If you need me and I can help, all you have to do is ask and I will fly with all my might to help you. I live in the mountains to the west."

With that he launched himself into the air and after dropping below the level of the windmill platform, he spread his massive wings and flapped leisurely as his body lifted into the pale blue western sky.

Cordelia watched him fly away. She'd not said a word and she felt foolish letting him go without saying anything. Suddenly, Sid and Trev flapped up and perched next to her. Cordelia was initially shocked. "What are you doing here?" she asked as they landed.

"We've come to see if you're alright, darling," Trev said.

Before Sid added, "We've known all along about your secret wedge-tailed eagle, sweetie. But we felt it best to leave you alone."

Cordelia shrugged, her shoulder feathers puffing out and catching the wind. *Of course they had*, she thought. They all watched Gary disappearing toward the mountains in the west. Cordelia tried to hold in her tears, but she couldn't help allowing her sadness to spill out. Gary was gone, Bruce was gone and soon she would have to go too. *But where?* she thought. *Where do I need to go?*

28

The Picture Window-Box

Time keeps on slippin', slippin', slippin'
Into the future
Time keeps on slippin', slippin', slippin'
Into the future.

I wanna fly like an eagle
To the sea.
Fly like an eagle.
Let my spirit carry me.
I want to fly like an eagle.
'Til I'm free.

Steve Miller Band – 'Fly Like an Eagle' (1976)

CORDELIA RETURNED to her plans and preparation to leave. She flew further and further each day. She practiced mid-air fighting with Sid and Trev, sometimes attacking or defending herself against them both at once. Her skills improved and she was soon able to out manoeuvre, corkscrew fly, and tumble with her claws up in mid-flight. Her wing was healed, and she could stay aloft a long time without tiring or feeling fatigued. Trevor and Sid spoke with her each day about the possibility of staying, but Cordelia was adamant, that one day she would leave the station.

"If you don't know the way back to your valley, then where will you go?" Sid asked.

Cordelia was clear that she'd find away. She just didn't know how.

Bruce came back a few passages of Elppa after Gary had gone. He was not the same playful puppy though and Cordelia, while glad to find him alive was devastated by the state he was in. He'd suffered terribly from the snake venom and the treatment used to cure him.

Lilly and Chris were delighted to have him back. Although everyone noticed he'd changed. Chris blocked up the dogy-door in the fly screen, so he really was a housedog now. While Cordelia could see it made Bruce feel a lot more secure and safe, it meant he couldn't come out to play or stay with Cordelia unless a norzela let him out, and Bruce rarely sought to leave the relative safety of the norzela nest.

She watched him through the full-length kitchen window, from the top of her cage. Bruce seemed content to sleep a lot more and he stayed in the norzela nest most of the Elppa. Even if she banged her beak on the window to get his attention, he pretended to sleep and ignored Cordelia most of the time.

When they did talk, Bruce seemed less inclined to want to play or to leave even the safety of the veranda. The day he returned he'd gone into the garden and come scurrying back at the sight of a small lizard. Cordelia could see how the Yrarbil's venom had done more than poison his blood. It had robbed him of his enthusiasm, his playfulness, and his humour. *Bruce is back, but he isn't really here,* she thought. It made her sad and she sang her lamentation for the loss of Gary and the real Bruce.

Sid and Trev could see Bruce was a shadow of his former self too and as they listened to Cordelia's song each nwod, it was clear she was singing a sorrowful tune for Gary, and Bruce. Cordelia knew she was also singing a lament for her father, her mother, her valley and at being lost on the station. She wondered if she would ever get away from the hot, dry, mostly treeless station, and from under the sheet of depression that covered her more deeply each Egnaro. It was like she had been captured under Chris's leather jacket all over again. Darkness surrounded her and while she knew there was a way to the light, it alluded and scared her.

With Bruce's withdrawal, she soon found herself also retreating further and further into herself. Her confidence dropped and she stopped practicing her long test flights. Instead, she would perch on the blanket on top of her cage and watch Bruce or the colourful picture window-box she could see through the long kitchen window. It was always on about the time of nwad and she enjoyed the colours and images although she couldn't understand the sounds or words used. Sometimes she could hear the norzela in the nest laughing at it or see them reacting to images and stories coming from the picture window-box, but she was never sure what the stories meant or were about.

She tried again to reach out to Bruce, to get him to come out and play or just spend some time talking with her, on the veranda, but she was unable to convince him. She started tapping on the window more and more frequently, to try and get Bruce's attention. But he didn't respond. Although it did serve to annoy the still recovering older brother, who threw a sofa cushion at the kitchen window where Cordelia stood outside as he shouted, "Bugger off, bird."

Bruce, though, took offence at the older brother's reaction and leapt from his soft bed, and, barking, he ran across to where the older brother was sitting and bit him on the ankle.

"Bloody dog," he cried as he reached for his lower leg before buckling in pain as he stretched the suture line on his backside. "Bloody dog," he shouted again as he creased in agony.

Hearing the shouting, Mary shouted, "Leave the dog and bird alone. Don't let me catch you tormenting them, my boy."

"Bloody dog," he mumbled under his breath.

Bruce darted back over to his soft bed by the kitchen bench, before settling down to rest again. He made two or three turns on his bed to pad it soft, and as he did, barked once toward Cordelia, "I'll be right enough soon mate. I've got your back."

Cordelia knew then that Bruce would be okay, he just needed space and time.

The third nwad after the wounded older brother had come home from hospital, Cordelia was watching Bruce and the picture window-box when something amazing happened. Cordelia saw a norzela on the picture window-box, holding a long shiny stick with a black head on it, *Like a rigid mushroom*, she thought. The norzela seemed to be talking into it.

It made no sense to Cordelia, and she was wondering at the strange things norzela do, when she looked past the shoulder of the female norzela and saw something she'd only seen once before. She knew immediately where she'd seen it before, and she knew it had been in the valley. It was the norzela thing she'd seen when she and her father were exploring the Cor clan lands. Her father had pointed out the Kar lands and said that on the other side of the road were the Wayt clan lands, then further along the sealed road, she'd seen the norzela thing, at the start of the Dart clan lands, just before the norzela park. Her father said it was to tell norzelas the way to the park.

She saw it now on the picture window-box, the female norzela was standing in front of it and talking earnestly. Behind her was a thin veil of smoke that hung about the road. A strong wind blew the trees around her, and a large vehicle rushed past her along the sealed road, whirling the smoke into a whirlwind like the dust clouds she'd seen at the station.

Cordelia knew this was her valley, she just knew it. Here it was, on the norzela picture window-box. She was at first reluctant to believe it, but as she watched the image and saw the sign, the reality of what she'd seen settled in her mind. Suddenly, the image on the box changed and the familiar image was gone. *The norzela thing I know, the smoke is new*, she thought. She searched her memory, she ploughed her mind, then in an instant her confidence in what she'd seen grew, and she knew. She really knew, *'The valley is on fire or is about to be.'* Then she had another thought, *If I can find the smoke and fire, I can find the valley.* Suddenly she knew what she needed to do, and she flew off in search of Sid and Trev.

PART THREE

CORDELIA'S FIGHT

29

Departure

All my bags are packed
I'm ready to go
I'm standin' here outside your door
I hate to wake you up to say goodbye
But the dawn is breakin'

It's early morn
The taxi's waitin'
He's blowin' his horn
Already I'm so lonesome
I could die.

John Denver – 'Leaving on a Jet Plane' (1969)

AFTER CORDELIA HAD LEFT the valley, Lord Kratt paced furiously. "Find them," he demanded. "They can't all have just disappeared. Find the mum and find the son, and find that bloody female child, Cordelia." Lord Kratt was furious, his seizure of the valley was almost complete, but some of his adversaries had escaped, and it wasn't good enough.

One of his hunters landed beside him. "I found them, Lord," he said.

"Finally, some good news," Kratt cried, excitedly.

The messenger looked confused. "But they're dead, Lord," the hunter said unsurely.

"Great," said Kratt, "that's another problem sorted."

"No, Lord," the messenger said nervously, "Suca and Traps are dead, the tawny frogmouth spies. I found their bodies under a bush at the base of the Cor nest tree."

Kratt almost turned a dark shade of purple as his rage grew. "I'm looking for the Cor clan leaders, not my dead spies." The messenger turned to leave and was about to take to the sky when Kratt called him back.

"Wait," Kratt called. "You found Suca and Traps at the base of the Cor clan nest tree?" he confirmed. The messenger nodded. Kratt thought for a moment. "Spread the word. Anyone who finds the mother, her son, and their disappearing daughter, will receive all the Cor clan lands. Tell everyone." The messenger was about to fly when Lord Kratt stopped him again saying, "and tell everyone that the whole valley is now Lord Kratt's land... I mean Krat clan land," he corrected himself. "Every mytre in the valley is now a Krat clan member. Tell everyone." The bird hesitated. "Well, get a move on, to wing, to feather... fly," Kratt shouted. The messenger didn't wait and was soon flying across the valley with news for any mytre he located.

Lord Kratt signalled for Krattac and Kratatora to approach him. Krattac had blood on his face. It dripped from the socket where his eye had been removed by Karbett in their fight. Once they were nearby, he whispered to them, "Find the Cor clan rebels. I want them all brought before me. I want them destroyed."

"Yes, Lord," Krattac and Kratatora replied in unison. "We'll tear the valley apart and leave no hiding place unsearched," Kratatora reassured him. *They won't find them in the valley,* Kratt thought. But he demanded, "Do it quickly," before adding, "then you can start searching beyond the valley. In that eucalypt forest, and in the land to the east, and the escarpment lands to the north." Lord Kratt looked about at the dozen or so scared and broken Kar clan mytre still perched uneasily on the branches near the elpitlum. He looked at them with contempt, but knew he needed their support with his own Krat clan numbers dwindling.

"You can all go home now and remember, you are all Krat clan now. Serve me well and all will be well, serve me not... and you will find yourself in the Great flock of Elppa before you can say Elppa's blessings, now go."

-0-

Cordelia found Sid and Trev on the roof of the shearing shed. They were deciding what to eat and were contemplating a long flight to the west for insects in the scrubby, pale grassy paddocks or a short trip over to the fruit trees in the norzela's garden. "I feel like a long flight today," Sid was saying as Cordelia arrived.

"Who's this, dear," Trev said excitedly, as Cordelia landed in an excited flurry of tail and wing feathers.

"I know... I know that I must get to the valley now. I think it's about to catch fire and I must get back." Cordelia squawked quickly and Sid had to ask her to talk more slowly.

"I know... that it's time to go, I think the valley is about to be set on fire, and I have to get back." Cordelia sounded excited and insistent.

"But you still have no idea where the valley is, sweet," Trev reminded her with a dismissive wave of his wing. "How will you know which way to fly?"

Cordelia had to stop and think for a moment, leaving and getting back had occupied her mind so much that she'd neglected to consider the original problem of which direction to travel.

"A long flight today, I think, to the west," Sid went on, returning to their interrupted conversation about where to go to eat, as if the matter of Cordelia's leaving were settled.

As the three birds sat on the apex of the shearing shed roof, suddenly two rainbow lorikeets darted past them, they appeared quickly and disappeared almost as quickly as they flew at considerable speed, at roof height, right past Cordelia, Sid, and Trev.

They are beautiful birds,' Cordelia thought. *They have a dazzling colour pallet of feathers, and remarkable orange beaks.* Cordelia had seen many as she'd flown about the valley, and she knew their plumage in an instant.

"They're in a hurry to somewhere," Sid said as he watched them speed away.

"Must be late for something," Trevor said.

"Or trying to get away from something or someone," Cordelia speculated. As she wondered what it could be she saw two more lorikeets approaching from the east, also at speed. As they passed, Cordelia called out to them, "Where are you going so fast?"

One of the rainbow lorikeets kept flying, fast, west, into the distance. The closer one, swept in a long arc around the shearing shed roof and as it passed again it shouted out in a breathless spray, "Fire, smoke, fly, flee." Then it sped away after its mate.

Sid and Trev looked at each other confused, but Cordelia knew at once what this meant. Although the lorikeets had clearly travelled far, they were fleeing a fire and the smoke that it creates and they'd come from the east. That was the direction Cordelia needed to take. The revelation hit her like a gunshot to the chest. *Home is to the east,* she thought, and her relief was palpable. Although she still had no idea how far it was, she knew now which direction to take. "I have to go east," Cordelia said to Sid and Trev.

They had taken longer to identify the significance of the lorikeet's news, but as Cordelia spoke, they both knew the truth, that the valley was east, and this was the way Cordelia needed to fly to get home.

"So, this is goodbye, darling," Sid said lamentably.

"Oh, my luv," Trev said, as he grew emotional. "We knew you'd go… one day… but so soon." He was almost in tears as he spoke.

Cordelia hugged them both with her wings spread awkwardly around them and said, "I'll miss you both, you've been wonderful." Then she added, "But I do have to leave, and right away. I just need to speak with Bruce before I do."

Sid and Trevor understood and let her go. She flew off the roof of the shearing shed and darted back over to the top of her cage in a moment.

Bruce was outside, waiting near the cage door. "I've come outside to sit in the sun," he said. "I can smell the faintest hint of smoke and I heard the distressed lorikeet call out, 'fire, smoke.' I was alarmed at first, but I sense the fire and smoke are a very long way off. It's a gift we dogs have," Bruce clarified.

Cordelia flew down to the veranda floor and approached him. "Bruce," Cordelia cut in, "It means I know the way home, to the valley. It means I must go, now." She looked at him sympathetically. "I'm sorry, friend," she said, "for everything."

"I've been distant, I know, lost almost. I was at first afraid to come back here. It's taken me a while to see that no place is truly safe, no place is truly protected from the keere, if they're determined and savage," Bruce said.

"But we have to fight them," Cordelia replied. "It's why I have to leave."

"I know," Bruce said. "I understand now. The bullies want you to be afraid. They want you to feel weak and vulnerable, to lose your way, your hope, and your belief. I see now that I allowed the snake to steal the very things I was passionate about. My sense of fun, and humour, and it nearly took my life too." Bruce sat and then dropped to lay on the veranda. He nuzzled up to Cordelia and said, "Thank you, for helping me see this." He licked her face kindly. "I'll be fine now, I'll miss you… but I'll be fine here at the station. I have the yard-dogs and Sid and Trev to keep me company and to remind me of you." Cordelia was unable to stop crying.

Bruce went on, "You have your passion to fight for. Your home, your family, and your valley. I wish I could come with you, but I know this is a fight you'll have to face alone."

"No, not alone, I have my friends here at the station behind me, I have you in my heart, and with you, and Sid, Trev, and even Gary, I'll be unstoppable." Cordelia used her wing to wipe her eyes as she finished speaking.

Bruce spoke in a deep broken voice as he said, "Go… friend," and withdrew from their embrace.

With that Cordelia said, "Goodbye," one last time, and hopped up to the top of the cage. It was there she noticed Mary looking at them through the full-length kitchen window.

-0-

"I'd swear that bird and the dog were just talking to each other," she said turning to Lilly. "That's the strangest bird I've ever known," she added.

"Mum, it's just a magpie," Lilly exclaimed.

"Did you ever name it?" Mary asked still focused on Cordelia.

"No," Lilly said, "I wasn't sure it was going to live when we first found it."

"Have you thought of a name now?" her mother asked.

Lilly replied, "Yes, I think so, we were reading 'King Lear', by that Shakespeare bloke, just before I finished school. I was thinkin' of calling her Cordelia, after one of the king's daughters. She was the best of them according to the play. I thought that would be a good name."

"Cordelia," Mary repeated, smiling, "yer, I like it, dear… Cordelia, clever girl."

-0-

Outside, Cordelia took to flight. She spread her wings, now strong and ready, and flew over to the shearing shed to say a final farewell, but she couldn't see Sid or Trev there. *Gone to the west to find insects*, she thought. She lifted her head and pushed her wings up and down with her powerful chest muscles. Slowly she rose into the sky. Soon she caught an updraft as Gary had taught her. He'd said, 'Use them, they will save your energy and allow you to travel further for longer.' Soon she was higher than she'd flown before.

Below her, the station grew smaller and smaller. The yard-dogs kennels, the machine shed, the shearing shec, the windmill tower, the small garden, and the norzela nest with the all-round veranda and her cage. Soon they were too far behind to see, and she began her journey east, back to her valley home.

30

Danger from Above

The world's a nicer place in my beautiful balloon
It wears a nicer face in my beautiful balloon
We can sing a song and sail along the silver sky
For we can fly, we can fly.

The 5th Dimension – 'Up, Up and away'' (1967)

THE UPDRAFTS were a wonderful mechanism for covering great distances without expending huge amounts of energy. Cordelia had flown a long way by using the warm rising air and by circling with it, up and down instead of flying low and fast as she had aways done before. Korzela, the God of wind was with her too, coming briskly from the west. She could occasionally see rainbow lorikeets flying low and straight below her, heading away to the west. It confirmed her hope that she was going in the right direction. Although she had started to wonder what she was returning to. *Would she find the valley burnt? Would her family be gone, killed, or banished? Could she fight Lord Kratt?* She had no way of knowing any of this. All she knew and all she needed to focus on was getting home, back to the valley.

The land below her was still wide open plain, covered with sparce grass, low shrubs and weedy gum and eucalypt trees. Occasionally, she could see the outline of a creek or road as it curled across the landscape, or the sparkling glint of water in dams or reservoirs. She began to tire as Elppa set behind her and she started to look for a place to settle and rest. She'd flown over thousands of trees, but few looked to be well suited for resting in.

Below her she noticed for the first time her shadow gliding silently over the ground beneath her. It looked massive, far larger than she had imagined. She'd never seen it before, as it didn't show in the closed country of the valley, and she'd never flown so lofty to get a look at it from this high above. She studied it for a while as it flicked and rolled over the landmarks below her on the plain. It was almost mystical, as if there was another low flying black bird that flashed along the ground.

Suddenly, she was aware of a second shadow. Elppa was low in the sky to her rear, and the second shadow seemed to grow rapidly ahead of her own as she circled toward the ground. It looked like the two shadows were about to collide. Then Cordelia recognised what was happening. She'd seen this before when she'd practiced her arial fighting with Gary. In an instant she realised she was under attack.

Her attacker was almost upon her. Suddenly, Cordelia rolled and pitched onto her back and faced a brown goshawk. She raised her claws as she tried to deflect the assault. It worked, the hawk had never encountered prey that had dared offer resistance of any sort and Cordelia's enemy was stunned. It was too late to pull up though and the diving hawk tried to swivel away to Cordelia's right as it passed.

The brown goshawk had its own talors drawn up into its streamlined dive position and so had no strike weapon ready as they passed. It meant Cordelia managed to scratch the bird as it raced past her. She didn't have the power of Gary's talon, so she was unable to hold on to her attacker as it passed, but she dealt it a savage scratch on its flank that sent the bird into a tailspin. Cordelia dived after her attacker as it plummeted, taking up a corkscrew dive in pursuit as she twisted in yaw.

Cordelia's manoeuvre had so completely ambushed the hawk that it now felt in peril of its own life. Shrieking as it spun away, the attacker was soon able to correct its tumbling fall and regain some aerodynamic stability. However, as soon as it did, Cordelia was on it, sinking her claws into the hawk's shoulder and upper wing. They both dropped quickly as they fought, pitching, and spinning towards the ground. Then, the earth was suddenly there, rushing up to meet them as their combat continued.

Moments before they crashed into the ground, Cordelia disengaged from the fight, flapped her wings, and used her spread tail to pull up before the potential impact.

The goshawk plummeted on, only managing to gain lift as it spread its wings just above the height of the low shrubs of the scrub. Cordelia flew up to a sparsely leafed tree and came to rest on a branch. The brown goshawk flew to the ground and landed gracelessly, as it tumbled and fell into a small Dillwynia Floribunda bush, landing amongst the terete leaves and finding itself covered by petals from the yellow pea-flowers as they fell about it. It shook its head as it tried to recover from the unsuccessful ambush and failed combat.

Cordelia watched as the hunter looked around and tried to get its bearing. Soon she saw that the goshawk had seen her perched on the tree branch. She could see the look of confusion on the goshawk's face as it saw her, and she called over to the dazed hunter.

"I am Cordelia the brave. I was trained by the best," she shouted, "Gary the wedge-tailed eagle, only son of Garth, grandson of Graham, great grandson of George, and descendant of the Great Gus from the western mountain cliffs. In future, it'll be best if you avoid any conflict with my kind." Cordelia tried to sound bold and unafraid. Inside her heart was pounding and she could hardly believe she'd survived." *Gary would have been proud*, she thought.

The hawk flicked a yellow pea-flower petal off its head and stood defiantly facing Cordelia. They both regarded the other for a moment, across the short strip of plain between them. Then, to Cordelia's surprise, her attacker said, "My apologies, Cordelia the brave, I mistook you for a lesser bird. Pass in peace." With that the hawk bowed low and after shaking all the remaining flower petals off, it lifted into the air and flew slowly away back towards the west to preen its feathers and dress its wounds.

Cordelia decided to stay in the tree and rest. She'd flown a long way and although she'd not been injured in the fight, she was emotionally tired. As she'd flown, drifting on the air currents, she'd thought about leaving Bruce and Martin and the other yard-dogs. About Sid, Trev, and about Gary. She even thought about the norzela who had saved her life and helped her when she'd been injured and captured. The only things she didn't miss were Lilly's older brother, who kicked the cage, and the keere snake.

Darkness was approaching and she was still not sure where she was or if she really was going in the right direction. Nothing she saw around her or had flown over, looked familiar or reminded her of the valley. But, as she rested, she was aware of something new in the air, something she'd only smelt on cold nights in the valley, not long after she'd hatched: smoke. Now she was lower down it was clear for the first time that she was getting closer to the fire. Then she turned to look toward the east away from the setting Elppa.

The sky was full of a red glow. *It couldn't be Elppa*, she thought. She could see the smoke clearly, and beyond the smoke, the whole sky was a blaze of red. Then she saw the trees further away in the east. They stood starkly against the glowing blaze of sky. They were all black, barren sticks rather than trees. Some still held red, yellow, and orange smouldering embers in their cores and the dying rays of Elppa's light showed them clearly against the red glow. Others had burnt and crumbled, laying like shadows of trees on the ground. There was no grass, no green, just blackened, charred earth, and ash covered soil. Cordelia was in shock. '*Would the valley be like this? How could her family survive a fire that left nothing in its wake?*'

Then she saw the first one. It looked like a kangaroo corps laying stiff and black and unnatural on its side between two burnt tree trunks. Then she saw another. They'd had no hope, even with their long legs and speed, the fire must have been too fast, even for them. Slowly Elppa's light dwindled behind her as the sky darkened above the far-off red glow. Cordelia looked higher into the dark sky, toward the east, and towards Orion's belt. There, three bright stars that form a short straight line of the belt, were rising. *That is the way I must go,* she thought.

Everything was red, like a false nwad. She felt defeated and forlorn, tired, and confused. She'd beaten the goshawk, she could find her way east, but how could she beat Kratt, or the fire? How could she even find the valley if the fire destroyed everything she remembered about her home? *Will the three stars be enough?* she wondered. She decided to rest alone in the slender tree. *I'll deal with Kratt and the fire tomorrow. One victory, one escape, one day at a time will be enough*, she thought.

-0-

Kratatora and Krattac had taken a long while to search the valley. Much longer than Kratt had wanted. Krattac had wanted to go faster, but his missing eye hampered his flight, and this slowed them both. Kratatora didn't want to go fast. She was keen to be thorough and searched every likely hiding place in the valley. They found no sign of the Cor clan escapees or indeed any of the Cor clan members.

When they told the Great Lord Kratt that it appeared that the Cor clan had all moved on, he flew into a rage, flapping his wings and demanding servants he could trust. Krattac tried to explain, "The Cor clan lands are practically empty, even many of the other birds seemed to have gone, Lord."

"But gone where?" the Great Lord Kratt asked angrily. "Birds don't just disappear."

"Maybe it's magic, or some sort of Cor clan trick?" Kratatora foolishly suggested.

"A trick," Kratt bellowed, "A trick." He scoffed, shook his head, and pointed a wing at Krattac, "I can understand you not being able to find anything Krattac, you have just one eye, but you." He looked at the unfortunate Kratatora. "You're just a fool."

She looked deflated. "But Lord... we looked..." Kratatora stammered. The Great Lord Kratt looked at her. *Pathetic,* he thought.

"Kratjoa," he called, loudly.

"Yes, Great Lord Kratt," she replied as she flew down from a branch in the once Kar nest tree and landed at her Lord's side.

"Go now and search the forest to the south. If you find the traitors from Cor, report back to me, immediately."

"Yes, Lord," Kratjoa, said clearly and obediently.

"You two," Lord Kratt shouted at Krattac and Kratatora. "Search the escarpment, and don't let me down again. You," he said, pointing with a large black and white wing at three ex-Kar clan members roosting nearby, "search the eastern norzela park."

With their orders set, all the Great Lord Kratt's servants took to the air. As the hunt for Cordelia's mother, Corselia, her brother, Corxell and the disappearing Cordelia began to grow in intensity.

-0-

Corselia and her son, Corxell, flew west as fast as they could, stopping every now and then to look behind for pursuers. In the pale light of Egnaro, they saw none, and they flew urgently on. Corselia had never been this far west of the valley, and she was fearful but alert for danger. The dark of Egnaro offered some protection although it also increased their feeling of dread and trepidation. Egnaro was directly above them when they rested for a short while in a Ghost Gum near a creek in another valley. They'd not been in the tree for more than a moment when they heard a voice.

"You can't stay here," someone said in a deep, angry tone.

"We just need to rest," Corselia said calmly, although startled and unsure of where the voice was coming from.

"Well, you can't. This is our land, our place, and your kind are not welcome here."

Corselia couldn't see who was talking or gather were the voice was coming from. Then she looked up. Although the light was minimal, she could just see, perched well above her on a peripheral branch of the tree they were sitting in, a yellow-tail black cockatoo. It was holding a woody fruit with one foot while prizing out the seeds with its enormous upper mandible.

It looked to be black-brown in hue, but it had flashes of yellow behind its eyes and on the underside of its tail feathers. Its eyes were round and black, dark, and deep, most unlike the amber brown of her own. As well, it was large, at least a third larger than her. She was immediately intimidated, and her calmness evaporated.

"We're fleeing our nest tree and clan lands," Corselia said, anxiously. "Please, we just need to rest for a short while."

"No," the old Lord of the yellow-tail black cockatoo snapped in a booming voice. "We've seen it before. You say you're refugees, fleeing some imagined strife, some place where your life is in danger, some war, or famine or natural calamity. But you just want what we have. Our nuts, fruit, grubs, and larvae... our trees, our nests, our place." He paused. "Well, you can't stay, you're not welcome and we have nothing for you here that we can spare."

Corselia was taken aback but she gathered her wits and was about to argue and protest, when Corxell raised his wing and gestured for her not to bother.

"It's no use, Mother," he said, "we're not welcome. Let's find the Wayt clan lands, and our own mytre. We'll leave these miserly, miserable birds to the nuts and larvae... I hope they choke on them," he concluded, bitterly.

"But we just need a place to rest, can't they see we're tired and want to stop and rest for a while?" She spoke softly to her son, her exhaustion and frustration growing as she spoke.

Her son understood. He was tired too. "Let's just go, Mum," he said, resigned to their fate.

The old yellow-tail black cockatoo continued to eat, dropping bits of nut and seeds down through the foliage of the massive tree as he did. As the two mytre prepared to leave, they noticed other black-brown, yellow-tail black cockatoo distributed about the upper limbs of the tree, also eating their nuts and seed with their dextrous feet and powerful mandible beak. It was soon evident that a considerable colony of yellow-tail black cockatoo lived in the area.

As they noticed them, almost as one, the tree's residents began to call out in a chorused ear-splitting screech.

"Go, leave," they began to chant in a deep scratchy chorus. "Go, leave, we don't want your kind here."

Corselia and Corxell saw no point staying and although tired they each took to the wing. This time, Corselia led her son back, in a sweeping arc toward the eucalyptus forest, travelling southeast and away from the yellow-tail black cockatoo valley.

They had flown all night and nwad was breaking as they reached the edge of the forest. They both rested on a tall gum tree before daring to venture into the forest. They had no idea where the Wayt clan lived or if indeed they still lived in the depths of the eucalypt forest, but this was their only avenue after fleeing the valley. Elppa rose across the treetops of the forest before them, and as the early mist dissipated from around the tallest trees, they flew on to try to find the Wayt clan.

They flew above the forest canopy for a while, finding this easier than weaving their way between the tangle of trees, branches, and leaves in the canopy crown. Trees gave way to open ground in places, but they were few, and, even there, ferns, low shrubs, and bushes covered the ground. Corselia knew if they reached the creek they had gone too far, so when they flew over the banks of a narrow creek, she called out to Corxell to follow her back toward the west. As they turned, a large beaked bird flew up to confront them.

"Halt," he cried, then paused and added, "wait, I know you." Cordelia and Corxell were about to drop down to the banks of the creek to hide when, the big bird called again, "I know you… you're Corzell's partner."

Stunned and relieved in equal measure, Corselia signalled for the big bird and her son to descend to the creek bank. There, under the dappled light of the forest, where the creek line broke the canopy, they all landed to talk. The creek meant she and her son could quickly quench their thirst, but as the bigger bird landed near them on a boulder, she instantly recognised him as the bird her partner once chatted with in their nest tree. As he landed, she called out, "I know you too, you're Bill, the kookaburra friend of Corzell."

"Yer, that's right, luv. I've bin hiding out 'ear in the forest since those two mytre were killed by that Krat mob," Bill said, directly. Then he went on, "I tried to warn Corzell, I tried ta' tell him something bad was comin'. Too late now I'd say."

"Do you know what happened to him… to Corzell? I haven't seen him since the elpitlum and…" Corselia's voice began to quiver as her emotions and exhaustion overcame her.

"Nar ain't seen him… sorry, luv," Bill said sympathetically. Then he added, "He's not 'round here anyways."

"We're looking for the Wayt clan too… do you know where they are?" Corxell asked butting in.

Corselia regained her composure and put in, "Yes, we're searching for the clan that ran and hid in the forest. Do you know where they are?"

"Nar, not seen 'em," the kookaburra said, bluntly.

"Will you help us find them?" Corselia asked, hopefully.

Bill looked at the soil, he jabbed at it with his powerful beak as he thought. "Nar…" he replied after a moment. "Gunna go… I can feel something bad comin' again, worse than the Krat, I reckon."

"Worse than the Krat!" Corxell exclaimed, doubtfully.

"Yer, I reckon. Anyway, I ain't staying, and I reckon yuz should fly too." The kookaburra thrust his beak at a worm as he uncovered it in the soil. As he flicked it up into the air, he grabbed it with his beak, then, speaking with his beak full he said, "I was… on my… way when… I saw yoz two… and I thought… I'd say g'day." Bill finished speaking and swallowed the worm. "I thought you might be me mate, Corzell. I'm sorry he'z gone, he was a good bloke… for a mytre."

Corxell looked offended. "Oh, no offence meant, mate," Bill said softly.

Corselia ignored him, and asked, "Where are you going?"

The kookaburra made to take off. "North, over the escarpment… safer there I reckon. Yoz should come too." His offer was only half-hearted. He doubted these mytre would ever really leave the valley.

Corselia and Corxell were beat. Their fight to leave the valley, their flight west and run in with the yellow-tail black cockatoo, their flight back to the eucalyptus forest, and their fruitless search for the Wayt clan had left them both on the brink of collapse. Corselia doubted they would have the energy to fly north even if she had wanted to go with him.

"No," she said at last, "we'll only slow you down… and we have to find the Wayt clan… they might know what happened to Corzell."

"Suit yezself, but yuz have been warned… somethin' bad's coming. Somethin' worse than Kratt." He flapped his wings quickly and was soon well above the forest canopy. As he ascended, he shouted, "Good luck… yuz'll need it."

They watched him leave. Both birds felt utterly dejected. But with a look of determined resignation, Corselia led her son up into the sky again as they flew back towards the west. Taking to the air again, it was clear they couldn't go on like this. They were both getting fatigued and Corxell was starting to tire completely. Seeing him fall behind, Corselia slowed down and flew back to support her son.

"We can land there," she shouted as they approached a small break in the forest canopy. She led her son down and came to rest on a fallen tree trunk in a small clearing. The forest felt oppressive, dark, and musty, not at all like the open grassed areas and separated trees of their clan lands.

Corxell found a small pool of stagnant water in the hollow of a log and drank from it. It stank and tasted foul. He shook his head to clear his beak and nostrils of the pungent odour. The smell made his feathers curl and a shiver of revulsion quivered down his wings. *This was nothing like the sweet, clear, valley creek water,* he thought.

Corselia looked about at the forest floor and up through the high green canopy. She tried to see into the thick forest all about them, but even she was feeling the effects of their long journey, and her eyes were playing tricks on her. She thought she'd seen her partner Corzell hopping toward her through the thick fern fronds. *But it couldn't be, could it?* she thought. She blinked and tried to refocus her eyes and as she watched, a familiar black and white bird approached her.

"Corzell," she called, "Is that you?" She could hardly believe her eyes.

Corxell turned and saw the strange black and white bird hopping in their direction, then he saw another, and another. "It's not father," he called out, suddenly fearful.

One of the mytres coming toward them spoke. "Corselia, is that you and your son?"

Corselia was shocked into wakefulness. It wasn't Corzell before her, and as soon as she was sure, she was alert and braced herself to fly.

"Corselia, it's me… Waytbill, of the Wayt clan," the mytre called.

Corselia had bobbed low and held herself ready to fly, but a wave of relief suddenly gripped her. She'd found them, or rather they'd found her, and she and her son were instantly overcome by joy, relief, and a terrible tiredness that made them feel like stone.

"Waytbill," she said happily, "we've been looking for you." As she spoke another three mytre came out from the undergrowth and approached the log.

"You have landed on the elpitlum log of the Wayt clan," Waytbill explained as he approached. We were just coming to sing our ksud chorus, before going back into the forest to hide." He paused, "but where is Corzell and your daughter, and why didn't he call for our help with the Krat clan?"

"It's a long story and I only know part of it," Corselia said. "But we're hungry and exhausted from our long flight. Can we talk after we've rested?" she asked.

"Yes, yes, of course," Waytbill said, as he signalled for his clan members to help their two guests to their hiding place.

"Also, it might be best to avoid your carolling for a while too," Corselia advised as they hopped and walked away from the elpitlum log, adding, "Kratt is looking for us... for all of us."

The Wayt showed Corselia and Corxell the way to their clan burrow. *It's amazing,* Corselia thought. Waytbill explained that while there were many places to build a nest in the forest, they had discovered it was safer to take over the hole of a long past wombat. These were ancient dwellings, from when the forest was younger, and the wombat had first arrived. They were made within the network of a great tree's root system. The tunnel was wide, and deep, and warm, but most especially it was safe.

"When we first came to the forest we tried to live in the trees and began to build nests in a few suitable trees. But all the life of the forest is on the ground. We felt out of place high up and once we'd found and explored the abandoned wombat burrow, we decided to move in here. There was a small green snake, but we drove him out and cleaned up the tunnel to make it comfortable. Being underground means we are unlikely to be seen from above and it allows us to feed and live in comfort, here on the forest floor.

"It's very un-mytre-like behaviour," Corselia said, with a tone of admiration. *They've come to a new place and adapted to it*, she thought, *very impressive.* Corselia told Waytbill and the others of his clan what had happened at the recent elpitlum. She didn't know what had happened to Cordelia or her own partner, Corzell, but she explained that she'd seen Karbett, Kardelia, and Corhelia killed. It had been an ambush and the whole valley now seemed to be in the wings and beak of Lord Kratt and the Krat clan.

She explained that Corzell had sent for Bil 's help, and the Wayt clan, but Kratt had intercepted their messenger. Now she could only assume that her partner and daughter were dead or captives of Kratt. "Any hope I have that they live is smal ," she admitted. "We flew to escape and came to find you here in the forest," Corselia explained finally. "Thank goodness we have," she sighed at last.

"I'm sorry to hear about your failed rebellion, but you're both welcome here, with the Wayt clan. We have little in the way of land, but in everything else, we have all we need, and we're happy to share." Waytbill thought for a moment, then added, "so, we're all fugitives now... from Lord Kratt."

"And he won't stop," Corxell added, fearfully.

Waytjulia put a comforting wing around the young mytre. "You'll be safe with us," she said, cheerily, "he'll never find us here, underground."

31

Searching

While overhead, her birds fill the skies.
All around the cathedral the saints and apostles
Look down as she sells her wares.

Although you can't see it, you know they are smiling,
Each time someone shows that he cares,
Though her words are simple and few,

Listen, listen, she's calling to you:
"Feed the birds, tuppence a bag,
Tuppence, tuppence, tuppence a bag."

From Mary Poppins – 'Feed the Birds (Tuppence a Bag)' (1964)

KRATJOA LEFT THE former Kar clan territory every day and searched for the rebel base, and the home of the Wayt clan. She knew it was in the eucalypt forest somewhere, but until she'd started to search, she had no idea that the forest was so vast. She decided to take a systematic approach and started with the parts of the forest closest to the Yat and Wayt clan lands. She even searched in and around the old norzela nest on the Yat lands in the hope of finding some clues to the rebel's whereabouts. Searching systematically meant searching methodically, slowly, and carefully.

The two searchers who were looking across the escarpment had found nothing, and Krattac and Kratatora were disappointed to report their failure to their Lord.

"Useless, foolish, and blind," their Lord told them, before dismissing them from the nest tree. Those sent to explore the norzela park had also found nothing, and Kratt's frustration and anger grew. *I want their bodies or confirmation of where they have gone*, Lord Kratt thought resolutely.

Kratjoa was sure she would find them in the forest, but she didn't trust the others and she decided to search on, alone, even though it meant taking longer.

The Great Lord Kratt was at first frustrated and disappointed with Kratjoa's progress too, and almost replaced Kratjoa as the hunter assigned to the forest, but she explained that she was sure to find the traitors and locate their base, their leaders and to discover their plans. She just needed more time.

Lord Kratt's anger after the murder of his two spies, Suca and Traps, and the disappearance of the leadership of the Cor clan hadn't lessened with time, even as his dominance over the valley solidified. None of the former Kar clan dared oppose him, after he'd killed Karmann, Karbett and Kardelia. Their fear of him was palpable and Lord Kratt had snuffed out any resistance from within the valley. The Dart clan had long since ceased to exist and the remaining remnants of Kar, Cor and Yat clans bowed to him as if he were Elppa himself. Only the Wayt clan and the remaining Cor clan leader and their children remained unaccounted for, and they were likely weak and dispersed.

"I should feel confident," he told himself. "Kratjoa will find the rebels and I will soon be absolute master of the valley." He had established a new nest in the old Kar clan nest tree and taken one of the old Karmann's daughters as his partner. Soon his takeover would be complete. If Kratjoa took a little while longer to find the Wayt nest, so be it, he could wait. But his anger remained raw, and his frustration grew as time passed.

Kratjoa was indeed thorough. Each day she would fly to the same place she'd finished searching the day before and start a systematic sweep of the forest canopy. Sometimes she'd swoop in under the foliage and look along the banks of the creek, or explore possible nest sites in suitable trees, but after many passages of Elppa she was still unable to find the mytre who eluded her.

As she flew over the treetops on her way back to her own nest tree in the new Krat territory, she realised that she'd been searching so long she'd missed the nwad, nwod and ksud carolling. It was unusual for any mytre to miss these traditions and she knew that she'd become completely focused on her search. As she came in to land, she heard the finishing notes of what sounded like a forlorn hymn from some of the former Kar clan mytre. They stopped as she approached and scattered about the nest tree or flew away to their own nests.

Kratjoa thought, *These foolish birds don't know that their own tired devotion to their singing will see them give away their treachery to Lord Kratt one day.* She watched them fly and had half a mind to say something to her Lord the next rising of Elppa. But as she waited for the shadow of Egnaro to rise, she had another thought. *If the traitors here will risk singing of their loss as they always have, perhaps the rebels in the forest will sing at the traditional carolling times too. If I search for their songs as well as their nests, I'm sure to find them.* The idea came to Kratjoa like a revelation. *They will sing me to them,* she thought. The idea played on her mind for as long as Egnaro's glow rose and fell across the valley. In the growing glow of Elppa, she knew, she would apply herself to her new plan.

-0-

Once rested, Corselia and Corxell were able to give the Wayt clan even more detail about the ambush at the elpitlum and the desperate fight of Karbett and Kardelia.

"I don't know what happened to Corzell or Cordelia, but I saw a small flock of Krat warriors chase them from the elpitlum. After that, we left the valley and tried to find you here. If we hadn't stumbled into your clearing, we never would have found you in the vastness of the forest," Corselia explained.

"Or if we hadn't ventured from our tunnel," Waytbill said, with a chuckle.

"Underground mytre, who would have thought it," Corselia exclaimed.

They all strode about under the ferns and shrubs searching for grubs and insects, each finding plenty to satisfy their hunger. "I don't know why we haven't lived in the forest before," one of the Wyat clan members said, cheerfully, as he pecked at a loose piece of bark to reveal the grubs within.

"We are meant to fly and sing in the sky, not fuss about under thick ferns and in the close heat of the underbrush," another said, sounding unhappy and dissatisfied with the new Wayt home. "We haven't even sung to welcome Elppa or celebrated the nwod or ksud chorus since we've been here," the unhappy mytre complained loudly.

"You know we can't, it will give our new nest location away and if the Krat clan are hunting us we might be found and captured," Waytbill explained.

"Or worse," put in Corselia.

"But we can't go on living like this indefinitely," the unhappy Wayt clan member said as he saw a fat flying beetle and snatched it from the air in a flash with his beak.

"I like it here," said the more cheerful Wayt mytre as he flapped over towards a fern off to one side of the group. Suddenly, he was gone. All the others saw was the fern leaves flapping in the air, where the mytre had once stood.

A quoll had been hiding in a hollow space by a log and as the unfortunate bird passed the fern the quoll struck. The cheerful birds screech of surprise and pain was shocking, and all the other birds took to flight, each rising away to the nearest high branch. The quoll had been out hunting all night and was on its way back to its hiding place in a hollow log west of the Wayt clan clearing, when it saw the birds chatting and walking leisurely about the forest floor. It rarely caught birds, but today's catch had been simple.

All the quoll had done was lay still and wait for the foolish bird to wander closer as it came to be devoured.

The remaining birds watched from above as the keere dragged the once happy mytre away, back to its hollow log to feed itself or its family. Either way, one of the Wayt clan had been taken and suddenly the forest floor didn't seem as safe as they had first thought.

"And she was happy here," said the unhappy mytre, "Not so happy now," he added dismissively, and unkindly.

"She is with the Great flock of Elppa now," Corselia said solemnly.

The others retorted, "Flying with the Great flock of Elppa." They all went silent in respect of their loss. They were all aware that their normal response would be to sing a lament, a prayer, or a solemn carol in memory of the lost mytre, but as fugitives, their voices remained as hidden as they were themselves. Corselia knew that songbirds who had lost their song, their chorus... were truly lost.

After a moment, Waytbill spoke commandingly to them all, saying, "I'm sorry for this loss. However, we'll have to stay here until we know that we're safe, until we know that Lord Kratt is gone or until we can find another place to go." They'd all watched the quoll scurry away through the underbrush and disappear with their dead clan member, gripped in its jaw.

After this, no one ventured back to the forest floor for a long while. When they did, Waytbill suggested they feed and forage in two groups, with one group staying above the forest floor on low branches to watch for danger, while the others feed, safely observed from above. This reassured everyone but doubt about the safety of life in the forest had begun to grow and Corselia and Waytbill knew they couldn't survive forever living in the eucalypt forest.

Corxell was especially unhappy, but he said nothing. Instead, he waited for ksud to pass then he snuck out of the burrow and flew between the trees to sing softly to Egnaro from the elpitlum log in the clearing. He knew it was foolish, but he couldn't stand the heat, the dry air, and the claustrophobic conditions underground.

He told himself he was helping keep watch over the burrow site, but he simply hated life underground.

He started talking to the unhappy Wayt clan mytre, who he felt shared his dissatisfaction and soon they both began to sneak out to play fight, fly above the canopy and pretend to 'guard' the nest site. They knew to be on the lookout for Krat clan hunters but had no idea of the real dangers in the forest, especially at night, and although they tried to keep their activities quiet and secret, Egnaro's creatures, the quoll, the tawny frogmouth, the boobook owl, and other keere were watching and waiting for their chance to strike.

-0-

Kratjoa was having no luck and her search for the missing clans was going nowhere. Each day she would leave before nwad and fly over the eucalypt forest listening for any sound of the mytre's chorus. Each day she returned with no new information or any further clues about their whereabouts. Lord Kratt was becoming increasingly frustrated. Soon even the faithful Kratjoa was being suspected of treachery. *After all, how is it that no one could find my foe,* Kratt speculated.

"No news is good news," Kratjoa reasoned to her Lord. Then she added, "Maybe they have truly gone away and maybe, My Lord, you are indeed, the sole master of the valley?"

Lord Kratt wanted to believe his servant, but he was starting to feel he could trust no one. *How hard could it be to find a group of mytre in a forest?* he wondered.

"My lord, if they are there, I'm sure I'll find them soon," Kratjoa insisted.

"I'm sure they're out there. You have one more passage of Elppa to find them. Then I'll lead every mytre in the valley in a sweeping search myself. We'll cover every scrap of the eucalypt forest. I'll find them if you cannot."

Kratjoa felt betrayed, after all her hard work and devotion, now she was to be pushed aside.

"Send word that after the next Elppa every mytre is to assemble at my Krat nest tree and help search the forest for the missing rebels."

Lord Kratt's decree left Kratjoa in no doubt that she had no time to waste. The Wayt clan nest tree had to be found or her place at her Lord's side would be in jeopardy. Then she had a thought, *Send word. Send word*, Kratjoa said to herself. An idea flashed into her head.

"Yes, Lord, immediately," Kratjoa cried as she took flight in search of the willie-wagtail near the norzela nest on the old Cor clan lands.

She found the bird quickly and confirmed this was indeed the same willie-wagtail that Corzell had recruited to pass on a message to the Wayt clan and some strange kookaburra bird.

"I am," the willie-wagtail confessed, fearful of the larger bird and keen to avoid its wrath.

"Then Lord Kratt orders are that you to take them another message. Tell them the rebellion is over, all is forgiven, and they can return to the valley if they wish."

The willie-wagtail looked confused. "Tell who, Lord?" he asked.

"I'm not your Lord, but I speak with the authority of the Great Lord Kratt." She paused and puffed out her chest. "Now fly into the forest and find the Wayt clan mytre and tell them they are forgiven."

"Tell them Lord Kratt forgives them?" The small bird repeated, still unsure.

"Yes... and tell them they can come home. All will be well." Kratjoa sounded upbeat and even pleased with her plan. "You can go now?" she added insistently.

"Yes... err... Lord... err... Miss," the frightened and confused willie-wagtail agreed. Kratjoa watched him take off and fly south toward the forest. She waited until he'd flown a long way then took off herself, to stealthily follow the simple, hoodwinked bird as he led her to what she hoped would be the Wayt hiding place in the forest.

32

There'll be No More Crying

For you, there'll be no more crying
For you, the sun will be shining
And I feel that when I'm with you
It's alright, I know it's right.

To you, I'll give the world
To you, I'll never be cold
'Cause I feel that when I'm with you
It's alright, I know it's right.

And the songbirds are singing,
Like they know the score.

Fleetwood Mac – 'Songbird'' (1977)

THE FIRE STARTED when a faulty electrical connection on a powerline near a barren hilltop sent a shower of sparks plummeting toward the crisp, dry grass at the base of the pole. The location was isolated and gave the fire time to get a grip on the high fuel load spread near the pole. Within minutes, the fire had spread to a plantation of pine trees, and it was on its way. The heat helped. It was a hot day, hotter than many before and it combined with a powerful wind gust coming from the west and southwest.

Before any norzela had detected it, the fire had hold of the timber and bush, and it grew into a fierce, catastrophic bushfire.

The wind grew too and combined with a sustained high-pressure system over the central west of New South Wales. The thermometer climbed and the oven-like blast of wind fed the flames. The humidity fell, creating the conditions for a fire flume that was spreading wide and thickly across the lower slopes of the western Great Dividing Range.

The wind grew in intensity to twenty-five kilometres an hour, before picking up further. After three hours of life, the wind was at thirty kilometres an hour and driving the embers and fire front forward, relentlessly.

Once the norzela became aware of the fire and its predicted path, the local, and government agencies responsible for fighting the fire sprang into action. Norzela within the predicted fire path began to follow warnings on the radio, or RFS website. They filled wheelbarrows, wheely bins, buckets, gutters, and tubs with water. They checked pumps and generators, hoses, and connections. Despite the heat, they changed into sturdy clothes, strong boots, and had goggles close at hand, ready to apply at a moment's notice.

Many watered their lawns, raked up leaf litter, cleared rubbish and fuel from around their properties and tried to block places where embers could enter their homes. They showered their homes with water, all the while keeping an ear on the radio, for updates and warnings. Many had cleared tall trees from near their homes and faced the prospect of open fields or paddocks between them and the fire front.

But the embers didn't respect the open space and blew even more easily onto the exposed properties. Hoses ready, pumps checked, fuel loads reduced, water available in tanks and dams, everything a norzela could do had been done. But still the fire had grown into a raging inferno as it pressed on, like a living beast or evil dragon, with its allies the wind and heat.

Many had plans to leave. Some packed what they could into their cars and made ready to flee. They took their precious things, their pets, and their children, hoping they'd not left it too late, and were trapped. Hoping that a wind change would spare their home while they were away. Hope was not a powerful weapon against the terrifying force of nature, but for many, unprepared or caught unaware, it was all they had.

Few, even those who'd seen fire before, and were physically ready for the fight, were unprepared for the psychological burden of the coming battle. They were unprepared for the burden of the heat, the assault of the embers, and the noise. The noise transformed the fire and warned of the fire's intensity. When two norzelas stood close together, their voices and breath were stolen by the fire. The heat, wind, flames, and embers that swirled around them consumed the sounds.

Government agencies sprang into action too. Networks of fire towers, control centres, regional headquarters and state-based management centres became hives of activity. But coordination was not always achieved, as fire generals and regional headquarter staff became bogged in masses of disparate information they couldn't control or sift through. Soon all their plans and responses were hours and hours behind the wind, the heat, and the fire. Water bombers were called in, fire fighters were dispatched, strike teams on the ground cleared fire breaks or back burned. But the size and rapid advance of the fire meant control was lost before a response had been initiated. It was now up to local norzela and small firefighting crews to face the blaze and kill the inferno.

The valley was still not ablaze, but thick smoke had covered the district. The smoke was white, not dark, or black. The valley locals who had gathered to defend their homes knew it meant the fire coming their way was hot, extremely hot, and before long, embers began falling like wicked glowing sprites that had come to dance a spiteful jig in their faces.

The wind began to howl, the air felt like an oven, as sparks and smoke filled the air and the sound overwhelmed them, like a jet engine or a locomotive barrelling through their yard. Falling embers drifted and tumbled in the yards, in the paddocks, on the sheds, on the tin rooves, on their skin, eyes and hair.

The embers were fragments of burning leaves, branches, and forest litter, plucked up by the wind, and carried far ahead of the main fire.

The day became night. It felt like an ember attack, as if an imagined monster was throwing fire and sparks into their very faces. An eery red tinged darkness surrounded the whole valley. One of the norzela looking out from the veranda of their house, in what was once the Cor clan territory said, "It's coming, and we're in for it now," as a gust of wind filled his yard with sparks and embers. In the distance, he could see through the smoke, as flames began tearing through the crown of the eucalyptus forest, south across the road. Suddenly, the wind was erratic and utterly unpredictable, as the very atmosphere seemed to be sucked up in a whirlwind of smoke, fire, embers, and debris. The initial ember fall was past, the fire had come to the valley.

-0-

Kratjoa followed the willie-wagtail as it skipped across the treetops of the eucalypt forest. It flew a long way before dropping into a clearing. Kratjoa had searched this part of the forest and was sure there were no Wayt clan nests in the area. But she followed the willie-wagtail into the open space and waited, hidden high on a tree branch. As she watched, Kratjoa saw the willie-wagtail fly down to a log in the centre of the forest space. A mytre was sitting on the log and the two birds sang together for a moment, before the mytre, Corxell, called and sang for Waytbill to come over to the log. Nothing happened for a short while. Then Kratjoa saw Waytbill, hop-fly across to the log and perch upon it, talking to the small messenger while the other mytre listened.

Got you, Kratjoa thought, triumphantly.

Behind her, growing in density, smoke billowed ahead of the fire front. She had smelt it as she'd flown over the forest, but disregarded it, so focused was she on following the willie-wagtail. Now as she rejoiced in having located the Wayt clan home, the smoke that had become thicker and more evident about her suddenly distracted her.

Kratjoa flew up to the top of the forest canopy and looked east. The wind had increased, and the cloud of embers and smoke were drifting and falling about her. She cursed Korzela, the God of wind, *Not now*, she thought bitterly. It had happened so quickly.

Checking again that she had found them, she turned and looked down. She saw Waytbill and the other mytre, followed by the willie-wagtail as they flew over to a tall tree. *'This must be their nest tree,'* Kratjoa thought. But as she watched, Waytbill and the others dropped low and landed at the foot of the tree. Then, to her utter amazement, they disappeared into a hollow, a hole in the ground. Confident that she had finally found the hiding place of the Wayt clan, Kratjoa flew into the air.

The smoke was now thick about the forest crown and in the air about her. She took off, flying with difficulty, northeast back to the Krat nest tree. The smoke was choking, and the swirling wind and heat dragged at her speed. Still, she was desperate to tell Lord Kratt her news, that she had found the rebels. So, she pressed on through the growing haze. As she did, the smoke and embers trailed her all the way, growing in intensity.

-0-

Waytbill had landed on the log. "What are you doing here, Corxell?" he asked, angrily.

"I'm on guard, watching the sky and forest floor for danger," Corxell replied defiantly. "We can't just hide in a hole all our lives," he concluded.

"Fool, you could give us away," Waytbill shouted. Then, seeing the willie-wagtail, Waytbill asked, "and what is all this calling about?"

"This messenger has come with a song from the valley," Corxell explained, although he was feeling hurt with the earlier rebuke.

"The Great Lord Kratt wants you to know that you are forgiven and can come back to the valley." The willie-wagtail finished delivering his message and looked about himself quickly. He added softly, "I think it's a trap, the valley is a mess, birds are leaving, the clans of old are destroyed and Lord Kratt is hated by everyone but a few loyal mytre of his own clan." As the small bird spoke, an ember burning on a small piece of bark landed near the log. Then another drifted, spiralling down to the ground near them.

Waytbill looked up and saw the dark cloud of smoke drifting high above the treetops. He'd smelt it as soon as he'd come up from the hole, but he'd been too upset with Corxell to pay the smell any attention. Now with embers falling around them he took note. "Quickly," he said, "Corxell and you, willie-wagtail, come with me. We have to get underground now."

The willie-wagtail hesitated, unsure what was happening. He contemplated flying back to the valley, he'd never seen a fire, or smoke and embers falling before and wasn't sure what was happening.

"Fly and die, or stay and hide," Waytbill said as he and Corxell took flight, over to their burrow. Feeling he had no choice, the willie-wagtail flew after the two bigger birds. *What does underground mean?* the small bird pondered as he followed them.

There was no panic at the burrow, as Waytbill, Waytjulia and Corselia reassured the others. "It will be hot and uncomfortable in the burrow, but it will still be the best place to stay, to hide and to survive the coming fire," Corselia advised.

"We should fly away from the fire and smoke," one of the Wayt clan members called, fearfully.

"Fly where?" Corselia replied. "The forest will soon be a blaze; it is heading to the valley. Bill said a terror was coming," Cordelia asserted recalling what the kookaburra had said. She could see the confusion on the faces of the other mytre. "Look it doesn't matter how I know, I am sure I do though, and I think all the land and sky between here and there will soon be a blaze, if it isn't already. We have a chance if we stay," she concluded, adamantly.

"If we stay here, we have a chance, if we try to fly, we may die," Waytbill confirmed. "Now, everyone find a comfortable corner of the burrow and wait. It will be hot and dark, but if we are lucky, it will pass over us and we'll live."

As they waited, the fire came into their part of the forest, driving all those without burrows or hollows and water homes before it.

Corselia and Waytbill assumed positions near the burrow mouth to defend it should other fleeing creatures try to come in and take it from them. From their position, they could look out and see the red glow growing, the heat intensity build, and the smoke block out Elppa's light. All became red, orange and eery, black and choaked. Their world became smoke and embers, heat, and noise. Noise like they'd never heard before, surrounding, and confounding them.

As they waited, they looked at each other and began to sing to Elppa and Egnaro for deliverance. But even as they sang, Korzela raged, and a powerful whirlwind blew up all about them. The fire raged, the sound of falling trees, and the cries of other creatures dying and burning, filled their ears. They were sure even Elppa could not hear them. But they sang out loud in prayer, in fear and in hope.

Corselia knew that Bill had been right, this was a worse calamity than the Krat invasion, or the terror of Lord Kratt. The kookaburra had been right to leave. The fire tore through the forest, racing through the high crown and pushing embers ahead of the main fire. It was as if Elppa himself had come to the forest to play with them, bringing with him, his hate, his heat, and his fury. They sang in the burrow with all their might. But no one heard them, and as the heat grew, the very air they breathed was burned away. They soon went silent. Only the locomotive of the fire thundered on as they cowered in the ground, panting, baking, gasping, and waiting to join the Great flock of Elppa.

33

Together Again

First to fall over when the atmosphere is less than perfect
Your sensibilities are shaken by the slightest defect
You live your life like a canary in a coalmine
You get so dizzy even walking in a straight line

You say you want to spend the winter in Firenza
You're so afraid to catch a dose of influenza
You live your life like a canary in a coalmine.

The Police – 'Canary in a Coalmine' (1980)

KRATJOA ARRIVED BACK in the valley and immediately searched for Lord Kratt. She found him trying to prepare the clan to leave the path of the approaching fire. Embers had already sparked small spot fires near the old norzela nest on the former Yat lands, and all the mytre were looking to Kratt to lead them away from the impending disaster. Some of the former clan members had already flown east, ahead of the fire and smoke, hoping to out fly it.

Kratt knew this was futile. With the blaze coming so quickly, only a strong and determined bird could out fly a fire. But he let them go. "Cowards," he called after them as they left. Some of the Krat clan were about to try and stop them, but Lord Kratt held them back. "Let them fly or flee, let them die or be," he called.

Kratjoa landed next to him. "Great Lord Kratt," she began. "I have found the rebel Wayt nest in the forest. It's in a wombat burrow, a hollow in the ground, Lord. It's why I took so long to find them. But I know where they are now."

Lord Kratt was at first ambivalent to the news. He had enough to manage with the approaching fire. Then he turned to Kratjoa and confirmed, "You've found them... in a wombat burrow you said?"

"Yes, Lord, it's why I couldn't find them, they're underground."

Underground? Kratt thought. *Underground!* Suddenly awake to an idea, he called to all the mytres near him, "Come with me if you want to live." Without waiting for a response, he took to the wing and flew east, away amongst the embers and away from the fire front. The birds around him thought they were following the others, trying to escape the fire with flight. But within a short time, Lord Kratt landed near the norzela park and started searching the area near the old Dart lands for the rabbit holes. "Search quickly," he cried. "Krattac, did you find the entrance to the holes that had the blood of Karbett when he had tried to escape?" Krattac nodded, unsure of why he asked. "Quickly, can you find them now?" Lord Kratt shouted.

Embers and smoke were thick about them when Krattac shouted, "Here, Lord." They all looked to the one-eyed mytre. He was gesturing towards a steep bank with a rabbit warren visible on its slope.

"Quickly," Lord Kratt instructed, "everyone inside, everyone underground."

Kratjoa hesitated, "What of the foe?" she shouted into the gusting wind and above the roar of the approaching fire.

"First we need to survive the fire, then we will vanquish the rebel traitors," Lord Kratt cried. "Now into the warren... hurry."

-O-

Cordelia left early, before her Elppa chorus was due, so that she could locate the valley as soon as possible. Orion's belt was low in the west, directly behind her and she knew she was going the right way. The wind blew in the direction she was flying, and she was glad to be following the fire and not to have smoke blowing in her face. *Korzela is good*, she thought.

She flew high again, over the charred ash covered earth, although, she could not see her shadow flying along below her.

For kilometre after kilometre all she saw were burnt trees, black skeletons of their former selves. Burnt earth, burnt bush, burnt scrub. The nature of the land had changed. The flat plain gave way to rolling hills and what should have been open green pasture lands, but these too were black and destroyed. Every now and then she saw a burnt shed or barn, the white carcass of a norzela vehicle or other types of norzela structure.

She also saw norzela nests isolated and alone in the barren landscape. Some stood as islands of undestroyed wonder, having escaped the flames. Unburnt, their tin rooves had lost their reflective power and stood dull and lacklustre under a covering of ash and debris. Some though had been unlucky, the white ash lay all around the fallen structure of walls or twisted metal so that the nest was unrecognisable. The occasional single standing chimney stack stood in defiance of the fire that had destroyed the home around it.

As she flew on, she became more and more despondent with each collapsed norzela nest and each animal carcass she flew over. She saw hundreds of dead livestock, wild animals and even birds, choked by the smoke and fallen to their doom. As the burnt trees thickened, so did the number of dead koalas she saw, most laying stiff and black at the base of trees or frozen halfway between trees, caught where they had tried to escape the onslaught.

Although, Cordelia thought, *the cattle are the worst*. They were big and bloated, black and toasted. Many had all four of their legs pointing skyward and clearly their great size had been no defence. Worse even than the dead were the injured and partially burnt livestock and wild animals. Many were crying out for relief from the pain, many called up to her for help, for water and food. For most, everything they could eat had been cremated, and even those few who survived the flames and heat faced an ongoing struggle for survival.

She flew on, the ground seemed to rise a little and she saw what she thought was a familiar view of the escarpment in the far distance to her left. She was passing over a forest of destroyed trees, each black and scarred by the recent fire.

Many still smouldered and glowed through the smoke as embers continued to glow within them.

Then, as she looked down, she saw half a dozen mytre emerging from the ground. It looked like they had been buried, and not burnt and to Cordelia's surprise they seemed to have survived the fire. Everything around them was gone. The tall tree near them stood black and still, like a single finger pointing skyward. Smoke still billowed from small fires all around them, and Korzela carried the ash into their faces and eyes. Embers gave off heat and small fires still consumed the wood and ferns of the forest floor. It was as if a giant flame thrower or ball of power from Elppa himself had been strung out across the land and swept the forest floor of anything green or good.

Few creatures seemed to have survived, and Cordelia was surprised to see the small group of mytres below her. She was about to fly over them, not wanting to be distracted or captured or attacked for trespassing, when one of the mytres began to fly up towards her. *To intercept me?* she thought. She was beginning to tire and with the escarpment in sight and so near, the last thing Cordelia needed was conflict, so she increased her speed and began to climb away from the approaching bird. She was sure she had the stamina and power to fly away. Her wings were growing stronger, and her lung capacity had increased with her previous practice and the long flight to get to the valley.

But there was something unusual or familiar about the approaching bird that made her slacken her climb and slow her speed. She knew she could still escape the interceptor if she needed to, so she slowed a little waiting to see what the bird wanted.

They came within a short distance before each bird truly recognised the other, and it was instantaneous.

No sooner had Cordelia recognised her mother, than Corselia knew she had found Cordelia. They flew into an embrace, midair and tried to shout to the other about their joy and relief. About the fulfillment of their hopeless hope and about the gift that had come from so devastating a fire. Because they knew, had the fire not come, Cordelia never would have seen the mytres on the ground and her mother never would have seen Cordelia flying high over their nest warren.

On the ground, looking up, Corxell thought his mother had been attacked and he braced himself to take off and join battle with the intruder.

Up high, it was no use, it was too difficult to fly and embrace so Corselia signalled for them to land, and they both flew back to the expanse of soot, ash, and still smoking timber in the Wayt clan elpitlum clearing, near the burrow.

As they descended, the members of the Wayt clan and Corxell waited anxiously.

34

Firestorm

No more sunshine (sunshine)
It's followed you away (you away)
I'll cry, Birdie (Birdie)
'Til you're home to stay (home to stay)

Ann Margaret – 'Bye Bye Birdy'' (1960)

ON THE GROUND, the Wayt clan braced themselves to attack the intruder, not knowing Corselia had invited her daughter to join them. Once the two birds had landed, Corxell dived at the strange new bird. Cordelia parried his attack and was able to push her brother to one side, deflecting the force of his attacking blow. She sent him sprawling across the ash and he landed on his back, in a cloud of white dust, and ash.

"Corxell, stop…" Corselia cried out. "This is your sister, Cordelia. Don't you recognise her?"

Her brother sat forward. Ash and dust covered him and gave him a new grey covering to his chest and wings, he looked like a very young mytre again. Feeling foolish he blinked and held his wing up over his eyes to get a better look at her.

"Cordelia?" he said, unsure.

"Hey, Bro," she said, "you alright there?"

"Sis, it's you," he said at last, now sure it was her, "you're back,"

"I've come to kill Lord Kratt," she said defiantly. The small group of mytre gathered around her each offering their welcomes and greetings. Cordelia was overjoyed to have found her mother and brother, but she was suddenly aware that her father wasn't there. She knew why. "Mum," she said, softly, "Do you know what happened to Dad the night of the elpitlum battle?"

Suddenly the gathered mytre were silent.

"No, dear," her mother said sadly, "were you with him?"

Cordelia started to cry. "I was," she said, between sobs. The two mytre embraced. "I saw him die," Cordelia said. Adding between sobs and tears, "A car killed Dad the night of the elpitlum. We were trying to escape the Krat hunters, but Dad was hit and killed… I'm so sorry. The light took him." Corselia began to sob and the two mytre held each other amongst the ash and soot, smoke, and destruction, as they shared their grief.

I knew he was gone, Corselia thought. *Still, having it confirmed doesn't make hearing the news any easier.*

Waytbill and Waytjulia both threw their wings around their Cor clan friend, while Cordelia broke away to hug her brother.

"But where have you been, Sis?" Corxell asked.

Cordelia looked sad and choaked back her tears. She realised she'd come a long way and there was still much to do. She stepped back from her hug, and looking coy, she said, "It's a long story, best saved for another time. But I'm here now, and it's time to rid the valley of the Kratt tyrant."

"But how is it you're here with the fire?" Waytbill asked.

"The fire was my clue to finding the valley," Cordelia explained. "Now I want to use it to help rid the valley of Kratt and his clan of murderers and thieves… forever."

"How?" Corselia asked, as she too refocused on their current situation, "He's too strong."

"Not today, Cordelia said, "if he and his clan have survived the fire and smoke, he'll still be weak. If I strike quickly, I can retake the valley and see him off before he knows what's hit him." Cordelia spoke forcefully and confidently.

Who is this bird? her mother thought.

"We can help," Waytbill said.

"About time we did something more than cower underground," the unhappy Wayt mytre added.

Waytbill cried, "To wing, to flight, to fight!"

"To the elpitlum place," Cordelia cried. "If he lives, we'll find him there."

Corselia had prepared herself for the knowledge that her partner was gone, and as sad as she was, as bereft and empty as she felt, she was overjoyed at being reunited with Cordelia. Suddenly, she was facing the prospect of losing her again, and she was concerned that their attack on the valley might be premature. She wanted to wait and gather more information about the valley and their enemy. She wanted to make a more detailed plan, she wanted to be with her daughter and hold her. But the flock were in the air, their attack had begun, and Cordelia was leading the wing as it lifted into the still smoke-filled sky. Corselia wanted to call out, "Wait, stay." But she'd been too slow.

Seeing her daughter and son take off to battle, she had no choice other than to go with them; grief, worry, joy, and all. The willie-wagtail watching them decided to let them fly their way, to battle. He would fly to his home near the norzela nest and see if his family had survived the firestorm.

-0-

The norzela were ready. As ready as they could be when facing a firestorm of such magnitude. The first norzela nest the fire hit was on the former Cor clan lands. There, the mother and her two boys had been sent to a rescue centre near the norzela park on the far side of the valley.

Their father had stayed to fight the fire. He heard the roar of the approaching fire front, and felt the heat build around him. His hope crackled and burnt like a slice of bacon on the barby. His throat was dry and parched even before the fight had begun. He looked about him as ember fires started all over the property.

He had a pump running to drive water down from the dam. But would the pumps work if the power was cut? If the petrol ran out? If the fire burnt or melted through the hoses? He was about to run to the dam himself. There at least he would be safe under the water if all was lost.

Then, to his relief, a Rural Fire Service (RFS) truck rolled into his drive and came to rest just outside his main gate. Two RFS volunteers got out and ran over to him, "Need a hand mate," one of them shouted. He was dressed in yellow overalls, sturdy boots, and he wore a white hard hat, with a clear plastic visor. Another RFS volunteer, a woman, dressed the same way, came and stood at the side of the first.

"I'll take this side of the house, you take the other," the first volunteer cried.

"And I'll stand by the shed, and the pump," the father shouted above the din.

That was it. No great tactical discussion, no long or detailed strategic debate, time was against them, and the fire was upon them. Action was the only defence they had now.

The fire had one plan, destroy everything.

The volunteers rushed off to take their places. The father watched for a moment. He didn't know these people. They weren't even being paid to help him. Volunteers, risking their lives to save his home. *And who knew,* he thought, *maybe, at this very moment, their own homes might be in need of a similar defence. Yet here they were, at his home, risking their lives, to help save his family home.* It fed his courage and determination.

He strode over to the back of the house and checked the pump, flicked it on, and waited for the hose to start to churn out a steady spray of water, drawn from the dam. As it did, he directed the spray at the machine shed, and the back of the house, dousing embers and splashing spot fires as they appeared before him. The smoke was choaking, blinding, disorientating. He was hot all the time and blind most of the time, but he fought on, occasionally turning the hose on himself to try and keep cool or to stop embers from burning through his overalls and jumper.

The RFS volunteers did the same, using the pump and water reserve on their truck to feed hoses to spray fires wherever they found them. Time seemed to stand still. The deafening sound completely stole any sense of being in the world. Instead, they were in a sort of reverse snow globe, being assaulted by embers, smoke, and debris, tossed, and buffeted, by the wind's wrath, and the whirlwind of heat and embers.

At other locations, small tunnels of wind grew around the volunteers as they did their best to stand their ground. Every instinct said run, hide, go inside, and stay out of the fire storm, but they fought on, only stopping when the danger had passed. When the noise was gone and all that remained was the white ash field where a house had been, where a shed had stood, where a car had been parked, or where a body lay consumed and disintegrated.

At the norzela nest on the former Cor clan territory, the three fighters battled for three hours to keep the nest safe, to keep the shed from being obliterated by flames and to keep the water flowing into their hoses and from the dam.

By 2pm the fire had passed. The three fighters who had fought alone for the past three hours, staggered to the front of the property where they had parked the RFS truck. Its tires had melted or been burnt, and the truck lay smouldering and broken, but mostly unconsumed. The house stood too, as did the machinery shed. They had defeated the fire. The three norzela sat on the charred front lawn to drink a beer. Around them lay the snuffed-out bodies of a dozen or so little Superb-Fairy Wren, three Galah and two Willi-Wagtail. As she looked at them, fallen across the lawn, the female volunteer said, "Smoke and heat got 'em."

"Bloody fire," said the other, as he coughed and spat out a lump of black sputum onto the ground.

"I don't know how to thank you," the father said, humbly. "I couldn't have saved my house alone."

"You could give us a lift back to base," said the male volunteer, "it looks like the truck is toast."

"Gladly," the father said. As he did, he locked across the valley, over the creek and towards the norzela park. He could see both buildings on the other side of the valley in flames. One had already collapsed, and the other was sending flames metres into the sky as fire consumed it. *Shit,* he thought, *that could have been my place.*

"Why didn't some of your colleagues help the houses over there?" he asked pointing east.

"You're lucky we came here, mate," said the male volunteer. "This is the only fire truck in the valley, and yours was the first road we tried. You, Sir, are bloody lucky."

"And bloody grateful, I am too." As he spoke, he blinked a few times and couldn't help letting his tears fall, as his adrenaline dropped, his emotions overwhelmed him. He dropped to his knees, exhausted, and cried like a child.

-0-

Cordelia led the others in a quick loop over the valley. They looked down and saw that almost all of the Wayt clan lands had been destroyed by the fire. Smoke still drifted up and embers still rolled across the ground, driven on by Korzela's power, although they could feel it losing its potency. They flew on over the Yat clan lands. These too had been savagely torched, and the old norzela nest was in pieces, with only the old stone chimney still standing, like a single tall gravestone over the ash covered and smouldering remains of the norzela nest.

Not a tree is untouched. Cordelia observed as they flew on. Over the Cor territories, the nest tree still stood, but all its leaves were gone, and the branches were all scarred in some way. The low shrubs and bush between the norzela nest and the creek were gone. They saw a few blackened carcases of kangaroo and koala, and even the body of what looked like a fox or a cat laying near the creek.

Oddly, Cordelia thought, *'this norzela nest is unscathed.'* She also saw the three strangely dressed norzela, resting on the scarred lawn and she wondered if they might be the reason for the miracle.

They ventured over the old Kar clan lands too and saw the still burning norzela nests, and the total destruction of the Kar nest tree. The valley was completely changed, and Cordelia was heartbroken to see it this way after being away for so long.

It was Waytbill who signalled for them to land at the elpitlum site. Smoke drifted across the valley still and the small flock of Wayt clan mytre, Cordelia, Corselia and her brother, Corxell dropped to land on the still warm ground at the elpitlum.

"What will we do now, it looks as if the Great Lord Kratt and all the other mytre have gone," Waytjulia said, unsure of what to expect next.

"Or they have been consumed by the flames," Corxell suggested, cheerfully.

"No," Cordelia said, assertively, "they were not killed, they may have left or taken refuge, but they are not dead. I saw no mytre bodies." The land around them was empty and only the stench of burnt flesh and ash filled their nostrils. Smoke, began to choak them too and Cordelia said, "We shouldn't stay here. It feels unsafe, evil almost."

"No," Waytbill shouted, "if other birds have survived, they will come here, and this is where we should wait, safe or not. We need to gather in one place so we can decide what to do next, now it seems that Lord Kratt and his clan have left the valley."

-0-

The fire raged over the norzela park, burning the greens, the fairways, and the trees and shrubs at the side of the course. The heat in the burrows was intense. Kratt had to hold in a few mytre that found it intolerable and wanted to fly out, but by holding them back, he likely saved their lives in the process. When the smoke, heat, embers, and fire passed it was Lord Kratt who emerged first.

"Come out," he called back, "the fire's passed."

One bird had died in the burrow. It was Krattac. He'd found the stress, heat, and claustrophobia too much. Underground is not the natural habitat for birds, and he felt he couldn't breathe. His stress and panic rose so that even with Kratatora at his side, he simply expired.

"Leave the fool in the dark," Lord Kratt shouted, when he was told of the tragedy, "we have other work to do." Then he shouted, "Kratjoa, get everyone back to the elpitlum place, we need to plan for a raid on the Wayt clan in the forest. There is no time to waste."

"Yes, Lord," Kratjoa said, pleased that her information about the rebel base would finally be of use.

"I'll meet you there shortly," Lord Kratt said dismissively. With that, Kratt rose into the sky and flew off to survey the destruction across the valley.

Kratjoa, ushered the remaining Krat and other remaining clan mytre out of the warren. Then directed them to follow her, back toward the elpitlum place. There were less than a dozen mytre in the flock. Seven of them were original Krat clan members and the remainder were the rump of the five clans that had occupied the valley before the Krat clan's arrival.

As they flew the short distance to the elpitlum, the destruction of the valley stunned Kratjoa. Trees were still a blaze, the roadside was black, and still smouldering, and most shocking, the norzela nests near the Krat nest tree were white, ash covered wrecks. Even the Great Lord Kratt's nest tree had been destroyed. It was laying on its side, with the base of the trunk snapped and the upper tree all but completely destroyed. Nothing was left of Lord Kratt's nest and his partner who had refused to leave her eggs, and the eggs themselves, were gone. Their flight was a sad one, but short, and they soon reached the elpitlum area and settled on the ash covered ground.

Waiting for them were what Kratjoa thought were the remaining Kar clan mytre who had escaped the fire by flying east, but she was mistaken. When they landed, they found they were in the midst of the five surviving Wayt clan and the three Cor clan renegades. As the Krat clan mytres landed, they were set upon by the returned valley clans mytre.

"You helped kill my father and you tried to kill me," Cordelia said to Kratjoa coldly as Kratjoa touched down.

Kratjoa was stunned, "You vanished," she said, shocked.

"I did," agreed Cordelia, "thanks to you." She hopped over to where Kratjoa had landed and stood before her. "You tried to take my head off... you failed. Now I will take yours." Cordelia was as cold as stone. "I have been flying with the Great flock of Elppa," she lied. "But Elppa sent me back for justice. Are you ready to die?" she asked, menacingly.

Kratjoa was suddenly afraid. She'd seen Cordelia take her blow and drop from the air. She'd seen Cordelia vanish, simply vanish, out of the sky on the night she'd struck her. *If she had been in the Great flock, how was it that she was back? Had she been sent back to kill her?* Her mind was all confusion and bewilderment. The fire, the lingering smoke, and the smell of burnt flesh, burnt fruit, burnt wood, all began to make her swoon. *What is happening? Where is Lord Kratt?* she thought.

"You killed my partner?" Corselia shouted. She flew over to where Cordelia was standing and landed on the other side of the Krat mytre. Then she strode towards Kratjoa, getting closer, her footprints left in the soot and ash as she walked. "I have not been in the Great flock, like my daughter, but you soon will be. Enemy, traitor, murderer." Corselia spoke with venom in her voice. It echoed around the elpitlum space and resounded amongst the gathered mytre.

With that, she attacked Kratjoa savagely, flapping up and bringing her beak down hard across her enemy's collar.

Kratjoa tried to dodge to avoid the blow, but she was too slow and the full force of Corselia's beak smashed into the back of Kratjoa's neck. She staggered back reeling in pain. But instead of peeling away to gather her bearings, Kratjoa swung her head up from below and struck Corselia in the wing pit, under her right wing.

Corselia staggered back as Kratjoa followed up with an upper cut catching Corselia in her neck. Corselia staggered back further and Kratjoa, taking the upper wing, swung her claws up into Corselia's face scratching and scraping her claws down across Corselia's face narrowly missing her eyes. Corselia felt the three blows as if they had all come at once and she struggled to regain her focus.

Kratjoa stepped back and taunted her adversary. "Maybe it will be you who will join the Great flock of Elppa?"

Corselia spat out a beak full of blood and drew her wing over her head stretching out the underwing injury. Then without warning, she flapped into the air again, springing at Kratjoa. Kratjoa was too slow to see the jump and before she could react, Corselia had risen and hooked one claw about Kratjoa's neck. With the other she hooked across Kratjoa's beak and as she came down, she twisted and flicked with her feet. She broke Kratjoa's neck in an instant and the Krat clan's searcher lay dead at Corselia's feet.

Other Krat clan mytre moved to join the fight, but the few Wayt clan mytre confronted the Krat clan and although outnumbered, a standoff ensued.

Kratatora shouted to the few remaining Kar clan who had stayed and gone to the warren. "Kar clan, join us as Krat." He saw the defeated clan could help swing the balance of the coming fight.

The air was tense as each bird waited to see which way the old Kar clan would turn. Many knew Corselia and Waytbill. Few had any love for Kratt or the Krat clan after they had killed their leader and others of their clan. Waytbill knew that with the Kar clan mytre against them, they would be swiftly overwhelmed and their bid to wrest the valley back from the Krat clan would be short lived.

As the mytre stood facing each other, Cordelia called out. "There doesn't need to be a fight." As she spoke, she flew up to the still smouldering elpitlum log and looked down on the assembled mytre. "I only want Lord Kratt. Let us take him now, and peace will return to the valley clans again. I assure you, no harm will come to any bird who stands with us." A few birds relaxed their stance, and the Kar mytre began to contemplate joining with their old Cor and Wayt clan allies.

Then Lord Kratt struck.

35

Elppa's Kindness

Little darlin', the smile's returning to their faces
Little darlin', it seems like years since it's been here
Here comes the sun
Here comes the sun, and I say
It's alright

The Beatles – 'Here comes the Sun' (1969)

THE WILLIE-WAGTAIL FLEW cautiously toward the norzela nest and his own nest within the thick hedge near the back of the still standing building. He could see the three strangely dressed norzela talking and drinking on the lawn. *'How odd,'* he thought. *A fire has almost destroyed everything and here they are relaxing, drinking and chatting.* He flew past them, giving them a wide birth, before arriving at where he had last seen his nest and partner. The ground and plants near the norzela nest were still burning in places, but he could see, through the lingering smoke, the main structure of the norzela nest was still standing.

He saw too that a few birds lay dead on the lawn or on the gravel driveway, some he saw were small, superb fairy-wren that had died from heat stroke as they lay unburnt, but unmoving on the driveway. His heart sank, but he flew on. As he flew past the norzela nest, he saw the hedge where his home had been. Although ashen and with dry crinkled leaves in places, it was still standing.

As he flew towards the hedge, his partner chirped a greeting when she saw him. "I thought you'd been consumed in the fire," she said, beside herself with worry, and brimming with relief at his safe return.

"No," he replied, "I was hiding in a wombat hole with some mytre." She hugged him to her and showed him that the eggs were still warm, and miraculously, safe.

Then she asked, "Really, how did you avoid the flames?"

He could see she wouldn't believe him. "I was just lucky, my love," he said. Adding cheerfully, "Sometimes Elppa is kind to the little folk."

-0-

Kratt flew in low and fast, skimming the ground in a silent glide at the height of the fallen elpitlum log.

Corselia saw him at the last moment, but it was too late to cry a warning to her daughter.

He hit Cordelia from behind and she was flung to the dust and ash of the valley floor. The fall knocked the breath from her and in the ash cloud that blew up about her she struggled to breathe. She was flipped quickly over onto her back, but she tried to rise. Strangely, she noticed that the earth was still warm. Apart from this, she was only aware that she was in pain as she tried to get up.

Kratt landed quickly and firmly on Cordelia's chest, knocking more air from her lungs. He landed with one claw on her chest and the other on the shoulder of her previously damaged wing, she felt a twinge where her old wing injury had been.

"Finally, we meet," Kratt said, in a deep menacing voice. "Cordelia, is it? Like the hero from our legends. Come to save the day, the valley, your mother's life, your friends." Kratt lifted one claw and brought it down hard on her injured wing. He lifted his head and gazed about at the assembled mytre that surrounded them.

Cordelia let out an anguished cry, and looking up, she stared at Lord Kratt. He looked like all mytre she thought, *He's not much bigger than average, not more beautifully graced with plumage, not more intelligent, or courageous. Not more charismatic, not more powerful in strength or skill. Even the small star of white feathers on his brow gave him no more power. Why has this bird risen so high?*

As she thought about her adversary, Lord Kratt cried out, "Seize them all." The few Krat faithful were slow to respond. Like the Wayt clan and the two remaining Cor clan members, Kratt's return stunned the Krat clan. No one moved.

"I said seize them," he bellowed, sweeping a wing to indicate the traitorous, Wayt and Cor clan invaders. "I saved your pathetic lives; I led you to the rabbit holes and saved you from the fire that destroyed your homes in the valley."

A few of the surrounding mytre mumbled their agreement. But still none moved.

"You are the fire," Cordelia stammered with difficulty, looking up at Lord Kratt. "You brought the curse of the fire to the valley. You destroyed the valley."

"Fools," Lord Kratt shouted. "I am your saviour, your Lord. Don't listen to this young imp." Then, he saw Kratjoa, lying dead in the pale ash on one side of the elpitlum space. "Who did this?" he demanded. "Who killed loyal Kratjoa?"

"I did," Cordelia said still with difficulty as she struggled under Lord Kratt's claw. She didn't want her mother to suffer if she died under the claw and foot of Lord Kratt, so she lied to save her.

"You?... you're too young, too foolish, too puny to kill an experienced Krat warrior." He considered her, cautiously. Her dark 'horned', feathered tuft above her beak made her look somehow otherworldly, defiant, or special. *As if she has magical or superpowers.*

"Well, I did," she lied.

He looked suddenly perplexed. He felt something he'd not felt in a long while ... doubt. He wasn't sure if he'd underestimated the Cor clan. *Maybe, I should have established my nest in their territory first,* he thought. He caught himself and his thoughts before they overwhelmed him. *But I have them now,* he reassured himself.

He looked at Cordelia as she lay sprawled out on her back on the warm earth under his feet. *Puny,* he thought as his brow grew black.

"Well, now I'll kill you, then your mother, then your brother, then all these foolish Wayt clan traitors. Have you forgotten my rule is law by claw?"

The fire had devastated most mytre. Their underground experience had tested their courage, and fortitude. The loss of their nest trees, the valley burnt… it had all been enough for most of the gathered mytre, Wayt, Cor, Kar and even the surviving Krat mytre. All of them had been through enough. They had no more to give, no more fight in them. As much as they had wanted to strike Lord Kratt down, their energy and determination were sapped, their courage spent, their spirit broken, destroyed. It was why most mytre turned their faces away, not wanting to see Cordelia's end.

Her mother, brother and the remaining Wayt clan mytre, were exhausted, silent, and simply hid their faces under their wings. It was all they had the power to do in the face of this final blow.

"Now… you really will disappear this time," the Great Lord Kratt declared, in a quiet voice to Cordelia, before looking around at the gathered mytre. "Time to die," he shouted. The few remaining Krat clan mytre looked terrified, and they averted their gaze. *Fools and cowards*, he thought. Smoke from a brush fire reignited near the orchard over the creek and it drifted over the gathered mytre and filled the elpitlum space. An eery silence surrounded the elpitlum area and it was cast in red and grey shadow even though Elppa was high.

Cordelia looked into Kratt's eyes, she could see the keere there, she could sense his malus. But she wasn't afraid.

Kratt saw her resolve, her courage and he felt puzzled. *Why wasn't she begging for mercy?* he wondered, confused as a swan on ice, he hesitated a moment longer.

He was about to raise his foot to crush Cordelia's throat, when she said defiantly, but just loud enough for Lord Kratt to hear, "I am Cordelia the brave. Friend of Gary, only son of Garth, grandson of

Graham, great grandson of George, and descendant of the Great Gus from the western mountain cliffs. I will not die today! I have seen it."

Kratt turned his head in confusion, looking down at the smaller mytre under his feet, within his power. *What did she say?* he thought. It was almost his last thought.

Suddenly, Cordelia thrust up with her powerful feet and lifted Kratt up so that while he was still above her, his grip on her neck was loosened. Then, in a woosh that was lost amongst the smoke and noise of the firestorm, Kratt was gripped and swept up and away into the sky, soon to be lost in the smoke and heat haze of the devastated valley sky. Never to be seen again.

Cordelia flipped over onto her feet, pushed herself up, then flapped her wings, and although in pain, she took to the air after him. Soot, ash, and smoke billowed all about the elpitlum as the birds rose and disappeared into the dark sky, and away toward the escarpment.

It had happened in a flash, in a hummingbird's heartbeat. No one saw Gary snatch up the Great Lord Kratt, no one saw Cordelia dart into the sky behind her friend, and no one knew what had happened as they raced away, escaping, northward. When the assembled birds looked into the space at the centre of the elpitlum, Cordelia and Lord Kratt were gone, vanished, it was as if they had disappeared, in a cloud of ash and smoke.

36

Resolution

He clasps the crag with crooked hands;
Close to the sun in lonely lands,
Ring'd with the azure world, he stands.

The wrinkled sea beneath him crawls;
He watches from his mountain walls,
And like a thunderbolt he falls.

Alfred Lord Tennyson – 'The Eagle' (1851)

NO ONE AT THE elpitlum saw exactly what had occurred. For a long time after there was speculation that Elppa himself had taken the Great Lord Kratt and destroyed him. Others said it must have been a norzela intervention, some sort of wicked craft like a gun but with more power. Others speculated that the smoke and fire in some sort of bushfire whirlwind had taken Kratt into the sky to join the Great flock of Elppa.

Only Cordelia knew the truth. She had seen her one footed eagle friend, Gary. She saw him swoop in and take hold of Kratt with his one strong talon, and carry him away into the sky, to destroy him with his powerful beak or crush him between his claws. She'd taken off and followed him at once before any of the mytre at the elpitlum site had realised what had occurred.

She and Gary flew up to the high escarpment cliffs above the valley, above the destruction of the fire, above the elpitlum and away from the conflict of the clans. There they landed and talked quickly. Lord Kratt was not with Gary though.

"How did you find me?" Cordelia asked.

"Trev and Sid came to see me after you left. They told me you had flown east, towards the fire. I set off at once and followed you. I saw you fight the brown goshawk. You were masterful."

"I was so scared," Cordelia said, "but you taught me well."

"I saw you land and rest with your kin at the burrow. The fire was all around, and I flew high to avoid the heat and smoke. The up drafts were strong, and I flew up above the fire and smoke, destruction, and death. When I came down, I saw the elpitlum and your fight with Lord Kratt. I waited and waited, until I saw my opportunity and I came through and took him away."

"Where is he now?" Cordelia asked.

"With the Great flock of Elppa, or somewhere else, I do not know the way for birds who break the laws and who offend the Gods." Gary paused. "But I can assure you... he's gone."

Cordelia let a long sigh escape her beak. "What will you do now?" she asked.

He didn't hesitate when he replied, "Go home, back to my mountains. Look about you there is nothing in this valley to sustain life. There is nothing moving about to eat, ash has polluted the water, and the green plants and seeds are gone. You should come with me. Return to the station and live with Bruce and the norzela, live with Sid and Trevor... I can visit you every now and then as I fly over the station," Gary concluded. He could see she was considering his proposal.

Then she said, "No... no... this is my home, green and blue, black, or ashen. I can't leave my family and my mytre friends, not again."

Gary understood. "Then this is goodbye again, Cordelia the brave," Gary said sadly.

"Thank you for saving my life," Cordelia cried, as they embraced high on the northern escarpment. "Look high for me if you need me again," Gary said, adding, "from the west." He then spread his wings and pinions wide and dived over the escarpment's cliff edge.

Cordelia watched him flap his wide graceful wings almost leisurely, as he climbed into the sky above the valley. Behind him a bank of clouds had rolled across the valley from the south. *'Rain's coming,'* Cordelia thought, *'Xervinu, the God of rain, is finally awake.'*

-0-

At the elpitlum site, none of the birds understood what had occurred. The mystery of Cordelia and Kratt's disappearance left them all stunned.

Waytbill reacted fastest. "We need to call a truce," he cried, loudly. "Until we know what has occurred to Lord Kratt and Cordelia."

A number of the birds mumbled their thoughts to their neighbours, but none spoke out against his proposal.

Corselia and her son were in shock. Kratt had been about to kill Cordelia and now he and she were gone, vanished. Corselia had only just found her daughter after ages of uncertainty and grief, she'd only just been told that her partner was dead, and she'd only just survived the fire, the confines of the burrow and the fight with Kratjoa. Now her daughter was missing again. "Did anyone see what happened?" she asked desperately.

The gathered birds had all suffered from the fire or the confines of their underground escape and every one of them was spent, physically and emotionally. Their valley homes were gone, their relatives, friends and partners were dead or spread, burnt, or hurt, all was lost, and here they were on the brink of further territorial conflict.

"A truce," Waytbill called again. The gathered birds all looked at each other. There were just under two dozen at the elpitlum, and few had the heart to fight on.

"A truce?" one of the Krat clan mytre said, in a low smoke choaked voice.

Waytbill suggested they should search the valley for other survivors and assess the state of their former homes.

Kratatora was the only remaining senior Krat clan member and she was at first inclined to fight on. She couldn't conceive that Lord Kratt was gone for good. But she was also tired and traumatised by the loss of her partner Krattac in the rabbit warren, and with the ongoing loss of life about her.

"We three should wait here," Kratatora proposed. "Myself, Corselia and Waytbill. We should wait here for Kratt's return."

"Or Cordelia's return," Corselia interjected, hopefully.

"We wait," Waytbill agreed. Adding, "Until ksud, no longer. But there should be no fighting or treachery while we wait, we have all suffered and seen enough. Let's allow peace to come to the valley in place of the ash."

There was no celebratory chorus, no sound of glee, or rejoicing. Just a silent resignation as each bird from each of the surviving clans took to the wing to search the valley for lost, ash covered things. The three clan leaders each sat on the cooling elpitlum log and waited, each nursing their own grief and loss, and each pondering what had happened to the duelling mytre, Cordelia and Kratt.

As they waited, a mytre flew into the middle of the elpitlum site and landed before them. He bowed low and said, "I have come to report that I saw an eagle near the escarpment. It didn't look like it was coming to the valley, but I thought I saw it talking with a mytre."

"A mytre, are you sure?" Corselia quizzed the bird. The bird looked anxious and replied, "Yes, err...no...no... I'm not sure. They were a long way off and the smoke was still thick toward the head of the valley. I was sure, at least, that I saw the eagle, but it could have been the smoke playing tricks... Lords." The mytre seemed hesitant and wasn't sure who led the valley or the clans now.

"Thank you for your report," Waytbill said, kindly.

"What else did you see?" Corselia asked as the mytre made ready to fly.

"Destruction, ash, soot, trees burnt and in splinters, nests destroyed and gone, bodies and," he hesitated and stammered as he finished, "death, just death."

"And your nest and partner?" Corselia asked, sympathetically.

"Gone… flown with the smoke, burnt with the flames… gone." The bird looked at the three senior mytre and said forlornly, "Only the norzela nest on the old Cor clan lands is unburnt. Everything else from east to west is gone." With that he took off, to resume his search while the three senior mytre waited on, in silence.

-0-

Cordelia returned to the elpitlum site as Elppa crossed towards the west in a high arc across the slowly clearing sky. It was dim still under the smoke that lingered in the valley, even though Elppa was passing slowly, moving west. When she landed there, Corselia, Waytbill and Kratatora were waiting, still sitting on the log. They had dragged Kratjoa's body away through the ash, and the three birds waited patiently, in silence, as Cordelia landed. As soon as she was amongst them their questions began, breaking the silence.

Corselia was overjoyed, Kratatora was troubled and Waytbill was stunned.

Corselia spoke first. "Cordelia you're alive, I hoped that you would return, what happened to you?" Her questions came in a flurry of words, chirps, and were sung without a pause for breath.

Kratatora demanded sternly, "What has happened to Lord Kratt?"

While Waytbill simply stammered, "You're alive."

Cordelia held up her wings, signalling for a moment to compose her response.

"One moment you were under Lord Kratt's claw then you were both gone," Kratatora said, "How did you escape? Where is Lord Kratt?"

Cordelia held up her wings again, and when the three mytre were still and quiet, she spoke. She did so, slowly, deliberately and with great care. It took a moment for the three clan leaders to settle, but Cordelia was patient and calm and waited with her wings aloft until they had settled. Then she began.

"Elppa took us. He wanted one of us for the Great flock. He chose Lord Kratt and asked me to come back here and lead the valley mytre," she lied.

"No… Lord Kratt can't be gone?" Kratatora cried incredulously.

Cordelia waited again for silence then she repeated, "As I said, he's gone… to the Great flock of Elppa, or somewhere else, I do not know the way for birds who break the laws and who offend the Gods," she said repeating what Gary had said on the escarpment.

"So, he's dead?" Kratatora and Waytbill clarified simultaneously.

"He will never be coming back to this valley," Cordelia explained, "ever."

"One of the Kar clan mytre said they saw a mytre on the escarpment talking with a wedge-tailed eagle," her mother said, reporting what the mytre had told them earlier. "Was that you or Lord Kratt?" her mother asked, hesitantly.

"A wedgie?" Cordelia exclaimed, sounding surprised. "No… they must have been mistaken. I was on the escarpment, after Lord Kratt had left me, talking to… talking to… a representative of Elppa himself," Cordelia explained with as much conviction as she could muster.

She added, "Mother… an eagle took my brother, your son, why would I be talking with a wedgie?" she scoffed, dismissively as she finished talking.

Her mother was unconvinced.

Behind her back Cordelia crossed her two wings as a superstitious protection from her lies. "But we have to move on here in the valley," Cordelia said quickly, changing the subject.

"We've established a truce between all the valley mytre clans until we knew what had happened to Lord Kratt and yourself," Waytbill explained.

Cordelia considered what Waytbill said, and after thinking for a moment longer she replied, "I believe we should go further than this. A truce or treaty is of no value if the leaders of the clans are dead or gone."

She hesitated, took a breath, and offered a proposal, "I believe we should have no more separate clans in the valley. We will achieve more and fight less if we're all one. One big valley clan. This should be a 'mytre' valley and we should all be one 'mytre clan.'"

Corselia could see the wisdom of the idea immediately.

Waytbill was also easy to convince. He was tired of hiding and living in the stuffy wombat hole.

Kratatora reflected a moment longer. "So, the Krat clan can stay in the valley, in harmony, without further conflict, or retribution?" she clarified.

"Only if you all agree to become part of the 'valley clan'. With the rest of the mytre that live here," Cordelia explained.

Kratatora hesitated a moment longer as she pondered the proposal's 'pros and cons.' She looked at Cordelia, smiled and said softly, "If only we'd done this before Lord Kratt tried to take the valley by force and deception."

Cordelia was overjoyed and reaffirmed, "We have a chance now to unify all the clans and mytre in the valley. We just need the will and wit to do it. With faith and kindness, we can share the resources and gifts of the valley and grow trust and respect for each other so we can share responsibility for our valley."

Cordelia could see it clearly, one valley, one mytre clan, one community. All it would take was a willingness to trust and respect each other and believe in their shared contribution.

Corselia stepped over to her daughter and threw a welcoming wing about her shoulder. "Cordelia the brave," said her mother.

"Cordelia the wise,"' said Waytbill, as he too moved into the hug.

"Cordelia the forgiving," said Kratatora, generously as she shook wings with both Corselia and Waytbill, before bowing low to Cordelia.

Cordelia knew that really, she was, 'Cordelia the lucky'. Lucky to have a friend like Gary, lucky to have a valley and family to come back to, and lucky that the fire, as well as destroying the valley, had presented her with an opportunity to propose a new way forward for the valley mytre.

-0-

Above them the smoke was settling, as a bank of clouds rolled up from the south. A short time before Elppa set, a light rain began to fall across the whole district as Xervinu showered her blessing on them. The rain grew in intensity and extinguished the large bush fire, washed away the ash, and killed the spot fires. Xervinu brought the rain, and it flowed down the valley, washing debris and ash, dead things, and soot.

At the next rising of Elppa, the valley was still scarred, and black tree trunks stood like sentinels over the barren ground. The fruit trees in the orchard were stripped of fruit and leaves, but their trunks and branches still lingered, clinging to life. The valley had survived, to grow again.

Life in the valley was not easy after the fire had destroyed the nest trees, the orchard, and the lawns at the norzela nests or at the norzela park. But the mytre's song rang out about the valley each day, joining with the other birds in a celebration of their having survived the fire and joined together in a peace that ruled over the valley again.

The fire had stolen much of their food and the birds still faced starvation unless they could secure a suitable food source. Again, it was Cordelia who thought of a solution, and each day she would take several mytre up to the norzela nest where she encouraged them to sit on the lawn, or what was left of it, and sing a chorus for the norzela. Without fail, the norzela female would come out from the

312

house and throw bread or food scraps onto the lawn to feed the struggling mytre.

Don't the magpies sing beautifully? she thought as she called to her husband to come and listen. When he came out, the two norzela listened to the magpies' wonderful carolling. They watched them for a short while, before the two norzela boys came outside to kick a ball about on the barren lawn.

The majority of the mytre immediately took to the wing and flew away, scared by the sudden activity around them. Only Cordelia stayed to continue her song, lifting her voice in celebration of her friends and family, the valley, and the station. Singing for her own children to come and singing of survival and gratitude.

"Yer, they do a lovely job," the norzela father admitted, "beautiful."

ACKNOWLEDGEMENTS

This book would not have been made without the wonderful support of Elaine Ouston from Morris Pub ishing Australia. Her contribution to the cover, editing and general advice about the story structure and writing process has been invaluable, my first and primary acknowledgement is to her and the publication team at Morris Publishing Australia.

No work of fiction comes completely from the author's mind. This story is no different. Reading similar books about the world from an animal's perspective inspired me to write *Cordelia's Song*. Most notable amongst them is Richard Adams *'Watership Down'* (1972).

However, the magpies that come to feed at my back door and back garden mainly inspired my story. As I watched them feed and sing, I started to wonder if magpies might also have a story of their own to tell. Watching them, I started to view magpies in a different way. As a result, I read Gisela Kaplan's wonderful book, *'Australian Magpie: biology and behaviour of an unusual songbird'* (2nd Ed) (2022). This gave me all sorts of insights that I was able to lend to *Cordelia's Song*, and I hope I have done justice to magpies in the same way she has with her book.

My love of the Australian bush and my encounters with the harsh realities of living in rural Australia also inspired parts of *Cordelia's Song*. Therefore, I have also tried to capture something of the magic of the Australian outback and Australia wildlife in *Cordelia's Song*. Mostly though, the unique behaviour, songs and habits of the many magpies that visit my garden each day inspired me. This book is for them.

I have borrowed Cordelia's name from a character in William Shakespeare's play 'King Lear.' Lear's daughter, Cordelia, is too honest, and is subsequently banished from his kingdom because she will not over-play her love for her father, the King.

314

Really though I just liked the name Cordelia and Shakespeare's character lent her name to the lead character in this book.

I also consulted a number of other written sources in developing Cordelia's Song, these include:

- John W. Wrigley and Murray Fagg's book *'Australian Native Plants; cultivation, use in landscaping and propagation.* (Concise Edition) (2023)

- Louise Egerton's *'Know your Birds; Australia's Most Common Birds'* (Revised Edition) (2019)

- Matthew Jones and Duade Paton's book, *'Australian birds in pictures'* (2021)

- Jeff Davies, Peter Menkhorst, Danny Rogers, Rohan Clarke, Peter Marsack, and Kim Franklin's little book, *'The Compact Australian Bird Guide'* (2022).

- Peter Stanley's insightful and heartrending book; *'Black Saturday at Steels Creek'*, (2013) the story of the Black Saturday bushfires that killed in total, 173 people on February 2009.